I0612772

On Earth as It Is in Heaven;
Omens and Prophecies

Authored by Merri Patrice
With special love to Jamilyn, Kimberly and Nicole
xoxo

"God put Angels on Earth as it is in Heaven…
He must have had a good reason."

On Earth As It Is In Heaven ~ Omens & Prophecies

ISBN-13: 978-0692611166
ISBN-10: 0692611169

This is a work of fiction. The included miracle story is based on true occurrences. However, other parts of our story were inspired by media accounts and in no way reflect real events. Names, characters, businesses, places, events and incidents are either the products of the author's imagination or are used in a fictitious manner. Any resemblance to actual persons, living or dead, or to actual events is purely coincidental.

Dedication

My story, real or imagined, has captivated my mind and emboldened my spirit so that I might share it with you….

It is made possible to share my story due to the support from my loved ones ~ the ones who know me as crazy or a wee bit off, but always loving.

To my best friend, the love of my life, you are the brighest star in my universe. Thank you for letting me 'dream on.' I will always & forever be 'crazy on you.'

And thank you Karen Moss-Chassman. You prove that Rotary friends are the best type of friends. I love your red pen. Your keen eye is matched by your big heart.

I love you all higher than the birds can fly,
And my love goes deeper than all the oceans.

xoxoxoxo

Preface

The Gnostic Gospels are a collection of 54 ancient texts which are based on teachings from Spiritual leaders dating back to the second century. The word Gnostic derives from the Greek word gnosis which is translated to "Knowledge" or "Enlightenment."

Gnostic texts, written in Coptic and stored at the Nag Hammadi Library in Egypt, were recovered partly in 1945 and over time. It is thought that Gnosticism stemmed from a Jewish movement which emerged directly in reaction to Christianity. The belief is rooted in an understanding that we are created in a mirror image of God's likeness in which our souls carry an internal knowing of our Father.

Our story brings to life an interpretation of The Gospel of Truth, one of the Gnostic texts, where we meet Pistis Sophia. She is a troubled soul with many names and identities. After being seized by a longing for clarity, Pistis Sophia is separated from her consorts. In her journey she incurs the hatred of Authades, an evil soul. Deceived by Authades, Sophia is enticed into the depths of chaos, where she is deprived of hope. She must be made humble, and believing in supplication to a higher power, she prays for deliverance.

Imagine that Pistis Sophia were a real soul on earth today. Thrown into chaos by her enemies, her journey to find her family transforms her but she will need divine intervention to save her soul.

Valentinus, a father of the Gnostic teachings, was born in the northern part of Egypt and migrated to Italy as a Catholic priest. Passed over for a promotion to become Bishop around 136 A.D., he left the church. He began to save souls in his own way. Unveiling Pistis Sophia's story, Valentinus's followers show us that there is more to the sacred texts than what we have been taught.

His Gnostic ideas present the conception of the Godhead, both in its original essence as the True God and in its debased manifestation as the false or creator God. Valentinus tells us of Aeons, the intermediate deific beings who exist between the ultimate True God and ourselves. Archons, on the other hand, may influence the negative energy within us.

The Aeons and angels, together with the True God, comprise the realm of Pleroma or Fullness wherein our souls reach their fullest potential of divinity. The Fullness of our souls stand in contrast to our existential state which, in comparison, may be referred to as emptiness.

"God's will be done On Earth as it is in Heaven," the words Jesus gave us. There is a duality in life and in death… a Fullness and an emptiness.

Valentinus introduces a labyrinth of the heavens that in addition to Pleroma includes the Kingdom of Light, the Light-Treasury, The Region of the Right, The Middle Region, The Region of the Left, and the Formation of Souls to bring back lasting obedience and reverence demanded of the rebellious souls, or Archons, in our story. In essence, Valentinus's vision of seven heavens helps us in obtaining gnosis or knowledge, taking our souls on a celestial journey.

The labyrinth of the heavens may seem fantastical but when viewed through religious or mythological cosmology, the seven heavens refer to the seven divisions of Heaven, the abode of immortal beings or the visible sky, as well as the expanse containing the Sun, Moon and the stars. This concept dates back to ancient Mesopotamian religions. A similar concept is also found in some Indian religions such as Hinduism, and in some Abrahamic Religions such as Judaism, Islam and Catholicism.

"Allah is He who created seven Heavens or Firmaments and of the earth a similar number. Through the midst of them (all) descends His Command: that ye may know that Allah has power over all things, and that Allah comprehends all things in (His) Knowledge."
Quran 65:12 Yusuf Ali

Religious leaders throughout the centuries have provided various interpretations of sacred texts which have erupted in wars. In years past and still today, millions of innocent men, women and children have been slaughtered and displaced over dueling "religions."

Valentinus's fiercest opponent was Irenaeus, a Bishop in the Roman Empire. Born in Turkey, Irenaeus traveled to France during the time of persecution under Marcus Aurelius, the Roman Emperor (161–180 A.D.). Irenaeus famously wrote '*Adversus Haereses,*' known by scholars as '*Against Heresies,*' that provides a detailed attack on Gnosticism. As an early church Father, his writings were influential in the initial development of Christian theology.

Imagine if Valentinus and Irenaeus faced each other today, if the Catholic religion and others collapsed under the weight of their created anarchy. Imagine if people today realized that, in a world born of religious chaos, they did not need any organized religion to reach fullness in one's soul.

While Historians tell the story of our past, and while Scholars debate it, it is up to us to decide our future. Our souls, buried deep within, can lead us to eternal salvation or to purgatory.

"He who is to have gnosis, or knowledge, knows where he comes from and where he is going." ~ Gospel of Truth

Introduction

"It's no wonder that truth is stranger than fiction. Fiction has to make sense." ~Mark Twain

Lightning strikes the basilica, a meteor strikes Russia. "An omen?" The old man ponders. His faith is shaken as chaos seeps deep within his church's foundation. The Pontiff resigns and a new leader is chosen but the new leader will face competition.

Coincidences, angels, chaos and murder make life complicated for Sophia, an unassuming Italian scientist who made finding her biological family a priority- until destiny calls her by name.

Cardinal Valentinus de Marcosi tried to ignore his family's controversial past as Gnostic followers. After being shunned by his Catholic peers, he seeks revenge in the only way his knows —by stealing souls from his fiercest enemies, especially Cardinal Irenaeus Smyrna. Valentinus will have to fight for his life, and to save his soul.

Ben, an attorney originally from India, and Michael, a U.S. Army Lieutenant stationed in Italy share a common bond with death that leads them to join an international fight against terrorism.

Yin Quan, a respected journalist, brings us the latest updates from around the world. Everything is an illusion or so it seems…

And the seer prophesized: "I saw an Angel with a flaming sword. The flames appeared as though they would scorch the earth. The angel pointed to his right, where an immense light shone and I knew it was our Father. The light was almost too bright for my eyes. It was like I was looking through a mirror. I saw religious leaders on their knees at the foot of a mountain. Coming from their own houses, they were making their way up to a large Cross that stood at the top. Each one was killed by their enemies who set their weapons upon them. In the same way I saw others slaughtered, men, women and children of different faiths. Two Angels on each side of the Cross scooped up the blood using a crystal basin filled with holy water. I could see they sprinkled the souls with the holy water as they were making their way to our Father."

A world born of Chaos will die enslaved by Ignorance...

Chaos you are not my friend,
Ignorance to you my mind I will not lend,
Ah but through you, Gnosis, my soul transcends.

TABLE OF CONTENTS:

Heaven on Earth emerges into Hell on Earth.

This is where our journey begins…

Chapter 1

THE OLD PONTIFF

The winds were changing, a storm was coming. Gray clouds were moving surely and swiftly. Saint Peter's Square was busy with travelers from all over the world. You could hear the chatter of many different languages whispering in the wind. People would stop and stare every so often, entranced by the beauty of the enormous ancient buildings and statues from long ago. The visitors were oblivious to the storm fast approaching.

An Obelisk, given to Rome by an unknown Pharaoh of the Fifth dynasty of Egypt, stood in the middle of the square and around it were paving stones that varied by radiating lines in travertine. At noon, when the warm Italian sun shines in the middle of a clear sky, the obelisk finds its shadow washing over circular markers set to track the sun's motions through the zodiacs. Today however, there would be no sunshine. Only shadows of a troubling past were visible, a dark future was still obscured.

Unsuspecting sight-seers marveled in awe of St. Peter's Square. The symmetry and orderly arrangements of the almost faded white ash columns were reminiscent of a medieval time. The Basilica stood prominently in the square, towering over the visitors as if they were tiny ants.

Little droplets of rain began to trickle from the sky, scattering the travelers like ants trying to find cover. From a high balcony in the Basilica a man stood in front of the window overlooking the square, staring down at the people he remembered days of long ago.

"The first time I laid eyes on this holy place, I was in awe too," he then looked up into the darkening sky.

Desperately he searched for answers to the questions that plagued him. He clutched a curtain in each hand to hold him steady as he searched the sky with hope to see a sign.

1

Gazing down on the piazza, then across the tops of the buildings, and again to the sky, he pleaded softly to the All Mighty.

"*Bitte*, I beg of you, *mein Gott* in heaven," he whispered, "I need a sign. I need you to show me that I am following Your path."

"I can feel my bones aching," he sighed. In a brief moment, he could hear news reporters distantly in his mind referring to him as the old Pope. He was, after all, one of oldest Pontiff's ever elected. His Eminence, Pope Gregory XIII, stood there mumbling to himself, ignorant of the man who now stood behind him.

Antonio Lombardi was his butler and friend. For a second Antonio watched the short thinning man stand as a silhouette; a shadow of the man he used to be.

"Hmm, *scusami*.. your Eminence," Antonio muttered, "are you ready?"

Pope Gregory turned around slowly, a little unsteady on his feet. He looked at Antonio as he shook his head slightly, "*Kein Antonio, ich brauche ein paar minuten*," the pope softly said in his native German tongue.

"Of course, as you wish. I will leave you for a few more minutes," Antonio answered. He turned back to the door and closed it behind him.

Again alone, the Pope stared once more up towards the sky. There over the buildings he could see the enormous blackened clouds drifting in from the south. They looked heavy and seemed to speed towards Rome with determination, eating away the slow moving white clouds with a furious hunger. Pope Gregory thrashed the curtains closed in disgust.

"I am tired, so very tired," he grumbled.

In the corner of the neatly appointed room, there was an old tattered chair. It almost looked out of place in the richly decorated office that had served many Popes before him.

Walking over to the corner of the room, he collapsed into the chair relieving his legs of what seemed to be the weight of the world.

"I am happy I at least have you, old friend," he said, rubbing the arm of the comfortable worn out chair.

2

He brought it with him from his homeland in Bavaria, Germany. Quite often he would rest in his little piece of home to think and pray.

"I do not fit here anymore." Looking around the room he thought, "I am the tiny ant in this enormous world." His stomach was tied in knots, his heart was broken. Clasping his hands he prayed again.

"*Bitte...*, forgive me Father." He looked over on his desk and gazed upon the large stack of labeled folders with the word "*Confidenziale*" in red lettering.

"Could it be that my opponents elected me knowing I am an old man?" He questioned himself, "Did they anticipate working around me? How could such an honor, to be the leader of the Church of God, be so damning?" He could not help but speculate as his mind raced.

The sound of the rain came faster, the rhythm of each drop clashing against the balcony like the beat of a fierce orchestral arrangement, both angry and soothing. Pope Gregory knew it was time. He meekly rose from his chair, seeking courage as he found his feet and walked toward his desk.

Picking up the phone, he called Cardinal Giacomo Antonelli, his personal secretary, "I need you to set up a meeting with my advisory council immediately. It cannot wait," the words gushed from his lips.

Antonio returned with his Eminence's papers and one more *confidenziale* folder.

"*Grazie*, Antonio," frowning he paused, "...after my meeting, it will mark an historic time for millions of Catholics around the world. God help us!" He prayed as he took the marked folder.

Making his way to the meeting, "I am glad I chose meeting in an office furthest away from my own." Pope Gregory mused, "I can distance myself from the chaos that I am sure to start."

The room's decor elegantly dressed the floor to the ceiling. In the middle of the room stood a long oversized wooden table at least two hundred years old tailored with a red and gold embroidered silk cloth tabletop runner. Matching chairs cluttered close and complemented a rich style.

Gifted from French royalty, the *fleur-de-lis* boldly ornamented each of the chairs.

3

Windows were on the right side of the table, covered in long red and gold draperies. On the other side of the table, an oversized fireplace gave the room a soft glow.

Above the fireplace mantle hung a portrait of da Vinci's Last Supper. As with each apostle sitting around Jesus, each Cardinal took his place when Pope Gregory entered the room. Bowing their heads to recognize his presence and then taking their seats, they waited nervously. Each had noticed profound changes in their boss. In recent months he seemed to grow more frail and distraught.

Cardinal Antonelli was the first to break the thick silence as he asked, "May I get you anything, my Eminence?"

"No, I believe we should get straight to the point of this meeting," Pope Gregory flatly responded.

The air was thinning. A hot cloud rose, making it feel as if there were twice as many bodies occupying the large conference room. The portly Cardinal Korsig swept his sweaty palm across his face to dry his dampening brow. Their attention was directed to the Pope as he spoke.

"As you all know, I have received results from some of the various investigations concerning Mother Church and our Vatican Bank. News is starting to circulate outside the Vatican about misappropriated funds." He gazed at the Last Supper portrait and continued, "There have been allegations of fraud by people within these very walls." Sighs and chatter began to grow louder. The Pope's strong German voice overshadowed the Cardinals' growing protests and concerns.

"For overseers...," he paused, "as God's stewards, we must be above reproach! We must not be arrogant or quick-tempered or drunkard or violent or greedy for gain." Pope Gregory lectured, "We have moved in a direction of authoritarianism and absolutism which does not acknowledge anything as certain. One's ego and desires cannot be above the needs of our collective obligation. Our church needs to prevail over temptation. Even people who are trying to do the right thing will fall into traps that Satan uses to ensnare us, but we must not fall prey to his trickery."

The Cardinals seemed to focus on his every word, staring intently. Sitting across the table were Cardinals Toulouse and Le Bourge.

4

"What is going on?" shrugging his shoulders, Cardinal Toulouse mouthed to his French colleague.

"I do not know," Cardinal Le Bourge shook his head. Their expressions reflected their confusion.

All the Cardinals were dressed in their black cassocks, ornate with red piping, scarlet fascia sash and a pectoral cross on a chain accompanied by a scarlet zucchetto cap. In a picture, they would look like a flock of red-hatted penguins clamoring about in the chaos.

"We must not be led into temptation ourselves. We need to be shepherds leading the flock away from temptation. Let us pray that the Holy Spirit illuminates, inspiring and guiding the work of God that pushes us to charity, agreement and the service of the truth," the weary Pope warned in a sorrowful tone. "Truth is not determined by a majority vote and we must face the truth even if it is evil..," he paused before pouring out more of his words, "It is the purity of heart which enables us to see clearly. The only thing necessary for the triumph of evil is for good men to do nothing."

The Pope stood up and looked each of the sitting cardinals in the eyes and continued, "We are taught that it is a fraud to conceal fraud. We know that all things gained through unjust fraud are never secured."

His Eminence choked up as tears welled in his eyes, "My time would not be served well to continue on this path. It is another fraud. And after much soul-searching and prayer, I realize for the sake of God's flock, I must step aside or the fraud would continue."

Gasps of shock echoed in the room. Each Cardinal reacted in disbelief, but the Pope was not to be deterred. Sternly, he went on, "I plead with you to work together. I ask you, what shall it profit us to have churches if we suffer the loss of souls?"

His last words to them were to the point. "Together we must trust in our Father. We must renew our strength. We will then soar on wings like eagles. We will fly to the heavens and not grow weary. You, gentlemen, must not be weary!"

He scolded them like children. "This obscure administrative Roman system that runs our headquarters is over shadowed with darkness and we must bring the Curia into His light and good graces."

Raising his voice still higher, and pointing his finger, he demanded, "These are serious issues that MUST be addressed to ensure the sustained life of our beloved church. May God have mercy on us all!"

Murmurs in various accents, united with tension, filled the air. Cardinal O'Brien, with his Irish brogue, was the first to protest.

"My Eminence, we understand there are issues that need to be addressed, but please tell us what can we do to help change your mind?"

"No, this is the way it must be." Pope Gregory shook his head, his eyes filled with even more determination, "I will end my reign by the end of the month, thus allowing for time to choose a new leader." Already standing, the Pope blessed the befuddled Cardinals with the sign of the cross. "May God bless you and guide you," he then quickly turned to leave the room.

The Cardinals were now left to their own devices. The heat in the room has unbearable. Succumbing to the heat, Cardinal Korsig took out his handkerchief to wipe the now dripping sweat from his brow. Shaking their heads, Cardinals Toulouse and Le Bourge talked in their native tongues, but could not hear each other over everyone else.

"Pope Gregory XII would be the first pontiff to resign in over 600 years! How will we explain this to the people?" Cardinal O'Brien cried out in disbelief.

Their panicked voices were shouting over each other in concern, confusion and fear. Cardinal Antonelli was the target for the Cardinals requests for answers.

"I am just as blindsided as you," he assured them.

"What about these other issues. What was he referring to?" Cardinal Jaworski demanded in his thick Polish accent, "how bad could things be that Pope Gregory is willing to resign?"

The Cardinals were stunned and left to debate the situation amongst themselves.

The Pope walked swiftly back to his sanctuary and returned to the old chair that gave him comfort. Hours passed, but he did not take notice. He was in a trance state of prayer. "Please God, show me a sign," he begged.

As the hours rolled into early morning, the raging storm poured down upon Saint Peter's Basilica. He listened intently to the rain.

"It is teaming as if the heavens are crying too," he bowed his head but was startled by a loud booming thunder. In an instant there was a glowing light that seemed to illuminate the whole room. In that same moment, lightning struck the top of Saint Peter's Basilica.

Pope Gregory smirked, "It is as if You are sending me Your messenger Uriel, the archangel of light, to be at my side." His heart raced, "…Thank you. Brrrr…." Goosebumps sent a shiver down his spine such as he had never experienced.

"In my heart I now know I am not alone. I must be making the right decision but alas, I am saddened for the world," and he began to weep.

The night was long and lonely, the hours ticked by one minute… then another. "This is the longest night I have had on this earth. I just want this to be over, my Father," he pleaded.

All through the night Gregory prayed. Sometimes walking in circles, sometimes sitting in his favorite chair, he prayed the entire night. He stood at the window of his office for what was sure to be one of the last times as Church Father. He could see the sun rising slowly and surely.

"Holy Father, help me to do your will, *bitte*, I beg," he stood again and steadied himself.

Antonio walked through the door with his morning tray of coffee and Italian taralli biscuits, Gregory's choice snack.

"*Buon giorno*," Antonio gestured, placing the tray on the table as he usually did. Gregory just looked at Antonio, staring through him as if he was in a daze.

"My Eminence, you look like you have slept in your clothes," Antonio sounded concerned for his friend. "What can I do to help you?"

"*Scusa…*, my Eminence?" Antonio tried to get Pope Gregory's attention.

"A-hmm, no I am fine," Gregory responded.

Antonio was heartsick for his boss, "*per favore*, tell me how I can help you?

"*Per favore*, Antonio would you pour my coffee and ready my extra garments from my office wardrobe?"

"*Sì*, very good my Eminence. You have the mass at the Apostolic Palace in a short while, is there anything else I can do?"

The Pope walked closer to Antonio, placed his hand on his shoulder and looked him in his eyes, "You know how you can help me and Mother Church?"

Antonio looked at his friend and then down to the floor, "Yes, my Eminence, I am your loyal servant."

Gregory half smiled at Antonio, "You should leave the Vatican shortly." Gregory then left for the restroom, gathering his tattered pride. Changing his garments, he readied himself for the day's events.

In the later morning, though weary and frail, Gregory attended a celebration at a large hall on the third loggia of the Apostolic Palace in the Sala del Concistoro in the Vatican City. Looking more like a ballroom, it is in the residential wing of the palace, added by Pope Sixtus V and lavishly decorated by Pope Clement VIII.

"All of these riches, how many poor went hungry?" he nodded slightly in disgust as he gazed upon the elaborate paintings and marble floors.

Gregory stared for a brief moment at Clement's coat of arms featured on the ceiling of the hall and then gazed up over the people before him.

"It is time," his inner voice spoke. He stood and addressed the crowd, "and it is with my deepest sympathies that I must announce my resignation," he told them in Latin. As he spoke, gasps of surprise filled the room. Gregory ignored them all.

"A Vatican holy day mired in scandal," Cardinal Antonelli whispered to himself as his eyes set upon the altar watching the Pope. "The devil lives in the shadows of history, creating hell on earth and making it necessary for the need of martyrs. But I think Gregory's announcement will overshadow our celebration of the canonization of the Catholic martyrs, he is making his own history today." Antonelli then remembered Shakespeare, "Hell is empty and all the devils are here."

Pope Gregory cited his deteriorating strength, "it is due to my age, and the physical and mental demands of the papacy."

His voice cracking, "I am declaring that I will continue to serve Mother Church in another way, through a life dedicated to service and devotion to our Blessed Mother."

After making his historic announcement, he arrived at the Papal Palace of Castel Gandolfo and awaited news from his counsel regarding the beginning process of his transition. Already anxious he turned on his television.

"World news headlines are already exploding," he thought, "that did not take long. These reporters will hover over the Vatican like buzzards looking for fresh prey," he sneered.

Reporters focused on a church plagued with scandals as yet another developing story was uncovered.

One newscaster almost gleefully reported, "We have learned the Vatican document leaks involve the Pope Gregory's personal butler, Antonio Lombardi. Our sources tell us he is soon to be arrested for leaking the Pope's personal files. We will have more on these Vati-Leaks as more information becomes available," he promised.

"It seems that these reporters think they are clever in titling these scandals. I suppose it sells more newspapers and increases viewership," Pope Gregory was deeply troubled because Antonio was his friend.

The Pope kept an eye on the news coverage, both good and bad. He followed more scandalous headlines that were surfacing.

Another newscaster reported, "Vati-con is the latest scandal concerning the Vatican." She went on to explain, "Delaney Mills the well-known American actress was engaged to then-boyfriend, Rodolfo Solleirio, who with the help of a few rogue Cardinals, defrauded the billionaire, Warren Blake, over church property land purchases. Rodolfo Solleirio was arrested in the United States and more arrests are pending. We will bring you latest news when we have more details."

"*Bitte* God, on top of the sex abuse scandals that are ever present in people's minds and in active court cases, how much more can we take?" His frustration grew into anger.

Sickened and weak, Pope Gregory turned the television off and sighed, "There seems no end in sight to the deluge of these reports. The news is everywhere!"

There was no escape for the old Pontiff.

Chapter 2

SOPHIA OF TRASTEVERE

Televisions were set on the news in almost every household. In a medieval looking neighborhood known as Trastevere, the 13th district south from the center of Rome and separated by the Tiber River, there was a report of an Italian mobster that caught the eye of a twenty-seven year old Sophia Pistisi. She was walking toward her kitchen while passing her television set stationed on the local news reading the headlines, "Vatican Took Money from Cosa Nostra."

"There are reports that Enrico De Pedis, the former boss of Rome's notorious Magliana gang, is buried in the sacred Basilica of Sant' Apollinare," the middle aged male anchor made the announcement. Sophia stopped in her steps. She stared at the television screen.

The reporter went on as if almost talking to only Sophia, "Investigators stated that there is a possible connection to the mobster and that of a missing 11 year-old girl, Emelia Franco."

Sophia stood mesmerized as the anchor continued with his story, "It was widely speculated that Emelia was kidnapped about 15 years ago, possibly in retaliation for her father's willingness to show evidence linking the Vatican Bank, Istituto per le Opere di Religione or IOR, to organized crime. Sources cite there may be evidence that Emelia was snatched to keep her father silent."

Sophia's heart dropped as her mind became flooded with memories of Emelia. Her mind flashed back to a happy time when they attended the same Marymount International School in Rome. Sophia remembered vividly the day Emelia disappeared.

On their way to school they usually sat together on the bus. Clad in their uniforms, Eme seemed agitated. Her long brown hair and brown eyes matched the brown jacket she wore, which Sophia had admired.

11

"I love the tweed breaded lines running up and down in the front of your coat," Sophia complemented, "Eme, *sei bella*."

The complement went unnoticed. Using her finger to twirl her hair, Eme confided in Sophia, "I overheard my parents talking about what my Papa should do about his job. Sophia, he seemed afraid of something, I could just tell." Eme's eyes grew wide with concern, "but they realized that I was there in the hallway and told me to go to my room. They told me everything was fine but I just know something is wrong."

"Eme, if they said everything is fine then believe them," calling her by her nickname, Sophia tried to assure her friend.

"But I could sense my father's fear. There is something wrong I just know it. And he never tells me to go to my room!" Eme countered.

Sophia remembers the day like it was yesterday. They walked up the steps of the school as they had done for so many years. The sky was blue, there were white angelic clouds passing overhead. It was a beautiful day.

It haunted Sophia as she remembered the concern in Emelia's voice. "Don't worry Eme, your dad will be OK. He knows a lot of powerful people in the Vatican so don't worry," Sophia reassured her friend again as they passed through their school doors. Those were the last words Sophia ever spoke to Eme.

Ring, ring… Sophia's mobile snapped her out of her trance.

"*Ciao* Mama."

"Sophia, are you listening to the news about Emelia?" Her mom asked with concern.

"*Sì, sì*, Mama," Sophia replied.

"Are you all right? Do you need me?"

"No Mama, really *sto bene*. I will see you this weekend for Sunday dinner," Sophia assertively answered her mother. But as Sophia ended the call, she could still feel the anguish from the loss of her best friend. The wound felt fresh and unhealed.

She sat down to collect herself. There were so many mixed feelings, so many unanswered questions.

12

She closed her eyes and began to remember Eme.

They were perhaps as young as eight years old, playing in Eme's room and dressing up in Eme's father's white shirts, their lab coats.

They were going to be scientists together. Two little girls, they had such high hopes of making a difference in the world.

"Don't just make a wave in this world," Eme's mum would say. "Girls, you need to make tidal waves! You girls need to make this world know you were here!!"

Sophia could hear Eme's mum encouraging them as she handed them treats. Eme and Sophia would pretend the treats were their own inventions for lifesaving ways to help people in far off lands. They pretended to hold secrets to powerful medicines and they held many other secrets just between each other. They were like sisters.

Sophia remembered when she first told Eme that she was adopted.

"When I was a baby, they left me on the steps of an orphanage." Sophia explained.

Eme looking a little confused at her friend, "On the steps? Were you cold?"

"I don't remember," Sophia replied, "I was a baby. My parents told me when I was about six months old they adopted me." Mario and Patricia Raiti, a kind older childless Italian couple, doted on Sophia.

There were no secrets about Sophia's adoption. It was on Sophia's 21st birthday that she seriously questioned to her parents about her birth parents. They took Sophia to a fancy restaurant, and as the waitress came with a small birthday cake and a lighted candle, staring at the flame Sophia could not help but wonder if her birth parents knew she was 21.

"Do they even care?" Her inner voice questioned anxiously.

"*Ti amo con tutto il mio cuore,*" Sophia looked up and exclaimed without too much enthusiasm to her beloved Mama and Papa.

"We love you with all of our hearts too," Mama responded lovingly.

Sophia looked sad. Her expression was telling. It was what her parents dreaded. They could feel it.

"I just want to…" Sophia's voice trailed off as the candle burned. She stared at the candle and looked over at her parents with tears in her eyes.

"We know Sophia, we understand," her Papa gently whispered as he reached to hold her hand.

"We knew you would want to know about them. Really, we do understand," his eyes seemed to glisten with his own tears.

"Make your wish Sophia," Mama insisted and blew a kiss touching her two fingers to her lips and then motioned them toward her, blowing a kiss her way. It was Sophia's sure, safe signal that everything was going to be OK; something Sophia had recognized as long as she could remember.

Sophia nodded. "I just want to know who I am and what my life's purpose is," she mumbled as she blew out the candles.

With her parents' blessing, she started to investigate. Over a few months' time she found that her last name was Pistisi, and she legally changed her last name.

"Maybe changing my last name will make it easier for my birth family to find me." Not wanting to alienate her adoptive parents she hyphenated her name to Raiti-Pistisi.

Sophia's childhood was wonderful by most standards. Gazing at other pictures on her wall, she remembered the beautiful pink frilly dress she wore on her ninth birthday. She loved to twirl in it and the fancy holiday red and white overcoat complemented her white hand muffs. It brought back fond memories.

"But there is something missing," she sighed.

A picture with Sophia and her "Nonna Jo," short for Johanna, gave her a happy and guarded grin. She loved Nonna Jo with all her heart and remembered that Nonna always made Sophia special personalized birthday cakes. However, this picture snapped of a younger Nonna and herself flaunted Sophia in a white dress after she received her Confirmation while standing in front of white cake.

It gave her an uneasy feeling because of her emotions regarding the Catholic Church, Eme's warning of her Father's fears, and Eme's disappearance.

"Ahh but I loved that angel shaped cake Nonna made me," she then stared at the white orb looking spot above Sophia's head.

"What is that white spot above my head?" Sophia remembers asking Nonna of the picture.

"That is a spirit orb. It is Poppy looking over you from the heavens," Nonna responded affectionately.

They had lost Sophia's Grandfather years earlier. "He always loved being in pictures. He was such a big ham," Nonna smiled.

She managed to ignore the Confirmation dress and its meaning, focusing more on the cake and the white spot orb of Poppy. As a religious family, Sophia and her parents had attended their Catholic church every Sunday and she continued with religious instruction throughout her school years. However, after Eme's kidnapping something inside her changed. Over the years, Sophia had learned to either change the topic or to just walk away when a religious conversation came up. Now older and somewhat wiser, Sophia realized that she could not change other people; she could only change the way she reacted to them.

Looking at another picture of Sophia and her adoptive parents, one could not help but notice that she did not resemble her portly olive-skinned parents. Sophia was fair, tall and thin. Her long, straight black hair framed her face, featuring her high cheekbones. But it was her bright green eyes that captured the attention of anyone who looked at her. They seemed to change with her mood: a fluorescent green when feeling well or happy; a dark hazel when angry; or a mix of blue and green when she felt insecure or confused.

"You are like a living mood ring," her Mama teased, "I can always tell how you are feeling."

Sophia's favorite family photo was of Mama, Papa and herself hugging after her high school graduation. Mama came up to Sophia's chest in the photo.

Papa stood to Sophia's left as they smiled broadly, Sophia's eyes shining bright. She towered over them as they all mugged for the camera.

Now, as her adoptive parents' only child, she felt obligated to protect them and to make sure she included them in her adult life.

"But I just want to know more about my birth family," she whispered. "Were they religious? Were there many of them? Did they love me? Why did they give me up?" These inevitable questions streamed through Sophia's mind.

Breathing in and out slowly, Sophia tried to meditate.

She remembered what she had been taught by her counselor, Caterina. It helped her to maintain control of her feelings, but it was difficult.

Her unanswered questions and memories of Eme were too powerful. Tears ran down her cheek.

"Sophia, when it is the right time to find your birth parents, you will know it," Eme had responded to her friend's questioning about her "other family," as she referred to them.

"Eme, I can almost feel you, as if you were sitting alongside me," she said aloud, sitting on the small sofa that took up most of the living room.

Sophia looked around her little flat. Her queen-sized bed was on the other side of a nicely decorated wall partition, the television was perhaps ten feet away from her sofa, with two extra chairs, a small coffee table and two folding tray tables.

The kitchen consisted of a few cupboards, a hot plate and sink; the bathroom had a toilet, small corner sink and the shower pretty much filled the room. The faded pale yellow walls bore family and friend photos scattered about. A bit melancholy, she stared at the photo of herself standing between her parents, smiling, the day she graduated from her university.

She refocused, and reminisced having moments with her friends, Eula Sabio and Navaeh Farai from her last birthday.

After university, they had remained close friends. "I miss you guys," she thought.

Eula was just as much of a science geek as she, having a penchant for astrology and numerology.

Navaeh was different. After three years she had dropped out of the university and pursued her passion for fashion.

Navaeh's father, an engineer from South Africa, was not pleased by his daughter's decision. But as a fashion designer, at least Navaeh always looked stunning, her black skin reflecting elegantly with anything she wore.

Sophia had learned a lot about class from her fashion friend, unlike Eula, who came from a traditional poorer Italian family.

In Eula's household, fashion was not a highlighted concern, but intellect was.

The picture of the three sitting in a park illustrated a humorous combination of their personalities.

"You both really would have loved Eme," Sophia whispered. And there, in the corner of one frame, was an old picture of her with Eme, faded from the times Sophia's hand had clutched it, crying, talking to her long-lost friend.

Sophia began to inventory her possessions, her mind wandering as she recounted family memories. Her middle-class family had some luxuries others might have taken for granted, but they knew what the real treasures of life were, and she never felt unloved. Sophia grew up feeling like a princess. Christmas had been magical with what seemed to be a thousand gifts under the tree. There was singing and music at every holiday. The extended family gathered for suppers filled with the seafood and Italian delicacies that Sophia loved most.

Even thinking about searching for her birth family made her feel a bit guilty. It held her back from aggressively focusing on finding her biological family. She had done some research on the internet, and field work, as she liked to think of it, reviewing the few available orphanage records and talking to several people at the orphanage, but she had not learned much beyond her name. Even changing her name had made her feel like a traitor, but she was grateful her parents were so encouraging. With limited information, time went on as she settled into her job and living her new independent life in her flat. Months then turned into years.

Wiping her tears away she turned off the television and sat back on the sofa. She recalled Eme's voice, "You will know when it is the right time."

Sophia sat straight up, posturing herself, continuing to deeply breathe in and out. With each breath she could feel Eme's presence becoming stronger.

"What are you waiting for?" she thought.

Allowing herself to feel a little excitement, she thought, "Maybe the time *is* right." A calmness came over her.

This time she felt more determined. "If Eme's disappearance must remain a mystery, maybe I can gain some control in my own life by finding out where I came from. I do think it's time!"

Opening her laptop, she searched the internet for private investigators. She knew few details of how she came to the orphanage, having been left with a pair of crystal rosaries and a note that she had read thousands of times. *"Per favore, take care of our little one and let her know she is loved."* That was it. Further inquiries had only yielded her name, Sophia Pistisi. Her adoptive parents loved the name Sophia and they decided to keep her first name, which helped to trace her birth parent's last name, Pistisi. But that was all she knew.

Clicking the keyboard, Sophia searched until she came across D Rock Investigations. It was the website of Dennis Schiano, a retired investigator for The *Direzione Investigativa Antimafia* (DIA), the Anti-Mafia Investigation Department, a joint organization of *Polizia di Stato, Carabinieri* and the *Guardia di Finanza* who fought against organized crime.

"The website is impressive. Hmm…, his mission statement says that he had twenty-eight years on the job before he retired, and he has been running this small private investigative company for ten years. *Bene,*" she thought.

"We are dedicated to helping solve our client's problems." Something clicked in her mind. "Perhaps this would be more fitting for my budget. Hiring a former investigator could help me to find loopholes around the law that prevented adoptees from finding their birth parents if they didn't want to be found."

Before losing confidence, she picked up her mobile and dialed the number listed on the website.

"Ah…, Mr. Schiano, *per favore.*"

"*Sì*, this is he," the deep voice answered.

"Oh, ah..." Sophia felt like a child unsure of what to say.

"Can I help you," he asked directly.

"*Sì*, I mean I was looking for a private investigator to help me find my birth family. Do you do that sort of work?" Sophia inquired.

"*Sì*, I do," Mr. Schiano replied.

"*Bene*. Ahh..., how does this work?" Sophia hesitated. "I've never hired a private investigator before."

"Well, how about we first meet? This way I can see what information you have, see if I can help you and I can review the terms of my employment with you," he countered.

"*Va bene*," she agreed. "Can we meet at Café Trastevere on Wednesday? Let's say at two o'clock."

"Two p.m. is fine," Mr. Schiano replied, "I will look forward to meeting you."

Ending the call, Sophia had wondered what this man would look like, since there were no photos of him on the website. As he answered her questions, she was impressed with his phone etiquette in smoothing over her obvious lack of experience. "Having never hired a private investigator, I don't really know what to expect. Mama at least would approve of my meeting in a public place," she reasoned.

Her only previous contact with the police had been after Eme was kidnapped, and that impression was damaged. She remembered the police sitting in Sophia's living room beside her parents and asking, "How did Eme dress? Did she have a boyfriend? Did she do drugs?" Sophia felt that they had been overly intrusive. "We were too young for all that business. The *polizia* were foolish," she recalled.

The investigation unfolded after weeks, then months, then years, and Sophia became disgruntled. "It was either a politician's ego or an investigator's politics that upstaged leads in Eme's case." After some time, there was little compassion during the encounters with *polizia*. Sophia felt anger, recalling their interrogations.

"But perhaps this experience will be better. After all, Mr. Schiano is a *retired* investigator," she reasoned.

She had a good feeling about their meeting. "It WILL work out," her inner voice recited over and over. And her inner voice had never let her down before.

The few days passed quickly. Waiting at the café not far from her flat, she sat outside at a small table. A feeling of nervousness stirred within her as she anticipated Mr. Schiano's arrival.

People milled about the busy quaint café, with perhaps a dozen tables outside, and a half dozen inside.

It was unseasonably warm for February, as the sun had made a welcome appearance. A few of the outside tables were covered by umbrellas and they were scattered in no particular order close to the café's wide open door. The cobblestone streets were reminiscent of Italy's ancient history.

Looking around, Sophia occupied her time with reading the blackboard menu which hung on the outside wall a table away, and then she would glance at her cell phone as if expecting a call.

No umbrella obscured her view when she squinted at a tall strapping man with blond hair and blue eyes walking toward the café. Sophia looked at him and somehow knew that had to be him. He carried a certain presence, almost intimidating. Mr. Schiano looked around for a moment and fixed his eyes on Sophia. As he approached, she sat at attention.

"Miss Sophia Pistisi?" Mr. Schiano asked.

"*Sì*, a-hmm," clearing her throat, "that's me."

"I am Dennis Schiano; we spoke on the phone." His deep voice almost boomed over the tables.

"*Per favore*, sit. Would you like some coffee?" Sophia gestured.

"No, *grazie*, I prefer to get right into business if you don't mind," he responded. He was about thirty years her senior, with handsome features.

With her coffee cup held tightly between her hands, she told Dennis of wanting to find her birth parents. She could sense his gentle-giant energy as he listened.

Sophia could sense a person's energy in an instant.

20

She considered herself to be a good judge of character and was rarely wrong.

"As an orphan, I need to understand more about where I came from," Sophia went on with her story, showing him the rosaries, the note and what little information she had from the orphanage.

"I can understand. I have worked on similar cases," Mr. Schiano acknowledged.

"Then we can agree?" Sophia asked.

"I will contact you with weekly updates, but after my first update I request payment for services in advance," he said matter-of-factly.

He reached out to shake Sophia's hand. She looked a little surprised. But offering her hand, she could now sense his strength as they shook on their deal.

Mr. Schiano then rose to his feet, "I will contact you in a week's time with your first report." Sophia stood as well, registering his height.

"That would be great. I look forward to hearing from you with any news," she excitedly replied as he was leaving.

But having this added expense, she realized she would now have to work extra overtime. "I hope he comes up with information before I go broke," she mused.

After graduating from The Institutions, Markets, Technologies (IMT) Institute for Advanced Studies in Lucca, Italy, Sophia worked at the forensic science laboratories of Carabinieri Scientific Investigations (RaCIS), based in Rome, so the commute was as frustrating as it was costly. As a junior research scientist she made €100,000 yearly, which may seem like a lot of money but living near Rome was not cheap. Rent, taxes and living expenses were a drain on her bank account and lifestyle. But having had previous experience with investigators, she felt drawn to the field of science.

"I do want to help people, but more," she had earnestly explained to her parents. "Maybe there is something I can do to find out what happened to Eme."

She realized, however, that it would take time to make her way to the top levels. "One day, I will get that promotion and I WILL find out the truth. I promise Eme."

21

Her position as a junior researcher was in a sub-department in the field of forensic analysis. It was not glamorous to analyze evidence and oversee the process of identification, preservation and presentation of admissible evidence for court cases, but she loved it. Her job was tedious on the technical research level, but it was a bonus that she seldom had to speak publicly, if at all. That her small lab cubicle was no bigger than the kitchen in her flat did not bother her; she was used to being in confined quarters.

Large stone walls surrounded the institution, which stood in ironic similarity to Sophia's life.

About twelve feet high, brick mortar outlined the many buildings in the compound. Her laboratory was located near the parking lot.

The entire compound was heavily guarded, and it was not unusual for her to need to show her identification badge two or three times a day. As with her inner feelings, everything was well protected.

After her café meeting, Sophia felt a little lighter, a little calmer. She felt confidence in Mr. Schiano's ability. Still, she decided she didn't want to share her new arrangement with anyone just yet. "I'll wait to tell Mama and Papa," thinking of her parents at Sunday dinner.

She tried her best to have supper with her parents each week, and this Sunday was special because her Nonna Jo and her cousins would be there too. Not having seen them in a few months, it would give them time to catch up and be together again. "The conversation will be lively enough without mentioning Mr. Schiano. And besides, Mama will make my apple stuffed pork chops."

Getting onto her red Vespa, her mind drifted away, just thinking about smelling the appled pork chops. She was used to driving the Vespa LX everywhere when the weather allowed. Better than taking the public transport, and having few parking alternatives, this was the least expensive. Besides, she didn't know how to drive a car. Thinking about Mr. Schiano being able to help her and the appled pork chops, Sophia almost didn't see the pothole in the road until someone beeped their car horn.

"*Santo Merda,*" snapping out of her daydream just in time, she swerved just before hitting it.

The next day, alas, the weather was returning to the normally colder conditions even though the sun shone brightly. "I guess the bus will have to do," she sighed. Sophia picked up a few grocery items to get her through the weekend, and made sure she got the rolls for Sunday supper. She even splurged on a new red dress.

"Clothes shopping could be my hobby if I could afford more of it," she laughed. Instead, her hobby was limited to on-line window shopping, sparingly indulging her love of shoes and pocketbooks.

Her mobile rang with a familiar ring tone, "*Ciao,* Eula. What's up?"

"Nothing really, just wanted to see if you wanted to catch up; get a drink, and maybe some dinner tonight?" Eula's voice was pleasant, sounding more like a young girl. She could seem introverted, until you got to know her, and then she wouldn't shut up.

"*Bene,* that sounds great! Same time at Big Mama's?" Sophia suggested.

"Oh…got another call, see you tonight." Eula ended the call abruptly.

"*Bene,* I will…mmm, OK, I look forward to seeing you there," she mumbled to herself.

Big Mama's was one of Sophia's favorite places. The jazz and blues nights mixed with other nights of rock and funk offered a release from reality. Young people made up most of the audience. The American University of Rome was nearby, and it meant there was a chance to meet people.

"Perhaps I will a meet a nice guy," Sophia thought hopefully.

The night air was cold, and dampness crept into Sophia's bones. Taking the subway to Big Mama's was fast and easy. It was an unassuming building with white faded bricks outfitted with two red steel poles holding up the black awning over a heavy black metal door. "It gives the impression you need a password to enter," Sophia snickered upon arriving.

The place was packed with people. Girls were dressed to attract; guys were dressed to accommodate any female attention. Pushing through the crowd, passing the bar Sophia could see that Eula was lucky enough to get a small table to the right of the stage. She headed toward the back of the room, where above the stage hung a big red heart with "Big Mama" written across it.

Walking up to Eula, "*Ciao*, my friend," she leaned down to give Eula a kiss.

"*Ciao*, Sophia, how are things with you? I ordered your drink."

"OK, the next one is on me." Sophia gratefully acknowledged her friend's thoughtfulness.

Eula was always thinking of others; her near-poverty Italian background gave her a unique realization of the value of friendships.

"Hey, I like your sweater," Eula responded.

"Thanks, and I could say the same about your jacket. Is it new?"

"I was hoping you would ask. I think Navaeh would be proud that I finally went shopping," she laughed. Eula's new black leather jacket added character to her short brown hair and thin frame, almost giving a biker-chick impression. Her brown eyes were dark but soft.

The music started, drinks were poured, and the two old friends found it was like old times. "Did you hear about the meteor that exploded over Russia today?" Eula asked seriously, with glazed eyes.

"No, I didn't," Sophia was half listening, the music blaring in her ears.

"*Sì*, it exploded just about eleven kilometers above the ground, and people were hurt by breaking glass. I can't believe you didn't hear about it. Your head is always in the clouds," teased her friend.

"This is the only thing I care about right now," Sophia replied, putting the straw in her mouth and taking a big sip from her cucumber martini.

"Don't you find it odd that the night the Pope announced his resignation, lightning struck Saint Peter's Basilica, and now a meteor that could have killed many people exploded above Russia? It is like an omen; like God is trying to get our attention, don't you think?" Eula asked with a serious expression.

24

"Eula, you worry too much. If God wanted to get our attention I'm sure He would let us know," she sounded confident.

"Well, I am taking a new numerology and astrology class, and I'm trying to figure out what these signs mean."

"Again? Don't you ever get tired of these classes?"

"No, Sophia, and you should pay attention to the stars. They were here before us and they will be here long after we are gone. Prophets believe they can dictate our destiny." Eula was confident.

"*Sì, bene.* I have you to help me, then."

"Hey, look over there." Eula pointed to a young woman about their age with long blond hair wearing a black mini-dress.

The woman was talking with another girl and two young men near the bar. "Isn't that your old friend Shala?"

Sophia squinted and stared at the woman who did look like a former friend from her troubled past.

Watching the woman's movements, Sophia remembered the girl she had once called friend. It seemed like a lifetime ago when they partied together, passing a blunt and sharing a toot. They had not seen each other for a long while until she and Eula happened to run into her at a party a year ago.

"Her name is Sakla. *Sì,* I think that's her," Sophia responded as the woman took notice of being stared at.

Gesturing to her companions, Sakla pointed to Sophia and Eula, then excused herself and made her way through the crowd to them. Sakla walked with a sway that drew the attention of men, young and old.

"*Mio Dio!* Sophia! How are you? You look wonderful," she broadly smiled. Sakla was sincere, but ignorant to a fault. Both of her parents were drug users and she did the best she could with the assets God gave her.

"*Bene.* How are you?" Sophia stood up and kissed Sakla on the cheek. Directing her finger toward Eula, "You remember...?"

Before Sophia could finish, "*Sì,* Eula, right?" Sakla answered, "I remember because your name ended with *A,* like mine." Sakla was always trying to act smart, contriving little games to help her memory.

"You know, Sophia, I work at "The Via Medii Art Gallery" in Via Principe Eugenio." Sakla's movements seemed on cue.

"Next Saturday we are having an opening night for a new artist to debut her astrogeology art pieces. Perhaps we can catch up on old times if you would like to attend?" Sakla sold her employer's product well.

"*Grazie*, but I am not really..."

"That sounds great! Can anyone come?" An anxious Eula interjected, excited by the prospect of astrology and art mixed together.

"It's Eula who is interested in astrology," Sophia explained.

"Oh, I thought you were interested in the stars," Sakla referred to Sophia, then looking at her friend. "*Sì*, Eula, you can come. I can put aside two tickets if you'd like."

"*Sì*, that would be wonderful!" Eula enthused.

"OK, great. I look forward to seeing you then." Sakla leaned toward Sophia, kissing her cheek in farewell.

"That would be wonderful?" Sophia looked down, questioning Eula.

"Oh *per favore*, come with me!" Eula begged.

"I'll see," Sophia negotiated, and left it at that. It was a good night especially sharing it with Eula. Working hard was taking its toll on Sophia, and this weekend promised to be restorative, relaxing with friends and family.

Feeling rested the next day, she got ready to visit her parent's home for Sunday supper. "This new dress is lovely," she thought. Its red color accented Sophia's dark hair, and the low V-neck gave just a hint of cleavage.

"If I wear this with black stilettos, I could wear this dress out to a club. Navaeh would be jealous! This gives me options; I like it," nodding her head as she slid her hand down her hip and then to her thigh.

"But I think to be conservative for Mama, I'll wear low heels with a top sweater."

Checking the weather through her window, "I think this visit requires calling a taxi."

"This particular dress would not do well on the Vespa," she chuckled.

The thirty minute ride to her parents' home gave her time to check her makeup again, and daydream as she looked out the taxi window. Just south of Sophia's flat, the roadway to her parents was scattered with a mixture of modern and traditional Italian buildings and homes. New construction was diverse with old-styled dwellings, making each trip home more unfamiliar as time went on.

Arriving at Mama and Papa's house in Infernetto, Latium, she smiled. "*Bene*, I love coming home." Leaving the taxi and walking up the cobblestone walk to the blue-shuttered house flooded Sophia with memories.

"Mama, Mama, I'm home," she would call out, running up the two steps when she got off the public bus from school. She couldn't wait to see what treats Mama had for her. Her stay-at-home mother had given Sophia every comfort of a loving home, including her favorite biscuits.

The narrow stone porch held two chairs to the left of the front door where Papa and Sophia had had many serious talks, and shared an equal number of jokes. Papa taught Sophia about generosity.

He owned his own custodial company that regularly did work for the Vatican and was a longstanding member of a local Rotary club.

"We are a group of business people who raise money for different causes, like the Gift of Life program," she recalled him saying, "and we can save children's lives with heart surgeries that they would not otherwise get." He told Sophia many stories of the children being saved in foreign countries, even introducing a few of them to her. It meant a lot to her, changing her view of the world, and making her own life feel blessed.

Sophia looked up to her Papa, her hero. Her most prized treasure was the dollhouse he had made when she was seven, a miniature of their home.

Walking under the roof overhang, she was reminded of being sheltered on the hot, summer rainy days when she and Papa would sit together for hours on the porch chairs. She held those moments close to her heart.

Opening the large oak wood door, as she had done all her life, gave her a famaliar comfort. The open-concept living area was small, but charming. "Ah, Papa set everything up." Sophia looked to the left, toward the living room with its large red sofa and two brown leather reclining chairs taking up one end of the narrow room. The dining table with its matching chairs and three folding chairs dominated the room, spilling into the living room area to provide more space for their extended family. The small kitchen was behind a half-wall breakfast counter and two stools, which afforded some separation between the living area and kitchen.

On the right side of the front entrance was the long hallway leading to the bathroom and three bedrooms. Closing the bathroom door, Mario, Sophia's stout, balding father, was just coming down the hallway.

"*Ciao,* Papa... Mama *io sono a casa*!" She shouted excitedly to her mother who was bent over the oven in the kitchen. Sophia walked to her Papa to kiss him hello.

"Oh, *il mio bambino*, you are home," Mama exclaimed, as she straightened and ran toward Sophia with her arms opened wide.

"Oh, Papa, she's home!" Mama gushed.

Mama was wearing her best blue dress with her favorite yellow apron over it. Mama stood a mere 5 foot 5 inches to Sophia's tall, thin 5 foot 9 inch frame. But her black curly hair that granted an inch more, and Sophia could recall her mama's round face as always having a smile on it.

"*Mama Mia*, Patricia, she was only here last week," Mario teased as he shook his head, hugging Sophia.

"Let me help you with supper," Sophia countered, kissing Mama, putting her things down, and following her mother.

"*Sì,* you can help finish setting the table while I check on the appled pork chops. Uncle Egidio is bringing the lamb, and your cousins, Rosey and Little Tony are coming with Uncle Tony and Aunt Rose. So be sure to set enough dishes." She turned to the oven and added, "You did remember to go to church on Ash Wednesday, Sophia?"

"Mmm... yes Mama, I *saw* the church," she mumbled quickly, picking up the china dishes to set the table.

The light yellow and reddish terra cotta tile floor announced every step Sophia took, and she hoped the noise would hide her answer.

"Did you say Nonna Jo is coming too?" Sophia inquired, changing the subject as she picked up glasses and utensils.

"Of course. Aunt Rose is picking her up," Mama replied happily.

"*Bene,* Mama. I prepared the rolls already so they only need to be warmed up," Sophia motioned.

Uncle Egidio was the first to arrive. He was always on time, especially if there was a meal. Recently widowed by Aunt Assunta's passing from cancer, he was starting to show signs of depression. Their only child, Sophia's cousin, Pietro, lives in Messina with his own family so Mama, Papa and Sophia were his only family near Rome.

Papa and Uncle Egidio were from a large family that hailed from Turin in northern Italy where many relatives still resided. While they looked like opposites, with Uncle Egidio being taller having broad shoulders and a full head of wavy jet black hair, Papa was balding with a stout frame. However, of the twelve siblings, they were the closest of brothers. And Uncle Egidio loved Sophia as his own daughter.

"You are our little Flaming Star...," he would say to a young Sophia as he lavished her with gifts.

No toy or dress was too expensive for his Sophia. His position as a top security official in the **Gendarmerie Corps of Vatican City State** provided well, even in retirement.

When she was a small child if he and Aunt Assunta came for supper, Mama would let him tuck her into bed and he would make up stories that she loved to hear. "The night your Mama and Papa brought you home, they had just laid you down to sleep when we went out on the porch to thank our lucky stars and count our blessings. Looking up at the beautiful stars in the night sky, we saw a huge red star pass over your house. This comet was larger than anything we had ever seen. We felt so blessed to have you in our lives, so that is how we got our Flaming Star." Mama, Papa and Uncle Egidio would repeat that story over and over, and she loved hearing it.

"It was a blessing to help your Papa and Mama to adopt our little Flaming Star. You are so special," he would remind her as he kissed her forehead.

"*Ciao, Zio* Egidio," Sophia went up to him giving a warm greeting to her kindly, eccentric uncle.

"*Ciao*, Sophia, how are you, my Flaming Star?"

"*Sto bene, grazie*," suggesting a chip on her shoulder.

"What's the matter, my love? I can tell something is bothering you," he said, handing her the lamb dish.

"Mama asked me if I went to church for Ash Wednesday. I hate lying to her, but you know how I feel about the church," she charged.

"I know, Sophia, but you must follow your heart, no matter what others think," he wisely answered, meaning to comfort her. Sophia looked at him, smiled approvingly and turned toward the kitchen with the warm lamb dish.

Aunt Rose, Uncle Tony and Nonna Jo tapped on the front door as they entered the house, **bearing** food, wine and flowers for Mama.

"*Ciao*, Nonna!" Sophia ran to her grandmother planting a big kiss on her slight cheek.

Nonna was also on the petite side, standing 5 foot 3 inches, with grey curly hair, but her feisty attitude implied extra height.

"*Ciao*, b*ella*," she exclaimed, wrapping her arms around Sophia's **waist**. "*E' bello vedere che il mio amore.*

"*Si*, Nonna, it's good to see you too. I've missed you," Sophia whispered as she hugged Nonna tighter.

The twins, Little Tony, or "LT" and Rosey, named after their parents in the Italian tradition, soon arrived. Mama's brother, Big Tony, looked almost identical to his sister, with the same large nose and roundness. An unfortunate difference was that Mama had not been able to bear children.

Little Tony and Rosey were like Sophia's siblings. There had been times that Rosey might have been jealous of the attention Uncle Egidio paid to Sophia, but as they grew up, Rosey set her attention on more important issues; she had a new boyfriend every other month.

"So what is your flavor for this month?" a curious Sophia asked Rosey, a beautiful petite young woman about twenty-five, with big, dark round eyes. Her short black pixie hairstyle flattered her plump red lips, an alluring feature.

"His name is Amil, and he's gorgeous! We're going out dancing next Saturday. Why don't you join us? You can meet him then."

"I'll see."

"That's what you always say."

"Well, I bought this new dress so maybe I will this time."

"And you look delicious in it. You would be sure to attract much needed attention," Rosey teased Sophia.

"Mmmm… it smells so good," Little Tony interrupted as he exhaled in anticipation, sitting next to Sophia. His combed, greased-back hair accented his Italian nose, while his overdose of cologne conflicted with the smell of Sophia's appled pork chops. However, it was Little Tony's sense of humor that Sophia most loved about her cousin.

"Hey, did you hear about that Italian chef who died?" he asked Sophia and Rosey, looking very serious.

"No, where?" Rosey replied genuinely.

Sophia, being cautious, just nodded.

"*Si*, he pasta away!" Little Tony laughed. "Get it? He PAST-A away!" He was laughing so hard he didn't notice as his father came up from behind and lightly smacked the back of his head.

Sitting down, Big Tony pointed his figure, and in jest he added, "*LT mente le buone maniere.*"

"*Si*, Pops, I will mind my manners, just for you," LT jokingly snickered.

As the food was being placed on the table, Papa brought the last dish. Uncle Egidio was delighted to bring such a prized lamb to the table, making everyone *oooh* in anticipation; everyone except Sophia, who hated lamb because it reminded her of the unnecessary sacrifices referenced in the Bible.

"And now, we will say our prayers. Sophia, will you lead us?" Mama encouraged. Sophia's eyes shot a dart at her Mama.

31

"She did that on purpose," Sophia thought. "All right then, let us bow our heads. Blessed Mother, *per favore,* bless this meal we are about to receive. From the sacrificed blood of your Son, we recognize that we are not perfect and that your church is not perfect. *Per favore,* forgive us all, and make us worthy of Your mercy. Amen."

"*Grazie.* Sophia that was, hmmm, nice," Papa offered. Mama's stern face revealed she was not too pleased about the church comment.

"That was nice, *Bella,*" Nonna spoke softly. "The Blessed Mother holds a special place in my heart too."

Looking a little puzzled, Sophia tilted her head to Nonna, "Yeah, me too," not really giving it too much more thought.

"*Bene,* pass the lamb and the biscuits," LT chimed.

"*Sì,* and pass the *vino,*" Sophia added.

The seafood, artichokes, lamb and Sophia's favorite apple stuffed pork chops were passed from one person to another. Mama's cooking made any tension forgotten. With light traditional Italian music in the background, the meal and dessert were devoured within two hours.

"The preparation always takes longer than the eating," Papa muttered as he patted his stomach. Coffee, espresso and cordial were served and the hour grew late. Aunt Rose and Uncle Tony were taking Nonna to their home and the twins had just left.

"Sophia, how are you getting home?" asked Papa.

"Well, I was hoping you could take me."

"*Bene,* we shall go."

Sophia gathered her belongings and went to her mother.

"*Ciao,* Mama. The pork chops were the best yet. I love you so much." Mama returned the loving energy, giving her a bag of leftovers.

"*Ciao, zio* Egidio, I will see you soon."

"*Sì,* I hope so. And remember, listening to your heart can help you to see things that you cannot see through your eyes," added Uncle Egidio, fortifying his wisdom with a hug.

As Papa and she left the house, Sophia glanced up at the night sky. "Ohh, Papa…look at the stars. They are talking to us tonight, *sì?*"

Looking up, "*sono belle come te,*" her Papa replied, "but you shine the brightest, my Flaming Star."

"Ohh, *per favore*." Accepting another of his corny sayings, she hugged him before he went around to his side of the car.

Midway to Sophia's flat, stopping at a traffic light, Papa could not resist, "Sophia why don't you learn to drive? I will teach you."

"Ah, Papa, *per favore,* I have told you. I don't need to pollute the earth any more than it is already. Besides, I'm not crazy. Look at these people trying to cut each other off to get to where they have to go," Sophia smirked.

"But one day you may need to know…"

"Papa, then I will call you when I need to know."

"*Bella*, I will not be here forever…."

"Stop it, Papa. You will be with me forever," she insisted.

"*Bene*, my Flaming Star, I will be with you always."

Arriving at Sophia's flat, Papa idled the car in the no parking zone, put the car in park, and sat up straight. His arm around Sophia's shoulder, he leaned in toward her, looking into her eyes and tried to express what was in his heart.

"Sophia, I…," he began.

"*Sì*, Papa, what is it?

"I… I just want you to know…."

"What is it, Papa?"

"I just want you to know how much Mama and I love you."

"I know, Papa, I know," she smiled.

Looking at him for an extra few seconds, she could sense he might be troubled by something.

"Papa, are you sure you're all right?"

"*Sì, sto bene. Ti amo,* Sophia…, you should go in before the night chill gets in your bones."

"Ahh, *bene…* Papa, I will call you in the coming week. I love you, too." As she opened the car door to get out, she blew him a kiss.

"It was a nice Sunday supper," she reflected.

Chapter 3

INTERROGATIONS AND ANGELS

Monday morning came quickly enough, and Sophia went to work in the afternoon for a double shift. The unusually warm sunny day allowed her to wear her favorite blue pantsuit, which today seemed to fit her mood best.

"This weather is like a rollercoaster: warm; then cold; but today it's nice and you should not be locked up all day," she stroked her Vespa, readying for her ride to work. It helped to clear her mind, racing through the alleys and streets.

"Ahhh… my freedom has come to an end, too," she shook her head while locking up the Vepsa. Entering the building, she followed the long maze of hallways to her lab in the rear.

"*Buongiorno*, Carmine," she greeted her supervisor in route to her desk.

Carmine Greico, a sixty-something single man, had been designated "The Lab Rat" by cafeteria gossipers, with more hair on his bushy eyebrows than on his head. A short thin man, with a receding hairline, he desperately tried to cover his balding head with hair paint. Carmine was Sophia's direct manager and she tried to stay on his good side; his Italian temper could get the better of him.

"It's funny, he never talks about family or a lover; he gives hermits a bad name," Sophia snickered. "Hmm…but he may not have family, how sad..." Sophia had a passing thought of her own situation, not knowing her biological kin.

"*Buongior…mm*," he stammered under his breath as he handed Sophia the next batch of her case files.

"See that this information is analyzed right away, and give me your report," he demanded, swiveling his chair to return to his own work. "Oh, and by the way, Rosario was looking for you. You must have done something to get under his skin," he grumbled.

Rosario Lorino was the Chief of Staff with a gruff exterior.

He was an intimidating tall man, and Sophia did her best to avoid him. She flashed to the memory of rounding a corner in the hallway near her office with coffee in her hand just as Mr. Lorino was coming round from the opposite direction. "Oh... *Scusami,* I am so sorry," she had exclaimed as coffee went everywhere. She felt sick just thinking about it, Mr. Lorino's expression still haunted her.

Trying to compose herself, she began her work when the door flew open. It was Mr. Lorino. Cringing, Sophia turned around.

"Ms. Pistisi, *per favore,* would you come with me?" he asked as if it were her option.

"*Sì* of course, Mr. Lorino," she almost whispered, clumsily rising from her chair and following him out the door.

Side by side they walked down one of the many long hallways. All the buildings seemed to have that in common; a maze of long white hallways. Among the secured lab rooms of various sizes were several conference and storage rooms. Sophia noted the many laboratory doors that warned of caution upon entering.

"Ten caution doors. The number ten. I hope that's a good number," thinking of Eula's love for numbers and their meaning.

She knew the lab building inside and out. Badges and key cards were required to enter, but it was the building's café that Sophia liked best. It had wonderful coffee, especially when freshly brewed late at night, when she often worked.

"Mr. Lorino, have I done something?" Sophia asked, unsure of where they were headed.

Looking down at her, he asked, "Do you remember the event in your laboratory last May 13?"

"Of course I do, it was the day someone poisoned my coffee!" she exclaimed.

"You know you are not supposed to drink coffee in the labs," Mr. Lorino reminded, not flinching.

Sophia choked a bit.

"*Bene,* the laboratory attorneys are here in the conference room." Mr. Lorino continued, "They want to know more about that incident."

He barked his orders at Sophia, "You are to tell the truth. Do you understand?"

She nodded nervously, as they entered. Mr. Lorino introduced the two people at the large conference table.

"Sophia, this is Mr. Dhara and Mrs. Potter. They are part of our legal counsel and they will ask you a few questions," he directed, as Sophia felt her knees get weak.

"Please sit down." Mr. Dhara stood, motioning for her to sit, as he pulled out a chair for her. Talking to lawyers made Sophia's eyes sparkle with a hue of green and blue, and Mr. Dhara noticed.

Not much taller than Sophia, he was a slender man who appeared to be a little older than she. "From his accent and his appearance I'd guess he's from India," Sophia thought. He was impeccably dressed in a dark gray suit. His large dark brown eyes with small pupils were the first facial feature she noted. Then looking more intently at his very white teeth and the dimple in his left cheek, she could sense he was a gentle soul.

However, that could not be said of his older counterpart. Mrs. Potter was a well-suited mature woman with a stern face. She reminded Sophia of the character "M" from the Bond movies, but taller, and dressed in what was certainly a designer outfit. "I can tell she's very matter-of-fact straight off." Sophia mused, "In other words, she looks like a *cagna*!"

"Ms. Pistisi, I suppose Mr. Lorino told you why we are here?" Mrs. Potter asked in her uptight English accent.

"*Sì*, he told me that you want to know what happened on May 13 here at the lab," Sophia acknowledged.

"Correct. If you could tell us in your own words, we would appreciate it," Mr. Dhara added in his thick Indian accent.

"I did complete a report, and spoke to investigators," Sophia answered.

"We know. However, we need to also hear it from you, personally," Mr. Dhara stated.

"*Va bene*, I see...." Sophia continued with her version of events, "I was working late in the lab. My boss, Mr. Greico, went home early."

"It was around ten p.m. and..," Sophia was interrupted by Mrs. Potter.

"Do you often work late?" She was straightforward; like a bullet.

"*Sì,*" Sophia responded guardedly.

"Fine, please continue," Mr. Dhara gestured as he looked Sophia over. She was starting to feel the energy in the room getting heated, and was beginning to sweat.

"Perhaps you need a drink of water?" Mr. Lorino reached for a cup attached to the water cooler, observing Sophia's testimony.

"*Sì, grazie,*" Sophia went on. "As I was saying, it was about ten p.m. and I had just gotten my coffee from the café. I went back to my lab when I heard a noise in the corridor. I went to see if anyone was there, but I saw nothing so I went back to my work. I think I I drank a bit more of my coffee as I worked, but then I started to feel dizzy and sick to my stomach."

She stopped for a deep breath.

Mrs. Potter did not look pleased. "Please continue, Ms. Pistisi," she prompted, pointedly.

"*Sì..* mmm, I was feeling dizzy and the next thing I remember I was lying on the floor. A man was kneeling beside me, hovering over me. He told me that everything would be OK. I could see that he wore a security guard uniform and he said his name was Raphael. The next thing I knew I was in the ambulance, being taken to the hospital. They told me that I was poisoned with GHB, a date rape drug," Sophia's voice trailed off. "It was a horrible experience."

Mr. Dhara could see that Sophia was shaken up recounting her story. "Ms. Pistisi can you think of anyone who would want to hurt you?"

"No, I could not think of anyone. I don't have much of a life outside of work, so I can't think of anyone," she replied in jest.

"And this security guard, Raphael, had you seen him before?" Mrs. Potter was deliberate.

"No, I had never seen him before, or since that night. I was told the regular security guard, Mr. Bernadetto, was out sick. I would imagine it was the same illness Mr. Greico had," Sophia shrugged.

"Ms. Pistisi, did you know that there are no records of a security guard named Raphael?" Mrs. Potter asked in a more accusatory tone.

Sophia began to feel more confused, but still she insisted, "The guy was kneeling next to me just as real as you or Mr. Dhara…"

She paused, catching her breath, "he was kind, and he comforted me until I got to the hospital!" Sophia contended, almost to the point of being argumentative.

Mrs. Potter stood, bending over into Sophia's face, "Ms. Pistisi, I can only tell you what the records show, and there was no guard named Raphael. The replacement security guard was not even aware of your situation until the ambulance arrived. Did you know that?"

"I don't understand." Sophia looked puzzled.

The meeting went round and round, confusing Sophia. "*Per favore*, tell me what is going on," Sophia stressed.

Mr. Dhara sat back in his chair. "We are just trying to learn whatever information you may have to help this case." Sophia shook her head as Mrs. Potter scrutinized her every movement.

He went on, "The night you were poisoned, someone tampered with crucial evidence needed in the criminal trial of a Canadian student and her Italian boyfriend who were accused of killing her American flat mate. You must have heard about the case in the news?" he asked, studying her reaction.

Sophia gave a blank stare; her mind racing. "I'm sorry…, I'm confused," she shook her head.

"It is simple," Mrs. Potter stated, "someone tainted the evidence and according to the records, you and Mr. Greico were working on that case. Does that make sense to you now?"

"*Mio Dio*! Do you think I tainted the evidence and then poisoned *myself*?" Sophia shot to her feet.

"No, no, no, Ms. Pistisi we do not think that at all," Mr. Dhara assured her, "we are simply trying to understand what happened."

"Ahhh….," Sophia was stunned. "I didn't…"

"*Per favore,* sit down Sophia," Mr. Lorino requested.

"Look, I would like to understand what happened, too. After all, I was poisoned and could have died." Sophia shouted.

"I had an allergic reaction to that drug and if it were not for that security guard I might not be here today. Besides, I couldn't know what case I was working on because all I get are case file numbers." Sophia decried her innocence.

Her eyes changed from their green/blue hue to a darker florescent green as she got angry. But no one seemed to care.

Exhausted from the run-around conversation, Sophia insisted, "No matter how many times we go over this, I did not know about the evidence tampering and there was really was a security guard named Raphael who saved my life. I am certain of it!"

After a private conversation among Mrs. Potter, Mr. Dhara and Mr. Lorino, they finally released Sophia. "*Grazie*, Ms. Pistisi, for your cooperation. You may return to your lab," Mr. Lorino said apologetically.

Relieved, Sophia was at the door when she turned back to glance at Mr. Dhara again. There was something about him; something about his energy that Sophia intuited. He smiled in return as she closed the heavy door behind her.

The meeting with the attorneys had been emotionally exhausting, and Sophia went to the ladies room to collect herself. "I just don't understand. Who would poison me, and who was Raphael?"

She flashed back to conversations she had had with investigators soon after the event, and was more than disappointed that they had not found out who was responsible for her hospital visit. "Did they know about the evidence tampering back then?" No one had mentioned it before this, she thought.

Standing in front of the mirror, she breathed deeply, in... then out. Noticing a bit of her blue jacket sticking out from under her lab coat, she mused, "and I thought my favorite suit would bring me luck today."

Needing to calm her nerves, she placed a wet paper towel over her face to refresh herself, and had a flashback to the hospital.

The doctor in the emergency had been kind and caring with her. "I am sorry to say that the lab results of your blood work came back positive for Gamma Hydroxybutyric Acid or GHB."

"It is a tasteless and odorless substance, frequently used in date rape." His tone showed concern for her wellbeing.

Another flash and she was talking with investigators who seemingly took their notes. Then she was home, she would have been alone sick and vomiting if it had not been for Navaeh stopping by to drop off a pair of shoes Sophia had bought from her.

"You look terrible." Navaeh's concern and honesty gave Sophia a little comfort. Caring for Sophia, Navaeh bought chicken broth, nursed her friend to health and gave her a shoulder to lean on as she described her ordeal.

Sophia had confided in Navaeh, but had chosen not to tell her parents. They would worry and be overprotective, but it was two days of hell before she began to feel better. She researched GHB and found that it was not something they kept in the lab, but was easy for a common criminal to get his hands on.

Wiping her face with the towel, her memory wandered back to sitting in an attorney's office. She wanted more answers, and had even considered suing her employer.

"Are you sure you want to proceed with this lawsuit, Ms. Pistisi?" the older man, who resembled Caesar with glasses, asked. Sitting behind his large dark wooden desk with many degrees and certificates hanging on his wall, she thought he might be able to help her.

"*Sì*, I do," Sophia responded confidently.

But she then made the mistake of mentioning something to Mr. Greico, who then told Mr. Lorino.

"Sophia, I like you," Mr. Lorino pointed out, while Mr. Greico was conveniently out of the lab. "And I would certainly like for you to continue your employment with our laboratories. If you were to leave us, just know that we would be happy to provide recommendations. Please understand that we know many important people."

Sophia just nodded, not knowing what to say.

"However," he continued, "we are happy to have you on our team, and we have decided to move your employment evaluation up and grant you a raise to show our appreciation of your... talents."

Sophia recalled his solemn tone. All she had mustered in response was a simple, "*grazie*."

Thinking further, "Was that a quiet hint that I could lose my position at the lab and perhaps be blacklisted from getting a similar job anywhere in Italy or Europe? *Merda!* I was the victim. I shouldn't be punished." But her options were few, and she came to realize there was little she could do, and she had not pursued hiring an attorney.

Water dripped from the towel, bringing her back to the present. She shook the the water from her hands and gave herself a pep talk to get herself together. "*Va bene,* one more last deep breath," then stepped out of the restroom, head down, barely noticing the figure in front of her.

"Oops, *scusami*." Sophia had bumped into Mr. Dhara.

"It is not a problem Ms. Pistisi," Mr. Dhara gestured. "Listen, I know we were hard on you at the meeting but you do understand we needed to see how you would react in pursuing this matter further."

"You mean you needed to test me," she shot back, standing her ground.

"If you prefer to say it that way, then yes," he countered, "but let me make it up to you… as you are not a suspect, perhaps I can take you out for coffee."

"A suspect?" she stammered defiantly.

"Please understand. I was only doing my job," he reacted intently, "but I can tell you are a good person."

"That's funny," Sophia thought to herself. "I had the same thoughts about him… there was just something about him." She left him with, "*bene,* I'll think about the coffee," and she continued on back to her lab.

Sophia had a hard time concentrating on her work, yet she had to push forward. "How else am I going to afford to pay my rent as well as a private investigator?"

She worked through the day and into the night, finishing her shift early the next day, and hoping to get some very much needed rest.

On her way out she stopped at the café for her chocolate. It was her new regular routine after finishing work.

"Stop smelling the coffee," she argued with herself on the queue. "I will *not* get another cup of coffee from this café after last May 13 …but the chocolate? That's different." She held two bars in her hand, thinking "it's safe and I do need my fix."

"May I help you?" the girl at the register asked. Sophia was not paying attention.

"*Scusami.., signora,* may I help you?" the girl asked again.

"Oh, I'm sorry, just these two chocolates," Sophia smiled sheepishly.

"And I will pay for that," came a man's voice over her shoulder. It was Mr. Dhara. "It is the least I can do."

Sophia nodded, graciously accepting his offer.

"Can you sit for a moment, Ms. Pistisi?" he asked gently. "Mrs. Potter and I have returned this morning because we have more work at the lab, but I can sit for a few minutes, if you have the time."

"All right, but just for a minute," Sophia agreed, sensing his calm presence.

They chose a corner table, away from the busy queue and the food counters. He sipped his coffee while she held onto the two bars of chocolate.

"Mmm, *bene,* that smells *magnifico.*" Smelling the coffee watching him sip was a challenge for Sophia. She loved the aroma and taste of coffee, but could not get over her distrust of coffee from this café.

He started the conversation with, "Please call me Ben."

"*Va bene*, I am Sophia, as you know," she gestured, half kidding.

"Do you like working at the lab?" Ben asked, to be friendly.

"It pays my bills. Do you like being a lawyer?" Sophia responded.

"It pays my bills," he retorted jokingly.

"How long have you been an attorney?" Sophia wanted to know.

"Almost five years."

"…And working with Mrs. Potter?"

"About two years. I know she is a little crass but you get used to her…"

"A *little!*" Sophia interrupted with sarcasm.

"OK, maybe more than a little. But she is good at what she does and I have learned a lot from her."

"Well, Mr. Dhara," Sophia went on, but he interrupted.

"Please call me Ben," he insisted.

"*Va bene*, Ben. *Grazie* for the chocolate, but I really must be..."

"Look, I know being... interviewed," Ben interrupted her again.

"You mean interrogated," Sophia corrected him.

"All right..., interrogated. I know it is not easy," Ben was apologetic.

"I should say not," she went on.

"But, I don't believe you had anything to do with the tampering of any evidence," he continued with sympathy.

"*Dannatamente giusto!*" Sophia clamored as she hit her fist on the table.

"But I could not help but wonder if you thought it could have been anyone within the lab who poisoned you," he asked, making his point.

"Of course I had wondered about that, but I couldn't find anything or anyone to shed light on what happened that night. It is yet another mystery in my life."

"What do you mean?" He was surprised by her choice of words.

"Nothing," she was embarrassed by the slip of her last words. "Do you have any ideas?" she asked.

"You know I could not tell you if I did, but the issues in this case will certainly stir the pot. So please be careful," Ben suggested with concern.

"Do you mean I am in danger?" Sophia was now alarmed.

"No more than yesterday or the day before," he shrugged. "I just thought you should be alert. And if something does turn up or causes you concern, you should call me right away," Ben insisted, reaching to retrieve his business card and extending his hand to Sophia.

Instinctively, she reached for the card, with both of them now holding it for a few long seconds.

Sophia could feel warm energy emanating from his touch. She was a bit taken aback, and felt even more confused. Not knowing what to make of Ben, she accepted his card.

"*Grazie* for your concern," she added, tossing the card into her already cluttered purse. Standing and ready to walk away, she said, "If anything comes up I'll call you," sounding a little caustic.

"Please do," he persisted.

She gave him a half smile and started to walk away.

"By the way, what was the noise?" Ben asked.

"Noise, what noise?" She stopped in her steps.

"The noise you heard in the hallway," Ben made her think. "That night, that made you leave your lab?"

Sophia's face was blank. She had tried to remember everything that happened that night but she had been in a smog of confusion from the drug. "I'm not sure, exactly. I've tried to remember, but it's strange. I feel like I walked from my lab toward the bathroom but I have done that so many times I can't be sure what I heard or what I did."

"Well, if you do remember anything, please let me know."

She gave him one more half smile and left him at the table.

"There is so much to take in, my head hurts. I can't wait to get home," she thought as she hurried from the café and out of the building.

She felt as if she flew home, but it was much colder than the day before. "Maybe it wasn't such a good idea for the Vespa," but her mind was free to race as fast as she rode.

She could see her breath in the cold air surrounding her. "The weatherman promised to cooperate, but even he's turned against me," she thought, feeling betrayed. "Breathe in and then out. Breathe. Just breathe. *Accidenti!* I need *vino*!" She felt wide awake and looked forward to holding a wine glass.

The morning sun was hidden behind a few clouds as Sophia returned home. She felt aroused by the recent interrogation episode and almost welcomed the clouds to dampen the effect of a bright light hurting her tired eyes.

"I'm tired but awake at the same time. I know what will help me," Sophia assured herself as she made a beeline to her wine bottle and poured a large glass.

For the rest of the day Sophia kept thinking about her interrogation. "Being poisoned months ago, with no arrests and no information about who could have done that to me, makes me all the more sick to my stomach."

Sitting on her sofa, she stared seemingly into space.

She recounted the experience of lying on the lab floor. Sophia remembered her eyes fluttering and trying desperately to open them more fully to see the large man in a guard uniform kneeling over her.

"Do not be afraid. I am here to help you." His voice was so comforting she hadn't felt fear.

"Mmm, mmm," Sophia had moaned, shaking her head back and forth as if in a bad dream, trying to get up.

"My name is Raphael. You will be all right. Have faith," he assured her.

"It seemed like a dream but it was real. *Wasn't it?*" Sophia was starting to question herself, taking another sip of wine.

"Was he real? Why was there was no listing of a guard named Raphael on duty? Why would someone poison me? And why haven't I heard about tainted evidence before this?" She muttered to herself.

Before long she realized she had drunk the entire bottle of wine.

As the sunlight started to fade, she felt hungry. Getting up from the sofa, she went into her kitchen and opened the refrigerator door. "I should have bought more food," she murmured, poking her head low enough to see the fairly empty shelves. "Ah, but there is the leftover pasta from Mama and Papa's. This will do nicely." She took the container out and opened it.

"Mmm, it still smells fresh," she smiled. "*Grazie,* Mama."

Warming up her pasta, she looked over to the counter and saw another bottle of wine. "Hmm, I think I'd like just a little more to go with supper." Sitting alone for dinner was something she had grown accustomed to. She liked to listen to classical music to aid her digestion and comfort her loneliness.

Each sip of wine made her more tired, and looking at the second bottle she had finished, she realized it was time to go to bed.

"*Per favore*, let me sleep well," she spoke into the air with hope that someone would grant her wish. But, a good night's sleep was not in the cards for Sophia. "Groan, grrr...," she tossed and turned, her body increasingly tense with each passing hour. Images of the mysterious guard, Eme and the interrogation plagued her mind.

"*Accidenti*! This is not rest." Sophia got up and began to pace the floor. Stumbling through her flat in the near dark, her left big toe hit the sofa.

"*CAZZO!*" she exclaimed, grabbing her foot and sinking onto the sofa. Rocking back and forth to alleviate the pain, she glanced at the candle on her little folding tray table. Deciding the soft light might help soothe her mind, Sophia lit it. The glow of the white candle enveloped the room and the voice in her head spoke once again.

"Pray," she heard a faint whisper.

Looking up at the pictures on her walls, she remembered praying the rosaries often when she had been much younger. "But I can't pray the rosaries, I don't remember it. It was too long ago," mumbling to herself. "That was a time when innocence was familiar to me, before Eme's disappearance." But praying after Eme was kidnapped had been mostly in anger and confusion.

"Why did You have to take her away from me," she would shout out at God. After a while she had reasoned that the best revenge was to stop praying to Him altogether.

Looking at one picture of her eighteen-year-old self dressed in dark clothes in front of a car, she could remember that time of her life as being more rebellious. Drugs, alcohol and sex filled the emptiness that had consumed her.

In another picture, she sat on the steps of her childhood home with a young university student. The memory of those friends was hazy; they were users like her, but then there was Dominic.

Looking more like a male model, Dominic was tall and slender with light eyes that pierced through her. His muscles spoke to all of her senses.

Gazing at the picture after having too much wine prompted her to recall their lovemaking sessions. She closed her eyes for a brief moment, realizing that sex with him had not been making love. It was lust, but she had enjoyed it; perhaps too much.

Her troubles had seemed endless; staying out all night; all the lies…. Desperate to save her, Mama had urged Sophia to speak with a counselor she knew from church. Sophia certainly did not want to go, but she caved in after listening to her mother crying over the stress she had caused, and after her father's near-fatal heart attack.

Sophia's eyes wandered to the shelf of her television stand. "That little angel," she was reminded of the little angel statue her counselor had once given her.

She would never forget her first visit to Caterina's office. At 5 feet 6 inches, Sophia towered as Caterina stood to greet her.

"*Ciao*, I am Caterina," she said, extending her hand to Sophia.

Sophia returned the greeting with, "It's nice to meet you, Cat."

"*Scusami*, but my name is Caterina!" This little woman was quick to correct Sophia. A woman perhaps her mother's age, she had beautiful, wavy blond hair and blue eyes.

Caterina could show her Italian bravado with the best of them, but angel pictures and angel statues covered almost her entire office, exposing a very tender soul.

"*Strano*," she thought to herself.

Caterina read the look on Sophia's face.

"*Sì*, I know it may seem strange to have all these angels in this small room, but having angels around me can never be a bad thing. Don't you agree?" she tested Sophia. Shrugging her shoulders, Sophia sat down for her first meeting.

Over time, Sophia had been able to release some of her negative energy and eventually pulled away from her friends, including Dominic. It had been a difficult thing to do, but her life was spinning out of control and she needed to save herself.

In their sessions Sophia would often challenge Caterina about the goodness of the church. "Did you see the news was filled with priests raping children?" Sophia would antagonize Caterina.

47

Caterina's response to Sophia was always the same: "The church is filled with bad apples, contradictions, politics and even fraud. But the one thing that is real is our Father and His love for us. That is why He sends angels to help us. That is how *we* met, is it not?"

Sophia eventually learned more about Caterina's angels and, more importantly, how to control her emotions when negative feelings crept in. The breathing exercises still helped her.

After years of counseling, she and Caterina had become more like friends, and she began to accept that maybe Caterina was not so *strano*. Maybe it was the world that was strange.

Sitting on the sofa, breathing in… and then out…

Sophia tried to focus, but the wine was confusing her thoughts and making her drowsy. The voice in her head interrupted again.

"PRAY!" The voice rose higher as if someone else were in the room. It gave her chills, and the hairs on her neck stood up.

Still rubbing her foot, Sophia realized the pain in her toe was gone. She stood up, reaching for the small picture of Eme. "I wish you were here," she whispered.

"PRAY!" The voice again called to her.

The chills up her spine returned. "*Bene,* I will pray," she thought, still feeling the effects of the wine.

On Sophia's bedpost hung a pair of rosaries that she had received from her parents when she turned sixteen: the rosaries that had been left with her at the orphanage. They were the only concrete thing she had from her birth parents. Sparkling like diamonds, each of the size six millimeter clear crystal beads shone as a prism of light shimmered onto the floor, ceiling and walls.

The rosary beads were held together by a tarnished silver chain with five groups of eleven crystal beads close together. Each grouping of the beads was separated by one single bead in between each grouping. A gently used miraculous medal of the Blessed Mother Mary centered the rosaries, and on the back of the medal was what looked like a Christogram symbol sprouting up from a five-petaled flower.

Under the symbol there were faded words which appeared to be Latin, but she couldn't figure out their meaning.

Sophia lifted the rosaries from the bedpost and returned to the sofa. "You are not the usual rosary beads, are you? We are both different. Ah, but the candlelight is soothing," she thought, putting Eme's picture on the folding table. She sat down and held the rosaries in her hand as if they were supposed to do something.

She had stared at them countless times, sometimes pretending they were magical and other times simply to feel her birth parent's energy. The candle flickered and caught Sophia's attention. It seemed to glow over Eme's picture on the little table, and Sophia could sense Eme's presence again.

Closing her eyes and feeling the rosaries in her hand, she heard Eme's voice start the rosary prayer in her mind. Without realizing it, she recited the prayers as if she and Eme were the young girls of so many years ago.

It seemed like second nature to her as the words just poured out. Holding the rosaries closer, she could feel their energy increase.

Her heart was beating faster, yet she felt calm, almost in a trance-like state. The Hail Mary prayer released a warm feeling throughout her entire body. Over and over she repeated the prayers. The candle flame seemed larger and larger as she prayed, and took on a yellow and gold glow. She could hear Eme's voice louder, saying the words with her. In her imagination, she could see Eme's face and sense her energy right next to her, feeling each bead slip through her fingers.

An intense feeling came over her as they finished the last prayer together. With the last prayer bead in her hand, Sophia looked up at Eme's face next to her. Light beamed all around, and she could hear Eme's voice.

"Each time you pray the rosaries, I will be with you," Eme declared softly.

"But I don't like praying. God took you away," Sophia explained.

"No, No Sophia. Men took me away. God gave those men free will, and they used it poorly," Eme countered.

"I miss you so much Eme." Sophia's tears came easily.

"But I am right her with you, always," Eme went on. "I have made friends here in heaven. They want to be your friends too, Sophia."

"Friends?" Sophia was surprised, "…who are your friends?"

"Well, you have already met Raphael," Eme pointed out.

"Raphael!!" Sophia raised her voice in shock. "The security guard, Raphael? Who is Raphael," she demanded.

"Sophia, Raphael is an Archangel. He is God's angel of healing and travel, among many other wonderful things," Eme smiled. "He came to your rescue in May. Our Father spared your life when He sent Raphael to help you. Do you remember?" Eme asked.

"Raphael is an angel? And he saved me?" Sophia was confused. "But why save me, and not you?" Hot tears streamed down her cheeks.

"We all have jobs to do on earth, but also in heaven, Sophia." Eme smiled, "and our Father has called upon you to help him. Eme's voice was calm, and as endearing as ever.

"Help *God*? Why would God need *my* help?" she cried. She began to tremble. "I am only one person. What can I do," Sophia challenged.

"Sophia, listen. My time is limited here. If you help our Father, I can help you, and we will see each other again soon," Eme assured.

"Oh, Eme. I miss you so much! I will help Him and help you. *Per favore,* don't leave." Sophia begged.

"I told you, I am always with you," Eme reminded. "You will meet Raphael again and he will help you at the lab to find the answers you seek. Remember, angels can disguise themselves as they help people. So stay alert. And keep praying the rosaries!" The candle grew dim as she spoke, and Eme's image faded into the dark room.

"No, Eme, don't go," Sophia pleaded desperately. Seeing Eme had been overwhelming for her, "I need to see you again. I want to hold you and talk to you!" She whimpered, feeling abandoned; alone again in her dark flat.

"Sophia," a voice outside her door called for her.

"Sophia," the voice seemed familiar. Sophia stood, drying her tears, and went to the door.

"Who's there?" She asked, yet somehow felt an inner calm.

"Sophia… come," the voice repeated.

Sophia listened as a female voice called to her in a tranquil, steady tone. "I will help you," the voice assured her.

Putting her hand on the door, Sophia felt compelled to open it, as if she were being guided to follow.

"Who are you? Do I know you?" Sophia asked the seemingly familiar stranger. The door was open slightly and an almost blinding light caused her to cover her eyes.

"Sophia, come. Do not be afraid. I am here to help you."

Sophia could not help herself as she walked out into the glowing white hallway. No one else was present but she heard the serene voice again.

"Come this way, and I will help you."

"How will you help me? I don't understand," she countered. But she heard the voice down another hallway and followed it.

"You will understand soon enough."

Sophia was led along another long white corridor.

She recognized the corridors at her job. Rounding a corner, she saw a large, dark figure ahead.

"Who are you? How can you help me," she pleaded.

"Do not be afraid. We will help you." The figure expanded, dissipating into the air.

"Wait! Don't go! Don't leave me!" Sophia shouted into the empty space. Whimpering and alone, she collapsed to the floor, hands to her face, and sobbed.

RING, RING, RING…

Her mobile was so loud, Sophia almost jumped out of her skin. Sitting straight up, she was wide-eyed, looking around the room, and realized she was still on the sofa, with dim daylight coming through her window.

RING, RING, RING…

The phone vibrated on the table where she had left it. Sophia stood up, and felt dizzy from the wine the night before.

RING, RING…

"*Bene*, I am coming," she said to herself, putting her hand to her aching head.

"*Ciao*," a groggy Sophia answered.

"*Ciao il mio amore, come stai*," Mama asked in concern.

"*Sto bene*, Mama, no worries. How are you and Papa?"

"We are fine. Do you remember about supper on Sunday and you are bringing the rolls?"

"*Sì*, of course, Mama, I will be there like every Sunday."

"*Bene, il mio amore*, then have a good day. *Ti amo,* Sophia," Mama blew a kiss in the phone.

"Yes, Mama, I love you too,"

"Wow, that was some night," talking to herself again. She looked at the clock, realizing it was early morning on another dreary day.

"I should lie down for a little while. I need the rest," she thought, having a few hours off before having to return to work.

In the bathroom, brushing her teeth, she looked into the mirror and told herself that she would never drink two entire bottles of wine again.

Just then, the lights flickered. She looked into the mirror again, and the voice in her head whispered, "Stay alert."

Then Sophia recalled the conversation with Eme. "Was that just a dream?" she wondered, "…but it felt so real."

"Raphael, an angel? I really must be having Caterina's dreams. Angels don't come to earth in security guard uniforms," Sophia laughed, convincing herself, as she went to bed.

Lying there, she thought about Eme and the way she looked. "Even if it *was* just a dream, Eme looked *magnifico*. She looked happy, and she had made friends. And angel friends at that," Sophia giggled.

Closing her eyes, Sophia could remember herself and Eme when they had been about ten years old at school. Eme walked over to a little red haired girl who was being teased, and was ready to cry.

"You should pick on someone who cares what you have to say," Eme scolded the would-be tormentors.

She then put her arm around the little girl and made her laugh. If someone was Eme's friend, they became Sophia's friend, too.

Sophia recognized being shy was a negative trait, but Eme made it easier for Sophia. The memory faded and the reality set in that Eme could no longer help her. She began to tear up, and placed her hands over her heart. She felt something.

"What is this?" Sophia wondered. Sliding her hand under her shirt, she realized she was wearing the rosaries. She sat up in bed to remove them from around her neck, but she didn't remember putting them on.

"The *vino*," she figured, "it must be the *vino*." Holding the rosaries in her hands, she remembered more of her conversation with Eme.

"It was either a hallucination or a dream," but she remembered Eme's words, "Raphael saved your life and he will come to help you to find the answers you seek."

"The lab!" Sophia realized why she drank so much wine in the first place. "It was the lab, the interrogation, the questions of why someone poisoned me and what about the tainted evidence?" Her focus was starting to return.

"I need to find out what's going on." Sophia got out of bed and grabbed her laptop. Making a mental list of what she would need to do, she devised a plan to learn what she could on her own.

Sitting on her bed, Sophia turned to her online news websites, coming to a site that was covering the problems in Rome, finding a new Pope and the alleged fraud by the Vatican bank. Clicking on other sites, she stopped on a site covering the Canadian student accused of murdering her flat mate. Sophia's eyes bulged from their sockets.

"The Case of Murdered American Kerry Dempsey is NOT Over."

Clicking on the attached video, "Trisha Hedrinx, the accused Canadian student, is appealing her case to the Italian Supreme Court," the female news anchor announced, continuing with, "Hedrinx was arrested along with Roberto Callesino, her boyfriend at the time."

Looking dismayed, the anchor continued, "They were convicted, and each was sentenced to twenty-five years in prison. Some suggest that Hedrinx's troubled character was more in question than the hard evidence itself."

"It seems the murder of Kerry Dempsey captivated the world audience with intrigue," Sophia thought, feeling sorry for the victim and her family. Listening intently to the anchor go on about the dead student, Sophia could not help but be drawn to her. She was taken away, like Eme. It was almost as if a gravitational pull drew her into a story that just yesterday had seemed abstract, along with so many others.

Sophia clicked on another website intoning, "The deceased victim and the accused are being paraded around like animals in a circus. Reporters hold the attention of their viewers much like the ringmaster." As Sophia listened, the cast of characters was played before her:

"The Canadian student accused of this heinous crime had a romantic relationship with an Italian architecture student, Roberto Callesino," the male anchor reported. "Upon returning home from a party, Trisha Hedrinx claims she noticed a broken window."

The reporter continued, "She said she called for her flat mate to open her door, but when there was no response, Hedrinx called the police. Dempsey's bedroom door was broken open, and her body was found on the floor, having died of stab wounds to her neck."

As if he was a judge, the news anchor read the findings, "Interviewed by police, Hedrinx said she had spent the entire night with Callesino at his flat close by. He corroborated her alibi, but in a subsequent interrogation Hedrinx incriminated herself and Billy Norton, the bar owner she worked for. Following that interview, Hedrinx, Callesino, and Norton were arrested and charged with the murder of Kerry Dempsey."

A picture of the crime scene flashed behind the anchor. "Norton was released after an examination of the crime scene exonerated him. Shortly thereafter, forensic traces of Hedrinx and Callesino's friend, Jude Broude, were found on Dempsey's body. Billy Norton has now sued Hedrinx for slander."

"Broude, Hedrinx and Callesino were promptly charged with committing the murder together. We will bring you more information as it becomes available." The announcer used his finger to flick his computer screen to the next story.

"This reads like a bad novel," Sophia thought, shaking her head. She clicked onto another web news site, where a different reporter wrote, "After the murder, while waiting to be questioned, Hedrinx was witnessed doing jumping jacks and kissing her boyfriend."

"She *should* be guilty! Perhaps not for murder, but at least for poor manners." Sophia was disgusted. "The reporters were ruthless hounds tracking their prize. Because of Hedrinx's character, they were sure to find her guilty of something. *Anything* to sell a story!"

Sophia was all too familiar with the media circus. She flashed back to the memory of one woman who appeared to be a teenager, befriending Sophia. Sadly, she eventually learned that her new "friend" was a reporter wanting information about Eme years after she disappeared.

"If I'm going to understand this case, I'll have to understand the victim and the accusers without all this fanfare."

Click, click, click…. Sophia's fingers were ready to shake off the boozy effects of the wine.

"Maybe I can investigate this case, which might then lead me to the one who tampered with evidence and poisoned me"

Click, click, click….

Chapter 4

CELEBRATING THE LAST MASS

Italia News reported another article about the Pope's resignation:
"Pope Gregory Celebrates Last Mass."

"Pope Gregory celebrated his last mass as pontiff. Presiding over Ash Wednesday services, he shared his heart in a bittersweet moment with the audience," the article stated.

News photographs showed Pope Gregory standing above the ancient tomb of Saint Peter as he offered his final homily.

Videos showed Gregory looking frail, aided by two young priests as he moved beneath the vaulted canopy of the papal altar in Saint Peter's Basilica.

"It is upon much reflection that I stand here before you, and before our Father," he pronounced. "We must confront internal divisions in our house, in our minds and in our own hearts. Our hearts shall remain veiled from our Father's truth and His love if we do not recognize the hypocrisy within ourselves."

Ending his homily, he warned, "It is said that power tends to corrupt, and absolute power corrupts absolutely." Tears came to his eyes. "With great distress, I have recognized that our hearts have been afflicted with the disease of spiritual corruption. Sins within the church will cause disease to flourish in the body of the church, and in the Christian world. We must rid ourselves of spiritual corruption if we are to live with our Father in peace. We are His temple and His Spirit lives in each of us. Honesty, humility, unity and prayer are the remedies needed to live in His harmony, and to heal our own hearts. Let us pray for mercy."

His words carried suggestions that swirled around into a frenzy of rumors, as most major news outlets conveyed his last words as pontiff.

One newswoman reported, "The Pope appeared to implicitly address the Vatican power struggles and scandals plaguing the church, which may have potentially hastened Pope Gregory's departure."

Following his last Mass, Gregory was secluded at the summer residence, the Papal Palace of Castel Gandolfo. "I am sure my words will be analyzed," he thought to himself. "Let the sensational journalism begin. I just pray my sacrifice will be acknowledged."

His concerns over the security of the conclave were growing, and there would be no rest. "There are many spying eyes; no longer can my friend Antonio bring comfort to me," he sulked in his new temporary office quarters.

Gregory picked up a newspaper from his desk, noting yet another report: "Antonio Lombardi, Pope Gregory's butler, has just been arrested for allegedly leaking his private papers to the press." He shook his head. "In my heart I understand Antonio's behavior. God bless you, my friend. We have worked together for years and you have cared for my every need as a mother would for her own child. I miss you already."

As the hours went on, the Pope's health became more fragile as the Vatican had come under attack yet again. "These sex abuse cases are never ending," Pope Gregory read one report after another. "I have tried to reach out to the world community, offering support to the abuse victims while addressing the punishment of accusers, but I am overwhelmed. My disgust for these clerics goes far beyond measure. *Bitte,* my Father, show me how I can better serve You," he prayed..

Alone in his new surroundings, he mused, "At least they have brought *you* here to me, my old friend." He sat and rubbed the arm of his favorite chair.

"The pressures and the scandals continue to build, my Father. I feel more alone than I have ever felt in my life," Gregory moaned in emotional pain. "*Bitte,* where are You, my Holy Father," he cried, clasping his hands, "the frauds and the abuse from within the walls strike at my very heart with an evil blade."

Looking around his new bedroom he spotted a newspaper left on a side table next to the small sofa. It had a child's picture on the cover. Leaning over, he picked it up, his curiosity getting the best of him. "This is disturbing," he sighed heavily, noticing yet another sensational headline: *"Vatican Bank under Investigation."*

"A nine-month-old investigation has revealed mismanagement in the Vatican Bank." As reported in The Global Net Report, "A small castle-style building behind Saint Peter's Square has assets exceeding seven billion euros. This inconspicuous building is its own small empire. As a result of the investigation, a Vatican cleric, along with a former Secret Service agent, and a financial broker have all been arrested by Italian police and charged with fraud and corruption. The three are suspected of smuggling 24 million euros by private plane across the border from Switzerland." The article included a picture of the Vatican with an inset of each accused man's photo.

"Their faces are plastered across the world in shame," Gregory shook his head. "The world will judge our church based on these men," he sighed as he read further. "Prosecutors allege that the Vatican cleric, Cardinal Meade Rosotti, a former banker, was using the Institute of Religious Works or IOR, the formal name for the Vatican Bank, to transport money for a Naples businessman, who has long been considered a leader in the Mafia organization."

He read aloud, "Cardinal Rosotti, recently arrested in the Vatican, was at the head of a primary accounting department in the Treasury of the Vatican, the Administration of the Patrimony of the Holy See. The scandal gives the Bank of Italy as well as the Bank of International Settlements or BIS in Brussels, the necessary information to begin investigations and demand potential regulatory changes at the Vatican Bank."

Sickened by more scandals, Gregory threw the paper down, "Is this to be the legacy I leave for the new leader?"

He sat back and closed his eyes, thinking, "Cardinal Rosotti, you are Judas."

Knock, knock, knock. Gregory was interrupted.

"*Scusami*, Your Holiness," a concerned Cardinal Antonelli entered the room.

"*Sì*, Giacomo... Tell me, what is it?" Gregory invited his personal secretary and confidant to join him.

"We have more information regarding the other problem we discussed," Giacomo cautioned, approaching the aging Pope. The assistant's pale complexion and thick, black-framed glasses reminded Gregory of a nervous old schoolmaster.

"What is it?" Gregory grew impatient, shaking his head.

"As you know from the media, there is another cleric who used his influence, along with the former boyfriend of an American actress, to swindle the wealthy businessman Warren Blake out of millions of dollars in bogus church real estate deals."

Gregory lowered his head, as if defeated. "So I have heard. Tell me more...," gesturing for Giacomo to sit down and continue his report.

"We know the actress, Delaney Mills, was not involved in the scheme. She apparently had severed ties with Rodolfo Solleirio, who was arrested in the United States on charges of wire fraud conspiracy and money laundering. We have found that he was acting as a real estate developer and misappropriated Mr. Blake's $55 million investment intended to buy our church land in the States..." Giacomo's voice trailed off.

Gregory sat silently, looking appalled.

"Are you all right?" Giacomo asked, anxiously.

"*Per favore*, continue, so I can understand the extent of these issues," Gregory instructed, waving his hand.

Giacomo nodded, continuing, "Solleirio was charged with helping the church to sell off properties in the States. As you know, my Eminence, the funds were to be used to pay lawsuit settlements. In light of recent pedophile cases, we needed to liquidate more property than we had anticipated. However, it was revealed that these properties had been bought at a good insider's price and then sold for a profit," Giacomo frowned.

"Who from the church was involved?" Gregory asked, with distain.

"Bishop Stephen Alfieri, of the Diocese of Camden, in New Jersey. He was implicated by a news article linking him to Solleirio, who had bought the bishop's beach house for well over its $400,000 market value. It was implied that the transaction included a bribe, and occurred shortly after Bishop Alfieri's announcement that half of the Diocese's church properties would be sold."

"What other information do you have?" Physically drained, his Holiness tried to maintain his composure.

"Following a disclosure of the bishop's involvement in what the press is calling the Vati-Con, the Council of Parishes in Southern New Jersey demanded a complete halt to the Bishop's planned church closure program. It caused a scandal in the States and the problem is growing." Giacomo continued, "It was reported that the Bishop's beach house was later put back on the market shortly after the initial controversy. It was sold for just $310,000, which raises questions about the truth in the dealings between Bishop Alfieri and Rodolfo Solleirio. But I am so sorry to have to tell you there is more." Giacomo was distressed in having to further upset Gregory.

Adjusting his glasses, Giacomo continued, "Solleirio's father is an attorney, and sometimes works as a journalist. He is said to have been previously convicted by an Italian court of embezzling €200,000 from a company whose assets he'd been asked to manage."

"Oh my F…," Pope Gregory tried to interject.

Giacomo spoke over the Pope's sigh, "…there is talk that this family has also been seen at various Vatican events and has enjoyed relationships with Cardinals and Bishops here in Italy as well as other clerics around the world."

"It is these types of relationships that I am most concerned with," the weary Gregory added, "but you cannot trust *all* men of the cloth."

"*Sì*, I agree. I just thought you needed the update on this latest situation. While we are proceeding with the process of conclave, the reporters are relentless, and as you know, the enemies of the church can be especially vicious." Bowing his head, Giacomo sighed heavily.

"Unfortunately, it is not difficult to find fault within the church these days," Giacomo had to admit.

"I know that within these sacred walls there are secrets people have guarded for centuries," he mumbled as he looked around the room and back to Giacomo. "With all this unintended attention, seekers can distort the truth. There needs to be a delicate balance between the truth and some mysteries of the church which must be preserved."

As if reading Gregory's mind, Giacomo replied, "I am aware there is information that could destroy our church."

Giacoamo reached his hand to pat Gregory's knee, "I pledge to you, for the benefit of our Lord's flock, that I will oblige our responsibility to protect Mother Church."

"We must communicate these issues with the visiting Cardinals. You will need to schedule a meeting with a small group of Cardinals who will help us. I will let you know who to invite; they need to understand what diseases plague our home and the home of our Father." Gregory was tired. "When the new leader is appointed, he will need a miracle to restore faith in what is left of our church."

Adjusting his position, Gregory regarded Giacomo with sorrowful eyes. "*Grazie,* Giacomo. I will continue to pray. Let me know what other issues come up, and after some reflection, I will advise you on how to proceed."

"*Sì,* of course, Your Holiness, I am at your service." Giacomo stood, sensing that Gregory needed solitude. His folder tucked under his arm, Giacomo bid his Holiness well, closing the door behind him.

Chapter 5

THE MAFIA, THE CHURCH
AND THE TRAITOR

Following his meeting with Pope Gregory, Cardinal Giacomo Antonelli returned to his office at the Vatican and worked to prepare for the conclave. "All of this negative publicity and the chaos within Rome, it is so stressful, my blood pressure is out of control," he worried, rubbing his forehead. He felt physically ill from running the extraneous errands involved with welcoming the visiting cardinals, while still trying to assist Gregory.

"*Per favore,* help me to perform my duties to keep the visiting cardinals informed, and aid them with the transition to elect a new Church leader," he prayed.

"Ping," his laptop sent an alert. At his desk, with a much-needed coffee, he tapped the screen to open yet another report from *Italia News, "More Secrets of the Church."*

Reading further, "Information that was once regarded as open secrets is coming to the surface in light of recent scandals. But few insiders were surprised to learn of organized crime connections to the Vatican's own bank." Antonelli shook his head, "Oh, *mio Dio* in heaven, *per favore,* save us from ourselves!" The article continued, "The ties between the Church and the Mafia may not be so far off from the movie *The Godfather.* Investigator Michael Farina referred to the ongoing investigation saying, "There were scant records of early relationships tying the two organizations, but today we have technology and ways to uncover fraud."

Giacomo now recalled a conversation with Pope Gregory a few months earlier. "Giacomo, do you know what the Mafia's preferred name means?"

"No, I don't," Giacomo had replied, as they sat in the Pontiff's office preparing the documents needed to begin the process of reform.

"It means *Our Thing*." Gregory smiled, "Well **our thing** is to join Moneyval. For far too long the Mafia and the church have shared traditions. *Fuhgeddaboudit*! No more," steadfastly shaking his fist.

Giacomo was shocked at the Pope's use of Mafia slang, particularly with a German accent, but he was curious. "Moneyval?"

"*Ja*," Gregory looked pleased with himself. "They are the Committee of Experts regarding the Evaluation of Anti-Money Laundering Measures and the Financing of Terrorism. This monitoring body involves the Council of Europe, and it will help to secure the Vatican bank against fraud."

"Ping," Giacomo's alert again rang from his laptop. Clicking it off, he was reminded of his meeting with Cardinal Karl Korsig, who had held a high position in the Roman Curia for nearly ten years. He and Korsig had become friends over time. While the cardinal, a three hundred-pound big-bellied man, had a kind heart and an agreeable disposition, his staunch pursuit of righteousness had landed him in hot water. More than once, Giacomo had covered for his friend.

"It's time to go," he murmured, closing the laptop.

Arriving at Cardinal Korsig's office within the Vatican, Cardinal Antonelli was deeply troubled by the nagging reports of a Mafia connection being aired to the world like dirty laundry hanging on a very public clothes line. "Korsig, *bene,* it is good to see you, my friend," hugging and patting his back.

"You look like you can use a friend," Korsig replied.

After their greetings, they sat down for a serious conversation.

"The Corleone Clan of the Sicilian Mafia," Antonelli began, "has been using the Vatican bank as a way to launder Mafia money and the media is now exposing these schemes."

"I know. And to think these criminals would then attend church in an effort to cleanse their souls..." Korsig retorted with sarcasm. "Those media hawks should step back before they blindly follow the Mafia heathens into hell. However," Korsig put his finger to his lips as if in deep thought, "I also understand that the Cosa Nostra is having a difficult time with all of this unwanted attention."

"Investigators at the Vatican Bank have begun to close suspicious accounts," he remarked. Korsig smiled with gratification, "The authorities are moving closer to implementing His Holiness's plan. You can relay this much to him."

"I am sure he will be delighted to hear that," Antonelli acknowledged.

"However, Giacomo, there is yet another important matter I need to discuss with you." Korsig's tone grew more dismayed, "There is a leak within the Curia that we must identify immediately."

Cardinal Antonelli was not surprised. "I identified this problem to His Holiness this morning," Korsig smiled, as if he knew a secret. "As Dean of the College of Cardinals, I sometimes come in contact with information that I know is not meant to be shared, which is why I spoke with his Eminence immediately."

Korsig looked at Giacomo very seriously, "Even as he tried so desperately to reform the IOR, he unknowingly enlisted a traitor to help him." Korsig lowered his voice, not wanting the heavens to hear another church confession. "The media will soon report what is being labeled as the *Gay Lobbies*. This traitor secretly recorded a private conversation between Gregory and two Latin American clerics pertaining to this newest scandal."

"What? ...What are the *Gay Lobbies*?" Giacomo almost didn't want to know.

"There are a few clerics who apparently have been caught sinning against God." Korsig frowned, "...At this point, we are not just concerned with Cardinal Rosotti, who is very much involved in this *gay lobby* business but he was working with someone else from within the Vatican, and he is afraid to talk." Korsig was resigned to the ugly truths.

Antonelli was stunned. "Rosotti, yes I know him. He was helping us with joining Moneyval and he was recently arrested for money laundering. But I saw his Eminence yesterday and he did not mention this *gay lobby* business to me."

"I have just received this confirmation. It seems this *gay lobby* issue has yielded dangerous Curia leaks and blackmail." Korsig dared not raise his voice.

64

Returning his focus to Giacomo, "You know my capacity is limited, but whatever I can do, I will help." He lifted a manila folder marked *"PRIVATE- IMPORTANTE,"* and handed it to Giacomo.

The bewildered Giacomo regarded the folder. "As you know, I have had experience in my field of studies associated with the church's financial fraud... but I have not heard of this *gay lobby* you speak of."

"*Per favore,* read the file. And above all else, keep this to yourself," Korsig instructed.

"Gregory trusts us to help him, and we shall," Giacomo assured his friend. "Before the conclave begins, we must identify this traitor who recorded the *gay lobby* conversation, and find out if he has ties to the Mafia. His Eminence would not want undue influences to play a part in the conclave if this traitor is to participate."

Cardinal Korsig stood, reaching for a photo on his cabinet, "I know that over the years many priests and bishops have accepted the presence and influence of the Mafia, but few have had the courage to stand up to organized crime." He handed Antonelli a picture of his younger self, standing next to another young priest.

"Do you see the man standing next to me?" Korsig asked, "His name was David Perpino, from Casal di Principe, just outside of Naples." His face framed in sadness, he explained, "He was a brave priest, and he gave the ultimate sacrifice. He was murdered in March of 1994 for being too outspoken against the Mafia's use of the Catholic Church and its traditions to serve their *own* nefarious goals... and he was my cousin."

Giacomo looked surprised, holding the photograph and staring at the now-deceased cleric.

Korsig's tone was stoic. "I keep his picture here to remind me of the dedication it takes to serve God. We have long suspected that the Mafia's Camorra clan may have sent hitmen to silence my cousin, but they could not silence his love for the Church. I cannot think his sacrifice could be in vain."

"His sacrifice will not be in vain, my friend." Antonelli understood Korsig's emotion well. "It is His Eminence's last wish that we find this traitor and help to rid our church of this evil."

Growing more concerned, Korsig said, "While he takes up this last task to exterminate the vermin of the Church, as you know, it is taking its toll, and his declining health is evidence of that. I am more than a little concerned."

Antonelli then added, "Unfortunately, the world is intently watching Rome. Pope Gregory's reign is ending and his health will suffer," he paused with a sigh.

"But with God's grace, his legacy of reform will live on with our help. We need to restore our allegiance to God and to Gregory, however difficult." Korsig would not settle for defeat.

"You need to know that Gregory has only temporary residence in the Papal Palace of Castel Gandolfo," Antonelli went on. "He will soon be moved again. The Swiss Guard, as you are aware, served as his personal bodyguards, but they will terminate their service at Castel Gandolfo, following his effective resignation." Giacomo stood, to relieve his aching back.

"The Vatican Gendarmerie will then provide for the security of the Papal summer residence, and they will become solely responsible for his personal security. Following renovations, Gregory will then begin moving to a permanent address at the Vatican City's Mater Ecclesiae, the same monastery previously used by nuns," Antonelli explained. "I mention this, so you can appreciate that our methods of communication must be guarded." Agitated, Giacomo paced the floor. "We agree with other Vatican officials that Gregory's continued presence in the Vatican City could assist with the provision of security, and prevent his retirement location from becoming a place of pilgrimage, as well as providing him with legal protection from potential lawsuits." Antonelli made it clear, "This is unprecedented in our history, so the transition will be made easier if we identify the traitors from within these walls."

"I agree. *Per favore,* tell me how I can help," Korsig replied, retrieving the picture from Antonelli and carefully returning it to his cabinet.

"I will call tomorrow to ask for your help in scheduling a meeting," Antonelli answered. "I will let you know whom we need to invite. Until then, let us not mention this conversation to anyone."

"Preparations for conclave will begin soon, so we do not worry people unnecessarily."

"I understand, and will await your instructions," Korsig agreed.

Antonelli bid his friend farewell, and drove to his office to update Pope Gregory. The process of picking a successor was officially getting underway with more than one hundred of the cardinal electors already arriving, but the date of the papal conclave could not be set until all the electors are in Rome.

Giacomo recalled Gregory instructions, "And, Giacomo, you will see to it that of the 113 cardinals eligible to vote, the ones already in Rome will become better acquainted at the pre-conclave meetings and congregations. *Per favore,* ensure that all goes according to plan." He entrusted Giacomo with this sacred mission and added, "While waiting for the missing cardinals, I will have time to establish additional instructions. I will issue *Normas Nonnullas,* to allow for a schedule change, giving the cardinals more latitude to start the conclave earlier or later, instead of the usual fifteen to twenty days after the See becomes vacant. This long-held tradition of conclave will be especially historic."

"As it stands now, not having all the cardinals present gives Korsig and me more time to investigate the Curia leaks and the *gay lobby* issues," Giacomo thought. "In the meantime, I must be sure the visiting Cardinals are kept busy. They can pray together, share meals, talk over coffee and, of course, gossip together. After all," he mumbled aloud, "gossip is a part of human nature."

As he drove, Giacomo heard a news bulletin on his car radio:

"People are bewildered by what Pope Gregory's new historic role will be. Historically, the Pope has died in office before cardinals were summoned for this particular duty. It will certainly give the world more to pray for and more opportunities for gossip," the reporter announced.

Giacomo turned the radio off, his mind wandering, "Reporters from all over the world are gathering to record this momentous event. Even now, Saint Peter's Basilica is mobbed with throngs of worshippers singing and praying together, in their diverse languages, for the common goal."

"*Per favore,* help us to obtain that goal with dignity," Giacomo prayed, glancing over to the closed folder on the passenger seat. "I can see the image now," Giacomo thought aloud, "the new leader of millions of Catholics from around the globe will not only have the job of cleansing the Church Curia from the evils within, but also he will be charged with uniting the people with our Father, no matter their religious affiliations." Giacomo prayed, "The world is falling apart and we are in dire need of unification. *Per favore,* Holy Father in Heaven, hear our prayers!"

Parking near his office, Antonelli could not help but ponder. "Religion has been a constant point of reference for wars, yet it is also the spiritual force governing the most intimate decisions for the people of God."

Inside, Vatican staffers were kept busy; their energy in full force. As the cardinals arrived for the conclave, they were greeted by Cardinal Antonelli and others. Each was shown to his quarters in Domus Sanctae Marthae, the hospitality residence within walking distance of Saint Peter's Basilica, where they were given a daily schedule.

At his desk, Antonelli opened his laptop and began to organize his notes.…

"Attendees for pre-conclave PRIVATE meeting"

1. Cardinal Karl Korsig, Dean of Colleges *Trust*
2. Alexander Borgia, Cardinal Secretary of State of his Holiness the Pope. *presiding over the Holy See Secretariat, performing all political and diplomatic functions of the Holy See and Vatican City. *Trust.*
3. Valentinus de Marcosi, Italian Cardinal-Bishop of Suburbicarian Diocese of Velletri-Segni. He aspires to be the next pontiff and to bring the church into the future as he so wishes. * *Full of himself, but trust.*
4. Irenaeus Smyrna, Turkish Cardinal *living in Lyons, France, he emphasizes the traditional elements of the church. Many influences, strong opinions – *whose side?*

5. Ignatius "Gus" Theophorus, former Bishop of Antioch *lives life in imitation of Christ. Now living in Italy, he writes letters to churches around the world - too outspoken for reforms within the church. *Trust?

6. Pietro Gasparri, Spanish Cardinal *Headed the secret nine-month investigation of corruption within the Curia, per Pope Gregory. Dossier on his findings already delivered to His Eminence. *Trust.

7. Anton Oriolli, former Archbishop of Palermo. Worked closely with Gregory and now works with Cardinal Gasparri conducting investigations. *Influences unknown.

Antonelli needed discretion in organizing his private meeting. "I know the arriving elector cardinals are already aware of recent church scandals. It is good that Pope Gregory has imposed pre-conclave and social media blackouts. There are too many leaks to the Italian press."

Recalling Korsig's conversation, he told him, "The first of the pre-conclave congregations is set to begin in just a few days to allow the cardinals time to focus on introductory matters. There is no time to waste."

He typed and printed seven invitations to an informal luncheon meeting, during which the attendees would discuss recent church developments and conclave matters of concern. He titled the invitation "Spreading the Word in Today's Church," and went on to say, *Your attendance is required."*

Finishing his task, he gave the invitations to his assistant, Jozef Giordano, a Slavic Bishop and longtime friend, to deliver them personally.

"Holding the meeting at the Papal Palace of Castle Gandolfo will give the appearance that Pope Gregory will attend," Giacomo mused, "and one extra measure to ensure our attendees will come."

Closing his laptop, Antonelli smiled. "It's time for us to change the course of history."

Chapter 6

RELIGION and POLITICS

In Marseille France a television news reporter, Yin Quan, was broadcasting a special report on a controversial topic.

"Religious Authorities using Mind Control over Their Worshippers and The Subsequent Abuses Within those Religions."

"Just as the Catholic Church has struggled especially in light of recent developments involving various scandals," Yin Quan announced in her story, "Also troubling is that Jewish communities have dealt with their own sins. Media reports have featured more than one Rabbi abusing children who were left in their care. Recently a U.S. Rabbi in Massachusetts, a long time spiritual leader, resigned as a direct result of allegations that he used nearly a half million dollars of the synagogue's discretionary funds to pay hush money to an extortionist in effort to hide his relationship with a 16 year old male."

She went on, "much like the bible, the Torah teaches against these sinful acts. However, it appears that religious teachings do not deter the determined sinner."

Yin Qaun, of Asian descent has been living and working as a news reporter in Marseille for several years and this was her big break. She struggled to survive in a predominately male environment even going so far as to have plastic surgery. Looking into the reflection of the camera, she was happy that her eyelids did not droop as they used to. However it was not something she took lightly as her critics chastised her for it. Being on television, her appearance, physical or other, was a part of her contract. Her shoulder length black hair was usually neatly feathered on both sides of her face, giving a thinner appearance to her roundness.

Having a low raspy voice made her distinctly recognizable to her growing legions of fans.

Yin knew the more fans she had the less likely she would be harassed in the business. Using this to her advantage, she worked hard to develop a fan base on Twitter, Facebook and many social outlets.

Studying journalism in China, France and England she spoke five languages and had a unique experience understanding various cultures.

"The Jewish tradition prescribes the Torah to be read in public at least once every three days in the presence of the congregation." Yin Quan explained, "Reading the Torah publicly is one of the many tenants for Jewish communal life. These faulted Jewish leaders, even after participating in their religious obligations, were at the end of the day mere mortals. No matter their religious teaching, men have given in to evil. They have given in to sinning against the very God they worshipped. Religion is the common thread to bring people together. However, it is also a common threat able to destroy mankind!"

Staring straight into the camera she hoped to engage her audience, "The Catholics and Jews are not the only religion to be making headlines these days." She countered, "The Church of Scientology has been involved in a number of controversies involving abuse. And just as the Catholic Church has experienced, there are equally egregious violations by Protestant clergy and others. The list is long, but there is a new religious order that is dominating the news headlines as much as the ones we have mentioned."

A picture of the war torn city of Damascus appeared behind Yin as she introduced, "The Islamic State has declared themselves as the Islamic State of Iraq and Syria, or otherwise known as ISIS, and they are spreading their Sunni Jihadist views at an extremely fast pace. Claiming religious authority over all Muslims across the earth, ISIS aspires to bring most of the Muslim inhabited regions of the world under its political control." She wore a school teacher expression.

"It began in Iraq, Syria and other territories in the Levant region which included Jordan, Israel, Palestine, Lebanon, Cypress and part of southern Turkey." She continued with, "ISIS is the new kid on the block. Breaking away from al-Qaeda in Iraq, it has become a battlefield force to be reckoned with."

"Its former leader was recently killed and its new leader Mohammed al-Barabbas has gained more support in Iraq resulting from the surrounding chaos. A master opportunist, Mohammed al-Barabbas is seizing the moment as the Middle East hierarchy is collapsing." A map of the Middle East appeared behind Yin Quan's head.

She resumed with her report, "Beginning but certainly not ending in the Middle East, ISIS has self-proclaimed their status as a caliphate, meaning its succession. The caliphate is an Islamic State led by a supreme religious and political leader known as a caliph or the successor of Muhammad, the original Islamic prophet."

A picture of a man dressed in a black turban and black robes was displayed. Referring to the picture Yin stated, "This is Mohammed al-Barabbas who has proven to be a shrewd strategist and a vicious killer. He is also now caliph. After the U.S. had killed his superiors, he began to move forward with his hard line reform of Sunni Islam ideals. He has built up his reputation based on his Islamic studies and is a Sunni extremist who is as much an enigma to his followers as he is to his enemies."

Explaining ISIS's short history further Yin continued, "After the United States invaded Iraq in 2003 the Muslim radicals led a Sunni militant group that fought against American troops. Captured by U.S. forces in 2005, these extremists were held for four years at Camp Bucca, a U.S. military prison in Umm Qasr, Iraq. There, they met several al-Qaeda commanders. Unbeknownst to the Americans, Camp Bucca became a feeding ground for jihadist in the Middle East. The Americans, not understanding the local languages, allowed these al-Qaeda commanders to commune and foster a dynamic plan to later unfold. It gave Mohammed al-Barabbas the tools he needed to become the leader he is today."

Yin used her finger to move from one note page to another on her flat screen computer built into her desktop. "Later, the U.S. turned al-Barabbas over to Iraqi authorities as part of the President Bush administration agreement with the Iraqis."

A picture of an American soldier appeared next.

"Colonel Timothy Stringer, who oversaw Camp Bucca, recalls al-Barabbas taunting his American captors at the time, "I'll see you guys in America." Unfortunately the U.S. has unleashed the Titans." He was quickly released by the Iraqis and used his prison contacts to take over an al-Qaeda aligned militant group, the Islamic State of Iraq. Shortly after, he began the offensive to seize territory."

Yin's facial expression was sober and dead on.

She was showing her viewers that her report was to be taken seriously as she presented a picture of what appeared to be terrorist training camps taken from a drone.

"Mohammed al-Barabbas was growing his ranks faster than world leaders cared to admit. Even the current President of the United States, Thomas Chamberlain, referred to ISIS as a JV or junior varsity player in terrorism. President Chamberlain also stated the recent violence in Benghazi at the American consulate was a result of a protest over a video gone awry that ended the lives of four Americans. He later had to admit it was actually the work of these terrorists. President Chamberlain and many others doubted the facts in front of them."

She stared into the camera unapologetic, "Many recognize terrorists for what they are. Unfortunately young disillusioned people from around the world are taking notice of Muslim fanaticism and other terrorist groups and they have started to join in this radical movement. The internet provides an alter to profess extremist beliefs and ISIS's right to destroy those refusing to show allegiance to them." Yin Quan turned another note page.

A background picture showed the ISIS flag over a captured building. "ISIS rejects the political divisions established by Western powers at the end of World War I in the Sykes-Picot Agreement as it absorbs more territory in Syria and Iraq. By rejecting this Western agreement it gives them, in their minds, the God given right to expand their religious and political beliefs. They believe it is their duty," Yin reported in a serious manner.

Showing pictures of various websites, "With their effective use of propaganda, Muslim radicalism spreads through the media.

They provide CDs, DVDs, posters, pamphlets and web related products. Targeting Western audiences, materials are available in English, German, Russian and French. Muslim radicals use social media which has been described as comparable to the most sophisticated U.S. companies. Its violent messages of hate are becoming increasingly comforting to despots and to the ignorant." Yin starred into the camera in disgust, this media production company appalled her.

"We must remember that propaganda is not NEWS!" she insisted to her critics.

The next picture presented behind Yin was that of a British soldier. She went on expressing, "The ideals of Muslim extremism are growing all over the world, the terror groups are gaining new eager members everyday."

"These enthusiasts are keen to show their allegiance. In May of last year, in London, the murder of British soldier Stanley Gibbens by two would be Muslim defenders was carried out. The attack was to avenge the killing of Muslims by the British armed forces," she paused.

"…Each killer was raised Christian but converted to Islam. This is and should be a concern for all established religious organizations. It is and should be a concern for world governments who fear terrorist attacks on their home soil." Yin's expression started to lighten up on cue.

"Join us next week for a deeper look into Muslim extremism and other religions that can destroy our world. For News Today, I am Yin Qaun. Good night." The pretty smiling reporter peered into the camera as the television screen cut off and went to a commercial.

Ben Dhara was sitting on his bed in his hotel room in Rome as he listened to Yin Quan's report. He had watched Quan's reports previously and respected her style of reporting.

Clicking the remote of his television he found a news station reporting on the life sentences for the Stanley Gibbons murder defendants. The news was static with updates on the sentencing surrounding the murderers of this fallen British soldier. As Ben ate his curry chicken he shook his head and gave a sigh of relief.

"Another two bite the dust," he thought out loud.

Ben started to recall his own personal experience with terrorism in his home country of India before moving to England with his mother and two sisters. He could remember like it was yesterday.

He recalled how his father gave him a kiss goodbye before leaving for his business trip, but he never returned. On a Mumbai train, his father was killed when a bomb exploded after being planted by terrorists.

Remembering his father was painful as he recounted news reports, "It was July 11, 2006 when there were a series of seven bomb blasts that took place over a period of 11 minutes. In all, 209 people died from pressure cooker bombs that were set off by terrorists."

Ben recollected, "A few days after the blasts, a terrorist organization possibly linked to Lashkar-e-Taiba or LeT, claimed responsibility for the bombings. They are all cowards!"

"We need a new beginning Benjamin," his mother told him early one morning. She could not sleep and was up all night. "You, your two sisters and I will move to England to start a new life."

"England?" Ben gasped, "Mum, that is extreme I don't want…"

"Benjamin, it is away from this terrorism," his mother reached to touch the face of her only son. "We need to be safe."

"So it seems, Mother. So it seems," Ben was reminded of his Father's words when things looked out of sorts. His anger and frustration over his father's murder never waned.

"The phrase time heals all wounds, does not apply to me." His memory flashed to their comfortable Mumbai home. His older sister, Bijoya, alerted Ben to the breaking news reports that interrupted her favorite television program. The channels became flooded with images of the train wreckage and announcements about a series of bombs that exploded on the Mumbai trains. It was unknown at the time if there were any survivors. Ben's frantic mother tried desperately to call her husband of thirty-three years but to no avail.

Panicked, but maintaining a sense of awareness, "Let us keep praying," his mother insisted. "Perhaps he cannot talk on his mobile, perhaps he lost it …or maybe the battery died."

The images were hard to watch but the family was desperate for any news. Time passed slowly.

Across from Ben sat his sisters in smaller chairs. The small television was positioned on a T.V. stand in the corner of the room.

"He is fine," Ben tried to reassure his mother and sisters as he gently rubbed his Mum's back. He gazed around the room, family pictures graced the walls.

"You will be fine, right Papa? Please call us Papa," Ben secretly prayed. His stared at one of his favorite pictures, his dad was smiling over an eight year old Ben who was standing beside him.

"I know he loves us," Mum reminded them in a hush, "he will come back. You will see."

They were all huddled together watching the images on their television. Pictures of mangled steel appeared no stronger than tin. A large hole exposed the seats where passengers once sat.

Clothing and debris was strewn about. Gazetted officers were careful with each step they took around the damage. Some people were running, others were crying while holding their arms or legs as smoke was bellowing from one explosion.

"It is chaos," Bijoya pointed out the obvious. "Even if he is injured, that will still be OK?" She imagined the possibilities.

In slow motion it played in Ben's mind. He and his mother were sitting on the sofa as he tried to comfort her. The soft patterned brown and green sofa against the main wall centered the living room. It was the main space of the barely 1400 square foot flat. Two matching chairs were neatly arranged across the room on each side of the sofa with a small coffee table in front.

KNOCK, KNOCK, KNOCK...

"Mum?" Ben whispered, hearing the heavy knocking at their door.

Ben's youngest sister, Aja, was sitting closest to the door. Instinctively she sprang up. Her long black straight hair swung back and forth as she reached for the door knob and opened the door. A Gazetted officer in his khaki uniform, like the ones on their television set, stood on the other side of the door way.

"I am sorry to inform you..." The officer spoke softly and sorrowfully. Their worst fears were confirmed.

"Your father owned his small business on Abdul Rehman Street in Mumbai and did very well for himself," the lawyer in India recounted to Ben in their meeting before leaving India. "I understand he worked hard to support his family, and as the only son, you are now left with the responsibility of caring for your Mum and sisters. Do you understand Benjamin?"

"I understand," Ben's face was expressionless. Life was never the same for them.

"Your education must come first," Mum realized that Ben's education would allow for him to fulfill his family obligation. They sold his father's business and after a short time they left for England.

"We can live comfortably now Mother," Ben hugged his mother after settling in Princes Gate, Knightsbridge in London.

His father managed to save millions of euros that helped his family with their transition to a comfortable home.

"Becoming a lawyer, that is how I can combat terrorism," he remembered telling Aja before he graduated the university, "but more than that, maybe I can avenge our father." Hatred filled his heart.

"I am so proud of you and your father would be too," Mum hugged him after receiving a full scholarship to the London School of Economics. Ben obtained his law degree with a LL.m or masters of laws degree.

"The best way to fight terrorism was not on the battlefield but to destroy its funding," his law professor chided him for a pitiful revenge filled report on terrorism that Ben had handed in. "Use your head, not your anger!" His professor scolded Ben.

Looking back, Ben flashed his memory to just after graduating. He was so excited that he landed his first job working for a small London law firm. His experiences and determination led him to Mrs. Potter.

"Ben, you have the right drive but you need more experience," Mrs. Potter told him, "how about working with me at Orion and Zeita's? It is a large firm that has a partnership with Davidson and Davidson in the United States."

Mrs. Potter informed him, "You know they are based in Washington D.C. and their specialty is fighting terrorism through funding. I think here you can gain the experience in various fields that you need to fulfill your heart's destiny."

"I will be committed to you," he promised her after he had confided in her about his father. Mrs. Potter seemed to take him under her wing.

Working hard, he hoped to obtain a promotion and be transferred to Davidson and Davidson's international anti-terrorism unit stationed in London.

"You will be required to travel even more than you do now," Mrs. Potter reminded him after receiving a promotion.

"That's OK, I am still young," Ben remarked. "If I do not do it now... then when?"

The alarm on his watch went off.

He was brought back to the reality in his hotel room.

Opening up his laptop, he was still thinking of his family. A picture of Mum and his sisters from their last holiday together was his screen saver.

"You put so much of your energy into work and caring for our family, but when are you going to settle down and make me a grandmother?" Mum asked on every occasion. "You are neglecting your love life," she was not shy in reminding him.

Many of the dates that he had been on were arranged by his impatient mother, but they only lasted for a short time. Ben's required travel for his employer was a constant issue in any of Ben's relationships.

"Mother, when the time is right and I meet the right person, you will be the first to know," he always reassured her. Ben was in no hurry, he had other pressing matters to grapple with like finding the people who killed his father.

Reading his emails, he read down the list and could see one from his mother.

Subject: "Fiana broke up with her boyfriend."

He had wanted to open this e-mail as his mother's match making skills drew his curiosity. It almost became amusing, the girls or possible brides selected by his mother ranged in shape, size and occupations.

"I remember there was Hadi, the 24 year-old secretary who was well rounded in every sense of the word. Then came Naaz, the 27 year-old seamstress with long beautiful hair which would be better served covering her face," he snickered.

"Ah... but there was one hopeful, Fiana," she came to Ben's mind. "She was as beautiful as she was smart. There was only one problem- her former boyfriend." After six months of courting, her former boyfriend won Fiana back to his arms. "The bastard," Ben sighed. He was devastated. For the first time he actually started to believe in love. The experience hardened Ben's heart. His work became his lady fair.

"Shhhit...," He put his hands to his mouth, drawing his jaw down. Thinking about Fiana and the painful past, he shook his head slightly and sighed. "I can't do this right now."

"I am getting too close to my next promotion," he ran his hands through his thick black hair and put the thought of Fiana to rest drawing his attention to his work.

Opening the folders on his hotel coffee table, Ben began to review all of his notes and other material relating to the Canadian student case including Sophia's interview.

"At the Corte d'Assise, Trisha Hedrinx and Roberto Callesino pleaded not guilty to charges of sexual assault, murder and simulating a burglary. They requested their acquaintance, Jude Broude, to testify but he refused." Ben read the first trial notes.

"The murder of American Kerry Dempsey is attracting international interest," Mrs. Potter exclaimed as he recalled. "Can you handle it Ben?"

"I am confident I can. I had a good teacher." He then smiled thinking about his sweet talking response. He knew he could sway Mrs. Potter into allowing him to work on any case.

He now looked upon the piles of folders that surrounded him.

Ben moved his sticky note making reference to a few Canadian lawyers who were troubled by the character evidence regarding Hedrinx.

"So much of this centers on matters of a sexual nature and heard without the strenuous objections from Hedrinx's defense attorneys," Ben read his notes. "There is no way defense attorneys in a Canadian court would not have objected to that line of questioning," Ben talked aloud.

Thumbing through his papers he came across another of his notes, "Canadian politicians are faulting Italy's legal process and starting to make accusations of fraud. Lawyer Lacey Brenner founded the Friends of Trisha, a support group started to help raise money for Trisha's defense expenses. A Canadian Ambassador issued a statement that the evidence against Hedrinx was inadequate. A not-for-profit organization was now dedicated to proving the innocence of Hedrinx through DNA testing."

Ben paused and shook his head, "the politics in this case are intense."

He reached for another folder, the official report from the Carabinieri Scientific Investigations.

The label read it was completed and verified by supervisor Carmine Greico, case serial number KD22TH02RC. Ben labeled everything so he could keep his notes in order...

Item 1. The cover page included references of finding two knives, a large carving knife at the crime scene and a 6 inch kitchen knife that was later recovered at Callesino's flat. Hedrinx's DNA was obtained from the room where the victim was killed.

Item 2. The large carving knife was found near the victim with DNA of only the victim on the blade. On the bottom of the report page appeared a summary.

Note: inconclusive DNA materials found on the handle.

Item 3. The 6 inch kitchen knife that was later recovered at Callesino's flat had Hedrinx's DNA on the handle. Investigators say it was used to slit victim's throat. The knife was removed, taken from Callesino's apartment and transported in a shoe box.

Note: Minute amount of victim's DNA was indicated on the blade.

Item 4. Kerry Dempsey's white bra indicated possible DNA from Callesino on the clasp.

Note: Evidence inconclusive.

Picking up the crime scene pictures, Ben gasped. "Oh my God, this is so gruesome," Ben's jaw dropped. One picture showed the 22 year-old American student under a duvet on the floor by her bed, covered in blood. In another picture, a bloody handprint was streaked on the wall above her.

"It was indicated that the victim was held down while she was strangled and stabbed. The kitchen knife is seen in one picture and the carving knife in another," he repeated to himself.

Looking closely at one photograph, Ben could see Dempsey's bra. Staring at it and then reviewing the report, he was confused.

"The report said the bra was white but the picture showed it as nearly black in color." He tried to assess, "perhaps there was a shadow over the evidence when the picture was taken."

Looking back at the picture of the victim, "WOW, this is messed up!"

There was also a DVD copy of crime scene video and one of a trial video that Ben obtained. Putting one of the first DVD's into his laptop, he could see investigators milling about the crime scene.

"Oh my gosh, I cannot believe this... DNA has run amok." Smacking his hand to his face in disbelief. Noticeably, Ben could see some people were not wearing gloves and a female investigator looked as if she had her hair draping on the floor kneeling and leaning over the victim while looking under the bed.

Rewinding the DVD, Ben noticed in a dark corner of the bedroom an investigator was standing in front of a window. He played it over and over.

"I can't quite see in the shadow...," Ben squinted, "could it be that the investigator used his elbow and crashed it into the window?"

Ben strained to look at the DVD. "At this point, the same investigator looks like he is throwing something outside the window. Is that evidence?"

Fast forwarding the DVD, he noted, "these two police officials are hovering over the victim and putting their fingers in Dempsey's puncture wound. This was just wrong on so many levels," he sighed.

Reading from his notes, "on the night Dempsey was killed, Hedrinx and her boyfriend say they were at his house watching a movie and smoking hashish. Their recollection of events, they admitted, was hazy from the drugs, but both swore they went back to the house the next morning. Hedrinx says she was unable to gain entry into Dempsey's room and called police."

Ben talked aloud as if someone else was in the room, "questions over the validity of the DNA evidence are more than concerning."

Taking out another DVD and putting it in his laptop, Ben saw footage of the first trail. He could see the jury sat intently listening to a defense expert who was a geneticist and private coroner in Italy.

"Of the 6 inch knife found at Callesino's flat, the DNA sample on the blade was too small to be definitive," the expert countered the prosecution's questions almost taunting the prosecutors.

"The reasoning for the presence of Ms. Hedrinx's DNA on the knife handle should be no surprise because the couple had dinner at his house occasionally," he smirked.

Another expert testified for the defense, "there is no way that 6 inch knife could be the murder weapon. Considering the test results from the lab, the knife taken from Callesino's apartment wouldn't have made the slash wounds found on Demspey's body. It also doesn't match the size or shape of the puncture wounds. Further I would state that Mr. Callesino's knife doesn't match a bloody outline of a knife left on the bedding."

Ben got out his legal pad and pen. He made a chart that often helped him to decipher the facts in these tough cases. Drawing the lines on the page, he started to separate the facts.

For their case, prosecutors had to prove that Hedrinx and Callesino, who had recently started dating, were lying and they had to place them at the home when Dempsey was killed.

On one of Ben's sticky notes: "One police officer's report noted more than one person was around the house on the night of the murder. It was a positive lead for prosecutors but nothing was mentioned in court."

Ben opened another folder and began reading, "The prosecution contends there was evidence in the form of a bra clasp. The one that fell to the floor after the murderer cut Dempsey's white bra in half before she was killed. They maintain the minute DNA on the clasp was Callesino's. The dirty looking bra clasp was the only evidence that placed Callesino at the scene."

Reading his sticky notes: "The defense maintains that evidence on the clasp is fundamentally flawed, like much of the evidence collected from the crime scene."

"Hmmm…," he sighed as he continued to read more of his notes, "A prosecution source maintains the crime scene was handled properly and the evidence shows what it shows. At least one suspect had confessed to being at the murder scene."

In a side note Ben wrote: "Prosecutors maintained the victim had never been to Callesino's apartment and wouldn't have come in contact with the 6 inch knife yet investigators say her DNA shows the knife played a role in the murder."

"This is an International nightmare. I cannot believe this case has gone forward," he sighed in disbelief.

Ben picked up and looked at the picture of the 6 inch knife again, "If I could get answers to this case, my promotion would be guaranteed."

He started to jot down notes.

"How would the victim's DNA get on the knife if the prosecutors maintain the victim was never at Callesino's flat?"

"If this is the only real evidence linking all the suspects to the victim, this is not right. The Bra clasp had, admittedly, a DNA sample too small to confirm. It has to be the knife that was tainted. Think, think, think you can do this," he gave himself a little pep talk.

He picked up another of his sticky notes: "6 inch knife transported in shoe box. A shoe box! This is like a dark comedy, where did the shoe box come from?" He was stunned by reading his own notes.

"Perhaps Ms. Pistisi can shed some light on this perplexing shoe box or this kitchen knife."

Working through the night, Ben focused on his research.

"Morning has come fast…, too fast," Ben stood up from his makeshift desk and stretched. …Yawning… "I am so tired, I need a shower. Then I will go back to the lab."

Chapter 7

WORKING WITH A LAB RAT

Sophia stared at her computer screen with glazed eyes. Yawning, she threw her arms up and around her back. After a good long stretch, she slowly picked up the coffee she had made earlier, still looking at the screen.

"Ewwww, *che diavolo*?" Spitting the cold coffee back into the cup, she thought, "I should make some more." Then, glimpsing at her watch, she realized the time.

"*Dio mio*, I have to get ready for work...," she took a step forward and stopped.

"Ahh, my head." Pausing, Sophia put her hand to her forehead, feeling a shot of nerve pain to her head.

"*Accidenti*, I am getting a headache," she thought, feeling a little shaky as she reached for a fresh towel, heading straight for the shower.

"Breathe in... then out..." She coached herself as the water hit her body, "I have to focus. Eme, if you are listening, I could use your help today."

Dressing and grabbing her jacket, helmet and a leftover biscuit from Sunday supper, she left her flat. She finished Mama's biscuit with two bites, tucking the plastic wrapper into her pants pocket as she climbed onto the Vespa and sped off.

"*Grazie a Dio,* the weather is not too cold, but this traffic is terrible," she mumbled, "especially when feeling a little woozy from the wine and lack of sleep. Perhaps I should have slept a bit more."

She focused on driving, but was also deep in thought. "If I can review Greico's file on the deceased American student case, I may get more answers. Carmine doesn't *have* to share his files with me, but maybe I'll just have to lay on the charm."

Sophia arrived at work, parked the Vespa and proceeded into her building. Standing on the queue waiting to show her identification card, a funny feeling came over her. She felt flushed and looked around to see if anyone had noticed.

"Ah-hmm, Mmm," clearing her throat, she passed through security and headed toward her lab.

"*Dio m--*," she gasped. The maze of white hallways was too much. The walls were closing in on her. She stopped, standing still for a moment to collect herself.

"Sophia, come," she heard a woman's faint voice.

She looked around and saw a man in the adjacent hallway walking away from her, but no one else. Standing there, she started to sweat.

"Sophia, come. I will help you," the voice called to her. But she was frozen in place.

"Breath in... then out... you are fine," she convinced herself. Taking one step, then another, a warm tingling feeling ran down her spine. "Wow, that was weird," she mumbled to herself.

"Sophia," an unfamiliar voice called to her again.

"What!? ..." She heard the voice, now behind her.

She turned and saw Ben approaching. "Ben, you are back!"

"Yes, I have to review some information. Are you all right? You look like you saw a ghost!"

"*Sì, sì.* I am fine. I did not sleep well, that's all," she sighed with regret.

"I know what you mean. I was hoping I could talk with you. I have reviewed the American student murder case and I have additional questions, if you have the time."

"*Bene*, but I do have to go to my lab and check with Carmine first."

"Fine. I'll walk with you." They stepped together, side by side, to her lab.

Opening the door, Sophia could see Carmine standing over his desk.

"*Scusami*, Carmine," she said, putting her helmet and jacket down and picking up her lab coat.

"The lab attorney, Mr. Dhara, wants to ask me a few more questions," she advised him.

Carmine stood to acknowledge Ben. "Sure, just come back as soon as you are done. We have a lot of work today."

"*Va bene*," she replied, donning the lab coat and escorting Ben out the door.

"Do you have an office in mind?" she asked, as they walked.

"No, any one will be fine with me. It should not take long."

"OK, we can go in here," pointing to the adjacent office. She opened the door to a small room with a gray oversized desk, four black leather chairs, a state-of-the-art computer system setup on the desk, and two side tables. Like so many others in the building, it was a cold room.

"We use this room for our weekly internal lab audits, but that is not until tomorrow so we should not be bothered. *Per favore*, have a seat." As she took the large supervisor's chair behind the desk, she gestured for Ben to sit in the subordinate's chair. It suited her well.

"Now, how can I help you?" she asked, posturing herself.

Ben smirked, "Well, I was going through my records regarding the kitchen knife that prosecutors say was used on the American victim and I need more information about it. I saw in Carmine's notes that it was analyzed in your lab."

"*Si*, what about it?" she answered, focusing on him and realizing he looked as tired as she felt.

"In your lab report it was stated that the 6-inch knife had a small amount of the victim's DNA on the blade, and Hedrinx's DNA on the handle, although that knife belonged to Mr. Callesino. The second large carving knife was found at the crime scene but did not appear to have his DNA, only the victim's... and so the only knife linking Callesino, Hedrinx and the victim was transported in a shoe box?"

"I see your point." Sophia seemed a little bewildered.

"How do you think the victim's DNA got onto that kitchen knife?" Ben pointedly asked.

"Honestly, I don't know," Sophia shrugged.

As her thoughts broadened, she felt the energy in the room increase. "I also reviewed my personal notes on the case last night and I was going to see if Carmine would share his files with me about the knives and the bra."

"You said your personal notes?" Ben perked up.

"*Si*, I keep a separate file on all my cases, for the *C-Y-A* backup. Don't you?" she countered.

"*C-Y-A* backup?"

"What, you have never heard the expression? You're kidding." Laughing at Ben, "I am sorry…." Composing herself, "it means *Cover Your Ass.*"

Ben smiled, "Yes, a *C-Y-A* backup is a very good idea. And yes, I guess I do," the expression sounding a little funny in his native Indian tongue.

Adjusting her seat, Sophia continued, "Carmine gives me the evidence or material after he vouchers and tests it. I review it and then retest it for verification purposes. Initially, it seemed that all the steps were followed. However, after there were questions about the tampering, last night I looked again at my personal notes. My backup notes do not indicate that Dempsey's DNA was on Callesino's 6- inch knife. Perhaps I was incorrect, which is why I'd like to see Carmine's files."

Ben listened intently, thinking to himself as she spoke. The sound of the doorknob jiggling interrupted his train of thought. The door opened, with Carmine standing in its frame.

"Oh, I didn't know you were in here," he said, sounding a little surprised to see Ben and Sophia in the next office.

"I hope it's all right. We won't be much longer," Ben insisted.

"No problema. Is there anything I can help you with?" Carmine asked, uncharacteristically.

"No, thank you, I will be finished with Ms. Pistisi shortly," Ben replied.

"*Va bene*," Carmine turned around and closed the door.

Sophia looked a little baffled at Carmine's interruption. "As I was saying, I was going to see if Carmine will let me see his testing results."

"Hmmm. I don't think that he will help," Ben responded flatly.

"Why not?" She pressed on.

"I'm not sure, but I think this whole case is a political mess," he subtly suggested.

"I agree. I heard last night that Hedrinx and Callesino are being released and that there is a demand for a new trial. As I mentioned earlier, I didn't know what case I was working on until now. To know who these people are certainly changes my perspective. But why don't you think Carmine will let me see his files?"

"Because I have reviewed his report, the one that was introduced in the first trial and he, as your supervisor, signed off that there was a small trace of Dempsey's DNA on the blade of that 6-inch knife. I believe her DNA was added later, so I doubt that asking him for his records will help."

"Ahh... OK. What do you think happened?" She looked surprised.

"I am afraid this has become more like a political football game. So playing on the right side will be essential, if you know what I mean. It is just unfortunate the poor victim is the football." Ben's expression grew concerned. "It's like you say, *C-Y-A*."

"I do understand that." Sophia slumped in her chair and bowed her head, thinking about Eme and Kerry Dempsey. "It's not fair, is it?"

"No, I would say not," Ben agreed. "Do you think Mr. Greico would have any reason to intentionally tamper with the evidence?"

Surprised by the question, Sophia sat straight up, pondering the question, "Carmine is a bit off, but I'm not sure he would risk everything and do something like that."

Ben sat still, trying to read Sophia's reaction.

"Sophia, do you think Mr. Greico could have put the GHB in your coffee?"

"*Dio mio!*" she gasped, stunned by the insinuation. "I ..."

"I know it is hard to think that someone you have worked with for several years could do such a thing. It seems far-fetched, but someone put the GHB in your coffee and someone tainted that knife. I am sure of it," he insisted.

"Tainting evidence?" Sophia quizzed Ben. "I just don't think he could."

"This whole case is obviously fucked up," Ben countered, surprising her with his blunt assessment.

Sitting back in her chair, she tried to remember the night she was poisoned. "Carmine gave me a few case files, putting them on my desk, and as I worked testing the knife, he left early. I don't know...," she nodded.

"I am sure the person who put the GHB in your coffee probably didn't know you were allergic," Ben added, "I don't see him as a killer, but more as someone who may have been put up to it."

Feeling a little relieved at the prospect that Carmine would not intentionally kill her, but rather just hurt her, she repeated, "I just don't know."

"OK, let's review it again," Ben stressed. "What time did he leave the lab?"

Thinking about it carefully, "I think that I went for my coffee about 10:00 pm, just after he had gone home."

"OK. If he left just before 10:00 and you went for coffee after that, you then came back and drank it. Is that right?"

"*Si.*" She was trying to follow his train of thought, "he could have compromised the evidence while I was getting my coffee, so why use GHB?"

"Did you finish the testing and finalize your report before you went for coffee?" he asked.

Sophia thought for a moment. "I had finished it, since I had already entered the summary into my personal backup. But I must have been sidetracked and didn't get the chance to record it in the official files. But I don't understand. The night before, he could easily have put the DNA on the knife when he had the material, so that when he gave it to me the evidence would match."

"I thought about that," Ben responded. "What if he was asked to change the evidence *after* he tested it and before you verified it?" Now he couldn't just take it away from you, could he?"

Ben was convincing in his argument.

"No, he could not, but this is so bizarre. I cannot believe it." Sophia was fidgeting nervously in her seat.

"If he wanted to make sure that he was not going to be suspected of any wrongdoing, he would make sure that you would be able to say he was not there," Ben reasoned.

"But he could simply have said that he had to adjust his test findings." Sophia tried to defend Carmine, and added, "I just have a hard time believing he would be involved with something like this."

"If he was approached after his final test results were recorded and after yours, and then saying he had a problem with his results, it would be suspicious. His changed results would be suspect."

"I... I see," she paused, not wanting to agree with Ben. In a flashback she had the memory of Carmine reaching his hand over Sophia to put the other case files on her desk. She could see his hand in slow motion putting the folders down and noticing a large band-aid below his left thumb.

"Oh, I scraped it in my bathroom. *Che una cagna!*" Carmine responded to Sophia's concern, seeing that it was still a little bloody.

"Sophia," Ben distracted her, "I am sorry to be telling you this and perhaps I have already mentioned too much. But...," Ben went to say.

"It was a voice. I heard someone calling my name," Sophia remarked, point-blank.

"A voice? That is what you heard that night leading you out of your lab?"

"*Sì,* I am certain of it... but it's like a dream. I heard a woman's voice calling my name. I opened the door and saw no one. I thought I then heard it down the adjacent hallway, in front of this office leading to the bathroom. So I walked a little farther and looked around and still saw nothing. I was going to turn back but I heard my name again around the corner, closer to the ladies room." Sophia was trance-like as she retold her story.

"And you did not see anyone?" Ben cross examined her.

"…It was late, so you don't have many people around. I mean the security team is usually milling about, but the regular guard was out sick."

"Well, that makes sense to me," Ben observed confidently.

"It does? How?" She had to know.

"I saw the security video of that night and it looks like you were looking for something, or someone. There is no voice feed so I could not hear anything."

"But if the video does not show anyone else but me, where did the voice come from?"

"Hmmm, that's a good question." Ben considered the possibilities.

Sophia stood up to stretch her back and legs. "Yaaaaw, I am so sorry," she said, stretching her arms over her head. "I have to replenish my energy. I'm not feeling my best today."

Stretching her arms behind her back, she looked up at the ceiling and she noticed the industrial-sized vent. "Hey, do you think someone could fit in those vents?" she asked, pointing up.

Ben looked over his head. The vent above him was perhaps 3 feet by 5 feet in diameter. "That is a good question, Sophia."

"Wait, even if someone could fit in the vent, how would they do it?" Sophia countered herself.

Ben looked around the room. "Hmm…" He got up and moved the computer then picked up one of the side tables, placing it on the desk. Moving behind the desk he pushed it just under the vent.

"Ohhh, my…," she gasped in disbelief.

"If someone got into the vent and put small recorder transmitters at certain intervals from your office going to the ladies room, no one would see what you are looking for. When you went to the ladies room it would have given anyone time to put the GHB in your coffee. Yes?" Ben suggested.

"I don't know. I just don't know." Sophia shook her head, "I just cannot imagine Carmine, the lab rat, doing something that needed guts to do."

"Sophia, if you want the truth we don't have much time."

"What do you mean?" Sophia was puzzled.

"The only way to know for sure is for one of us to go into the vent to see if there is anything there."

"You're crazy!"

"I know it sounds crazy, but what happened when you told your supervisors you were poisoned? How far did they investigate?"

Sophia remembered the conversation with Mr. Lorino, and the hint of blacklisting her.

"OK. Who is going to go in?" Sophia was nervous, but also began to feel angry that she could have been the bait for whoever tainted the evidence.

"Well, it would probably look bad for me to get my suit dirty and then go to the security office," Ben said, brushing a piece of lint from his pressed suit jacket.

"Ugggg," Sophia locked the door and took off her lab coat. Ben climbed on the desk and looked at the screws securing the vent.

"Hmmm, one of the screws is missing." He took out the pocketknife his father had given him on his thirteenth birthday. "This will do," he started to unscrew each of the remaining five screws holding the vent to the ceiling, as Sophia paced to and fro.

"OK, let me first put my head in to see." Ben peered into the vent, trying to be protective, "OK, you are good to go. But you have to hurry. Just try to find the vent outside your lab door to see if you find anything."

Sophia didn't have time to think. As she looked at Ben, she had the stomach-churning feeling that he was right. Sitting on the desk, she unzipped her Christian Louboutin boots.

"I'd rather die than wreck these," she looked up at Ben, who was less than impressed by the style.

Climbing onto the desk with Ben's support she nodded her head, giving a sign that she was ready.

"I can't believe I'm doing this!" One big boost and she was in the darkened vent, head first. Through the vents, she could see the hallway lights illuminating the distance.

"My stomach is turning. Be calm, be calm..." She was convincing herself. Then, army-style, she used her arms to pull herself forward toward the hallway vent and light.

"*Dio mio...*, it's filthy!! I don't think this was a good idea!" Then a frightening thought came to mind. "What if I get caught? I'll lose my job." She started to panic before hearing Ben's voice.

"Sophia, are you all right?" Ben whispered.

She blew the dust out of her mouth and whispered back, "Yeah."

Slowly, quietly, she crawled toward the light. The first vent she came to was connected to others, giving her the choice to crawl straight, right or left. Looking down the metal vent walls, she saw light coming up from the vent in front of her lab door.

"Dust and dirt is everywhere," she thought, proceeding as quietly as she could. Holding her breath, she made her way to the vent outside her lab. Peering down, she could see people walking in the hallway under her.

"It's weird being here, looking down on people as they go about their business," she mused, stopping for a second. "I feel like a spy," she smirked, reaching the vent.

"Hmm, it seems normal." She analyzed the edges, lightly tracing her fingers around the corners.

"What, the..," she whispered. In the top right corner she saw a small piece of cloth tucked under the lip of the vent.

"*Merda*, this is sharp!" Feeling the lip of the metal vent, she almost sliced her finger. "What is this? ..." She took out the plastic wrapper that had once held Mama's biscuit, and turned it inside out to preserve any evidence.

With the plastic wrapper in her hand and the cloth securely inside, she scooted backwards, her legs guiding her return through the vents.

"Uggggg,' she yelped. "Oh, *Cazzo*! What the hell is...?" She put her hands in front of her. "...A decaying rat!"

"...I hope no one heard me," she whispered as she continued her crawl.

"I need to get out of here fast." One arm and leg moved backwards, then the other in rotation, until she was back at the vent where Ben waited.

"*Dio mio*!! Get me out of here!" she whispered loudly.

Ben helped her down onto the desk, and then to the floor. Her clothes were filthy as she tried to wipe her hands together and straighten herself up.

"Well, … did you find anything?" an anxious Ben inquired.

"*Si*, I saw that we need to do a better job of cleaning this place. It's gross up there, and there was a dead rat!" she exclaimed, disgusted.

"But did you see anything else?" Ben asked anxiously.

Sophia showed Ben the wrapper and the little piece of cloth. "I found this piece of cloth and I could see that the dust was less dense in the area around the frame of the vent. It could be possible that a recorder or transmitter, whatever you said, was placed in that spot," she reported, spitting more dust out of her mouth.

"This cloth, do you have any idea what it is?" Ben was curious.

"Perhaps, but I would like to verify it by testing it when Carmine is not in the lab." Sophia looked at the plastic wrapper.

"OK, that's a good idea," he concurred.

"What do you think we should do from here? I can't tell Mr. Lorino that I'm partial to poking around the vents," she stated, after dusting off her clothes as best as she could and putting her boots back on. Fixing her hair, she put on the lab coat to cover her dirty clothes.

"I think I need to do a little more research. If Mr. Greico was the one, he was not seen on any camera, so that needs to be addressed. You will need to go back to work and act is if nothing has happened. Can you do that?" Ben was hopeful that Sophia also had a passion for the truth.

"I am not sure, but I hope so. What other options do I have?" Sophia countered, without making any promises. "Then what?"

"How about we meet privately?"

"*Va bene*, we can meet at a Café Trastevere, near my flat. How about on Thursday? I have the day off."

"That will work. Let's meet about three P.M.," he suggested.

Ben returned the desk, computer and side table to their original places as Sophia collected herself. When she finally opened the door, they stepped into the hallway where Carmine had just opened the lab door.

"And, Mr. Dhara, if you want to speak to me again, you will need to have my boss, Mr. Lorino, present." Sophia shouted. "I did not do anything wrong! And I am tired of you and your questions!" She stared at a wide-eyed Ben, who was initially taken aback by her outburst.

"Ahh, well I…" Ben could not muster any words.

"This is the last time, Mr. Dhara. Do you understand me?" Sophia demanded.

"Yes of course, Ms. Pistisi. I am sorry to have upset you."

Carmine seemed not to know what to make of their interaction. Sophia pushed Carmine aside to enter the lab, going directly to her seat. For a moment, even she didn't know how to react.

Sensing movement behind her, she heard Carmine ask, *"Stai bene?"*

"I guess so. I am just tired and I don't feel well. And that guy, I don't know what his problem is. I don't understand anything." Sophia cried. She could feel herself letting go. A strange feeling came over her, and for no apparent reason, she began to sob hysterically.

Carmine was caught off guard. He was awkward around women, particularly crying women.

"Why don't you go home? I will let Mr. Lorino know you are not feeling well. But tomorrow, please come in early. We really do have work to be done," he reassured her.

"Grazie, Carmine. I do appreciate that. Perhaps I just need some rest," she said, wiping her eyes as she rose and picked up her helmet and jacket. "I will be in early tomorrow."

She walked out of the lab, leaving Carmine just as confused as she felt. "What the hell was that?" Even *she* was surprised by her ability to lie and cry on the spot.

After wiping her tears, she noticed how dirty her hands were, and entering the bathroom she realized the extent of the grime. "I have to get home!"

Chapter 8

YOUR BROTHERS ARE COMING

Sophia arrived home and immediately put on a pot of coffee. She took the plastic wrapper from her pocket and held it up to the light.

"This little piece of cloth can catch you," she thought, referring to the one responsible for drugging her.

"Carmine, I just hope it's not you. While I may not be your number one fan, I still have a hard time believing that you would intentionally hurt me."

"But there's only one way to find out. Tomorrow I will get his DNA and do a test on this cloth."

Ring, ring, ring...

"*Ciao*," she answered her mobile.

"*Ciao* Sophia, it is Dennis Schiano."

"Oh, Mr. Schiano. *Come stai*? Did you find anything?"

"How about we meet so I can show you what I have uncovered."

"*Va bene*, when can we meet?"

"How about Thursday, at the same place as before?"

"Can you tell me what you found?"

"No, I need to show you."

"*Bene* at the Café then, how about two o'clock?"

"*Si*, I can meet you at 2," Dennis responded.

"*Va bene*, I will look forward to it."

Ending the call, Sophia could not help but wonder what Dennis had found. Her mind was on overload. On the small counter next to the coffee pot there was an already opened bottle of Cabernet.

"One glass won't hurt. I mean just to calm my nerves," Sophia reasoned with herself while she poured a glass of wine and turned off the coffee pot.

"Wait. Thursday, *Merda*! I'm going to have to cancel my hair appointment with Marlene," she remembered.

"I knew Thursday sounded too familiar, with also meeting Ben," she thought aloud while calling her hairstylist to cancel the appointment. "Questions, questions and more questions. Maybe now I can get some answers," she mused, holding up the plastic wrapper again.

"So, how am I going to manage to get Carmine's DNA, and how will I analyze this little guy?" referring to the cloth. "Hmm, I'm going to have to think on this."

As the hours passed, various ideas came to mind. "Ahhh, I need sleep," she thought, finally tucking herself into bed.

But the conversation she'd had with Dennis mixed with her plans. "I have to get Carmine's DNA and meet Dennis."

"*Dio Mio*, I have to get some rest." Sighing, "B-r-e-a-t-h-e in… then… o-u-t." She got up, lighting the candle next to her bed. "I hope you can help me to focus." Fortunately, its soft glow and her deep breathing relieved her nerves through the night.

Sophia was back at work and took her daily case files from Carmine, as usual.

"Aaachew!" Carmine sneezed.

"*Dio ti benedica.*"

"*Grazie.* Damn cold!" Carmine blew his nose.

As she worked, she periodically looked over her shoulder to be sure Carmine was busy. She pulled out the wrapper with the cloth, and using her gloves and tools she removed the cloth from the wrapper and placed it on the glass tray in front of her.

Sophia had anticipated Carmine throwing out his used tissue, and waited for an opportunity to get it when he went to the restroom. Quickly, she rose from her chair and grabbed the tissue from the waste bin. As she stood up the door flew open.

"Carmine!" She whispered in surprise. His bulging eyes glowered at her as she held the tissue in her hand.

"Your brothers are coming!" He proclaimed, his eyes so wide open it seemed he was in a trance.

"What?" Sophia's heart began to race, and she felt frozen with fear.

Buzz, buzz, buzz, buzz, buzz...

Sophia's alarm clock sounded, and her eyes flew open in shock and confusion. Her jaw gaped open, slime leaking from the side of her mouth.

"*Dio Mio*! What a weird dream!" She jolted up, sitting on the bed.

"That was crazy." Stretching to wake up, she looked out her window, "What a *pessima* day." The rain was steady, splashing against her windows.

Relieved from her nightmarish dream, she got ready for work and called for a taxi. "These rainy days are no match for bus stops," she reasoned, paying the few extra euro on a taxi.

"You can do this." Excited and nervous, Sophia tried to stay calm by talking to herself.

Approaching her lab door, she looked up at the vents she had climbed into the day before, giving her a different perspective as she stood under them now.

Hesitantly, she twisted the doorknob and saw that Carmine was already in the lab.

"*Buongiorno*, Carmine," Sophia greeted, trying to act as normal as she could.

"*Buongirn...*," he sounded off in his usual muffled response.

She hung her coat, reached for her lab jacket, and after she got settled, she asked Carmine for her work.

"It's over there," he pointed, sounding nasal.

"*Stai bene?*"

"I just have a cold."

"Oh, feel better," pretending to sound somewhat concerned for him.

"I'll live," he responded sarcastically, then added, "Let me know if you have any questions."

Sophia took her work to her desk. "That sure was a crazy dream," she thought, shaking her head and thinking about the coincidence that Carmine had a cold in her dream. "I haven't had that kind of dream in years."

She continued her work, listening to Carmine sniffle and cough.

"Ahhhmmmm," he tried to clear his throat, "Ahhhhmmm." He grabbed for another tissue and tried to clear his nose, then threw the tissue away. After a few minutes of trying to clear his throat he got up and left the room.

This was Sophia's opportunity. Having already put on her gloves she stood up, moving quickly.

"*Accidenti,*" she exhaled, remembering her dream. Her heart raced as she retrieved the tissue from the waste bin and sat back at her desk.

As she began looking at her evidence, the door flew open and Sophia's head spun around, almost lifting her from the chair.

"Oh, I forgot my mobile," Carmine indistinctly muttered through his nose as he walked in, reached over his desk to grab his phone and quickly left again.

"Wow, that was close," Sophia sighed in relief. She reached into her pocket to retrieve the wrapper holding the cloth she'd salvaged from the vent. Using her tools, she placed the cloth on the glass tray and a piece of the tissue on another tray.

"*Bene,* now it's time to see about this DNA," she said as she began the testing process.

Trying to keep up with her assigned work was difficult enough, but Carmine soon returned to resume his coughing and sneezing song. The hours ticked by slowly.

"What if it *is* Carmine?" Waiting for the results, Sophia questioned herself.

"You'll have to remain calm." Convincing herself that she was a strong investigator, she finished one assigned case after another. Finally the last test result was at hand.

She waited until she was ready to leave work before reviewing the comparisons. "Just in case it is Carmine, I can't get weird in front of him," she reasoned, trying to absorb the information.

"*Va bene*, let's see," as she looked into her microscope and at the computer, "*Dio mio!*" she whispered.

"Did you say something?" Carmine asked.

"Aahh…, no. I was talking to myself again," she replied, abruptly turning and staring at the computer screen.

Carmine stood, and Sophia quickly closed the file. He walked toward her, stopping in front of the folders of her completed work.

"Are you finished?" he asked.

"Just about," she turned toward him. "I need to finalize my notes and then I'll be going home. It's been a long day."

She did not realize she was staring at Carmine; almost staring through him.

"Is there something wrong?" he asked, puzzled.

"Ahhh no. You just looked tired," she answered, to cover her weirdness.

"I feel tired," he answered, taking her completed files and returning to his desk.

"I'll bring the last of my reports over to you when I've finished," she said, keeping her last folder and notes in order. But before she closed the computer down she slid a USB backup thumb drive into the computer and clicked *save*. "I think I'll need this," she thought.

When it finished copying she clicked *delete* and erased the evidence of her private research.

Carmine was also getting ready to leave, and took her last report to organize for his review.

"I will look at these tomorrow," he muttered through his sniffles.

"Feel better," she offered, as she took off her lab coat and retrieved her personal belongings to head home. Her mind raced, but she couldn't show it.

"*Grazie*, I will see you tomorrow."

"Actually, I took the day off," she responded, with a nauseating feeling in the pit of her stomach. "*Arrivederci*"

She left the lab and called for her taxi. Walking through the maze of white hallways she couldn't help but feel trapped.

"I can't believe this is happening," she mumbled to herself outside, waiting for her driver. "The test results confirmed the tiny amount of blood found on the cloth from the vent was a 99% percent match to the DNA on Carmine's tissue. I just can't believe it."

Beep, beep. The taxi driver honked his horn for her. She returned home confused, trying to process what everything meant. "Why?" Sophia's mind raced as she struggled to grasp why Carmine would compromise evidence for someone, and use GHB on her.

"I just don't understand!" she repeated, sitting on her sofa, eating the roast pork sandwich she had bought on the way home.

With her laptop, she flipped to the various news sites, simultaneously watching her favorite TV show.

"Ah, HDTV's House Hunters International. Let's see where I could live." The shows expanded her fantasies of living in exotic places. "But don't worry, Mama, I won't leave you," she thought, gazing over to the pictures on her wall. "It is a dream that will remain my fantasy."

Ring ring, ring.

"*Ciao,*" she said, answering to the unfamiliar number.

"*Ciao,* Sophia. It's Ben. How are you?"

"I have more news to share with you," Sophia rushed him, sounding like an investigative reporter.

Interrupting, he said, "Yes, we will discuss it in person. Never on the mobile, all right?" offering her an important lesson.

"*Si, va bene,* I will see you tomorrow at three."

"*Addio, buona note.*" He wished her well, and Sophia smiled at Ben's attempt at an Italian accent.

Continuing her research, the night turned long, cold and damp. She put her laptop away, sitting still for a moment.

"I don't understand. *Per favore,* Eme, show me what's going on." She said a small prayer for Eme to help her to make sense of things.

Tick, tock, tick, tock. The clock nagged her.

Tired, she meditated, "b-r-e-a-t-h-e… slowly," she intoned, hoping for answers, and got ready for bed. But sleep evaded her.

Morning came slowly, but anxiety helped her to get up early. Still pleading for Eme's help, she dressed while the coffee brewed. Peering through her window, she thought, "Wow, the sun is surely welcome. I can't believe it's so warm for this time of year," and turned on the television for news on the weather.

"It's going to be in the 50's, *è perfetto*," she yawned. "…But I am so tired." Doing a few yoga stretches that Eula had taught her helped to calm her nerves. "Eula, my teacher, you would be happy," she giggled.

After further research on her laptop, she got ready and headed off to meet Dennis, and then Ben, at the café. "If I didn't know me, I'd think there was something strange about meeting two men at a café, one after the other," she laughed as she walked to the bus stop. "I hope you are with me, Eme."

Sophia arrived, and saw that Dennis Schiano was already seated at an outdoor table.

"*Perfetto*, it will provide extra warmth without an umbrella." Sophia walked up to the table, "*Ciao*, Mr. Schiano."

"*Ciao come stai,* Sophia?" He stood to welcome her, gesturing for her to sit.

"*Sto bene*, how are you?" She sat, as the waitress came to take Dennis's order. "*Bene..*, you've only just arrived?" Sophia asked.

"*Si, no problemo.*" He turned to the waitress, "I'll have *caffè*, milk and no sugar, *per favore*. Sophia what would you like?"

"I will also have *caffè*, black," she replied, then turned her attention to Dennis, anxiously waiting for him to tell her what he found.

"I do have some news, but Sophia, I must warn you, it might be a little shocking." His concern for her visible, seeing how anxious she appeared.

"I need to know. *Per favore,* tell me," she insisted.

Dennis pulled a piece of paper from a folder resting on the chair next to him, and passed it to her.

"*Per favore, take care of my little one and let him know that he is loved,*" she read from a copy of a small note-sized paper.

"I don't understand. It's identical to the note that was left with me. But 'he'? What is this?" She could scarcely utter the words in her confusion.

Dennis sat straight up, his posture implying he meant business.

"I looked into police reports from various districts in Italy for the days surrounding the night you were found on the steps of the orphanage." His tone was reassuring.

"It appears that there were two other police reports, filed for two other babies who were seemingly abandoned, the day before and the day after you were left at the orphanage."

"*Dio Mio!* …Two others?" Sophia sat back in her chair utterly amazed. As she processed the information, the waitress brought their orders. "May I get you anything else?"

"*Sì,*" Dennis replied, "we will have this pastry dish." He pointed to the menu, hoping he could help Sophia to swallow the news with perhaps a spoonful of sugar.

"*Dio mio!*" Sophia gasped.

"*Sì,* I know. I was able to track down this note which was left with the baby on the doorsteps of the Istituto Provinciale per l'Infanzia in Corso Giovanni Lanza Turin."

"A baby boy?" Sophia uttered the words, but couldn't process the idea.

"*Sì,* a baby boy, about six months old. I would say that there is a good chance that he is your brother, Sophia."

"*Mio fratello?*" The words sounded foreign to her.

"Unfortunately, I have not been as lucky in getting more information from the other police report in Palermo. However, I am still working on it." He was straightforward, sipping his coffee, and giving her extra time to process his information. "All I know is that the other baby was left at San Giovanni degli Eremiti, but you may know it as Saint John of the Hermits."

Sophia's expression was stunned, as she stared into space.

"Sophia, *va tutto bene*?" Dennis leaned forward with concern, as the waitress arrived with a small plate of pastries.

Then turning his attention back, Dennis asked again, "Sophia, *va tutto bene*?"

"I, I..," she stammered, "I just can't believe it."

"I know it is a lot to take in," Dennis admitted.

"Do you know anything about the boy left in Turin?" Sophia asked Dennis. "Is the other abandoned baby also a boy?"

"I don't know more than what I have just told you but I am still looking into it." He reached over and touched her hand, "As soon as I have any more information, I will certainly let you know."

Sophia shook her head, "*Grazie*, Dennis, I really appreciate this. I simply can't believe it. I just never thought..." She didn't even realize that she had improperly called him by his first name.

"I know it is hard to believe that you can have siblings and you never knew it, but we will learn more. I promise you," he reassured her.

"But I do believe they are my brothers; I can feel it," she responded, as a matter of fact.

"How can you be sure without any proof?" Dennis asked, surprised by her comment.

"I just know. I understand that this may sound strange to you, but I sense this deep within me. I just know it. Does that sound odd to you?" Sophia wanted his honest opinion.

"Actually, no. I have been married for more than thirty years, and my wife has such feelings all the time, so I understand strange," he chuckled.

"*Really*?" Sophia asked, relieved.

"I can assure you, after thirty years, nothing seems strange to me," he smiled.

"*Va bene*," she confessed, "the night before last, I had a dream that felt so real. My boss told me that my brothers were coming."

"Wow! *Questo* è *strano*," marveled Dennis, looking amused.

"But you just said...." She was embarrassed.

"Ha, ha.., no, no, Sophia. Sorry, I couldn't help myself," he apologized.

He failed at trying to lighten the mood. Realizing his poor judgement, he tried to reassure her, "Trust me; this is not so strange. The baby that I traced with this note is your age, so he could be a twin. Then, if the other baby, whom you sense is also your brother, then you are one of triplets."

"*Dio mio*! This is like like a dream *within* a dream," she mused, feeling her mouth move but felt otherwise numb.

"I can't imagine what you are feeling, but based on my years of investigation, I can assume that something or someone was threatening your parents. They went to such great lengths to separate you and your brothers to make sure that you were all safe," he assessed.

"*Sì* ..." she paused, "this other note was part of one police report. But you found nothing with the other?"

"Actually, I'm still trying to locate the third report, but because it was before records were computerized, it is taking longer."

"I understand," she gratefully accepted.

Dennis turned his attention to the pastries, allowing Sophia more time to absorb the information. "*Bene*, you should try one," as he tried to distract her.

Sophia absently took one of the pastries but didn't eat.

"Are you going to be all right?" Dennis asked, concerned.

"*Sì*, I am fine. *Grazie,* I am just trying to understand what is happening to me lately," taking a long sip of her coffee.

Dennis gave her a moment to think about what he had told her, but couldn't help but feel sorry for her.

"Do you know where he is now?" Sophia asked with a glimmer of hope in her eye.

"I am sorry, I don't; at least not yet. But I'm working on that too."

"May I see the police report? Or whatever you have?"

"In fact, this folder is for you. As you review the information, you may recognize something that I may not know." Dennis's serious demeanor returned.

"*Oh,mio*. What time is it?" She saw Ben approaching and looked at her watch.

"Dennis I hate to bother you with… but my own life is just as strange lately." She hesitated, fearing she wasn't making any sense. "And *mio mio*…" Sophia wasn't sure how to introduce Ben. "*Mio amico,* he is also to meet me here. I'm hoping that you will listen to us and, and," she stuttered. "Perhaps you can give us your advice on what we should do."

"Do, do about what?" Dennis asked with curiosity.

As Ben approached, the large band-aid under his left eye became more apparent.

"Ben, what happened to you?" Sophia exclaimed, gesturing to the empty chair next to her for him to sit.

A little surprised to see Sophia with someone else, Ben asked, "Excuse me, but I thought we…"

"Ben, this is Dennis Schiano, the private investigator who is helping me to trace my birth parents. I trust him," she rushed to assure Ben.

Dennis assessed Ben who seemed very nervous and agitated.

"But this is sensitive information," Ben insisted.

"*Sì,* and Ben, we need help. It was Carmine. The DNA was a match," Sophia explained.

"DNA?" Dennis inquired in surprise.

"Ben, what happened to you?" Sophia reached to touch Ben's face.

"I'll tell you later," Ben brushed her off, as the waitress came for his order. "I'll have coffee, black."

"Make that another round," Dennis added, "…and more pastries, *per favore.*"

"What is going on, Sophia?" Dennis urged, after the waitress left.

Sophia explained to Dennis who Carmine is and about the army-like moves she performed inside the vent where she found the cloth.

"Wow, I can tell you that none of my three daughters would climb into anything with spiders in it, much less a dead rat." Dennis remarked with a half smile. Taking a more serious tone, he asked, "What are you going to do about this DNA match to your boss?"

107

Dennis looked concerned for both of them.

"I don't know," Sophia replied with an uncertain grin.

"How sure of a DNA match are you?" Ben asked.

"There is a 99% chance that it's Carmine," Sophia assured them.

"I think you should tell your supervisors what you have found," Dennis said, alarmed for her safety. "As a father myself, I feel compelled to help you, Sophia. And I think…"

"I did try to go through the normal channels," Sophia explained. "There was an investigation, reports were filed and I even contemplated suing my employer. But I realized there were political issues with my employer, and my career would be destroyed."

Seeing that both Sophia and Ben were tense, Dennis asserted, "I understand. But I still think you should tell your supervisors."

"What should I tell them?" Sophia asked sarcastically, "If I reveal the DNA findings they will ask me how I obtained it. What will I say? That I just happened to be cleaning the vents and noticed you missed a piece of cloth?"

"Sophia, why would your boss, Carmine, compromise the evidence? What would he have to gain?" Dennis sat back in his chair.

"It's all politics, Mr. Schiano," Ben answered. "Isn't it always about politics?"

"*Per favore*, please call me Dennis," he turned to Ben. "From what you have said, this is serious and it must be dealt with through the authorities," Dennis insisted.

Ben sipped his coffee, remaining cautious, but a little more relaxed with Sophia's new friend.

"I'm not able to tell you everything that I know," Ben hinted, looking up. "In my official capacity I cannot tell you anything about an investigation or the accused, with regard to the death of the American university student."

Sophia looked at Ben as if reading his mind. "The *accused*?!"

Dennis tried to understand. "The death of the American university student? I read about that," he offered.

"Tricia Hedrinx and Roberto Callesino were accused of murdering Kerry Dempsey. And as I understood it, the evidence was questionable. I could see that politics played a part," Dennis pointed out.

Ben sat up, raising his finger, as if preaching. "Yes, politics has a lot to do with everything in our life today. Politics can determine the way we live, influence careers and even affect the way we die," concluding his sermon.

Dennis blinked away, dismissive of Ben's rant. "I read that Callesino's father is a politician who recently lost the election in the Turin City Council."

"I read that too," Sophia agreed. "It was suggested that the negative publicity about his son's case cost him his political standing...." Considering further, she exclaimed, "And the tainted evidence implicated his son!"

"I cannot confirm any such claims." Ben stated.

"*Bene*, so it's another avenue to explore. But what should I do with Carmine's DNA sample for now?"

"First off, you cannot really prove anything. You simply have a DNA match to a piece of cloth found in a vent. For all you know, Carmine could have been cleaning the vents," Dennis inserted. "You should speak to your supervisors and give them this information."

"Sure." Ben retorted, ignoring Dennis's advice, "and there was someone else who helped Carmine. If you find out who that is, we will have more proof."

"*Dio mio*! Sophia cried. "*Sì*, there must have been another person to mess with the cameras."

"Unless a security camera technician helped him...," Dennis answered in investigative mode.

"I can neither confirm nor deny," Ben said smugly.

"*Sì, sì* I know." Sophia got carried away. "I can find out. I can follow Carmine to see who he hangs out with."

"No, no, no! Sophia you should not be following anyone." Dennis's voice was deep and instructive, as if he were speaking to one of his own daughters.

He took out his pen and his notepad. "Write down what you know about Carmine and I'll see what I can do."

"Are you sure, Dennis? I don't want to put you out," Sophia asked, not wanting to take advantage of his kindness.

"*Sì,* I'm sure," Dennis responded, offering Sophia the notepad.

Looking up at him, "I will increase your fee for helping me. I want you to know that I really appreciate it."

"Listen, I can only try. *Per favore,* just promise me you won't start following people," Dennis grinned.

"I promise," Sophia assured him.

She picked up her coffee, took another sip and asked, "Ben what happened to you?"

Drinking his coffee, he winced with pain from his facial cut. "I had an accident," Ben stated, matter-of-factly.

"Well, tell us," Sophia insisted.

"It is an odd story," Ben sighed.

Sophia and Dennis looked at each other, then back at Ben. "Well, we were just talking about strange stories before you arrived. *Per favore,* tell us," Sophia prompted.

"I was walking to the corner store," Ben began, shaking his head as if he still did not believe it. "I wanted the curry chicken in the Indian shop across from my hotel. It was delicious the day before, so I decided to brave the rain yesterday for more. As I waited at the corner to cross, I felt a hard push on my back and fell, scraping my face on a bit of glass in the street."

"*Dio mio*, are you all right?" Sophia questioned.

"The glass was actually not my problem! It was the delivery truck that was fast approaching. *That* was my problem!" Ben raised his voice, "I was hurrying to get up when I felt two large hands on my shoulders pulling me up onto the sidewalk. I turned around to see a man with golden blond hair and sparkling blue eyes standing over me. He said that I would be fine, but that the scar on my face would be a reminder that miracles do happen."

"*Bene*, what an incredible story," Dennis countered.

110

"I can tell you that if this man had not been there I would probably not be here now. That truck would have killed me!" Ben tightly gripped his coffee cup, seemingly embarrassed.

"A large man with blonde hair and crystal blue eyes?..." Sophia wondered. "He sounds familiar."

"Yes, he does," Ben sighed with relief.

"He sounds like the security guard, Raphael, who helped me." Sophia marveled.

"It's crazy, but I thought of that, too," Ben answered Sophia with a confused grin.

"I know it sounds eerie, but it's true. I believe that man, Raphael, is an angel," Sophia insisted.

"A *what*?" Ben was surprised.

"I cannot tell you how I know but just that I know." Sophia was confident in her explanation. "Do you believe in angels?"

"I don't know," Ben replied, protecting his manliness. "It seems odd to me, but yesterday that man saved my life. I'm sure of that... but an *angel*?" Ben was unsure. "Sophia, that only happens in stories."

"What about you, Dennis, do you believe in angels?" Sophia asked.

"You should talk to my wife. She could tell you about a miracle that really happened. And, because of her I truly believe in angels," he answered.

"I would very much like to meet her," Sophia offered.

Dennis sat for a moment before responding, "On Sunday we're having a little party. I can give you my address and I'm sure she wouldn't mind if you came and talked to her. She loves talking about angels. You are both welcome, if you'd like."

"That would be great, *grazie*," Sophia sincerely responded. "I will really look forward to it."

"I'll be returning to London soon, so I don't think...." Ben tried being evasive, but Sophia interrupted.

"*Per favore* Ben, come with me," trying to persuade him.

"I'll have to let you know. I need to catch up on my work, so..." he began.

"Okay, but try, *per favore,*" she pleaded. "I'd really like to better understand these things, and it might help us both with Carmine," she argued her point.

Handing his business card to Ben, Dennis said, "If you can make it, you could come around three P.M." Then to Sophia, "I'm sure my wife would like to talk with you. In the meantime, I will look into this Carmine fellow."

Dennis stood, placing money on the table to pay the bill. "I must be going, but will be speaking with you soon. *Arrivederci,*" he bid them farewell with a nod and smile.

"*Grazie,* Dennis." Shaking his large hand, she uttered sincerely, "*Grazie*, it means a lot to me."

He nodded to Sophia, then to Ben, and left them sitting at the table.

Finishing their coffee, Sophia wondered, "So what do you think of Dennis?"

"I just met him, so…," Ben started to say.

"Well, I know I can trust him, just like I know I can trust you."

Ben smiled, "Are you hungry?" he asked, changing the subject.

"*Sì*, are you?" Sophia admitted.

"I'm starving. Shall we get something different to eat?" Ben was happy she agreed.

"I guess curry chicken is out of the question," Sophia remarked, with a laugh.

"How about it? Do you like curry?" He was curious.

"*Sì*, it sounds great.

"I know a place called Jaipur II, and it's not that far," Sophia suggested as they stood on the corner and motioned for a taxi. "Oh, and I got your email address from the business card you gave me. I sent you a copy of my *C-Y-A* file about the kitchen knife. Let me know if you received it."

"I will. Thank you. You know, I was happy that there was a curry house a short walk from my hotel. I thought I was lucky, until yesterday. I have five stitches, and the doctor said there is likely to be a small scar."

They got into the taxi. "I'm glad it's only five," Sophia added, as she scooted over for Ben to sit beside her.

"Yes, me too. I just can't help thinking about what that guy said. He lifted me up, telling me that I will have a scar to remind me that miracles do happen. It was surreal. His voice went through me." He was bewildered, not wanting to believe it himself.

"I know the feeling. Raphael has a deep voice, but it wasn't alarming; in fact, it was comforting," Sophia recalled. "Did you see who pushed you?" Sophia thought to ask.

"No, there were two women behind me but they saw nothing. Not even the man who helped me," Ben said with a straight face. "The man was gone as fast as he came."

"Do you think it was one of the women who pushed you?"

"I don't think so; one woman was about eighty years old, and the other was perhaps ninety, so I don't think it was either of them," he said with a straight face.

Sophia smirked, "Oh, I see. Hmm, maybe they lied."

"I don't believe that was the case," Ben looked serious. "But I am sure I felt someone push me."

"Why would someone want to push you?"

"I don't know, but I'll be looking over my shoulder from now on. I'm not a cat. I don't think I have nine lives," he grinned.

"*Sì, per favore,* you need to watch yourself."

"I can say the same to you."

"I am watching, and obviously the man who saved you was watching," Sophia acknowledged.

"What are the chances that this is the same person who saved you? …I can't believe it, but the thought has come to mind," he paused, starting to doubt himself. "Think of the odds; yet I can't help this feeling I have." Ben looked confused. "Until yesterday I had a hard time believing that angels would come down to earth and pull people out of the way of a moving delivery truck. Then I started to think about what happens to all the people the angels could *not* save." His face looked dejected. "I don't know what to believe."

"I don't know either," Sophia shook her head, thinking about Eme. "I just don't know."

They arrived at Jaipur II and were promptly seated in a booth. Ben was finally happy to have his favorite dish. "Chicken Tikka Marsala, my favorite. My mum would often make this for me. It reminds me of home," he said, looking a little nostalgic.

"I will have the vegetable samosas and for dessert, the kulfi," Sophia ordered, then turned to Ben feeling like she had walked into a wall. "I have to go to work tomorrow and it feels really uncomfortable having to face Carmine. I don't know how I'm going to act in front of him," she shared apprehensively.

"I can imagine that it will be uncomfortable, but you mustn't let on that you know anything until I can speak to your supervisors with you," Ben comforted her. "But there is just one thing that I must verify before you speak to your supervisors. Can you wait a day or two?"

"What do you need to verify?" Sophia was curious.

"I want to verify something with Callesino's father, the politician." Ben was straightforward, and then adjusted his seat, hoping to help Sophia face her anxiety with Carmine.

"You know, when I stand in front of people in a courtroom, I pretend that I'm an actor. It helps me to remove anxiety because it is just a show, like a movie," he smiled. "In a way, we can say that about life. Don't you agree? It's all a show with no dress rehearsals."

Sophia smiled back, "*Sì*, that's funny, and I do agree." She sat up straight. "During the week we will work double shifts depending on the workload and how involved the cases are. We generally will have the weekend off, but tomorrow I already know I'll be working a double shift with Carmine. I do hope the other lab desks are occupied. It would help if others were working in our lab so I'm not alone with him."

"I do hope so, too," Ben added. "I am going to look further into the father of Roberto Callesino and the Turin City Council election. Usually where there is dirty politics there's a trail, so I will follow where it leads. I'm sure there is something more to this." Ben looked confident.

"I agree," she replied, then thought for a moment.

"The tainted knife was an issue just before Councilman Callesino's election. What if Carmine compromised the evidence to help get Callesino removed from the Turin City Council?" Sophia suggested.

"There are possibilities, and I will try to look at all of them. I don't know why someone working at a lab would jeopardize his job for someone he may not even know," Ben wondered.

"The connection is lacking, but knowing Carmine, he had to have had a good reason. He loves his job; it's all he has," Sophia posed.

They finished their meal and had coffee. The dinner crowd was just starting to show up and the restaurant was getting noisy.

"Will you go to Dennis's house with me on Sunday? *Per favore*," Sophia asked in earnest, touching his hand.

"I'll try," he answered, looking into her eyes.

"It would mean a lot to me. I'm not sure why, but I feel like I have known you for years."

"That's funny, because I feel the same way," Ben replied, equally puzzled. "I don't understand what is happening, but I know you hold the key to questions that I must find answers to."

"I don't think I have any answers. I only have questions myself," Sophia differed.

Ben generously paid their bill, adding, "So I will call you when I have more information."

"*Sì*, if not before. I will call or text you before Sunday morning," Sophia said, as she grabbed her things. "And, *grazie*… for dinner."

"It's not a problem. I feel like you are my sister, and my mother would have it no other way," he smiled as they left the restaurant.

"And Ben, be careful of old ladies," she joked as she got into her taxi.

"Ouch, that hurt," Ben smiled. He watched Sophia's taxi pull away and headed back to his hotel.

MEETING OF THE MINDS

Cardinal Antonelli was pacing the floor inside an office at the Papal Palace of Castel Gandolfo. His anxious mind wandered for a fleeting moment. "I could see myself working in this office. No, no, no. Then I would have more meetings like this one."

The meeting room was not a typical office. Three large arched windows allowed light to illuminate the room. While its large Birchwood desk was a 200-year-old antique and a focal point of the room, the white-and-black marble fireplace was certainly the centerpiece. On each side of the fireplace, four chairs rich with red silk fabric and two large sofas were spaced far enough to allow free movement for guests.

"You must control your anxiety. Your high blood pressure will give you a heart attack." Cardinal Korsig could see Giacomo's hands were shaking as he tried to reassure his friend. "You will wear out your shoes if you keep pacing. Stop it and sit down."

Antonelli gave a faint smile. "I will feel better once this meeting is over. Are you sure everything is ready?"

"*Non preoccupatevi,*" Korsig assured him again.

"Giacomo, it must be this way." A heavy Spanish accent came from a tall man who stood behind the large wooden desk in front of the middle oversized window. Secretary of State Cardinal Alexander Borgia was noticeable because of his tall, lean stature and receding hairline. His small, beady eyes were hidden behind his glasses.

"You know that truth can restore our church, and lies will destroy it," Cardinal Borgia insisted. "We must pursue this course of action."

Knock, knock. Their conversation was interrupted.

"*Venite in,*" Cardinal Borgia said.

116

Bishop Ignatius Theophorus walked in with his limp, which exposed his past battle with polio.

As the assistant working under the secretary of state, Ignatius was able to speak his mind and advocate for church reform.

"*Mi scusi*, but I overheard your concern, Cardinal Antonelli. The church must be reformed. Our traditions must be reborn. It is the only way we will survive." Ignatius observed the tension in the room.

"*Sì*, I appreciate your input, and as dedicated to Christ and as well-intentioned as you are, your extremely traditional views have often gained you your share of critics," Korsig said with a nod and a grin.

"*Grazie*, gentlemen, your concerns are noted," Cardinal Borgia was trying to deflect tensions.

"Should I have the refreshments brought in now?" Ignatius changed the subject in his distinctive accent. The former bishop of the Hatay Province in southern Turkey was trying to be helpful to his boss.

"*Sì*, Gus that would be fine." Borgia turned back to Antonelli and Korsig. "I have known Val de Marcosi personally for many years, and I know he will be insulted about not having an opportunity to become our next pontiff. However, he is a man of God, and I am sure he will understand." Borgia was trying to convince the others as well as himself.

"There is no doubt about his love for God, but the church is another matter," Korsig said. "He wants drastic reforms."

"Too drastic!" Antonelli said. "He will quickly divide the church if he is elected."

Ignatius reentered the room carrying a tray of coffee cups and glasses. Behind him followed a man of above-average height with short black hair, graying sideburns, and a clean-shaven face.

"And to whom would you be referring?" The Cardinal-Bishop de Marcosi asked the question as he walked in. Cardinal Valentinus de Marcosi of Velletri-Segni, a suburbicarian dioceses in Rome, was a man of few words, but he was direct. A powerful and well-connected cardinal, he knew many influential people in and outside the Curia. With his refined stature, he was a man who was noticed entering any room.

117

"*Mi scusi*. Cardinal-Bishop de Marcosi has arrived," Ignatius tried to announce before being cut off.

"I can see that, Gus. *Grazie*." Borgia was looking annoyed at the lack of a formal announcement. "Val, *benvenuto il mio amico*."

"*Bene il mio amico*," Valentinus said in return as the two men gave a hug and patted each other on the back. They were in the same seminary years ago and had remained close friends.

"Val, you know Cardinal Antonelli and Cardinal Korsig," Borgia said, then turned toward Ignatius. "And you've just met Gus."

"*Bene*, it is nice to see you again," Valentinus said in his soft-spoken tone. "Now tell me, to whom were you referring?" Valentinus was curious to know.

"Well, I, a…" Antonelli stumbled on his words. "I was speaking to Cardinal Borgia about Cardinal Korsig here."

"I see," Valentinus replied. "I believe you, but thousands wouldn't." He shook his head in disbelief.

"Well, if you must know…" Giacomo stumbled to his seat but would not be taken for being weak. "I was speaking of your desire for church reform," he nervously offered. "I understand it is well received by many, especially the progressives who want to break from strict church traditions. We know they hope that they might strengthen the church's foothold in a world that is filled with chaos. But your methods are questionable, Cardinal. I think that is the issue…*signore*."

"Val, would you like coffee or some *vino* perhaps?" Borgia asked politely, trying to prevent an argument.

"It seems this meeting may require some *vino*." Valentinus grinned as he moved toward a table being set up with food and drinks, then turned to Giacomo. "Cardinal Antonelli, it may help you to reflect on the notion that you must be the change you wish to see in the world."

"*Sì, bene allora*. Gentlemen, *per favore,* have a seat. We are just waiting for a few other guests." Borgia gestured.

Gus made sure drinks and snacks of crackers, cheese, biscuits, and fruit were set up on a small buffet table. He stood near the door, joining his boss, Cardinal Borgia. "*Signore*, the other guests will be promptly announced as they arrive."

"*Grazie*, Gus," Borgia responded.

"I can see His Eminence will not be joining us. So who else is coming?" Valentinus asked.

"Cardinal Gasparri will be here to give us his updates regarding the investigations assigned to him by His Eminence." Borgia paused. "And his associate, Bishop Anton Oriollo, will also be attending." Borgia hesitated for a moment.

"Is that all?" Valentinus pressed. "No one else?"

"Cardinal-Bishop Smyrna will also be joining us," Borgia replied in a flat tone.

"Irenaeus?" A surprised look came over Valentinus's face. "This meeting is not just about the report on the investigations, I take it."

"Val, I understand your weariness about Cardinal Irenaeus Smyrna. However, we must be clear about the direction of our future as conclave is set to begin. You and Irenaeus have political clout within our ranks to either help the conclave process or destroy it. The outcome of this conclave could strengthen us, or it could destroy our relationship with the faithful even more than it already has been." Alexander said this quickly and directly to counter any more disparaging remarks.

Knock, knock, knock…

They were once again interrupted before de Marcosi could answer Borgia.

"*Mi scusi*, your other guests have arrived," Gus introduced. "Gentlemen, welcome Cardinal Gasparri and his associate, Bishop Oriolli."

"Welcome, gentlemen," Borgia greeted them. "I believe you know each other. We are just waiting for—"

"*Mi scusi, signore.* Your last guest, Cardinal-Bishop Irenaeus Smyrna, is here." Gus showed the cardinal into the room.

Cardinal de Marcosi was not happy, and his facial expression conveyed his displeasure at being in the same room with his longtime foe.

Valentinus's memory flashed back to years ago when he was working with Cardinal Irenaeus Smyrna.

Irenaeus was the former prefect of the Congregation for the Oriental Churches in the Roman Curia because he knew many powerful people. His congregation was responsible for continuous contact between Rome and the Eastern Catholic Churches.

"Cardinal Smyrna is tasked with protecting the church's rights and maintaining one Roman Catholic Church, uniting the Middle East with Rome. Through the liturgical, disciplinary, and spiritual patrimony of the Latin Church, Irenaeus has protected the heritage of the various Oriental Christian traditions." Valentinus remembered the then Pontiff Pius arguing for Irenaeus's promotion.

"He has authority over Egypt and the Sinai Peninsula, Eritrea and northern Ethiopia, southern Albania and Bulgaria, Cyprus, Greece, Israel, Iran, Iraq, Lebanon, the Palestinian territories, Syria, Jordan, Turkey, and Ukrainian regions," the former Pope Pius pointed out. "And as the world changes and terrorism besieges much of the Middle East, Mother Church, through Irenaeus, will become more prominent. He can help us."

Valentinus knew better. "Irenaeus is not afraid to show how important he is, especially to those he does not approve of."

"Welcome, Cardinal Smyrna." Borgia shook his hand and moved in for a bear hug.

"*Ciao bene*, it is nice to see you again, my friend," Irenaeus replied. He went over to Cardinals Gasparri, Antonelli, and Korsig to shake hands and greeted Bishops Theophorus and Oriolli.

Cardinal Valentinus de Marcosi was not happy watching the display of affection, and his discontentment grew. As Irenaeus worked his way around the room to greet the other guests, Valentinus stared intently.

"He always seems to have the right answers, and while he completed the tasks assigned to him, it did not matter who he insulted or stepped on," Valentinus slyly thought to himself. "Taking the jobs no one else wanted, that is what made him valuable. But despite his younger appearance, he only pretends to carry a mature presence that reeks with his infuriating opinions. Just look at him…"

"He is not polished in the use of his words, and his Turkish accent...ha, it is muddled with his Italian accent with an English translation. You can hardly understand him. He is not a leader!"

"*Ciao.*" Valentinus stood up to his foe and put out his hand. The two men looked each other in the eyes with disdain.

Valentinus remembered another conversation from long ago, when he argued traditional values were out of touch living in a modern society: "While traditional values are important, they need to be more modernized for the faithful so they can relate to the teachings of the church in today's time." Valentinus had made his intentions known.

The seeming distaste for each other stemmed from their two very outspoken points of view on the direction of church reform.

Lecturing in Turin, Valentinus was well liked. He also officiated over important Vatican meetings. He was known to hold some Gnostic views, which angered his counterparts, including Cardinal Smyrna.

Valentinus de Marcosi wanted to open discussions about women having more of a role in the church. He wanted transparency within the Vatican bank, and he was a key figure in helping Pope Gregory join Moneyval.

"If you change our traditions, you are a heretic." Irenaeus would counter opposing views in his letter-writing crusade to countless dioceses who, he felt, had loosened up too much on church traditions. He had as many foes as he did friends. After being elected as the Cardinal-Bishop of Palestrina Rome, another powerful position, he was a force to be reckoned with.

Irenaeus was a traditionalist and made his views well-known, even when no one asked. He appealed to the older clergy, who agreed that church traditions should be held in their strictest form.

Valentinus's memory flashed again, back to a year earlier when he and Smyrna took their aggression to a new height. As media rumors scandalized their beloved church, Pope Gregory had launched another investigation. Vatican officials and U.S. bishops raised concerns over several American nuns who had adopted a secular mentality of feminism.

The investigation involved over 300 religious orders and about 50,000 nuns. Irenaeus spearheaded the investigation on behalf of the pope.

"These nuns do not uphold church teachings sufficiently, and they are too involved in political issues regarding abortion and homosexuality rights," Irenaeus shouted out at their meeting. "They are exercising too much independence when helping the people. They do not realize that it is not theirs but our Holy See's order!" His stance was unyielding.

"Women can play an important role in our church," Valentinus had insisted. "People relate to these women. These American nuns can be an example of our truest form of compassion."

"You are showing the Gnostic side of your beliefs," Valentinus remembered Irenaeus sarcastically taunting.

Valentinus was not amused. While his family tree was rooted in Gnostic beliefs—and it was thought that Valentinus was related to the infamous first-century Gnostic father, Valentinus, who believed the role of women was essential—Valentinus was decidedly Catholic. Gnostics elevated women's statuses to teachers, priests, and even bishops. This conflicted with Valentinus's Catholic teachings and his dedication to the Blessed Mother Mary, which caused confusion in his mind at times.

"How could this ordinary woman give birth to the Savior of the world?" he wondered. "She performed her own miracles. She is honored in the Koran, Torah, and the Bible, and yet she is mentioned as just an ordinary woman."

Valentinus did not like or appreciate Irenaeus's reference to Valentinus's family in his remark at the Vatican nuns' meeting.

"Your mother must not have minded to bow to your higher power. God bless her," Valentinus shot back to Irenaeus. It was not his best comeback, but his tightened fist would make the second. It became a shouting match between the two men, and there was never any apology by either side since that time.

Now two enemies faced each other, sitting on opposite sides of the room. Everyone in the room could feel the strain.

"I understand that we may have our own differences, but I implore you gentlemen to set those aside so we may be able to save our beloved church from further embarrassment and further destruction," Cardinal Borgia said in his opening remarks after everyone was seated. "We have all heard about the reports and rumors regarding a few of our clergy. Cardinal Gasparri has brought with him an update to his report findings, which he has already shared with Pope Gregory and will share with others before conclave."

Borgia looked at both Valentinus and Irenaeus, knowing they were to be part of this process.

"His Eminence wants to share this report," Borgia responded. "Especially with those in conclave, so our new leader and those who elect him can understand the gravity of accepting the responsibility of becoming our new shepherd," Borgia went on. "Cardinal Gasparri, would you be so kind as to share with us the details of your investigation findings."

"*Sì, grazie signore.*" Cardinal Gasparri stood up from his seat. He picked up a folder he had brought in with him, then took out about a dozen papers. Passing one of each paper to the cardinals and bishops, he began.

"They say a man is not what he thinks he is but rather what he hides. Gentlemen, this report provides proof that some of our clergy have been participating in an act of sin against the church and against God."

Gasparri took out his reading glasses and started to read the first page of the report summary he had just handed out. He walked slowly in front of the sofa where Irenaeus sat next to Cardinal Korsig. Then he walked back in front of the chairs where Valentinus and Bishops Oriolli and Cardinal Antonelli sat, finally walking past Gus, who sat on another chair, and Borgia, who sat at his desk.

"The report summary highlights the illicit behavior of those named and unnamed clergy, as well as the impacts on our church in terms of the faithful, and of course, how it affects our church financially." Gasparri stopped and paused to take a breath. He continued solemnly, "It also points to the possibility that we have a traitor among us in the Curia."

123

Gasparri took off his glasses and looked at everyone in the room. "Gentlemen, you need to expose this traitor."

The men bore serious facial expressions.

"We believe he is close to one of us." Cardinal Korsig sat with his shoulders slumped due to arthritis.

"What are you saying? That one of us is a traitor?" Irenaeus shouted as he jumped to his feet.

"*Per favore*, sit down, Irenaeus. We need to discuss this matter civilly." Borgia rose up, his voice sternly deepened to attract everyone's attention. "Cardinal Gasparri, *per favore*, continue with your report findings."

Irenaeus slowly sat down again but only on the edge of his seat.

"What is equally upsetting is that information inside a secret red-covered dossier presented to Pope Gregory was leaked to the media. Specifically, the information leaked was regarding a private conversation between His Eminence and two Latin America prelates. You can see the words I highlighted on my summary which the media has reported."

Pointing to the middle of the page, Gasparri stated, "It reads that His Eminence reportedly noted that just as in the world, in the Curia there are good devoted people, but there are also elements of corruption. It is true what they speak of… a *gay lobby* among our clergy."

Cardinal Antonelli chimed in. "Our concerns about this leak are underscored with our concerns for the security regarding His Holy Eminence, our new leader, and also for the Vatican itself. I have just learned that the commander of the Swiss Guard, Colonel Albin Karim, has given his resignation as a direct result of these *gay lobby* scandals. He was the one who informed us of the extent of the immoral and illegal crimes committed by Cardinal Rosotti and others. It is my understanding the good colonel has been threatened and fears for the safety of his family. I believe he now is moving back to Switzerland."

"*Si*, the commander is a well-respected Swiss Guard, and his departure has not gone unnoticed," Gasparri commented "It is believed that Cardinal Rosotti was being blackmailed. It appears the blackmailing of one of our clergy for being gay can be politically useful."

"Our enemies can use information against us. You do not have to win by force when you can win by deception."

Anton Oriolli, the former bishop in Palermo and now the assistant to Cardinal Gasparri, added mercilessly, "They are heretics and heathens. They deserve to burn in hell!"

"Do you have any idea of who the traitor is?" Valentinus asked.

"No, but we are close," said Borgia, who pointed his finger. "His Eminence hired Cardinal Meade Rosotti as one of the five commissioners to help reform the IOR, and as you know, the Vatican bank has been plagued with scandals. Rosotti and the other commissioners had full access to documents and confidential information."

"However, Cardinal Rosotti was just recently taken into custody after finding incriminating information on his computer relating to money laundering and the *gay lobby* media leaks," Oriolli interrupted. "And we now know he was not working alone."

"What information was he found with?" Valentinus inquired.

"I cannot say at this point," Gasparri guarded himself, "but it points to having someone within the Curia. That much you should know."

"Valentinus and Irenaeus, each of you will take part in the conclave. His Eminence has asked for your assistance in helping us reveal this traitor so our new leader may be elected without this inside threat. May I tell him he has your full support?" Borgia was asking sincerely.

"I will do anything for Pope Gregory," Valentinus went on, "I am just wondering, however…My name has been mentioned as a possible candidate to become the new pontiff. How does this situation affect my chances of that happening?"

Borgia, his longtime friend, looked solemn. "Valentinus, we are asking for your help."

Valentinus hesitated. He could feel the rug being pulled from under him. "And you shall have it. I just wanted to know." He had worked hard to obtain his position, and it seemed his dream to be considered as pontiff was being taken away because of these scandals.

"The church is most dear to me, entrusted with the business of Jesus Christ in whom salvation of humanity resides," Ignatius preached, "We have an obligation to put our own egos and wants aside."

"Spare me the lecture, Gus." Valentinus darted his eyes as if to shoot him. "I understand what is happening here."

"We have a duty to guard our Savior's profound mysteries, which now are threatened, as is our future and our church," Irenaeus countered with a smug expression, watching his foe's dream of becoming pontiff being washed away.

Valentinus sat back in his chair, his muscles tight. He was infuriated that Irenaeus could take such obvious pleasure in his devastated emotions.

Bishop Oriolli stood up and walked over to Valentinus, placing his hand on Valentinus's shoulder. "For what it is worth, I believe you would have made a wonderful leader."

"And that is the point, Valentinus," Korsig insisted. "You can be a leader in helping us fight corruption within our church. We need you!"

"*Sì*, Valentinus, within the conclave there will be much talk and speculation," Borgia compassionately pointed out. "We need you both, you and Irenaeus, to calm the fears and to explain the situation of these investigations using the summary we will give you. You need to help the cardinals perform their duty in electing a new leader."

"Why Irenaeus and myself?" Valentinus asked with contempt in his voice.

"Because His Eminence recognizes that you both have many influences in and out of the Curia. While your political agendas differ, you both have influence over others that may be used for a common cause. United, you can help right the course of our church. If you work against each other, you will both further divide our church." Borgia warned them.

Valentinus looked at the report summary again. It vaguely mentioned the *gay lobby*. "Why isn't there any more information regarding Gasparri's investigation of this *gay lobby*?" Valentinus asked, feeling something was amiss.

126

"People don't want the truth. They want assurances that what they believe is the truth," Irenaeus contended.

Bishop Oriolli went further. "We are still working to gather more information to cure this disease before our new leader begins his reign. We are already working on damage control regarding our public image to ease the concerns of the faithful."

"It is my belief that if we take care to do all these things in harmony with God, people will see our new leader as presiding in the place of God," Ignatius insisted. "Tradition gives people a sense of stability. We must return to our traditions, weeding out infiltrators who threaten our good causes. It must be so for the sake of our beloved church."

Valentinus sensed the political rhetoric from each of his colleagues. He stood up and walked deliberately past each of them.

He did not say a word. Turning around to do an about-face, he put his finger to his mouth as if he was thinking.

Cardinal Korsig could see Valentinus was struggling. "The visiting cardinals are gathering, and their discussions are growing in fear. We need to work together if we are to calm their fears."

Still Valentinus did not say a word as he slowly paced in front of his colleagues.

Borgia interjected, "His Eminence thinks that Cardinal-Bishop Clemente Sisinnius may be able to unite the Curia and effectively lead the faithful." He was careful about the timing of introducing an opponent that Valentinus would have faced.

Valentinus darted a stare at Borgia, but still he did not say a word.

"I have worked with Cardinal Clemente Sisinnius in the past." Irenaeus said, agreeing to the former pope's possible choice for the new pontiff. "We have worked in Syria together, and he understands, more than many, the problems that plague the world. He is committed to Mother Church and to her people."

"Irenaeus, I also know him." Valentinus finally spoke up, choosing his words carefully.

"And I understand to whom Cardinal Sisinnius is committed," Valentinus slammed his foe.

Irenaeus would have his say as he stood up in front of Valentinus, blocking his next step. "Not that I am practiced either in composition or eloquence, but my feelings of obligation prompt me to help make known traditional doctrines that have long been forgotten, but which at last, through the goodness of God, are again being brought to light. There is nothing hidden that shall not be revealed, nor secrets that shall not be made known." Irenaeus went on, grandstanding in Valentinus's face. "I will give all I have to help rid our church of traitors and heretics alike."

"These doctrines you speak of are better left forgotten, Irenaeus." Valentinus took a step toward Irenaeus so that only an inch remained between them. "Can you not see that people are wiser to your rhetoric? Have you gone blind to the truths that the media has uncovered?"

Fearing a fistfight, Korsig stood up, providing an ample barrier between the two men, and begged, "Valentinus, we cannot do this without you. *Per favore,* will you help us?"

The room was quiet. The two men continued to stare at each other with Korsig still in the middle of them.

After a long pause Irenaeus took a step back and smirked at his rival. "We will see who the true servants of Christ are." He turned away from Valentinus and sat down on the sofa.

"Checkmate." Valentinus heard the voice in his head. He was stuck. Valentinus was fond of the game of chess, and usually he could outguess his opponents, but at the moment he did not know who was still on his side.

"Of course I will help to reveal this traitor and to bring order back to our Curia." Valentinus's tone was flat. "Living in silence is hiding from the truth. Silence will prohibit us from living by the words of Christ and shield us from receiving our Blessed Mother's grace. So I'm committing myself to your cause." He sat down slowly.

Valentinus's mind was racing.

"Not having any chance of becoming the pontiff is upsetting enough, but to have to work with Irenaeus is even more so. And *mio Dio* the idea of returning to the strict traditions of the church instead of progressing with society makes me ill. *Per favore, mio Dio*, help me," he pleaded in his mind's prayer. "Haven't I worked hard to listen to my parishioners? I have listened to other church leaders, and I have listened to my heart so that I may help bring your church closer to your faithful. What have I done wrong?" he wondered. "I fear that some church traditions disconnect the people from Your church. *Per favore*, help me…*il mio Santo Padre*!"

"Well then, we are all agreeing to work together," Borgia eagerly pointed out as he broke the awkward brief silence. "His Eminence will be pleased."

The men looked at each other, not really understanding the extent to which they would be needed but confident in their own commitment to the church.

"Cardinal Korsig and Cardinal Antonelli will assist us in keeping you updated on the investigation involving Cardinal Rosotti and his inside connection," Borgia instructed them.

"The first general congregation is tomorrow, and we will have most of the visiting cardinals in attendance. As you know, conclave will not start until all the cardinals are present. We are awaiting word on the arrival of two more cardinals before we can begin, and then we will suspend all media communications." Borgia looked more serious.

Borgia scolded them, "We must work with our visiting cardinals before we can work with our faithful. Blocking media communications will allow us to do this more effectively."

"We will communicate directly with you." Giacomo paused. "Of course, at least up to the point when Valentinus and Irenaeus go into conclave. It is our hope to unveil this traitor before conclave begins." Giacomo was optimistic.

"And how will you do this?" Valentinus countered, being skeptical.

"We are aggressively working on these issues and will call you with an update on your mobile," Borgia informed him.

Korsig then suggested, "In the meantime, we will need your cooperation in getting this report summary to the visiting cardinals to dispel the rumors and gossip."

"*Va bene allora*, are we finished here?" Valentonus asked, sounding in a hurry to get out of there.

"*Sì*, I believe so. Of course, the content of our conversation is to remain confidential," Borgia reminded Valentinus and the others. "I will call each of you later tonight to answer any further questions you may have."

Standing up, Valentinus nodded to all the men, even Irenaeus. "*Bene*," Valentinus acknowledged to Borgia.

"*Dio vi benedica e io e tutto cio che facciamo insieme,*" Valentinus spoke his final words slowly, asking for God's blessing. He looked at each of his colleagues, assessing whom he could still count on and who might be against him. He gave the sign of the cross, bowed to Borgia, then turned and left the room.

As soon as the door closed behind Valentinus, Irenaeus began to gloat.

"I am sure he is upset about not being considered for our next pontiff. I just hope we can count on him." Irenaeus grinned with satisfaction.

"He will do what is necessary," Borgia assured the others. "We will be in touch, gentlemen." He stood to bid farewell to the group and went over to Cardinals Korsig and Antonelli to shake their hands first. "You both did a good job, gentlemen. *Grazie.*"

While the cardinals and bishops said their farewells, Valentinus walked alone through the corridors of the papal palace, working his way to the exit.

"Valentinus." A man's meek voice called to him.

Valentinus turned around to see an old man with a cane standing in the doorway of another palace room. He was a shadow of his former self, but Valentinus recognized him.

"Your Eminence, I hope you are well," Valentinus acknowledged as he walked toward Gregory.

"Valentinus, will you come in and speak with me for a few moments?" Gregory's tone was sincere.

"Of course, your Eminence," Valentinus addressed him with reverence as he followed the small old man into a room that was attached to the office he had just left.

"I would understand if you are upset about not being considered as the next pontiff, but I want you to know that I personally and deeply appreciate your sacrifice." Gregory's sorrow was noticeable as he tried to ease the disappointment that Valentinus was sure to be feeling. "*Per favore,* have a seat, won't you?"

Gregory sat in his favorite chair which had been brought over from his Vatican office. "I know it looks like an old chair, but it reminds me of home. Besides, just because something is old, that does not mean it does not work any longer. Don't you agree?"

Valentinus smirked as he sat down across from Gregory. "*Sì*, I do agree."

"You must be?" Gregory asked.

"*Mi scusi*, your Eminence?" Valentinus tilted his head sideways, looking at the pope in confusion.

"You must be upset, no?" Gregory asked again.

"*Sì*, of course, your Holiness, but I do understand," Valentinus answered, covering his emotions.

"Do you?" Gregory asked pointedly.

"I believe so." Valentinus tried to hide his disappointment with no success.

"No, I do not think you do." Gregory tried to comfort Valentinus. "I appreciate your trying to appease an old man, but I do not think you truly understand what is happening to our church."

"I would like to try to understand," Valentinus conceded.

"I will let you know this. Once I had visions like you. I could see my role as a great leader to be a lasting legacy." Gregory teared up. "I dreamed of a legacy that brought the faithful closer to God's love and eternal life, but as you can see, I appear to be just an old man broken in spirit," Gregory confessed as he choked on his words.

"I don't see you that way, your Eminence." Now Valentinus was trying to comfort Gregory.

A little smile emerged from Gregory. "While I thank you, I can tell you that I am at least weary."

"I am sorry for your troubles, your Holiness." Valentinus could only imagine the sorrow that weighed on Gregory's heart.

"And I am sorry for yours, Valentinus, but I have great hopes that you can help our faithful and you can be the leader I know you were born to be." Gregory leaned over and put his hand over Valentinus's hand, which rested on his lap.

"But I am not going to be a leader. I'm not going to be the new pontiff." Valentinus's voice cracked.

Gregory looked into Valentinus's eyes. "Who said you have to be a pontiff to be a great leader, Valentinus? You know, your family name reminds me that the Catholic Church did not always exist. There was a time when people held deeply within their hearts their relationship with our Father. The relationship was based on knowledge. It was an inner knowledge that came from living in the way of Jesus Christ." Gregory's eyes sparkled in the truth of his words.

"There was no formal Bible at the time of your namesake, Valentinus, the great Gnostic teacher." Gregory smiled. "People had to develop their own relationship with God through their deeds and through their learning." The teacher taught his pupil.

"I understand," Valentinus agreed.

"I am sure you do." Gregory adjusted his position in his chair. "Let me be honest with you, Valentinus. Our church is in serious trouble. I am afraid the third secret of Fatima is revealing itself. No matter how well a secret is hidden, it always reveals itself in time, and its consequences are dire."

Gregory sat up to look into Valentinus's eyes once again. "I would like to share something with you. Something I would need your trust on. Can I trust you, Valentinus?"

"Of course you can. I am but your servant." Valentinus wanted to argue but his respect for Gregory was too great.

132

"The world is changing…You can see this not just from within our church but also from across the globe." The pontiff didn't want to admit it.

"While this is not a new concept, that people would fight and die in the name of a religion, what is new is that the faithful in numbers have been dwindling for some time now. The need for a strong leader in faith has never been so important." The old pope had promise in his words but it quickly changed to sorrow. "I have seen so much suffering, so much corruption…so much death." A hint of tears came to his eyes.

"For the first time in my life, I doubted how my church can guide her flock. The bloodline from the apostles has been corrupted." Gregory sat back in his chair, weary from the thoughts his words brought to mind.

Valentinus did not say a word. He let Gregory continue.

"People are homeless. They are sick and dying." Memories of the sufferings Gregory had witnessed brought more tears to his eyes. "Valentinus, I have to say these are very different times. These are dangerous times." Gregory's tone became stern, "I have seen inside this new extreme Islam under this so-called Islamic State. They call themselves ISIS. Do you know of them?"

"*Sì*, I have heard of them." Valentinus responded with a tense grin.

"I tell you, these Muslim extremists may be worse than Hitler." Gregory's voice went deeper. "History has seen the likes of them before. They are destroying people's lives and their spirit. It concerns me that Muslim fanaticism is spreading so quickly."

Gregory paused, "We have seen that when people's spirits are broken, faith may be lost. Without faith, humanity is doomed, and of course, Valentinus, without the faithful our church is doomed." Gregory looked as though the weight of the world was upon his shoulders. "Our new leader needs an understanding of this movement as well as other issues. He needs to be able to deal with the devil."

"Your Holiness, every day we all face the devil," Valentinus reasoned. "And if I may add, your Eminence, I believe I would be able to unite God's people."

Gregory adjusted himself on his chair and leaned a little closer to Valentinus as if to tell a secret.

"Through knowledge, Valentinus, people can better understand how to be free to follow their hearts, which will lead them to God...And through knowledge fewer people would be ignorant to the likes of these Muslim radicals. Wouldn't you agree?" Gregory half smiled with a small gleam in his eye.

"*Naturalmente*," Valentinus agreed, but was confused by the obvious question.

"Valentinus, I have followed your career. When you were a student at the Polytechnic University in Turin, you were working hard to become cardinal, and I have to tell you I was proud of you. I know you have a great desire to help God's flock. The greatest gift you can give to people is knowledge."

"*Sì*, I agree." Valentinus nodded his head.

"These walls have grown foreign to me. My heart speaks of change, and somehow I cannot help but feel you will be part of that change even if it is unconventionally." Gregory had hope for Valentinus.

"How can I make the reforms needed within our church if I'm not pontiff?" Valentinus asked.

"Give yourself to God. Be the servant of our Blessed Mother," Gregory directed. He adjusted his body in his chair. Sitting too long hurt his bones. Gregory could see Valentinus's despair.

"Valentinus, this may sound strange, but I had a dream. It seemed so real. Have you ever experienced that?" he asked Valentinus, hoping he would say yes.

Valentinus nodded.

"Do you remember when I first met you?" Gregory asked.

"*Sì*" Valentinus nodded.

"It was just before I was elected pontiff, and you were being elevated to my former position as cardinal-bishop."

"*Sì*, I remember."

"I knew there was something special about you. I am fond of the many discussions we have had about our Blessed Mother." Gregory relayed his shared pleasure.

"As I am." Valentinus was touched by the memories.

"One night after one of our many talks, I had this dream that our Blessed Mother was standing over you as you slept. I know it was only a dream," Gregory continued, "but to me, it felt very real."

Gregory looked kindly on Valentinus. He leaned over and patted Valentinus's knee. "Just bring forth what is within you. It will save you."

Then Gregory sat back. "But if you do not, what is within you will destroy you."

Valentinus sat up straight as he recognized the words of Christ.

"You know that suffering is but another name for the teaching of experience, which is the parent of instruction and the schoolmaster of life." The old pope smiled and looked upon his student. "Are you the teacher, Valentinus?"

Valentinus wanted to feel angry about his missed opportunity, but having this time with Gregory seemed to ease his pain. "We shall draw from the heart of suffering itself the means of inspiration and survival," Valentinus answered his mentor.

Gregory's face lit up.

Knock, knock, knock...

Their reminiscing was interrupted.

"Your Eminence, may I speak to you?" Cardinal Borgia had opened the door and stood in the entryway.

Valentinus stood up and acknowledged Borgia with a slight smile.

"*Sì, bene.*" Gregory took a minute to stand and steady himself. "I enjoyed our little chat, Valentinus. We must do it again." He nodded to Valentinus.

"*Sì*, I would enjoy that very much, your Holiness." Valentinus gently took Gregory's hand and kissed his ring.

Gregory moved slowly, meeting Borgia at the door. Turning to Valentinus, he said, "We will see each other again, my friend." He then left with Cardinal Borgia.

Valentinus was left standing in the empty room. He looked around and for a moment he imagined what it would be like to be elected as the next pope.

He imagined holding his audiences and having times sitting quietly in a chair next to the window.

"It would have been nice, I think." His face turned solemn as he turned and left the room. Leaving the papal palace, he felt every bit of his empty, aching heart. The drive back to his chambers was somber.

Chapter 10

SOCIAL TIMING

Sophia had an avocado-size pit in her stomach. Opening the door to her lab, she could see Carmine sitting at his desk. She took a deep breath and walked in.

"Be an actor." Remembering Ben's words, she walked right by his desk without saying a word and grabbed her lab coat.

"Sophia, are you all right?" Carmine gave her the once-over.

"*Sì. Sto bene,* I just did not sleep well."

"Those are your cases." He pointed to the stack of folders sitting near her desk. Abruptly he refocused on his own work.

"*Va bene,*" she answered him. "He is the same rude self," she thought, moving the case files closer to her desk.

Swoosh…the door flew open.

Sophia's head spun around to see it was Gabriella, a part-time lab worker.

"*Ciao,* Sophia, I hope you are well." Gabriella, a slender, thirtysomething Italian woman greeted Sophia and all but ignored Carmine.

"*Ciao,* Gabriella. *Sto bene,* how are your children?" Sophia greeted her.

"They are great. Lucas got his first tooth. It was so special…and Lydia had her first dance recital. So things are going very well. *Grazie.*" The proud mom smiled.

"*Che è meraviglioso,*" Sophia chatted gleefully.

"Yeah, I am working at station three today." Gabriella carried her folders to the lab desk to Sophia's left.

"*Fantastico!*" Sophia excitedly exclaimed. "I mean, it's nice to see you." She realized she might have acted a bit too enthusiastically.

"I'm glad you think so." Gabriella smiled.

"Mr. Lorino was making some changes to the lab room I was regularly using which means I will be in here with you." Gabriella got herself settled. She put a picture of her children next to her computer monitor. "And my mother-in-law just moved in with us, so I will have an extra pair of hands with the children."

"They say many hands make light work...at least that is what Nonna says, and having another woman in here, I think, is a good thing," Sophia joked.

Sophia liked Gabriella and certainly appreciated her timing. Talking to her most of the day made her work go faster. It made it a lot easier for Sophia to ignore Carmine and the twisted feelings she had. Before she knew it, it was time to go home and start the weekend.

"Well, I guess that's it for me." Gabriella stood up and started getting her things together. "I still have to give my cases to Mr. Lorino."

"*Tempismo perfetto.* I am finished as well," Sophia said gathering up her belongings and putting her closed case files on Carmine's desk.

She tried to act normal. "*Arrivederci,* Carmine." Her farewell was short and to the point.

"*Arrivederci,*" he replied, looking somewhat glum.

Gabriella and Sophia walked out together. "I hope you have a good weekend," Sophia wished to her new favorite colleague.

"And you too, Sophia. *Arrivederci.*" Gabriella walked away from Sophia down a different hallway.

It was cold outside. The weather was very much like the normal winter season. Sophia had called for her usual taxi, over time getting to know the same two or three drivers. Sophia had become friendly with a few of them, making small talk as they drove to her home.

When the taxi arrived, she got in, but out of the corner of her eye, she caught Carmine driving away in his car.

"Follow him," the voice in her head commanded. She'd never done anything like that before, but she had a strong compulsion to listen.

"*Ciao,* Raul, *per favore,* I know this sounds a bit odd, but could you follow that car?" She almost shouted at her driver.

Sophia pointed to Carmine's blue Fiat driving away.

"*Ciao* Sophia, *come stai?*" the taxi driver greeted her.

Raul, her Spanish driver, looked in his rearview mirror and could see Sophia was tense.

"*Sì, sto bene.* I just have to…" Sophia tried to think of a good reason to follow Carmine's car. "I have to give my friend something that I had forgotten about before he left work." She hoped that would be reason enough for Raul to help her. "I will pay you extra, *per favore.*"

"*Va bene*, I will follow that car for you." He smirked, having his suspicions.

They followed Carmine's car to the center of the Old Town of Rome, near a less populated tourist attraction of Mignanelli Square.

Sophia remembered visits with her family at Piazza Mignanelli, which lies at the foot of the Pincio Hill. To the right of the Spanish Steps was the famous poet John Keats's former home, which was converted into a museum. Nonna loved the author and had taken Sophia there many times. She recounted playing on its narrow stairways leading up to the Trinità dei Monti Church that Nonna Jo admired for its dedication to the Blessed Mother.

"Every year on December 8 the pope, as well as thousands of Catholics, visit the Piazza Mignanelli in order to celebrate the Immaculate Conception," Nonna Jo said, "which is symbolized by the statue of the Madonna on the pillar in the middle of the piazza." Sophia recalled Nonna telling her, "The pillar is called the Colonna dell'Immacolata. It is one of my favorite places, and do you know why?"

Sophia was about ten years old. "No. *Per favore,* tell me."

"Because I am sharing it with you," Nonna smiled, lovingly patting Sophia's small head.

Following Carmine's car was not easy. The numerous famous churches, museums and many restaurants made the streets very crowded.

"Hmm, I don't see him." Raul was having a difficult time keeping up with Carmine. "Ah, wait. I see your friend passing the Fontana della Barcaccia."

Sophia could see the Fontana della Barcaccia and the Spanish Steps where Audrey Hepburn and Gregory Peck made *Roman Holiday*.

Nonna's voice came to mind, gushing, "Oh, I love that man!"

"Look, there he is." She pointed Carmine out to Raul. Parking was hard to come by, but after a few attempts, Carmine's car made its way into a spot on a side street. Having no choice, Raul had to drive past Carmine's car as he was getting out.

"Keep going, Raul." Sophia nervously crouched down so she would not be spotted. Raul looked into his rearview mirror, confused by Sophia's actions.

"*Che cosa?*" Raul was baffled. "What are you doing?"

"I am…" Sophia was stuck. "I had an idea. *Mm…mio amico's* birthday is coming up, and if I could see what restaurant he likes, I can get him a gift certificate." She was unsure if that was even where he was headed as she cautiously sat back up.

Looking around before Raul turned with traffic, Sophia could see that Carmine was going into the restaurant Alla Rampa.

"*Fantastico!*" Sophia was impressed with herself. "Raul, if you could let me out here and pick me up in ten minutes, as I mentioned, I will gladly pay you extra for your time."

Raul looked at her suspiciously. Then, relenting, he agreed. "*Va bene* Sophia, just ten minutes. I have other runs I must attend to."

"*Grazie.*" She barely got the word out of her mouth when she opened the car door just before Raul made his turn. She leaped out into the middle of the street.

"Sophia, what are you doing?" Raul stopped short, yelling at her and raising his hands wildly.

"*Cazzo!*" She now realized it was not a smart idea and soon had regrets as the cars that were stopped in back of Raul started honking their horns.

"*Grazie*, Raul, it's OK. I will see you in ten minutes."

Raul sighed, shook his head, and took off.

"*Va bene.*" She gestured to the cars by holding her hands out as if to tell them to stop honking their horns.

Sophia ran across the street to the restaurant where small round empty tables were crowded under the awning with the restaurant's name displayed on it.

"Brr. It's too cold for people to sit outside." Sophia shivered. She walked by the empty tables and could see through the windows.

Watching for Carmine, she opened the door and was immediately greeted.

"Welcome to Alla Rampa. A table for one?" A tall, slender, older Italian man in a suit stood in front of her. Not paying attention to what was going on, she almost ran into him.

"Ah, *sì. Grazie*, and if you don't mind, I would like a table in the back," she hastily replied.

"*Ottimo.*" The host took a menu and turned around. "*Per favore,* follow me."

Her eyes were peeled for any sign of Carmine. She felt as if she were playing a spy game and sensed a tingle run down her spine.

Sophia followed the host, briefly noticing the beautiful archways dividing the dining table areas for more intimacy. The light-golden walls reflected a soft light.

"On any other occasion I would think this would be a wonderful romantic place, but this dimly lit restaurant is making it more difficult to find Carmine." Squinting, she searched, bobbing her head frantically as if she had a tic.

"There he is!" Exclaiming in her mind, she saw Carmine sitting at a corner table on the far side of the restaurant. She could see he was sitting with another man. However, she could not see the face of the man who had his back to her.

The host turned around, quickly stopping at her readied table. Sophia almost ran straight into him again.

"*Scusami*," she said, embarrassed.

"*Va tutto bene*," he politely replied. "Is this table all right for you?"

"*Sì, grazie*," she replied as she sat down. Sophia could see Carmine from a side view.

The host nodded, giving her a menu. "Your server will be along shortly."

She pretended to review the menu while she tried to study the man sitting with Carmine.

"It looks like they are engrossed in conversation. Hmm, the other man's head seems to overshadow Carmine." She strained to see.

"I think he is taller…and has a thinner frame." She was taking mental notes. "And he is wearing glasses. And I think he is dressed in a dark suit."

"*Mi scusi*, would you like to order now?" The waiter's words were directed toward Sophia, who took a second to realize he was speaking to her.

"Ah, no, I am still looking." She held the menu closer to her face to make it look like she was going to order.

"*Va bene allora,* I will come back." He smiled, then poured water into her glass and walked away.

Sophia drank the full glass of water in one gulp, having a dry mouth from dodging the cars just before coming into the restaurant. Staring intently through the dimly lit restaurant, she wanted desperately to see if she could recognize the man Carmine was sitting with.

"It almost looks like they are having an argument." She stared at them intently.

"*Mi scusi, signorina*, but a gentleman gave this to me to give to you." The waiter handed her a business card. "Is there anything else I can get you?"

"Not at the moment, *grazie*. I'm still looking at the menu." She took the card then watched the waiter walk away.

On the back of the card, she saw "GO HOME!!" in big capital letters. The exclamation points stood out. Sophia shot back in her chair, stunned, as she looked around the restaurant for a moment.

She turned the card over to see it was Dennis Schiano's business card. Sophia looked around again, but she did not see Dennis, and then looked at the card again with his instructions.

Contemplating for a moment, she stared at the card. Sophia liked Dennis and thought of how he was helping her.

"*Tutto Ok*...I guess I'll go." Sophia stood up as the waiter was coming toward her.

"Is everything all right?" he asked with curiosity.

"*Sì, va bene.* I...I just realized I had another appointment. I am very sorry." Giving him her plucky pout, she walked away, keeping her face hidden so Carmine would not see her heading toward the front door.

"*Pazzo!*" The waiter sighed, looking at her and shaking his head.

Outside she realized it was colder. "Brr, where is Raul?"

A car horn sounded. Looking across the street, she saw Raul waiting for her at the corner. Her breath showed in the bitter air. Huffing and puffing, she made it to the car, opened the door, and rushed inside.

"Did you get a present for your friend?" Raul asked with a bit of sarcasm, peering at her through his rearview mirror.

"Ah, *sì. Grazie.*" Sophia was relieved to be in the car. "*Per favore,* take me home, Raul."

"*Sono felice di.*" He smiled.

Once home, she gave Raul his money, hurrying inside her building, where a glass of wine awaited her.

"Home, sweet home." Sophia took off her coat, settling in for the night. After getting comfortable in sweatpants, she went into the kitchen. "One glass of *vino* will not hurt."

Ring, ring, ring...

Thinking it might be Dennis, she grabbed her mobile without looking.

"*Ciao*, Dennis," she rushed in answering.

"Dennis? Who is Dennis?" A surprised Eula wanted to know.

"Ah, no one. *Come stai*, Eula?" Sophia changed the subject.

"*Sì tutto bene.* You know you will have to tell me at some point," Eula teased. "What are you up to? Besides changing the subject."

"Nothing, I am just working a lot. How about you?" Sophia asked after she took her first sip of wine.

"You do remember we are going out tomorrow night?" Eula sounded anxious.

"*Sì, sì.* What time?" Sophia needed to be reminded.

143

"Well, I have to work until midafternoon, so I could meet you at your place at six, and then we can get dinner. How does that sound?" Eula was happy to be making weekend plans.

"Sounds great to me. I will—"

*Buzz, buzz, buzz…*Another incoming call interrupted Sophia.

"I have to go, but I will meet you around six at my place. I am looking forward to it. *Ti amo.*" Sophia rushed off.

"*Bene*—" It was the only word Eula could get out of her mouth before Sophia ended the call.

Buzz, buzz…

"*Ciao*, Dennis," Sophia politely answered the next call.

"Sophia, I have to make myself clear. Do *NOT* follow anyone again!" Dennis's tone was almost scary, his deep voice thundering through her mobile. "I do understand that I may sound like your father, but you never know when there are dangerous people around. So promise me you will not do that again, *per favore*," he ended trying to be a little less scary but stern.

"Ah…*sì*," Sophia replied to his request, crossing her fingers behind her back. "Did you find out anything about Carmine?"

"Did you say you are coming to my house on Sunday?" Dennis redirected.

"*Sì*, we are coming," Sophia confirmed and hoped Ben would also join her.

"*Bene*. We can talk then about Carmine and the rest of it, but in the meantime, *per favore,* listen to me. Do not follow anyone again. It could be dangerous, so promise me again." A concerned tone came through in his deep voice. "And if you don't listen to me, I am afraid I cannot help you in the future. Do you understand, Sophia?"

"*Sì*, I understand." She answered him as she would her own father. "I look forward to seeing you on Sunday," she assured him.

"You have my address?" Dennis asked to be sure.

"*Sì*, but can you tell me anything now?" She was anxious to know anything, any little tidbit.

"No, not now, but I'll see you at three pm on Sunday. *Arrivederci.*"

Sophia put down her phone then picked up a bottle of wine. "A second glass won't hurt me either." It was easy to reason with her self.

"Hmm. I hope he has some information about Carmine and my family. I wonder if he found more information out about my brothers." She spoke into the air.

The wine went quickly.

Sophia was ready for bed, but her restless night went much slower than the wine.

"Sleep is so overrated anyway," she told herself.

Her mind raced in circles as if in a three-ring circus. Each ring had its own characters. Carmine was in the first ring, and her adopted family and friends were in the second ring, with Dennis talking about his investigation into her brothers' whereabouts in the last ring. All the rings were spinning in her head.

"It is hard to get one complete thought about any one thing that has happened the last few days. I don't understand. I feel like I am in a time warp."

"B-r-e-a-t-h-e in…t-h-e-n out…," she repeated to herself throughout the restless night and into the morning hours.

"Ah, the sunrise, finally. I love the start of a new day," she restlessly appeased herself. She stretched out the kinks in her neck and back. "At least I am going out tonight. That should be fun."

The day went quickly. She did some research on her laptop, then laundry in the basement of her building. It was a common area for residents to meet, but it was not Sophia's idea of getting to know people.

"*Mi scusi*, you are stepping on my panties." She squeamishly evoked the memory of trying to pick them up from the floor, having missed them falling out from the drier. The old man who lived across the corridor was hard of hearing,

"*Mi scusi*, your foot…You are stepping on my panties." Sophia pointed to the floor.

She repeated herself louder each time until he realized the red and black lace thong panties were under his foot. The two other women in the laundry area giggled.

During the day, she called her mother and straightened up her flat. Before she knew it, it was time to play dress-up.

Getting ready for her night out with Eula was easy enough. Sophia wore the same red dress she sported at her parents' house, only this time she was ditching the sweater. Black stilettos replaced her flats.

She polished her nails with a deep red color.

"*È fantastico*. I think this will look the part." She held up her hands to her face and blew on her nails. She checked her appearance in her full-length mirror so she could get a better idea of how she looked.

"You think this looks OK?" She eyed herself and nodded. "I think you look damn good, girl!" She chuckled, running her hands down her dress to smooth out any last-minute wrinkles.

Knock, knock, knock…

"*Fantastico!*" Sophia exclaimed with anticipation, running to the door. Looking through the peephole, she could see Eula standing in the hallway.

"*Ciao, ciao.*" She opened the door to give Eula a big hug. "*Entra, entra.*"

"*Ciao.*" Eula returned the greeting as the two friends kissed each other's cheek.

"*Sì, guarda bella,* Sophia. That dress looks awesome on you. Navaeh would love it!" Eula always had a kind word to say and thought of Sophia as a sister.

"Eula, *si guarda sexy.*" Sophia went around Eula to peek at every angle. "*Bene.*" Sophia nodded her head in approval.

"Sexy? I don't think so. I don't think I look sexy." Eula was flustered. "Do you think so?"

"*Vieni qui.*" Sophia took her friend to her full-length mirror near her bed. "*Sì,* you do. *Tu sei bella,* Eula," she lovingly assured her friend.

Eula wore a black near mini-dress with off-the-shoulder straps and a sweetheart neckline.

While the dress was simple, a petite diamond heart necklace gave it just the right touch.

"You want some *vino*?" Sophia left Eula standing and gazing at herself in the mirror.

"*Bene,* that would be *fantastico.*" Eula smiled, staring at herself in the mirror, "I think she's right. *Sono sexy.*" She laughed then turned to Sophia.

"You know, at the art exhibit they have *vino* there too. Free *vino* is always a plus." Eula was hoping to lessen Sophia's hesitation about going there.

"I don't know about this art exhibit, Eula." Sophia had doubts.

"Ah, Sophia. *Andrà bene,* I promise." Eula encouraged Sophia. "I promise we won't stay long, but I really want to see the art, and you know I am studying astrology, and…" She ran out of reasons. "I have a good feeling about it. Besides, I read my tarot cards yesterday."

Sophia sighed and rolled her eyes.

Eula ignored her friend. "They said I will learn more about art and love." She was convincing. "It is in the stars, like destiny. *Accidenti*! I have done plenty of things for you over the years. Remember that test from—"

Sophia quickly interrupted Eula. "*Va bene*, we are going. I knew that would come back to haunt me." She smirked. "We will have one more glass of *vino*, and then we will be on our way."

"*Fantastico.* I'll call for the taxi." Eula dialed the number. "Did you know it's going to be a full moon tonight?" She was trying to get Sophia interested in astrology, even if it was only a little.

"*Sì*, I saw that," Sophia responded. "I thought of you when I saw that online."

"*Bene grazie*, I love you too." Eula got excited. "Do you know the moon cycles can help us to live better lives? You know a full moon gives people more energy and higher levels of emotions that maybe can lead to love. They even say women give birth more during full moons, did you know that? There must be something to this energy thing."

Eula's eyebrows rose in excitement, and she continued her lesson. "During full moon cycles, it is the best time to party. And while the last moon would be a good time to get serious, expand your awareness, and resolve problems, including completing projects"—Eula looked at Sophia's clothes needing to be put away— "perhaps it's also a good time to get rid of any doubts about love," she said in jest.

"During the first moon, it is a good time to be assertive and seize opportunities like new jobs, promotions, or even meet new boyfriends," Eula hinted lightheartedly. "And under a new moon, it is a good time to act spontaneously, maybe even start a new romance."

"*Va bene, va bene.*" Sophia laughed, impressed but not appreciating the information. "Here's a toast to the stars, the full moon, the new moon, and all moons for you, Eula." Sophia clanked Eula's glass and finished her wine.

"Here's to you too." They drank more wine and readied themselves for the taxi.

"The first stop is dinner. *Per favore,* let's go to Big Mama's."

Sophia gave directions to the taxi driver, starting off the evening with a bite to eat and live music. "It is not as crowded tonight," she remarked upon arriving at Big Mama's.

"Give it time. It's still early." Sophia smiled as they made their way through the maze of small, round, brown-topped wooden tables accompanied with black wooden chairs. They were seated a few tables from the stage, but in the corner up against a faded redbrick wall. It gave them some privacy, but they could not hide from the music that bounced off the walls, leaving them to practice their lip-reading skills.

"Have you heard from Navaeh?" Eula was almost yelling at Sophia.

"She sent me an e-mail saying she will be in town next week. I replied to her that I would talk to you, and we could have a girl sleepover at my place." Sophia moved her mouth slowly, shouting over the music.

"What?" Eula shouted back. "Tony is sleeping over? Who is Tony?"

Sophia shook her head. "No, no. Navaeh is coming next week. She wants to sleep over."

"Oh," Eula acknowledged and motioned. "*Posso venire?*"

"*Sì, sì,* of course you can come." Sophia laughed.

"That sounds great. I do miss her." Eula leaned in closer to Sophia. "So who is Dennis?" Not letting Sophia off the hook from earlier, she demanded an answer.

"Promise not to laugh." Sophia almost looked embarrassed. "He is my private investigator."

"Your what?" Eula look surprised.

"He is helping me search for my biological family."

"Wow, *è fantastico*!" Eula looked excited for Sophia and touched Sophia's hand. "Sophia, you cannot be a whole person if you feel you have a piece of you missing." She sat up and picked up her glass of wine for a toast.

Sophia smiled.

"Here's to you. May you find what you are searching for." Eula reached out to clink Sophia's glass.

"*Grazie*, Eula." Sophia was relieved. "It means a lot to me."

"So has he found anything?" Eula was curious.

"Well, maybe I have two brothers. I may be one of triplets. Can you believe that?" Sophia's eyes opened wide while describing the possible discovery.

"Wow and wow!" Eula was stunned. "*È incredibile*! I can't imagine having two other people like you in the world." She laughed.

"I know. I'm going to meet Dennis tomorrow to see if he found out anything else," Sophia excitedly blurted out.

Eula smiled and stared at Sophia for a moment.

"*Che cos'è*?" Sophia tilted her head as if looking to solve a puzzle.

"Nothing. I mean, it's just…" Eula paused.

"*Che cosa*?" Sophia insisted she answer.

"It's just that I have not seen you this happy in a while. *Si guarda bene su di voi*, Sophia." Eula chuckled.

"I think it looks good on me too." Sophia held out her glass to toast again. The music was louder as the crowd started to stream in. They ate their shared appetizers and had a few more drinks.

"The band is taking a break, so we better be going. I really want to see that art show." Eula was eager. Sophia saw the sparkle in Eula's eyes and could tell it meant a lot to her. They paid their bill and texted for a taxi.

Another taxi ride later, they headed to the art exhibit about ten minutes away. The cold weather prevented a lot of outdoor activities such as walking.

"Did you know that the planets are aligned in a position that hasn't been seen before in modern history, and it may be creating a weather vortex? Did you know that?" Eula wanted to make small talk.

"No, I did not know that, Eula." Sophia wanted to share the same enthusiasm, but she just didn't have it in her. "That sounds interesting."

"*Bene*, in case you wanted to know," Eula teased. "It may be one of the reasons why you have a lot of crazy things going on right now." Eula wanted to sound self-assured.

"*Bene,* I will think about that, and if you mention another planet thing again tonight, you have to buy my drinks." They both laughed.

"*Fantastico*, here we are." Sophia looked out the window. The car stopped, and they got out, back into the cold air.

"Of course it's just like you making that bet, knowing we are going to a celestial art exhibit, so I'm not sure it's a fair deal." Eula giggled, being grateful for Sophia going with her.

A banner above the door indicated they were in the right place.

"The Via Medii Art Gallery. You know I was happy to run into Sakla. It was nice of her to invite us to the art show. Don't you think, Sophia?" Eula wanted to get a rise from her friend.

"*Sì certo*, but there is a *queue*. Look." Sophia pointed. Six other people were waiting to be let in. They were cold and impatient, and when they did finally get inside the door, they realized they were missing something.

"*Mi scusi,* ladies. Your tickets, *per favore*." A woman stood behind a podium collecting tickets.

"Ah, ah, we do not have tickets," a disappointed Eula mumbled.

Sophia gently pushed Eula aside. "We're friends with Sakla. She has our tickets."

"What is your name, *per favore*?" the hostess asked with a snobbish attitude as if they were putting her out.

"Sophia Pistisi and my friend Eula."

The hostess held her clipboard and looked under the checklist.

After looking up and down the checklist, she said, "I do not have any tickets for a Pistisi."

"Oh, it may be under my other last name. Sophia Raiti."

"*Sì.* That is it. *Per favore,* come in and enjoy the exhibit." She changed her tone and waved her hand to allow them to come in.

"*Grazie.*" Sophia and Eula stepped into the gallery, where soft classical music played over the ceiling speakers. They were immediately impressed with the statues, paintings, and still photos of various stars and nebulous.

"Whoa. *È fantastico!*" Eula was ecstatic. "It's like we stepped into another world, like we are in heaven being surrounded by portraits of heaven."

"I am so glad you like it," Sophia responded. "Where's the *vino?*"

"Sophia, Eula, I'm so glad you could make it." Sakla came up from behind them.

Sophia and Eula turned around to see a pretty Sakla dressed to the nines in a blue velvet short dress. It exposed her cleavage at one end and her long legs at the other. Her natural curves spoke volumes. She looked like either a model or a high-priced call girl.

"Geez, *sei bellissima, Sakla.*" Sophia's words came out before she could think.

"*Grazie…*and you both look wonderful too. So how do you like our exhibit so far?" Sakla pointed around.

"*Lo adoro, è meraviglioso,*" an overly excited Eula gushed.

A server came by with champagne flutes on a serving tray.

"We will have one of those." Sophia grabbed two glasses, handing one to Eula.

"Which piece do you like the best, Eula?" Sakla asked. "This one is called *Making Wishes*. What do you think?" She showed them a painting that was diverse with colors. The sapphire hues swirled around a dark gold object in the center. The violet, yellows, and jade hues danced in contrast to the sapphire swirls.

"*È bella!*" Eula stood with her mouth gaping wide, her eyes almost popping out of her head.

"*Sì,*" Sophia agreed as she gazed into each of the colors.

"Sophia, I know one you would like. *Per favore,* follow me." Sakla sashayed around the room.

Moving about the people crowded into small groups as they stood in front of various paintings, statues, and photos, Sakla stopped in front of a painting entitled *The Flaming Star*.

"Wow." Sophia looked at the painting, and she connected to it instantly. The painting mesmerized her.

The black canvas background was dotted with golden streaks. Three white star-looking objects were off-center, with plenty of gold stardust encircling each star. Like a kaleidoscope, tiny bursts of brilliant magenta, emerald, violet, silver, and cerulean swirled around. Some were larger than others, but they all seemed to travel in a counterclockwise movement. They appeared to be paying homage to a red filmy mass that seemed to have no beginning and no end. The red mass formed a ghostlike figure in the middle of the painting.

Sophia could feel the explosions of color.

"Do you like it, Sophia?" Sakla studied Sophia's face.

"*Sì*, I…do." She paused, staring at the work of art.

"It is for sale," Sakla pointed out.

"Really," Sophia said, taking her eyes off the painting only for a moment to acknowledge Sakla. "How much is it?"

"One thousand euros," Sakla stated firmly.

"I'll take it," Sophia responded raising her voice.

Eula shot her head back in surprise. "*Che cosa*? You'll take it? Did you hear how much it is?" Eula was stunned.

"I know." Sophia was surprised herself but looked at Eula with confidence. "There's just something about it. It speaks to me. Isn't that what art is supposed to do?"

"*Sì*, but…," Eula stammered, not believing Sophia could connect to something other than science.

"*Va bene allora*, I will have it wrapped and delivered to you." Sakla went on, "You know, Sophia, I work for an old friend of ours."

"I told him I ran into you." Sakla's movements were on cue. "Oh, there he is."

Sophia's mind went racing, and before she could have a complete thought or say a word, a young, tall, slender Italian man with dark, wavy hair and a slimming goatee walked toward them.

"*Accidenti*, it is Dominic!" Sophia mouthed the words to herself. Her heart started pounding. The glass of champagne felt hot in her hand.

"*Ciao,* Sophia." Dominic's smooth, deep voice grabbed Sophia's attention.

Eula did not know how to react. She stood watching as Dominic took Sophia's hand and leaned over slightly to kiss it as he looked into her eyes. She had only seen pictures of him in Sophia's flat but he looked the same.

"Sophia looks like a statue just staring into Dominic's eyes. She looks like a doe caught in headlights. What is wrong with her?" Eula was confused.

"He is well dressed in that designer's suit. Wow." Sophia grinned. "And he is even more groomed than the teenager I remember." Sophia's thought passed through her mind as a cold tingling went down her spine.

A moment seemed like forever.

"*Come stai,* Sophia? *Sei bellissima.*" Dominic's sexy, black, wavy hair complemented his light almond-colored eyes. His strong jawline reminded Sophia of an actor on a television.

"*Ciao*, Dominic," was all Sophia could think to say. She could see his muscles bulging under his suit jacket. "It is certainly a fitted suit," she thought, sizing up his body.

"I was happy to hear that you might attend our exhibit." He was still holding her hand.

Sophia's eyes sparkled and seemed to change to a light-green fluorescent color. Still she could not speak.

Eula could feel the heat emanating from Sophia and lightly bumped into her.

"*Mi scusi,* I am Sophia's best friend, Eula," she said, making an announcement that she also was to be included in their little reunion.

Dominic released Sophia's hand and set his eyes on Eula. "Eula, *che bel nome*." Dominic complimented her. "How do you like our exhibit?" He gestured with his hand, showing the gallery as a whole.

"*È meraviglioso*," Eula enthusiastically replied.

"Sakla, why don't you take Eula to see our private collection while Sophia and I get reacquainted?" Dominic gave a subtle nudge to Sakla.

Sophia's heart was beating out of her chest. "I cannot breathe." Her mind raced. She tried to remember how to take deep breaths, but she could not connect her thoughts to control her reactions.

"Is that all right with you, Sophia?" Dominic slowly turned his head to look at Sophia. He made sure he would catch her looking into his eyes. Dominic could sense she was nervous.

Eula looked at Sophia for a sign. She was not sure how to read her friend's body language.

"Hmm...*va bene*." Sophia looked at Eula with a startled, wide-eyed look. "But only for a few minutes. We still have to go meet my cousin." Sophia's voice cracked as she tried to compose herself.

Dominic smiled like a black alley cat slyly coaxing his prey. "*Venire*. We will go to my office where it is quiet." He reached his hand behind Sophia's back to lead her into a small hallway.

Sophia could see a small office at the end of the short hallway.

Sakla took that as her sign to lead Eula across the floor to another room on the opposite side of the gallery.

Sophia could feel Dominic's hand on her back, then around her waist, giving her tingles down her back as she walked.

"*Qui*." Dominic opened a frosted glass door to his office. The office was small but well-appointed. The sleek, black metal desk with a glass top was complemented by what looked like a customized red leather chair. The red and black color scheme matched the art on the walls, but it was the life-size statue of two nude women lovers that Sophia took notice of as she entered the room.

Still having the glass of champagne in her hand, she guzzled it down.

"Ah, I have the good stuff in here. Let me refresh that for you." Dominic took the glass from her hand.

"No *grazie*." Sophia was determined not to give in to her feelings.

"Just one for an old friend?" Dominic's voice was soft...and then he did it. He raised his eyebrow and gave her his irresistible smile. She could remember all the times she had given in to him because of that look.

"*Va bene*, just one for an old friend." Against her better judgment, she agreed and hesitatingly tried to make conversation.

"So, how have you been? You look like you have done well." Sophia watched as he poured glasses of expensive champagne.

Snickering a little, he answered her. "*Sì*, I have been doing well. Art is like the soul, each piece being unique and very valuable to its owner. Don't you agree?" He handed her a glass.

"*Sì*, ah, *bene*," she said not really thinking about his words.

He held up his glass for a toast. "To old friends and to old lovers, may their love inspire new passions."

Dominic intentionally and slowly touched her glass, looking into her eyes all the while.

"*Va bene*." Nervously she sipped from her glass.

"So...what about you, Sophia?" He broke the mood.

"*Come stai*? I am sure your boyfriend must love that dress on you. *Sei così bella*, I cannot take my eyes off of you."

Sophia took a small sip and put her glass on his desk. "Ah, *grazie*. I'm a scientist working at Carabinieri Scientific Investigations in Rome. There is not much to tell." She did not know what else to say.

"Is your boyfriend working in the science field also?" He insisted on wanting an answer.

"I, um, well, I do not have a boyfriend. What about you?" She hesitated, wanting to avoid answering specific questions.

"I was married, but my wife died in an automobile accident a year ago." He backed away to reach for a picture on his desk. Sophia could sense his solemn tone.

"Oh, Dominic, I am sorry." Instantly she felt pity for him.

155

She was stunned, thinking, "I never thought about him as being married."

"*Grazie*. It has been difficult, but they say time heals. At least that is what they say." He handed her a picture of him with a smiling young short red-haired woman sitting in front of a white-brick fireplace displaying a large dark wood mantle above them.

"*Sì*, that is what they say." Sophia looked at the picture. "*Lei è bella*." She could feel the energy change in the room. She looked at the picture then handed it back to him. She became more aware of her surroundings. The abstract art on his walls seemed expensive, but it was the statue of the nude women that remained in Sophia's line of sight.

"Her name was Christina. We were married for two years before…" Dominic's voice trailed off.

"Do you have children?" The question slipped out of Sophia's mouth.

"No, we were waiting to start a family. We thought we had plenty of time, but the reality is time is short for all of us." He came closer to Sophia. "So we must make the best of the time we have."

"That is so true." She picked up the glass and took another sip.

"Speaking of time, why don't we have dinner tomorrow night?" His voice changed, switching to lighten the mood in the room. His deep tone reminded her of Marvin Gaye, in a sexy sort of way.

"Um, I can't. I am sorry." Sophia suddenly got nervous again. "He smells so good," she thought. His cologne wafted under her nostrils.

"*Per favore*, Sophia. What about the next day?" He softly tried urging her to change her mind.

"I'm sorry, but I am working all this week." Like a robot, she put down her glass again.

"*Per favore*, I cannot believe you're in front of me. Still after all these years, I have thought of you and questioned why you broke up with me. *Per favore*, I just want dinner, nothing more. I promise." He was pleading his case.

Looking at him, being so close to him, she could feel his breath.

"If I agree, we would have sex," the voice in her mind spoke up and her mouth opened.

"I am really sorry, but I can't. I really have so much going on right now. I am really sorry."

He took her hand and kissed it. "I promise I will be a perfect gentleman. You will see I have changed. *Per favore*, just one chance."

"Next Saturday is fine if that is all right with you." Reluctantly, but with an automatic response, she caved in.

"Sophia, you have made me so happy. I will call you during the week, and then we can make our plans."

"Wait…What did I just say?" She questioned herself, but when she looked into his eyes, they captured her. He stepped a little closer.

Feeling more nervous, she knew it was the right time to escape. "*Va bene allora*, that sounds like a plan. I should find Eula. We really must be going."

"*Bene*, Sophia. I cannot wait to see you again." He studied Sophia's body language as she turned to walk out of the office.

The lights were dim, with sixty to eighty people huddled in small groups admiring the various pictures, portraits, and statues positioned around the gallery. Light jazz music played over the ceiling speakers as she reentered the gallery. Sophia could hear people whispering and watched as they pointed to particular art pieces they appreciated.

"Ah, I believe you will find—" Dominic was about to say.

"Eula." Sophia could see her coming across the floor. "We must be going."

"Do you want to see—" Eula tried to ask.

"No, we should be on our way," Sophia interrupted with insistence.

"Sophia," Dominic asked, "did you see the name of this portrait?" He pointed to *The Flaming Star* painting, where they happened to be standing when they first said hello.

"Ah, *sì, è bella*, I am buying it," she declared, giving him a short answer.

"*The Flaming Star*. I remember your parents calling you that. How are they?" he asked with a hint of concern.

Sophia was touched by his gesture. "They are well, *grazie.*"

Smiling back at him she was smitten, "I will let them know you asked about them." She turned back to Eula. "Are you ready? I have to settle up at the front desk, and then we can meet Rose."

"I will help you, Sophia," Sakla politely offered.

"*Grazie*, Sakla." Sophia turned to Dominic. "*Arrivederci*. I will see you next weekend." They locked eyes for a seemingly long moment.

He took his time to say, "*Arrivederci*…and you will be all that I think about until then." He leaned over and gave her a kiss on her cheek.

Sophia could feel his shaven cheek and his soft lips, and she could smell him. Her heart skipped a beat. As she sniffed his cologne, a warm tingle made its way to her neck, then down to her breasts.

Sakla and Eula kissed cheek to cheek as if they were old friends. "I cannot wait to come back," Eula said, gushing.

But unlike Eula's farewell kiss, Sophia's kiss from Dominic made her face turn bright red. Sophia awkwardly stepped back from Dominic and smiled.

Eula lightly pushed Sophia forward, and they followed Sakla toward the front of the gallery.

"*Arrivederci*, my flaming star, until next weekend." He spoke softly.

Sophia nodded awkwardly and walked away, feeling his eyes on her, staring at her. She did her best to walk normally and pretend she was unaffected.

After Sophia paid for her portrait and agreed to its delivery on Monday, they left the gallery and hailed a taxi.

"*Bene,* onto the next stop. Akab awaits us," Eula declared.

Akab, a popular nightclub in Testaccio, Rome, was just about twenty minutes away.

"On their website I saw there was a good rock band playing." Sophia craved the live music. She was ready for a fun night out on the town.

A young audience filled the dance floor on the weekends, the music charging partygoers with rock, jazz, reggae, acid jazz, disco, funk, and soul.

"Dancing and drinking... it is just what we need." Sophia tried to change the subject before it got started.

Once they settled in a taxi, Eula gawked at Sophia, giving her a hard stare.

"Well, what was that?" Eula was a little tipsy and teased, "If you could see how red your face got, you would feel embarrassed."

"*Fantastico, grazie.* You know how to make me feel better." Sophia sat back and felt her cheeks.

"It's just that I've never seen you like that. What's the deal?" Eula had to know.

"I don't know, Eula. I remember when we dated it was strange...when we were together." Sophia paused. "He had this control over me. I could not help myself. I would lose myself to him. Of course the sex was *fantastico*, and there were the drugs. It was a crazy time. I felt I would kill my father or myself if I stayed with him." Sophia looked straight ahead as if she were entranced.

"*Bene*, he doesn't seem like he does drugs anymore, so maybe it will be good for at least the sex, yeah?" Eula nudged her friend, hoping to make her smile.

"I don't know. I just don't want to lose myself to anyone again. Not like that." Sophia wrapped her arms around herself for a self-hug. "He made me so nervous, just being next to him again."

"Sophia, you are now both adults. You are a strong woman. You will only find yourself." Eula gave a wonderful pep talk. "The stars in your destiny point to finding love..." Eula could not help herself. "Seriously, I read your cards before we came out tonight. One card read romance, and another was the number thirteen, which is like your favorite number, and the art gallery address had a thirteen in it."

"I guess we'll see." Sophia smiled as she poked Eula. "You and your cards," she laughed.

They arrived at Akab, the taxi letting them off on the corner.

"There are many people waiting to get into the club tonight," Sophia acknowledged.

"Saturday night electricity is in the air." Eula put her arm around Sophia. "Can you feel it?"

After a few minutes queued up, Sophia called Rosey.

"Where should we meet? The place is mobbed and the noise is deafening. I can't hear you," Sophia shouted into her mobile. "Say it again."

She shouted back at Rosey in response, "*Bene, bene.*" Sophia did not see the person in front of her.

Thump…

"*Scusa.* I am so sorry." She screamed her apology over the music after running into a tall, blond, blue-eyed, well-dressed young man about her age.

"It's OK. It is fine," the fair-haired, good-looking guy yelled, responding in his distinctive accent. "It's all good, and it just got better."

"You are American?" Sophia shouted.

"Yes," he shouted back. "Is that bad?"

"No, no. Your accent, is that New York?"

"You could tell that quickly?" he yelled back.

"*Sì,* it's nice. I love New York," she said still holding her mobile to her ear.

Eula nudged Sophia. "Your cousin?" she shouted at Sophia.

"Oh, *sì, scusami.*" She apologized again.

"No, don't worry about it. By the way, my name is Michael Barnes, so this way you are not bumping into strangers." He smiled and held out his hand.

"I am Sophia." She reached her hand into his.

"It's very nice to meet you, Sophia," he shouted over the crowd and music.

"It's my pleasure. Michael, have a pleasant evening." She smiled back, thinking, "his eyes are sparkling blue like a clear ocean. It is as if I could see through them. He must have a gentle soul."

With a nod to Michael, Eula and Sophia made their way to meet Rosey, who was waiting near a table about fifteen feet away from the dance floor. Rosey stood up, waving her arms to get Sophia's attention.

"*Ciao.*" Sophia greeted her cousin with kiss on the cheek.

"Sophia, Eula, this is my boyfriend Max." Rosey introduced them to a dark-haired, olive-skinned young man who remained seated.

"I thought you said his name was…" Sophia caught herself as she looked at Rosey's wide eyes. "Oh, Max. It is nice to meet you," she shouted over to him as he half stood to greet them.

"Maybe you girls can find a boyfriend tonight." Rosey smiled as she sat down.

"*Bene*, Sophia may have one already," Eula interrupted her.

"No, Eula." Sophia pushed Eula's shoulder.

"*Sì*, Eula, *per favore.* Do tell," the inquisitive cousin shouted aloud.

Eula looked at Sophia. "I'm sorry I did not know it was supposed to be a secret that you saw your old flame Dominic." Eula put her hands to her mouth. "Oops, I am sorry again."

Sophia gave Eula her death stare, her eyes turning dark green.

"Dominic?" Rosey gasped. "*Dio mio*, where did you see him?"

"I only saw him for a moment at an art gallery before we came here. It was nothing." Sophia tried to make light of her brief encounter.

"Well, how did he look? What does he do?" Rosey ignored her date to get more gossip.

"He looked fine. He owns the gallery. You remember he was always into art?" Sophia explained not to Rosey's satisfaction, but the rest of the story would have to wait. "*Bene*, the music, yeah?"

"Rosey, would you like to dance? This is our song." Max stood up and put out his hand.

"You are saved for now, but we will pick this up again." Rosey stood up, placing her hand into her boyfriend's and following him onto the dance floor.

Sophia shot a hard look at Eula. "*Per favore,* let's not let on about Dominic. I don't want Rosey to worry. She never liked him."

"*Va bene*, have it your way." Eula could see Sophia was upset.

The music was so loud, the vibration shook the floor.

Sophia felt the beat and started tapping her feet to the music.

"Excuse me, this is my friend Paolo. Do you girls want to dance?" someone with an American accent shouted over her shoulder.

Sophia turned around to see Michael. She could see a shorter well-built Italian man standing next to Michael.

The shorter man reminded Sophia of a smaller version of the American actor, "The Rock."

Eula was already standing up. Seeing Paolo made her forget about Sophia.

"*Ciao*, I am Eula, and it's nice to meet you. Now let's dance." Eula, feeling less inhibited from the alcohol she had already consumed, took his hand. They were off to the dance floor, meeting up with Rosey and her new boyfriend, as well as about a hundred other people.

Michael held his hand out for Sophia, who hesitated. "Come on. I am really not that bad of a dancer."

"*Va bene allora*, let's give it a try." Sophia smiled, feeling a little tipsy herself. His squared shoulders and confident stride attracted her.

The tempo was fast. All the dancers seemed to be shaking their hips, grinding, stomping their feet, and flailing their arms about.

Sophia could hold her own, at least giving it a good fake. Michael tried to look like a smooth operator. He was doing his best to impress her. They grooved to the beat even as the song changed to a slower, unfamiliar tempo.

Sophia leaned into her dance partner. "Can we sit this one out?"

"Of course." A polite Michael took her hand and escorted her to their table. She looked at Eula and Rosey, who were having the time of their lives, laughing at each other as the beat played on.

"Can Paolo and I join you?" Michael asked upon approaching Sophia's table.

"*Bene,* why not?" Sophia replied.

Michael took an empty chair from another table and sat down.

"So what brings you to Italy?" Sophia asked.

"I am stationed at Camp Darby near Livorno, west of here." He pointed over her shoulder. "I am on leave for a few days. My friend Paolo dragged me here, and I am happy he did." He looked at Sophia with a flirty grin.

"What do you do?" Sophia was curious.

"I am with the 509th Signal Battalion. I have been here for a year, and I have to say I love it," Michael enthusiastically exclaimed.

"When I get out, I would love to live in Italy." He was hoping to score points.

Leaning in closer to her, he smiled, exposing a small dimple on his right cheek. "Sophia what do you do?"

"I am a scientist. It can be boring, but I love it," she chitchatted. "What does a signal battalion do?"

"Cyber stuff, collect information and disseminate it. It's not glamourous, but a scientist, now, that sounds interesting. What kind of science? I mean, what is your specialty?" Michael smiled with a curious grin.

"Well, most of the time it's just about lab reports and testing materials and taking orders from my boss." She smiled.

"I can relate to that. That is the one thing I do well. I take my orders." He smiled back at her.

Sophia felt relaxed for the first time in a while. She felt comfortable talking with Michael, and he was very pleasant to look at.

They talked and danced more through the hours. The night quickly flew by. Eula was also enjoying her time with her new friend Paolo. They seemed smitten, especially when they danced to a slow song.

Normally it was not within Sophia's comfort zone to dance a slow song with someone she just met, but Michael made it seem right.

"He is a gentle soul. There is just something different about him." Looking into Michael's eyes, she wondered what it was. He was not forward, and he seemed to take his time. "He is a gentleman when he touches me as we dance." Sophia smiled softly.

Sitting back at the table, he made her laugh with his American accent, trying to tell jokes in Italian.

"How do you tell an Italian joke?" Michael tried a broken Italian accent. He hesitated before telling the punch line, "by looking over your shoulder." Michael and Paolo laughed.

Sophia and Eula were puzzled, laughing and shaking their heads. It was a silly joke that was made funnier by Michael's attempts to be funny.

"You should not change your day job." Eula was not too impressed, but she was polite.

"Tell me about growing up in America." Sophia was curious. "And I like the way he makes me laugh," she thought.

"Well, there is not much to tell. I lived in a town called Islip, on the south side of Long Island, with my parents, two older brothers, and my younger sister. Long Island is a cool place to grow up," he said, flirting with her.

He leaned into her. "I loved it because you can go boating, hiking, camping, skiing, see a Broadway show, and enjoy a beautiful sunset on the water all in the same weekend. It was great, but…I have never seen anything more beautiful than you."

Sophia did not realize his come-on. "*Fantastico.*" She was intoxicated with friends, new company, good music, and lots of liquor.

By the end of the evening, she had learned more about Michael growing up in America. There was something that clicked.

At the small table, the three couples drank and conversed. Michael told funny stories about his upbringing in New York that made Sophia laugh until her sides hurt. Sophia didn't realize the time until Rosey spoke up.

"It's getting late, and there are things I have to do tomorrow, so we have to go. But I am so glad you came out, Sophia. I really enjoyed hanging out with you and your friends." Rosey smiled and winked, looking at Michael. "Call her tomorrow."

"I am glad I came out too." Sophia kissed her cousin on the cheek. "Actually, Eula and I have to go as well."

"I am glad you came out too," Michael interjected laughing at Rosey's hint.

Michael had already written down his number and handed it to Sophia. "Please call me. Perhaps you can show me around Italy and show me things I've never seen before. I am sure you can do a better job than Paolo." He looked over at his friend, who was softly kissing Eula on her lips.

"*Grazie, è stata una piacevole notte.*" Paolo thanked Eula. "I will call you tomorrow."

"*Bene*, I will look forward to seeing you again," Eula babbled.

"*Arrivederci*." They said their farewells outside the club once again. Rosey left with her boyfriend while Sophia and Eula hailed a taxi to get back to Sophia's flat. As they pulled away, they waved *arrivederci* to Michael and Paolo.

"Wow, that Paolo could move! *Dio mio*, I think I am in love!" Eula was drunk but sounding almost serious.

Sophia looked at her with raised eyebrows.

"No, I mean it! We are going out next weekend. He's going to call me tomorrow. He is, well"—Eula paused and then sighed as she sank into the seat—"*così sexy*."

Sophia laughed at Eula.

"*Va bene*. You can laugh all you want, but you will see." Eula sat back up. "And what about Michael? He is handsome, and he seems very nice. What do you think?"

"*Che cosa*?" Sophia asked, not wanting to give an answer.

"What about Michael? Are you going to call him?" Eula insisted to know. "Or are you going to stay with Dominic?"

"I don't know. We will see." Sophia looked out the taxi window.

All the rest of the way, Eula talked about Paolo and tried to pry more information out of Sophia about her feelings for Michael.

Once they arrived at Sophia's flat, she set the sofa up for Eula to sleep on.

"You know I will make you tell me what I want to know." Eula pointed her finger at her friend, who was getting ready for bed.

"*Sì, sì, va bene*." Sophia brushed off the barrage of questions. "You can try, but I am strong. I will not crack," she teased. "Seriously, though, I am glad you had a good time."

"*Grazie*." Eula was getting her pajamas on. "I needed to have a good time."

Sophia brushed her teeth and headed to bed. Eula had made herself comfortable. "I had a good time too. *Buona notte*."

"*Buona notte*. Sleep well."

Getting into bed, Sophia pulled the blankets up to her chest.

165

"Eula?" Sophia softly spoke her friend's name. There was no response. Sophia poked her head around the room divider to see Eula was passed out.

"Hmm." She looked and admired her fast-asleep friend. Lying back down, she tried to fall asleep. However, it was met with the usual tossing and turning.

"B-r-e-a-t-h-e deeply, i-n…then o-u-t," she reminded herself.

"It looks like Eula is in love. She looks happy," a voice sounded out to her. It was a familiar soft-spoken voice that resonated within Sophia.

"Huh?" Opening her eyes to see who was talking to her, she gasped quietly.

Eme sat on the end of Sophia's bed, looking over at Eula. "She looks good when she is in love. Don't you think?" Eme turned her head and looked back at Sophia with a smile.

"Oh, Eme, you're back! I have missed you." Sophia sprang up, wiping the gunk from her eyes.

"I told you I was always going to be with you. Why are you surprised?" Eme tilted her head, looking over at Sophia.

"I know but sometimes I cannot feel you."

"*Bene*, I told you what you need to do." Eme's tone turned serious.

"*Che cosa*?" Sophia was seemingly puzzled.

"You need to pray. Do you remember?" Eme pushed for an answer.

"I know, but I was too busy."

"Life is busy, I know, but you must make time, Sophia. I am not the only one who wants to talk to you, but they need you to pray. Praying will open the realm of communication." Eme was somber.

"Who else wants to talk to me?" Sophia quizzed her long lost friend.

"I told you, Raphael and others."

"Raphael? The angel?" Sophia's shocked, high-pitched voice echoed, almost stirring Eula from her deep sleep.

"Why are you surprised? I told you they want to talk with you. Your friend Ben met Raphael. I know Ben does not believe he was saved by an angel, but he will," Eme insisted.

"What do you mean?"

"Ben is going to Turin. He will tell you this today. You need to make sure to tell him to visit the Shroud of Turin. There you will both find answers to your questions, but he must be careful, Sophia. He is being watched, not just by the angels but also the archons."

"The who?" Sophia looked concerned. "Eme, is he in danger? I don't understand. *Che cosa…?*"

"Listen, Sophia, I and the others will help him," Eme reassured her. "My time is up. *Per favore*, pray the rosaries. Your questions can be answered if you pray. Don't be surprised."

"Surprised?" Sophia grew frustrated. "Eme, what are you talking about?"

A mist that was once Eme disappeared before Sophia, causing her to blink several times…

Blink, blink, blink. Her eyes fluttered.

When she stopped blinking, her eyes were open. She realized she was looking at the ceiling, and it was morning.

"Another dream. Oh, *mio…*" She rubbed her head and realized she had a slight headache. She scooted out of bed to see Eula still asleep. Her attention was distracted by a light beam shining through the window.

She peered outside. The sun was out, but it looked cold.

"I guess it is still winter." She got up and made her way to the bathroom. After doing her business, she looked into the mirror. "Wow, you look terrible!"

Turning on the cold water, she washed her face and brushed her late-night booze-fueled mouth. "There. At least you look human."

She smiled at herself. "I need coffee."

Sophia walked toward the kitchen to see Eula starting to wake up. "*Buongiorno,*" she greeted her.

"*Buongiorno a te.*" Eula's response was muffled by her stretching and yawning at the same time.

Knock, knock, knock…

"Did you—" Sophia was interrupted.

"*Chi è quello?*" Eula sat up and covered herself quickly with the blanket.

"Ah, I don't know." Sophia was just as startled. She was not expecting anyone. Walking over to the door, she peeked through the peephole. "*Merda*, it's Dominic!"

He knocked again, hearing muffled voices coming from within the flat. "*Ciao*, Sophia. I brought you your painting. I thought I would deliver it myself. I wanted to make sure it got here all right. I hope that is OK." He leaned his head in toward the door.

"Ah. *Sì, sì. Va bene*, Dominic." Sophia was horrified. "Ah…but *per favore*, wait a minute. We just woke up."

Sophia looked at the mirror she had near the door. "*Dio mio*, I look so bad," she thought to herself.

There was no time. Eula shot up to watch the show that was sure to be talked about among the girlfriends.

Surrendering to the moment, Sophia opened the door.

"*Ciao*. You did not have to bring it here yourself. That really wasn't necessary," she stated in a huff, pushing back a few strands of wild hair from her face.

"*In realtà, non è un problema.*" Dominic stood outside in the hallway holding the twenty-five-square-inch painting. "Can I bring it in?" His deep sexy voice and sweet cologne was as rich as her coffee.

"*Sì.* I am sorry. We just woke up." Sophia moved to reveal Eula was still on the sofa bed. "You remember Eula?"

"*Sì, naturalmente. Ciao*, Eula. I hope you two lovely ladies slept well." He was polite as he followed Sophia into her flat.

"*Sì, grazie.*" Eula smiled playfully.

"Oh, you can put that right here." Sophia pointed to the half-wall counter that separated the living room from the kitchen.

"*Sì, bene.*" Dominic rested the picture on the counter as he was asked.

"I would invite you for coffee, but…," Sophia tried to say.

"No, no." Politely, he motioned with his hands.

Giving a small pause, he expressed, "*Bene.* I do not live far, so I thought I would bring it by. And besides, I got to see you again." He smiled seductively.

Sophia blushed, "*Per favore*, I look terrible."

"No, no, Sophia, *sei bella*. In fact, I like the way you look when you wake up. I remember staring at you while you were sleeping when we were together. I could not believe how lucky I was. I still think of you like that."

"Ah *bene…grazie*." Sophia's face got redder as Eula snickered. Sophia was reluctant to catch his eyes.

"Why are you surprised?" Dominic reached his hand out to touch Sophia's. "*Sei bella*."

Sophia's head snapped back, and her eyes grew wide. She repeated his words in her head as her eyes finally met his.

They were locked in a moment. Her eyes turned to a soft hazel blue, lost in the moment, remembering the words Eme had mentioned.

"Sophia, didn't you say you have to get ready because you have to leave soon?" Eula broke the mood. "Sophia!"

Sophia shook her head, glancing at Eula. "Oh, s*ì*," she stuttered. "I am sorry, but I do have to go."

"*Nessun problema*." He picked up her hand, bowed his head, and kissed it. "I will look forward to seeing you on Saturday." Smiling, he looked sincere. "I will see myself out. Eula, it was nice seeing you again." He turned to look at Sophia one more time as she came closer to walk him to the door.

"Until I see you again, *il mio amore*, I will be thinking about only you." He entered the hallway, nodded his head then turned toward the elevator.

Sophia slowly closed the door.

"Wow, he knows all the right words, doesn't he?" Eula couldn't help but sound a little sarcastic.

"*Sì*, I think he does." A little suspicious, Sophia answered her as she closed the door tightly. "What time is it anyway?" She remembered her appointment with Dennis and looked at the wall clock.

"Oh, I do have to get ready. I have to meet Ben at the train station to go to Dennis's house."

"*Bene*. Before you kick me out, *ho bisogno di caffè*." Eula laughed.

"Don't worry, I am getting your *caffè*. I am not going anywhere without my *caffè*." Sophia guffawed as she walked back into the kitchen to get her and Eula their desperately needed coffee.

They both got dressed and readied to depart from each other's company.

"Eula, *ho avuto un tempo meraviglioso*." Sophia hugged her friend.

"*Sì*, I had a good time too, but I want a full report about Dominic. And let me know if you hear from that guy from last night. What's his name?" Eula tried to remember.

"Michael." Sophia giggled.

"What's so funny?" Eula wanted in on the joke.

"Nothing. I was just thinking. It's funny. For two years I could not find a decent guy, and now I found two." Sophia grinned.

"Why are you surprised? Like Dominic said, *sei bella*. And what is really nice is that I met a guy too." She laughed.

"Why are you surprised?" Sophia repeated Eme's words in her head. "Wow!"

"*Che cos'è?*" Eula asked.

"It's nothing." Sophia paused. "It is just that I think I had a dream about Eme...but I can't remember it all. It's fuzzy, like trying to open a door I cannot unlock. I feel like it's déjà vu," she said looking puzzled and nodding her head.

"Well, you better be going, or you will miss your train." Eula kissed Sophia's cheek, and they parted ways, each going her own way.

Sophia walked toward the train station, calling Ben from her mobile.

"*Ciao*," he answered in a rushed tone.

"*Ciao*, Ben. I am on my way now."

"OK, I will meet you on the train. I got your text on which train," Ben was straightforward. "I will call you when I get closer."

"*Che cosa*?" Sophia was confused. "Are you all right? Ben—"

"I will call you shortly." He abruptly ended the call.

"Ben!" Sophia was concerned. She got on the train and waited to hear from him. "Eme, are you with me now?"

Glancing out the window, she watched the buildings and the people go by as fast as the train moved. Mesmerized by the moving reflections of the objects she passed, she stared out the window.

The train stopped at a station, and Sophia could see a reflection of a young woman sitting across from her. Opening her eyes wider, she could clearly see it was Eme. Sophia snapped her head around to see the seats across from her. No one was there.

She again looked out the window, and there was Eme in the reflection. Eme was sitting across from Sophia, grinning from ear to ear as if she had a secret. Sophia turned her head again but could only see Eme's reflection.

"Hmm, I must be seeing things." She stared at the window.

"You are not seeing things, Sophia. I am here." In the reflection Eme mouthed the word, "*remember*."

Ring, ring, ring…

She was still looking at Eme's reflection and did not look at the number on her mobile. "*Ciao*," she said, sounding a bit confused.

"Sophia, what car are you in?" Ben interrupted Sophia from her trance.

"Oh, Ben." She was relieved. "I am in car three."

"OK, I will be there in a minute. Save me a seat." He hung up on her again.

"*No problema*," she said to herself. She looked at the window, seeking Eme's reflection, but she was gone.

"*Ciao*." Ben came through the train door and sat down next to Sophia with a big thud.

"Ben, are you all right?" Sophia was concerned.

"I think so, but I think I was being followed." His tone was stark.

171

"I know." Sophia grabbed his arm. "You are being watched." She was just as serious.

"How do you know? By whom?" Ben's questions were rapid with concern.

"I just know that you are, but I don't know by whom." She did not want to startle Ben with her story of having strange dreams. "When you go to Turin, you must be careful."

Ben shot back in his chair. "How did you know I was going to Turin?"

"I just know. That is all I can tell you. How do you know you are being watched?" She wanted answers too.

"My hotel room was trashed yesterday when I came back from a meeting with Mrs. Potter. My clothes were all over the place. Whoever it was, they were looking for something." Ben's face showed concern for his safety. "Thank God I brought my computer with me to my meeting."

"Ben, why are you going to Turin?" Sophia expressed concern in her tone.

"I am surprised you don't know that if you seem to know—"

"Listen." Sophia leaned over as if to tell a secret.

"I will tell you how I know things, but you will think I am...*pazzo*." She pointed her finger to the side of her head and made circles.

"Try me." He looked her straight in her eyes.

She sat up. "I have a friend, Eme, who visits me, and she told me." Sophia's face looked distorted.

"Eme? Who does she work for?" He demanded to know.

Sophia laughed a little, but took notice of Ben's serious tone. "No, Ben, she does not work for anyone."

"Then how does she know to tell you these things?" His accent was endearing with a bit of confusion.

"Well, she knows things because she..." Sophia leaned in. "You promise not to laugh?" She paused, looking at him seriously. "She has passed on."

"Passed on where?" Ben tilted his head. He was befuddled.

"No, she…" Sophia hesitated, "she died." She searched his face for his response then sat up. "I guess you could say she works for God."

"God?" he repeated, his expression was priceless. "Are you joking?" His mouth was gaping.

"No, I am not joking. I know it sounds *strano*. I used to have a hard time believing it myself. But it started again with seeing that angel Raphael." She was confident in her assessment.

"Raphael! Yes, I think I know that guy." Ben sounded as if he knew him personally. He lifted his finger to touch his still healing facial wound. "What started again?" he looked confused.

"My dreams. Ben, I am not sure what is going on, but Eme said when you go to Turin, you need to visit the Shroud of Turin Church, and you will find answers there." She believed in her every word, as her memory was becoming a little more unclouded.

He sat back in silence for a moment.

"So why are you going to Turin anyway?"

"I spoke with Mrs. Potter. I told her about Carmine and the DNA test."

"You did?"

"Why are you surprised?" Ben countered.

Sophia's eyes grew wide again, remembering Eme's words.

"I mean, she is my boss, and I know she can be a bit of a hard-ass, but I do trust her." Ben was confident.

"And what happened?" Sophia softened her stance.

"She suspected a political game was being played here. She knows Mr. Callesino Sr. personally, and he had asked her to look into the tampering of evidence."

"Is that ethical?" she questioned.

"She told me she disclosed the relationship with her superiors and had me do all the legwork so she would not be biased." Ben sat back, more relaxed for the ride to Dennis's home. "I told her about Carmine, and she thinks the timing of the tainted evidence too coincidentally coincided with the election of the Turin City Council for the former Councilman Callesino's position. Mrs. Potter believes the tainting of evidence prejudiced his son's involvement in that murder."

"Mrs. Potter and I believe the implication of Callesino's son in the death of the American student had everything to do with the election."

"That makes sense, but why would Carmine do it?" Sophia could not believe her boss would be involved. "Do you think Carmine knows Mr. Callesino?"

"I am not sure who he knows, but I believe it had to do with blackmail. I am not sure of the details, but I have an appointment to talk with Mr. Callesino in Turin tomorrow morning at eleven."

"Ben, you need to be careful." She was concerned.

"Well, I guess we could ask your angel friend Raphael to watch over me." He smirked.

Sophia gave Ben a playful smack on the knee just as the train was coming to a stop. The train reached its destination at the Formia-Gaeta railway station.

"And we are here." Sophia started to gather herself and stand up.

"Gaeta. Not a bad place to live," Ben acknowledged the beauty around him. "It looks like a scenic seaside community." He admired the scenery then pointed out, "look at the traditional buildings and homes overlooking the ocean water. It looks like a picture."

"*Sì, è bella.*" Sophia half dismissed him as they walked out and stood on the platform heading toward a number of awaiting taxis.

"Have you spoken to Dennis after our lunch?" Ben asked.

"*Sì*, I did." Sophia got embarrassed remembering the message on Dennis's business card telling her to go home.

"Well, what did he say?"

"Just that he was looking forward to seeing us today." Then a thought came to Sophia. "Ben, how do you know you are not being followed now?"

"Believe me, after I checked out of my hotel yesterday, I have been busy trying to get lost. So much so, even I could not even find me. I even got more lost on where I was." Ben was serious.

"Where are you staying?" Sophia was probing for details.

"Don't worry. I'm with a friend," he reassured her.

They chose their taxi ride and told the driver the address. Dennis's house was a few blocks away from the water in Via Messina, Gaeta. It was not too far from the railway. On the way Sophia admired the seamless seaside landscape of the quant neighborhood while she made small talk with Ben.

"It is really a pretty place with all these colorful old buildings and homes, don't you think?" Sophia prodded him.

"Yes, it is one of the nicer seaside towns that I have seen," he eagerly agreed with her.

The taxi stopped at a white-stucco, single-family, two-story home with a small front porch and brown wooden door with glass inlay. The house had simple landscaping with a Blessed Mother statue positioned between two small rosebushes in the small front yard.

"Ruff, ruff, ruff, ruff," a small dog barked. Within a five-foot-tall white gate surrounding the property, a small, white, fluffy dog sat on the stoop outside barking wildly.

"It appears that Dennis has company," Sophia said, observing the cars parked in the street in front of the house.

As soon as they opened the gate, the white dog charged them, continuing to bark noisily. Snipping at Ben's shins, the little dog would not give up. Ben was his prisoner.

"Ah…Sophia." Ben's face was flushed.

Sophia bent down and held out her hand so the dog could smell her. It seemingly worked.

"*Sì*, you are a nice doggie." She petted it, smiling. "You just need the right touch."

Ben was not amused.

They walked up the brick walkway to the steps, but the little dog did not stay quiet for long. Sophia could see Dennis talking with one of his guests at the front door. Sophia knocked lightly on the door to get Dennis's attention.

"*Oh, entra.*" He gestured to Sophia and Ben, opening the door. "Charlie, *silenzio,*" he commanded the still barking dog.

"Everyone, this is Sophia and Ben," Dennis introduced.

175

They stood in a small living room with light tan-painted walls, glass coffee and end tables, and a brown sofa with chairs to match. Sophia took notice of two small angel plaques on the wall and people sitting on the sofa.

Dennis introduced Sophia and Ben to his two brothers and their wives. "It is my youngest daughter's birthday," he nonchalantly informed them.

As if prompted, a tall, slender girl with long blond hair came from what appeared to be the kitchen.

"This is my daughter, Nicole. She just turned twenty-one." Dennis was a proud papa.

"She looks just like you," Sophia had noticed.

Hearing that comment, Nicole pulled over the lower part of her blond hair to simulate a mustache. "Now I look like him," she expressed with a laugh.

"Yes, I see," Ben chimed in. "Happy birthday."

After the initial introductions, Sophia noticed Dennis's wife was not there. A car horn interrupted Sophia's thought.

That was Nicole's cue. She kissed her father's cheek. "*Va bene allora*, I will see you guys later. *Grazie...vi amo tutti.*" She made her escape to join her friends.

"*Bene*, I guess that means the party is over," Dennis's brother Ed hinted as he stood up, getting ready to leave.

Sophia and Ben stood to the side while everyone began their farewells. They started to feel a little out of place when a tall middle-aged woman with long, brown, curly hair entered the room. She started hugging her guests.

"*Arrivederci.*" She motioned to each guest until she came to Sophia and Ben. She was just about to hug Sophia in an automatic pilot mode when she realized her mistake.

"Oh, you must be Sophia." She stopped herself. "*È un piacere conoscerti.*"

"It is nice to meet you too." Sophia smiled.

Dennis finished his farewells and had just closed the door.

The last of his guests were gone. He then turned his attention to Sophia and Ben. "*Sì*, Sophia and Ben, this is my wife, Mariam."

She put her hand out to Ben. "*Bene*, it is nice to meet you. Dennis has told me a lot about you."

"You are American." Mariam's accent was hard to ignore as Sophia pointed out the obvious.

"*Sì*, I am from New York." Mariam shook Sophia's hand hard, in a New York fashion.

"It is funny. I just met a man last night from Long Island, New York." Sophia noted the coincidence.

"Wow, that is where I am from. It is a small world after all." Mariam chuckled as she gestured for them to sit. "*Per favore, entra.* Have a seat and make yourself comfortable. Can I get you something to drink? Some *vino*, perhaps?"

Sophia was reminded of the bottle of wine she carried in her bag. "That would be great. Here, we have brought this for you." She reached in her bag for the bottle of Cabernet and handed it to Mariam.

"*Grazie*, and it is my favorite." Mariam handed the bottle to Dennis for him to open.

"And Ben, what can we get you?" Dennis asked politely.

"I'll have a glass of the same," he answered as he sat down on the sofa.

"I'm sorry if we shortened your family gathering." Sophia was sincere.

"*Nessun problema.* We had a family brunch, so it was really time for them to leave. A gracious family knows when the party is over," Dennis smirked.

Ben and Sophia made themselves more relaxed as they were handed their wine. The presence in the room made Sophia feel comfortable. Candles were lit, providing soft lighting, and the soothing colors of gold, yellow, mauve, brown, and red mixed between the furniture and the fixtures. A large, arch-shaped, black cast-iron mirror centered over the back wall reflected sunlight. It was peaceful.

"Sophia, I wanted you to meet Mariam because she can share her miracle story with you," Dennis started the conversation.

177

"I think you'll find it interesting." Dennis presented Mariam as his loving partner.

"*Sì,* Dennis told me about your story, about meeting the angel Raphael." Mariam took a sip of her wine. "*Grazie a Dio per gli angeli,*" she toasted.

Sophia and Dennis joined her, but Ben was hesitant, holding his glass steady in his hand.

"I know that some people may find it hard to believe in angels." Mariam glanced over at Ben. "But angels are God's messengers. They are mentioned in the Bible, the Torah, and the Koran. They have been known by millions of people to help us and even perform miracles." Mariam's tone was confident as she put down her glass beside her on a side table.

"Mariam, *per favore,* can you tell them about your miracle story?" Dennis interjected before taking a sip of his wine.

"Her miracle story?" Sophia was more than interested.

Ben looked a little out of sorts. His mind was racing with thoughts of being followed and his hotel room being ransacked. He sat patiently, waiting to ask Dennis about finding information about Carmine. He didn't want to waste too much time chatting.

"Trust me, you want to hear about her miracle story." Dennis directed his comment at Ben. "She can tell it a million times, and it still sounds like the first time to me." He supported his wife.

"*Grazie amore mio…*But you still have the dishes to do," she playfully bantered.

They sat back as Mariam began the story. "I understand you also have had what I call a heavenly experience. So this might not seem too unrealistic for you to imagine." Mariam patted Sophia's knee.

"Actually, I have been experiencing the unimaginable. I mean, I am a scientist and things are not making sense." Sophia almost sounded desperate as a small statue of the Blessed Mother surrounded by family photos on an end table caught her eye.

"It is my hope that by sharing my story, it can bring light to others." Mariam was sincere, adjusting her seat in the chair. The light behind her almost made her glow.

"As I mentioned, I lived on Long Island in New York. Not too far from where I lived, there is a place called Our Lady of the Island Shrine. It is run by the Montfort missionaries, who keep the grounds beautiful. Anyway, there is a church and a small chapel on the massive grounds, as well as a very large stone statue of our Blessed Mother Mary holding baby Jesus as she overlooks the Great South Bay." She sighed as she tried to describe it.

"It is a beautiful place to walk through the Stations of the Cross that are forged in the woods along the grounds. They also have a rosary walk outlined with shrubs representing each bead. It just really is a beautiful place to go." She realized she was drifting from her point. "*Bene,* as I was saying…"

Sophia and Ben took sips of their wine. They could tell it was not going to be a short story.

"I started going there after my father was stricken with ALS. I would sit at the shrine for comfort. We have heard of miracles taking place there, but to witness one is something else." Mariam's eyes grew wide. "You know, I have to tell you that I have always felt someone was always with me, watching over me. Have you ever felt like that?" Mariam looked straight at Sophia.

"*Sì,* I can relate to that." Sophia was confused but agreed.

Ben grimaced, he could relate to being watched.

"My favorite place is the Our Lady of the Island Shrine, and this is where our miracle begins." Mariam folded her hands. "My cousin whom I have grown up with suddenly got very sick. He had contracted sepsis, a type of blood poisoning. He was hooked up to machines in the ICU unit of the hospital. His wife, Carolyn, and I were with him when the doctor came in the room and gave us a very serious prognosis. He explained that sometimes they don't know what causes these types of illnesses and said that my cousin could die." Mariam's face grew serious.

Taking a pause, she continued. "I did a double take at the doctor's name tag and saw it said Dr. Love." Mariam chuckled. "Can you imagine? That was his real name. I just couldn't believe it, and then I knew it in my heart. I knew he was not going to die."

Mariam leaned forward. "Opening my big mouth, I told the doctor that with a name like his, my cousin couldn't die. I was positive that he would be all right. Of course, the doctor just looked at me very strangely, but I didn't care."

Dennis took his empty glass. "Can I get anybody a refresher?"

"That will be great. Let me help you." Ben got up from his chair, taking Sophia's empty glass, and started to go with Dennis into the kitchen.

"*Grazie* for your help, Ben. Just put the glasses on the table and I will bring them in. You really need to hear the story," Dennis insisted, motioning for Ben to sit.

"Yes. OK, thank you." He did as he was asked, then he returned to his seat on the sofa. Ben knew he was caught trying to escape what he thought would be a boring story.

"Is your cousin all right?" Sophia was concerned.

"*Bene*, I will tell you, the next morning after speaking to the doctor, Dennis and I went to the shrine for mass," Mariam went on. "We went to pray for my cousin and buy another rosary bracelet." She held up her wrist, exposing a few crystal-beaded bracelets with dangling charms.

"We needed new ones since she seems to keep giving them away," Dennis added, shouting from the kitchen.

She smiled as if it were a compliment and continued. "After mass in the chapel, we were leaving when another couple followed us out and stopped us by tugging on my jacket. We turned around to see a woman and I assumed, her husband, standing in front of us." Mariam imitated the scene.

"The woman said she had a surprise for us as she held her two fists in front of her. She went on to say that she felt compelled to give us this…surprise." Mariam looked astounded, as if she were still in the moment.

"We had not seen these people before, so we were…well, surprised. I really didn't know what to think as she held her hands out in front of me. She just kept repeating she had a surprise for me." Mariam turned to Sophia. "What else could I do? So I smiled, playing along, and said, 'OK, I like surprises.'" Mariam laughed.

It made Sophia remember Eme's words about being surprised, and she responded with an uncomfortable laugh.

Ben at least did smile.

"The woman opened her hands and gave me two sets of wooden rosaries," Mariam recounted. "She just kept repeating that she felt compelled to give these rosaries to me." Mariam's Italian influence from Dennis kicked in as she flailed her hands about while retelling her story.

"I cried out, '*Dio mio,* my cousin really needs this!'" Mariam had a tear in her eye. "The woman told us that these rosaries came from Medjugorje and asked me if I had ever heard of this very special place."

"We have heard of it, but it was not a place we remembered at that moment." Dennis reentered the room.

He handed Sophia and Ben their glasses of wine. He sat down on the recliner chair in the corner of the room, giving Charlie the cue to jump on his lap.

Sophia took more notice of the little bichon dog, nicely groomed, with a red bandana on his neck. He sat on the strong, large-framed man's lap as Dennis petted his old canine companion.

Mariam motioned. "Through my tears all I could say was yes about having heard of Medjugorje. I hugged her and thanked her. I felt so overwhelmed with emotion that I had to go to the ladies room. I thought afterward we would thank them again, but we could not find them."

"It was strange. It was like they disappeared," Dennis interrupted again.

"We went to the gift shop and bought a few more rosary bracelets." Mariam looked at her wrist and twisted a clear crystal bracelet. "I would sometimes give them away when I saw people who may have a need for them…for encouragement."

Mariam took a clear, sparkling crystal bracelet off and handed it to Sophia. "I am sure you could use one now." She smiled. "I now make them. It's cheaper than buying them, and its therapy." She laughed.

"*Grazie*, but are you sure?" Sophia took the bracelet in her hand. It reminded her of a smaller version of her rosary necklace.

"*Sì, sono sicuro.*" Mariam went on, "We were paying for the bracelets when I looked down and picked up a colorful business card."

181

"It was on the counter near the register," Mariam smiled. Without reading it, I put it down, but something told me to pick it up again. This time I read it. It was a business card introducing a Medjugorje.com website. Of course, I was going to go online when I got home to see what this Medjugorje website was about," she cheerfully sighed.

Mariam's face lit up like a child. "I was excited by this business card and getting the rosaries, but first we needed to go back to the hospital to give one set of the new wooden rosaries to my cousin. However, before we could leave the shrine, we realized we had a flat tire. Dennis said we could change the tire at a gas station down the road from the shrine."

"It is funny, in all the years we had gone to the shrine, we had never gotten a flat tire before that day," Dennis agreed looking very serious.

"As Dennis fixed the flat tire, I prayed using the new rosaries." Mariam believed in her every word. "Now, because of the flat tire, we changed our route and took Main Street home. This way we could go slowly. Besides, it was a nice day to enjoy the view." Mariam gave Dennis a look of fondness.

Sophia could sense the true love between Mariam and Dennis. Feeling more comfortable with them, she put her new bracelet on her wrist.

Starting to wave her arms, Mariam tried to explain. "We were a few miles away from the shrine, on Main Street, or Montauk Highway, as it is also known, and noticed a man walking toward us on the opposite side of the road, carrying or dragging a six-foot wooden cross behind him. It's not something you see every day! Can you imagine?" Mariam looked at Ben. "I know it sounds...*pazzo*!"

"This man was wearing clothing like Jesus and had long hair and a beard." Mariam's voice was high-pitched with excitement. "All we could do was slow the car down to a crawl as our chins hit the floor. I don't know what this man could be thinking of us. We stared at him so intently it seemed to make him twitch..."

Dennis nodded in acknowledgment of the events.

"Of course, this man did not know we had just gotten these special rosaries *and* now we are seeing Jesus!" Mariam and Dennis laughed at the memory.

"We just stared at this man dressed as Jesus before traffic moved us along. I told Dennis *now* we really had to get to the hospital to see my cousin!" Mariam shouted.

"Wow, that is some story." Ben was really not all that impressed. He gave a double-take look toward Dennis with the dog on his lap. "Do you know he has his tongue sticking out?" Ben pointed in curiosity.

"He is not sticking it out at you. He does that all the time." Dennis smiled as he continued to pet his old buddy then refocused on Mariam.

"Wait, the story gets better." Mariam put the attention back on her. "I went straight to the ICU, where Carolyn told me the doctors would have to start dialysis because of the sepsis. My cousin was in a coma, and his body was shutting down."

Mariam was illustrating with her hands. "But I interrupted Carolyn with my story of the Medjugorje rosaries and seeing Jesus. And then as I handed Carolyn the rosaries, my cousin peed!" Mariam was happy to describe the events, no matter the depiction. "The doctors had already begun to prep him for dialysis, and Carolyn was so excited to see my cousin pee in that bag that all she could do was run to tell the doctor. Now there was no need for the dialysis!"

Sophia and Ben were mesmerized.

"Wow, that is a nice story," Ben admitted he enjoyed the story.

"Wait, it gets better," Mariam insisted again.

Sophia could only wonder what she meant, taking another sip of wine.

"I stayed with my cousin and prayed over him. My cousin from that moment on started to respond to the medication and slowly got better." Mariam's tone was more cheerful. Her New York accent and mannerisms made the story sound more interesting.

"A few days after giving my cousin the rosaries," Mariam recalled, "we had been invited to the home of our rela-friends, Eileen and Frank. As I walked up to her front door I saw something strange."

She paused. "On her doorknob, there was a set of rosaries! It's not something she had ever done before. So I hurried into Eileen's house and asked her why she had a pair of rosaries on her door," her voice screeched again.

"Eileen explained that her son was getting married in a couple of days, and she prayed for good weather. Have you ever heard of that, Sophia? Having rosaries on your door to pray for good weather?" Mariam questioned.

"No, never." Sophia was amazed.

"Well, I can tell you the rosaries and prayers worked! They worked for my cousin and for Eileen's son's wedding." Mariam sat back again. "And for me, the rosaries were a sign of the blessings we received and the true power praying the rosaries can have. This started, I mean, when we first saw Dr. Love was on May 13, 2012, which is also the Feast of Our Lady of Fatima."

"Ruff, ruff," Charlie barked.

Dennis hushed him, "*silenzio*." He then continued to pet him.

"Thinking about it now, I find it strange that the pope on May 13, 1917, when our Blessed Mother Mary first appeared to the three children in Portugal, shares the same name with the first pope to resign in six hundred years. Did you know that? I mean about Fatima?"

Sophia shook her head no.

"Unfortunately, we never saw the couple again." She sighed. Mariam's tone flattened. "I would love for the couple and the man dressed as Jesus walking on Main Street to know they were a part of this wonderful miracle that day."

Sophia and Ben did not say a word.

"*Bene*, a week after my friend's son's wedding, I saw an article in *Newsday*, the local newspaper, about this man walking around Long Island dressed as Jesus," Mariam recalled as if still surprised.

"The article mentioned his name, and I took notice that his first name is Robert. Can you guess what my cousin's name is?" Mariam asked enthusiastically.

Mariam did not give them a chance to answer. "My cousin's name is also Robert!"

Mariam reached into her pocket and pulled out a pair of timeworn wooden rosary beads. It had a weathered looking flat wooden crucifix.

"I do believe in miracles." Mariam displayed the rosary beads.

"Wow, that was some story." Ben was sincere in his disbelief.

"*Sì*, that is some story." Sophia looked at the rosary beads in Mariam's hand and shook her head.

"I know it is crazy, but what if an angel gave us a flat tire so we would have had to take Main Street, which led us to see Jesus?" Mariam asked. "I believe it was the Archangel Michael. He has always been around me."

"Stranger things have happened. Wouldn't you say, Sophia?" Dennis asked.

"*Sì*, I guess so." Sophia started to feel weird. She did not know what to make of all of this.

"Here, can I do something that might help you, Sophia?" Before Sophia could answer, Mariam stood up, went into the kitchen, and came back with a large deck of cards.

"Ben, let me get you more *vino*," Dennis offered liquid encouragement.

"*Grazie.* I was also hoping we would have time to talk." Ben smiled, trying to be polite.

"We will in a few minutes. I do have more information about Carmine." Dennis tried to relieve Ben's anxiety.

Mariam came and sat down next to Sophia.

She shuffled the overly large deck. "You see, they are angel cards." Mariam showed both Sophia and Ben.

"I should ask first: can I do an angel card reading on you, Sophia?" Mariam was sensitive to the idea that not everyone appreciated having angel card readings.

"I…I guess so," Sophia muttered. She had a distant memory of her counselor, Caterina, whose office had angel pictures everywhere.

Dennis came back and gave Ben another glass of wine. Ben took it from Dennis's hand in a tense motion that revealed his frustration.

"So many people believe in this stuff." Sophia's mouth opened as the words tumbled out.

"This stuff?" Mariam questioned her uncertainty. "You sound surprised that people believe in angels. Sophia, millions of people believe in angels just as they believe in the One who sends them to us."

Mariam pulled the thirteenth angel card. "Hmm, Michael, and look, the card says, 'I am protecting, you are safe. I am your shield against lower energies and guiding you and your loved ones.'"

Sophia looked at the card, which displayed a handsome bare-chested angel holding a sword in one hand and a shield in the other.

Mariam took out three other angel cards and placed them in front of Sophia. Each card was elaborately detailed with bold angel depictions and bright colors.

"Hmm, Raphael." She pointed. "This card says, 'Take deep breaths. Breathe in and exhale slowly. Renew your energy.'" Mariam concentrated on each word.

"The Uriel card says, 'Trust in your inner knowledge, your intuition. You know what to do. Act without delay.'" She flipped the next card over. "And lastly, Gabriel: 'It is time for you to assume your leadership power. Use your energy and position to guide others.'"

"Raphael?" Sophia repeated as she ignored Mariam, amazed to hear his name.

Remembering the security guard who saved her life, she immediately picked up the card. "*Dio mio,*" Sophia sighed, then slowly and deliberately she outlined the angel's face on the card. "If he were older, I would swear this is the man who helped me."

She showed the picture to Ben, who did not say a word. He just stared at the card and then back at Sophia.

Mariam looked at Sophia. "Look, the Guardians of the Four Winds, they are watching over you. You have a destiny that is as fixed as the stars."

"The four what?" Sophia was surprised and confused at Mariam's card-reading abilities and put the Raphael card on the table.

"These archangels are the Guardians of the Four Winds," Mariam informed her students.

186

"Michael is the guardian of the south wind, Uriel guards the north wind, Raphael guards the east, and Gabriel guards the west. So no matter the direction you travel, isn't it nice to know an angel is with you?" Mariam grinned softly.

"*Sì*, I guess—" Sophia was interrupted.

"Thank you for the lovely story." Ben tried to be polite, but he was running out of patience. "I do believe in God, but my hotel was ransacked, and I think people are trying to follow me, so I don't know how your story or angel cards will help us."

Sophia stood up. "Ben, I don't understand what is happening to me, but last night I met a guy named Michael, and he was from Long Island, New York. What are the odds that Mariam's miracle story happened there and the angel Michael was part of it?"

Sophia was confused, and her expression did not conceal her feelings. She studied the four angel cards. "*Per favore*, help me to make sense of all this." She didn't realize she spoke aloud.

Standing up, Mariam touched Sophia's shoulder. "Sometimes we don't understand what is happening, but we must have faith. I can sense that you will face difficulties, but you should give your worries and troubles to the angels. They will help bring God's solutions to you and give you peace."

Mariam took a serious tone, "I know how this sounds. It sounds *pazzo*, but trust me. It works if you believe. Miracles can happen to anyone, Sophia," she was reassuring.

Ben grew more anxious. "I just don't know what your angels have to do with my hotel room or the people following me or even Carmine." He was worried. "I had to go on and off the train at different railway stations to be sure I was not followed." His mind flashed back to stepping on the train at the last minute to ensure he was in fact alone in his travels.

"Ben, my friend Eme told me that archons were following you. I don't know who they are," Sophia reacted sympathetically to Ben. "But I believe her."

"Did you say archons?" Mariam questioned in disbelief.

"*Sì*, do you know who they are?" Sophia sat next to Ben, hoping to calm his frustration.

"Sophia, who is Eme?" Dennis's investigator skills turned on.

Sophia looked at Ben, her head tilted like a child not wanting to admit wrongdoing. "Hmm. She is a friend."

Ben saw the embarrassment Sophia tried to hide. He could not control his frustrations any longer. "Eme is Sophia's dead friend who came back to tell her of these things."

"Are you physic or a medium?" Mariam was curious.

Sophia looked at Mariam point-blank. "No, I am a scientist!" She shook her head. "I do not understand what is happening to me. Eme came to me this morning in a dream and told me not to be surprised. Then I have four people today telling me not to be surprised. I am trying not to look too much into it, but how does that happen?"

Mariam chuckled a little, as Dennis recognized what Sophia referred to as crazy.

"I can tell you from personal experience from being married a long time, things like this happen all the time." Dennis tried to lighten the mood.

Glancing at Dennis lovingly, Mariam smiled. "Yes, we have had many experiences with the unexplainable."

"We just know that it is God and His angels making sure we were paying attention," Mariam explained. "God has a way of emerging in our lives in ways we least expect." Then turning to Sophia and Ben, she added, "Let me show you something." She got up and picked up her iPad, which rested on a coffee table. Her fingers moved across the face of the iPad. She was searching for something specific.

"Oh, here it is." Mariam shared her husband's investigative skills. "This is who archons are." She passed the iPad around, starting with Sophia.

Sophia held the iPad so she could see the web page was open to a website "What Are Archons?" Her mouth opened silently, reading the words in front of her. "'Archon means ruler or lord. References are made to *Authorities of the Darkness.*' Archons are rulers? What is this website?" Sophia asked with curiosity.

Mariam took the iPad and scrolled down, pointing to the screen as she handed the iPad back to Sophia.

"Gnosticism?" Sophia mouthed the word. "I don't understand." She looked up at Mariam.

"It refers to several servants of the demiurge. Archons can be considered hostile powers. There are many who believe they are beings with devilish powers." Mariam's expression grew serious.

"What is this that you were talking about? I don't understand." Ben stood up. "This is crazy. Are you talking about aliens?"

"No, they are not aliens. I am only explaining what you asked about." Mariam was defending herself.

"Mariam, I have heard about Gnostics or Gnosticism. But what is it?" Sophia turned to Ben. "*Per favore*, Ben, just give me a minute." Her eyes were sincere as she played to Ben's sensitive side.

Reminded how he would respect his sisters or his mother, he sighed. "All right, but we really need to talk to Dennis about..." He hesitated. "About Carmine. We need to know if he found out anything. After all, that is why we came."

"*Sì*, and we will," Sophia assured him. "*Per favore,* Mariam, what is this Gnostic stuff about?"

"Sophia, I'm not an expert, but what I can tell you is that Gnostics believe in inner knowledge. It is through this inner knowledge that people can come to better understand God." Pausing, she sipped her wine.

"The people who believe in Gnosticism believe in the spiritual world beyond this material one. It is kind of like the Lord's Prayer." Then Mariam recited, "God's will be done on earth as it is in heaven..." Her voice trailed off.

"I don't get it," Ben answered her back shaking his head.

Sophia also looked confused. "I'm sorry, Mariam, but I still—"

"It's all right, Sophia. While I cannot tell you everything you want to know, I can say there is most certainly a spiritual world, and spirits or souls have energy. However you would like to describe it, they do come into this material world all the time. That is why people such as psychics and mediums can read people." Mariam smiled softy.

189

She explained further, "Psychics and mediums feel energy from the spiritual world." Taking Sophia's hand, Mariam held her palm on top of hers. "Like you, Sophia. You feel their energy. Don't you?" Mariam looked into Sophia's eyes.

Sophia nodded her head but could not say a word.

"Ben, this energy or these spirits are not all good. Some archons, they are working for the lower energy. Some might even refer to them as working for the demiurge or devil." Mariam's face bore concern.

"Whatever you want to call them, they can have influence over powerful people such as lawyers, politicians, and people in authority. They are usually attracted to people who have influence over others. It's a big part of how they operate."

"Politicians?" Ben for the first time sounded interested. "What do you mean, influence?"

"You know the saying, the devil made me do it?" Mariam sarcastically asked.

Sophia and Ben both broke out in smiles, wanting to laugh.

Mariam clarified, "There is energy in this material world that is negative, and while God gave us free will, we are influenced by good and bad energy. The archons use their energy to influence people to do bad things, to get us to make bad decisions. They get us to use our free will against others and against our Father. When someone cheats on a test and passes, they may feel better for a short while. The negative energy gets stronger, and over time they get emotionally blackmailed." Mariam paused. "Our ego blackmails us, the negative energy keeps getting stronger and people continue making bad decisions."

"Blackmailed?" Ben asked. "I don't see how all this talk of angels and archons has anything to do with my case," he deduced in his attorney-like manner.

"Maybe you don't see it now, but your mentioning the angel Raphael says there is something going on—something that is guided by a higher power. Sophia, your friend Eme, who has passed on, is helping you. I believe these archons are real, just as I know angels are real, and I hope that in whatever you are doing, you are careful. These archons are very powerful." Mariam spoke in a motherly, concerned tone.

190

Dennis stood up and reached for a large, sealed manila envelope that was behind the picture frame on the table.

"Open this later. It has information you wanted to see." He came toward Sophia and handed it to her. "And Ben, I have information about Sophia's boss, Carmine. It seems he's gay. Did you know that?"

"No, I didn't...But now that you say that, things make more sense about him." Sophia shook her head in realization of something obvious.

"It seems he has a high-profile lover, a Cardinal Rosotti. Have you ever heard of him?" Dennis was straightforward.

"No." Sophia shook her head again.

"No," Ben agreed with a nod.

"*Bene*, he was recently arrested. While the Vatican is keeping it hush-hush, my investigator friend tells me it was for bank fraud charges involving the IOR." Dennis went on. "I am looking into this some more. I have a few friends I am meeting with this week, and maybe I can find out what the connection is to Carmine in all of this."

"Dennis, I was just mentioning that I will be speaking to the senior Mr. Callesino in Turin, and maybe he can also give us more insight. The tainted evidence has to tie them together somehow." Ben inferred stating his case.

"I'll let you know what I find out this week," Dennis paused for a moment. "But, Sophia, you need to promise me that you will not be following people anymore." Dennis took a protective tone.

Sophia shrugged.

"No, I mean it!" Dennis was almost demanding.

"Sophia, we have daughters, so as big as Dennis is, he's really a softie when it comes to protecting his girls." Mariam defended Dennis's concern. "And it seems he has adopted you, in a sense." Mariam laughed.

"All right then. I promise I will try," Sophia gave in to his request. "My father is the same way."

"OK then, if that is all, I guess we should be going." Ben looked at his watch. "We can catch the next train in about a half hour. I will call the taxi."

"*Sì*, you are right." Sophia looked at Ben then back at her envelope with anticipation.

"Sophia, after you go through the information I put together for you, give me a call so I can answer your questions. I should have more insight for you next week," Dennis assured her.

"Oh, I almost forgot." Sophia reached in her purse and handed Dennis a check.

"*Grazie*." Dennis was appreciative.

"*Prego*. I really appreciate everything you are doing for me." Sophia was sincere.

"And Ben, I appreciate your spy moves to ensure you were not followed. What about your mobile?" Dennis probed Ben. "I hope you took care of that also."

"I did. I am only using burner phones," Ben answered confidently.

"*Bene*, where are you staying?" Dennis was concerned for Ben.

"With old friends. After my visit to Turin I will be leaving for London, so I hope to have some idea about what is going on before I return home." Ben's concern for his own safety was noticeable.

"*Va bene*, we will be talking. This is my number. *Per favore*, call me on one of your disposable phones," Dennis insisted.

Sophia heard the sound of a car pulling up in the front of the house.

"Oh, our ride is here." Sophia stood up, collecting her pocketbook. "*Grazie*, for everything! We will be talking again soon."

She turned to Mariam and gave her a hug. "I don't understand it yet, but at least I know there are people who also believe in this stuff, and I am not crazy. Now that I have more information, I will continue my search for answers." She paused. "And *grazie*, the bracelet *è bellissimo*." Sophia smiled.

"*Prego,* Sophia." Mariam returned the hug. "*Per favore*, just be careful."

Sophia and Ben bid their farewells then headed back.

They boarded the train to return to Trastevere. Sophia was numb, hardly realizing she was ignoring Ben.

Her thoughts were scattered. Gazing upon her new bracelet, she twirled it around. The clear crystal beads sparkled as she played with the two tiny charms, a silver miraculous medal and a silver heart that read "Made with love."

"I am going to give this to you." Ben pulled a small disposable mobile phone out of his pocket. "I programmed the number so you can dial me if you need me. I cannot return all the way back to Trastevere with you, so I will be getting off at the next stop."

"*Va bene*, just be careful." She encouraged him. "And let me know what happens in Turin." Sophia felt like he was somehow her new big brother.

"This is where I get off." The train stopped, and Ben got up. Nodding to Sophia, he said, "Be careful." He then turned and left as she looked at him, expressionless.

Sophia was alone, but she had the envelope she couldn't wait to open when she got home. As the train moved forward again, she watched the houses and the buildings. Passing the objects at such speed put her into a daze, as she remembered details of Mariam's miracle story and the talk of the angel Michael.

"It's been a long weekend." Once Sophia arrived home, she was exhausted. Partying the night before, seeing Dominic, dancing with Michael, and then going to Dennis's house took just about all of her energy.

"A nice cup of *caffè* should do it," she said to herself, hoping it would make her feel better.

She put the envelope Dennis had given her on the counter and started the water for her coffee. Looking at the envelope, her feelings were mixed.

"*Questo è così pazzo*." She recalled the crazy events of the weekend while tapping the envelope with her nails. She was nervous and excited at the same time. "But first I will renew my energy with *caffè*."

The envelope weighed only a few ounces. Sophia could feel its thickness and the paper clips inside that were used to hold papers together.

193

For a moment she imagined what her brothers would look like. She imagined them to be tall like her, with fair skin.

"People who look like me. That would be a nice change. But what if they don't want me? Maybe they can help to find our parents. Maybe our parents don't want us. Maybe, maybe, maybe…" Her mind started to spin.

The coffee machine beeped. It interrupted Sophia from her imagination running wild.

"*Va bene allora*." She got her coffee and sat on the sofa. She took the envelope with her. "Let's see what you have to say."

Tearing the top off with the knife that she used to stir her coffee, she could see the papers being held together with paper clips. Taking the papers out, she saw a cover page that Dennis had written to her.

"His handwriting is remarkably neat," she observed straight away.

Caro Sophia,

I have made a few notations as to the updates in your case. Please let me know if anything seems familiar to you.

1. The enclosed picture shows a man leaving what appears to be a large appliance-type box on the steps of Istituto Provinciale per l'Infanzia, the Turin orphanage. The picture is dark, but you can make out that the man is Caucasian and tall. He seems to be wearing a black overcoat and a black hat. There is not much to go on with this picture.

2. The enclosed DVD is a copy of what I believe to be the same man leaving a similar type of box on the steps of Casagrande Orphanage, where you were left. Again, the contrast is fuzzy at best, but the overcoat and hat appear to be the same.

3. The enclosed document is a copy of the police report, which is signed by an attorney for the orphanage where your possible brother was left.

Sophia looked at the note and quickly noted the attorney signature.

"A Salvatore Moretti, *rappresentante legale*…hmm. I think I read he is now on the Turin City Council." She quickly retrieved her laptop.

"That is interesting. This article says Roberto Callesino Sr. was not reelected and that Councilman Salvatore Moretti had won his seat." Sophia sat for a few moments.

"*Dio mio*." Sophia realized the coincidence before reading the final part of Dennis's letter.

> 4. I still have not found out more information regarding the child left at the Naples orphanage. My meeting with a source did not pan out as I had hoped. However, I am following up on another lead and will update you next week.

> "On a personal note, I am growing fond of you and do not wish to see any harm come to you. *Per favore*, call me if you need me. My invoices are enclosed.
> Sincerely, Dennis

The bottom of the letter, in big bold letters, read, *"AND DO NOT FOLLOW PEOPLE!"*

Sophia read the last line and giggled. She reviewed the envelope's contents more closely, hoping to find clues.

She reached for the DVD and slid it into her laptop, reviewing the DVD image. "This man…He does look like the same person in the picture."

Holding the picture Dennis had given to her in one hand and looking at the computer screen, she could see the tall man carrying a brown plain box about the size of her microwave.

On the DVD she can see him carefully putting a box down on the steps of the orphanage under a large overhang.

He securely put the box close to the door. He looked around, rang the bell, and then ran from the camera view.

"It takes all of one minute, and then he is gone," Sophia sighed.

She studied the DVD images and the picture. However, she could only make out his profile. He had high cheekbones, dark hair with sideburns, and a thin face, but that was it.

"This Moretti guy, he may know something. At the very least, I have to ask." Sophia took out her mobile.

"*Ciao*, Ben. I will meet you in Turin." She was assertive to a fault.

"No, Sophia, I cannot have you come with me." Ben sharpened his tone.

"No, Ben. I'm not going with you, but I will meet you anyway. *Addio*, and be safe." Sophia ended the call abruptly.

Ben was at Mrs. Potter's hotel reviewing the progress of his findings with her.

"I cannot believe it. She hung up on me." Ben was angry.

"What did she want?" Mrs. Potter demanded.

"She said she was going to meet me in Turin," Ben answered his boss.

"Ben, make sure she does not speak to Mr. Callesino," she insisted with her British sternness.

"I will make sure," Ben assured Mrs. Potter.

In the meantime, Sophia looked up train schedules and found the address to the Turin City Council building, hoping she would catch Mr. Moretti at his job.

"Yawn…" Sophia stretched. "I better take this with me." She put the picture of the mysterious man in her pocketbook.

Sitting down on the sofa, thinking about everything, she sipped her coffee and put the cup down on the small table. Her gaze went to the painting that Dominic had brought to her, which was resting on the counter.

Sophia stood up and picked up the painting. Taking the brown wrapping paper off, she rested it on the sofa. She stared at the painting, tilting her head, trying to figure out why it captured her attention.

"*The Flaming Star*." She repeated the name at the bottom of the picture. "These three white stars, one small, one medium size, and one that is larger than the others. Hmm…"

She gazed at the three stars. "What is it about you?"

The three stars were brighter than all the rest and formed an irregular long triangle. Red dust faded in and out of the black universe, with colors of magenta, cerulean, yellow, emerald, and gold being more prominent.

"It looks abstract," Sophia said to herself. She stared at it a long while. "I think I can almost see a face in the distance." Using her fingers, she traced a line of stars.

"The stars seemed to dance in and out of the red, gold, and blue dust. It is mesmerizing. It is like the picture is talking to me, but I cannot understand it." Her eyes were getting heavy, lost in her gaze.

"Yawn." She stretched again. "I better get some rest."

Getting ready for bed, she saw the rosaries on her headboard.

"Remember, Sophia, say the rosaries." Eme's voice came to her mind. Sophia picked up the rosaries, held them in her hand, and asked Eme's spirit to pray with her.

"Hail Mary, full of Grace," Sophia softy mumbled,
"Our Lord is with you,
Blessed are You among women,
and blessed is the fruit of Thy womb, Yehsua.
Holy Mary, Mother of God,
pray for us sinners,
now and at the hour of our death. Amen."

She recited it just as she was taught.

"No, no!" She heard a voice call to her. "The proper way to say it is, 'Now and at the hour of our *rebirth*.' Not death!"

"*Che cosa?*" Sophia replied in a state of shock as she turned her head toward the voice. It was Eme, sitting on the edge of her bed.

"Our Lady wants you to say it this way. 'Now and at the hour of our *rebirth*,'" Eme repeated.

"How do you know?" Sophia asked sarcastically.

"Because she told me so." Eme's voice was serious. "Men created that part of the prayer, *Now and at the hour of our death*, as a way to keep people in fear. Our Blessed Mother does not want you or anyone to fear Her or the time of our rebirth." She smiled softly.

"Rebirth?" Sophia mouthed the word in disbelief. "She told…you?"

"*Sì*, Sophia. You know we never really die. I mean, if you love and are true to our Father. Isn't that what the Bible, Quran, and the Torah all have in common? They all say we live eternally. So we are reborn into heaven."

"Oh, rebirth," Sophia repeated. "It does sound better."

"*Sì*, it does. So let's start over, shall we?" Eme started the Hail Mary prayer again.

"Now and at the hour of our rebirth," Sophia ended each of the Hail Mary prayers. After they finished the rosaries, Sophia laid her head down. It felt so heavy.

"What is She like, our Blessed Mother Mary?" Sophia asked as her eyes grew heavy.

"*Lei è bella*, and She loves you…" Eme's voice trailed off.

Sophia stared at Eme. Her image was fading with each blink until finally, Sophia was asleep.

Chapter 11

WOLVES and THE SHEEP

Valentinus was readying himself for the first of the congregations in preparation for conclave. He read his notes again...

"Each of the three congregations are scheduled to take place one day after the next. In this conference like-setting, the cardinals would be more relaxed to receive their instructions surrounding the process of conclave. It is also the time they are to make their vow of secrecy. To address security, the congregations are all to be held at the Palazzo Apostolico."

Valentinus sighed upon arriving at the Palazzo Apostolico and was witnessing the performance in its first act.

"It is time for the show." Valentinus sighed, *"Questo è pazzesco."* He cringed seeing the curious crowds of spectators.

At the majestic Vatican Apostolic Palace entrance of Portone di Bronzo, the scene was organized chaos. Swiss guards stood at their posts as cardinals with flowing red garments welcomed one another. Different languages overlapped one another as the cardinals moved forward toward the opened doors. They were guided swiftly like a herd of sheep by bishops and other Vatican staff. The cardinals obediently followed their shepherds through large corridors.

"Let me take the back-door route." Valentinus felt sickened by the pageantry with its pomp and circumstance.

The vast building held the papal apartments, various government offices of the Catholic Church and the Holy See, private and public chapels, Vatican museums, and the Vatican library, including the Sistine Chapel, Raphael Rooms, and the Borgia Apartment.

"Per favore, stay with me. It would be easy to get lost in here," Bishop Eagan announced to his group of shadowing visiting cardinals. "I am sure it could be quite overwhelming for many of you. I understand many of you have never been here before."

The cardinals obeyed their shepherd, wide-eyed in amazement, gazing upon the beautiful artifacts that richly dressed their temporary quarters.

"It is like having a secret." Bishop Eagan spoke to a visiting cardinal as he guided them through the numerous lavishly decorated corridors.

"Excuse me?" Nigerian Cardinal Arinogie asked in his thick accent.

"Tourists can see some parts of the palace, but not everything." He pointed down a long corridor they were passing. "Like the Sala Regia and Cappella Paolina. Even the Scala Regia can be seen into from one end, but it cannot be entered. The people will never see all we have," Bishop Eagan stated as a matter of fact. "All the history inside this majestic building, the history within these walls…It is like possessing a secret treasure."

"Oh, I see," Cardinal Arinogie answered him politely but he looked confused.

"Ah." Bishop Egan spotted Valentinus coming toward him. *"Buon giorno, il Cardinale de Marcosi."*

"Ciao." Valentinus realized he had been spotted. It was the only word that came to him. Seeing all these visiting cardinals made his soul sink. "They could have been voting for me." His mind wandered for a second.

"Will you help me?" Valentinus could see the bishop's mouth moving, but he did not hear the words.

"Mi scusi, Cardinal. Will you help me to show our guests the way?" Bishop Eagan asked again.

"Bene, of course, of course." Valentinus was back in reality, stammering as he turned around to show their guests the way to the first congregation.

Mixing in with the crowd, smiling and shaking hands, Valentinus tried to hide his disappointment.

"Ciao, benvenuto." Simple words he could choke on. Every handshake took a little piece of his heart.

"*Dio mio. Mio Santo Padre*, why will you not listen? I will do your bidding. *Per favore*, consider me," Valentinus begged silently.

"I plead with you, my *Padre*, *per favore*, make a clear path that I may help guide your flock." Valentinus's heart and mind begged his Father in heaven as he robotically found his way to his own seat in the Great Hall.

The cardinals were finally seated, and the first congregation started promptly with introductions. Listening to the various like-minded speakers, the attendees seemed to outwardly praise Pope Gregory and his courage, while inwardly they were feeding on surmounting gossip. Forming their own opinions, they forged ahead with the rituals, leading many to take the sides of the possible pontiff front-runners.

Speaker after speaker shared their praise and egos. However, not all the speakers were optimistic in their words. Brazilian Cardinal Di'Ortiz attacked the Curia in his speech.

"We are a body of ills that has been ravaged by divisiveness and corruption. We are sick with a cancer that must be cut out if we are to survive," he demanded while standing firm on the podium, using his thundering, gruff, deep voice to make his point.

His speech was well received by the reformers, who stood to give the cardinal a standing ovation. On the sidelines the traditionalists sat with stone faces like the ancient statues that surrounded them.

The very lines Di'Ortiz spoke of were being drawn at that moment. Valentinus remained seated, but not because he was taking sides.

"I have no chance of securing the votes I need." He sat watching everyone around him. "Look at these men of God." Some were applauding, while others jeered. "I am disgusted by the display of false worship. The 'sheep people' will blindly follow the wolves into hell!"

After the first congregation ended, Irenaeus began circulating Pope Gregory's memoranda listing the talking points as suggested by Secretary of State Cardinal Borgia during their meeting. He spotted Valentinus just as he was leaving the room.

"Val, I was surprised you did not stand for Cardinal Di'Ortiz. Many thought his speech was rousing."

After this apparent dig, Irenaeus smirked, hinting at his true emotions.

"I am on God's side," Valentinus shot back. "And whose side are you on, Irenaeus?"

Irenaeus stood inches away from Valentinus and leaned into him. "Despite what you may think, I also am on your side." He looked into Valentinus's eyes, studying his response.

"You are right. I do find that hard to believe." Valentinus got a cold chill down his spine, saying the only thing that came to his mind.

"We are on the same side, I can assure you." Irenaeus gave a half smile before his attention was diverted by a few visiting cardinals walking together in a small group.

"Ah, *scusami*." Irenaeus's expression turned serious. Departing from Valentinus, he walked toward the group of cardinals.

Valentinus watched as Cardinal Clemente Sisinnius was showered with attention. It made his blood boil.

"Irenaeus fits in with these conspirators." Valentinus talked to himself as he turned around and left for his temporary residence at the Domus Marthae Sanctae. "It is not a far walk," he thought, seeing the building was adjacent to St. Peter's Basilica. "Besides, it will give me time to think. I need to be alone."

When he was hidden away in his room, his thoughts could fester. "A cardinal from Syria! This world is not ready for that kind of reform," Valentinus grumbled under his breath, not ready to help support the talking points requested of him.

Valentinus did not underestimate Sisinnius. "He is known for his accomplishments as a financial reformer, helping Gregory to arrest Cardinal Rosotti and to clean up the Vatican bank. Clemente Sisinnius is a financial wizard as much as he is a strong leader who wants to unite the world church with an iron fist of traditional reform." Valentinus wreaked of bitterness.

"The problem is that Sisinnius is too well respected for overcoming obstacles, even as he was run out of Syria by terrorists before coming to Italy. He knows many important people," he grinned.

"His political connections reach far beyond Rome." Valentinus was thinking as if to hatch a plot against his enemy. "The world is full of politicians and leaders who promised reform. And what happens? The people these political leaders serve suffer more under the guise of their reform." Valentinus gabbled, in his own world, far removed from the gossip.

"I am hidden for now, safe from the crows of deceit." He sighed, feeling every bit of the emptiness in his heart. Standing at his window inside the Domus Sanctae Marthae residence, he could see people walking about in the distance.

"What they need is hope. They need hope that no matter their religion, they can stand united with our universal Father. They need hope that religion is not going to cause another world war."

A brief thought of watching the news came to mind, as he remembered how the reports were filled with acts of terror at the hands of Muslim fanatics.

"We have disappointed millions of people as we aired our dirty laundry, exposing unfathomable scandals." Valentinus stood silently pondering his words. "Jewish, Protestant, and other religious leaders had their share of scandals too. People all over the world are losing faith. Who will lead your people, *mio Santo Padre*?"

Valentinus began to pray. "*Per favore, mio Padre*, hear me. People on this earth need to know that their Father is residing within them here and now, in this moment of time. That you, Allah, Yahweh, Ehyeh, or God by any other name are the Supreme Reformer of souls." He closed his eyes, bowing his head.

He rhetorically asked, "Why can't people exist without the hierarchy of a church, a temple, or a mosque? Why don't they know they can have an intimate relationship with their Father on their own terms? I know they could acquire a relationship so powerful that it could unleash the secrets of the universe. *Per favore*, help me to show them the way."

Opening his eyes, he overlooked the blacktop-paved courtyard. "I know spirituality can be a powerful tool, even a powerful asset, and still, it can be a powerful weapon. *Mio Dio* in heaven, how can I help people to see Your truths?"

"How can I help them to be independent of these institutions that call themselves religions?" Valentinus's eyes teared up. Watching the people milling about in the courtyard below put him in a trance.

It brought him back to the memory of his letter-writing campaigns. He wrote letters to the cardinals and bishops around the world, encouraging them to spend less on the church decadence. It upset him to think of the excessiveness, even with millions of dollars used to restore Saint Patrick's Cathedral in New York.

"And senior worshipers cannot even use their restrooms as if our Father would turn away someone in need…pity the fools." Valentinus turned his head away, closing his eyes.

"Wouldn't it be better if we could worship You as one people?" Valentinus envisioned community centers of faith. He imagined Muslims worshiping alongside Catholics, Jews, Protestants, Scientologists, Episcopalians, and others, united in the common belief that there was a higher power.

"*Our* Father, under who all people could unite as a family and share in His unconditional love…That is what is missing. People today need a new kind of way to believe in their faith, beyond the houses they worship in," Valentinus argued.

"That is absurd! Val, you are not realistic," Cardinal Sisinnius once told him. More cardinals laughed at him. Still others indulged themselves in their favorite pastime, gossip. Valentinus's ideas were too foreign for the traditional establishments.

"While it may be a paper dream, the truth is that attendance in all major religions, including our own, has been on a steady decline around the world," Valentinus stated his conviction with vigor. "It is evident that people from across the globe are losing faith in the traditional religious institutions." He was opinionated and stubborn. "And, my dear Cardinal Sisinnius, you know this because the Vatican is running at a million-dollar deficit!"

Sisinnius was not amused at Valentinus's assessment. "You are not an example of the leader we need. Only fools would follow you Valentinus."

Valentinus, half smiling, shot his version of a familiar verse through Sisinnius's guilty heart. "If religion was not used as a weapon or a way to control people or even a way to extort money from people, we as people would be truly free—not using religion as a cover-up for evil, but living as servants of our Father and honoring everyone… loving thy brothers and sisters."

Peering again outside his window, he could still feel his passion burning within his heart. Valentinus wanted to make changes from within and outside the church. "Ah, *bene*." He sighed heavily.

"Through knowledge, people could better understand and believe in the light and in the energy of our Father's love for us." Valentinus blinked his eyes, and he was back in the moment. "*Per favore, mio Santo Padre*, help me to make this possible."

He grew weary from his thoughts. Valentinus turned away from the window and sat on his bed, bowing his head to pray. Folding his hands in front of him, he gazed down to the floor, where he noticed a piece of folded paper. Leaning over to pick it up, he realized it was the lecture confirmation letter that he, in the last minute, shoved into his suitcase as he left his home for conclave. The letter was from his old alma mater, Polytecnic University in Turin. Valentinus often shared his ideas and opinions through lectures. His favorite forum was Polytechnic, where his beliefs were widely applauded.

"Always a teacher in your heart." Valentinus remembered Borgia teasing him as Valentinus argued that formal organized religions were causing millions of people to stop believing in God altogether.

"The world is coming undone." Putting the letter down, Valentinus reached for the newspaper he had left on the bed when he first arrived. "Look at this. The front page headline is sprayed with evidence of the acts of terror. Pictures of burning cities make the front-page headlines courtesy of these Muslim terrorist newcomers. Where are the acts of kindness and love?"

Valentinus shook his head. "That which God has created, all in its beauty, is now being destroyed. Men are again killing in the name of religion."

"Allah is against killing, and yet as the Catholics, Jews, and even Hitler did long ago, Muslim radicals are now becoming the demonic serial killers of God's people."

Valentinus closed his eyes again. "Muslim extremism continues to decimate the ancient lands of the Middle East. They are the destroyer of souls and have preyed upon the ignorant, the abused, and the neglected. There have been religious leaders of all denominations who throughout history have acted in place of the devil. Their attendance have filled churches, temples, mosques, and political offices alike."

"Help me to help Your people, enabling them to better understand the inner knowledge they already possess," he implored his Holy Father.

"I want to help them achieve a deeper understanding of You within their soul and bring them closer to You." His desperation was clear. Tears flowed with each prayer as the minutes disappeared into the darkness.

Weary, Valentinus lay down on his bed to rest.

Time had no boundaries. Desperate for a heavenly answer, Valentinus continued to pray through the night.

Unaware of time, Valentinus had fallen into a deep sleep. Daylight had arrived without notice. Commotion outside in the courtyard roused Valentinus from his slumber. Not realizing the hour, he began to start up where he left off.

"*Per favore, mio Santo Padre*, do you hear me?"

Knock, knock, knock…

Valentinus stopped and stared at the door. "Could it be an answer to my prayers?" He allowed a foolish thought.

Cardinal Korsig called to him, "Cardinal de Marcosi? Are you in there?"

"Oh, that's not…" Still feeling exhausted, Valentinus got up from his bed.

"*Per favore*, Valentinus. I need to speak with you. It is urgent." The tone in Korsig's voice was noticeable with concern.

"*Dio mio, per favore*, now what?" Valentinus moved slowly toward the door.

"*Per favore*, Cardinal." Korsig sounded desperate.

Valentinus opened the door.

Korsig rushed in. "We need you. Why are you not in—"

"I have been praying. I needed time."

"The morning congregation is finished. There was much speculation regarding the scandals, and the visiting cardinals need direction." His voice rose with concern. "And I am afraid Irenaeus is pointing them in the wrong one."

"What do you mean?" Valentinus looked at his watch, now realizing the time of day.

"There is a consensus growing of foreign infiltration within the church that goes beyond the traitor we were searching for." Korsig's eyes grew wide with fear.

"I don't understand. What are you talking about?" Valentinus shot back with curiosity.

"I have to go back to my office to find some old files. After the lunch break, I need you to go to the afternoon congregation and watch whom people are talking with. Can you do that for me, or rather for the church?" Korsig pleaded.

Valentinus stood in silence for a moment, realizing what Korsig was asking. "I…" He hesitated.

"*Per favore*, Cardinal, I think there is something else going on. It's deeper than conclave, but I must be sure before I say anything further. *Per favore*! For the Blessed Mother. Her church is in danger of being destroyed from within!"

Now Valentinus's tired eyes grew wide with concern. "What are you talking about? I don't understand what you are saying."

"All I can say right now is that there will be a movement to recognize Palestine as a state and that Cardinal Clemente Sisinnius's nomination for pontiff may not be a coincidence. That is all I am willing to say without verifying some facts. *Per favore*, can you help us and our church?" The portly Cardinal Korsig looked terrified.

Valentinus thought about Korsig's concerns for a moment. "*Sì*, I will freshen up and leave immediately for the dining hall, where the cardinals do much of their gossiping."

"*Grazie*, Cardinal de Marcosi. I will notify you as soon as I can."
Korsig held out his hand to Valentinus.

They shook on their arrangement before Korsig took his leave.

Valentinus looked at his watch, realizing he had been in his room
all through the night and half the day. He put his hands to his face,
feeling his stubble.

"I must have blacked out or something. Time seems to have
stood still." He was amazed he did not feel the time go by.

The Domus Sanctae Marthae dining hall was a welcome sight.
Valentinus suddenly realized how hungry he was. Only two small groups
of visiting cardinals remained seated. As Valentinus walked by, he could
hear them gossiping in their native tongues.

"Ah, Cardinal de Marcosi, won't you join me?" The Latin
American–speaking Cardinal Perez tapped Valentinus on the shoulder.

Moving from behind Valentinus he offered, "I am afraid
everyone is just about finished with his meal. It looks like we are stuck
with whatever they have left."

"I see." Valentinus looked wearily at the one group of cardinals
taking their leave.

"You look tired. Are you all right?" The shorter cardinal, with a
bald spot and short thin strands of black hair sticking up, gazed up at
Valentinus.

"*Sì, grazie. Sto bene.*" Valentinus was short in his reply.

"I understand this is an arduous process. It can suck the life right
out of you if you let it." Perez grinned.

"*Grazie*, for your wise advice." Valentinus selected a chicken
dish as he sat down with the older-looking Cardinal Perez. "I am not
even sure what this is." He smelled his dish.

"I believe it is chicken marsala." Cardinal Perez tasted a bite of
his own chicken dish.

"So I understand there was much gossip today at the
congregation." Valentinus wanted to test Perez.

"*Sì*, the show was *interessante*. But I believe later will be even
better." Perez took a sarcastic tone while enjoying his lunch.

"*Bene*, can you give me the highlights?"

"At this point it is too early to tell, but I think Irenaeus is making progress touting his boss, Sisinnius, as the new pontiff. You really need to be present for the whole day tomorrow. And you really need to look the part. You have bags under your eyes."

"*Bene, grazie* again for your advice." Valentinus sneered.

"That is my job, to help people." Perez smirked, finishing some of his meal. "This was all right, but we have better food at home." He got up from his chair, taking his half-finished food with him. "I will look forward to seeing you this afternoon."

Valentinus watched Cardinal Perez leave the dining hall as the last of the cardinals followed him out.

"Never a dull moment," he thought, shaking his head as he finished the rest of his meal.

Getting ready for the congregations was likened to preparing for battle, but first Valentinus needed to know who was on which side.

The cardinals had returned from a congregation break when Valentinus finally arrived. Walking around, he noticed small groups of cardinals talking among themselves in pockets throughout the corridors and the Great Hall.

"There is Irenaeus, the snake in the grass." Valentinus watched Irenaeus slithering up to a few visiting cardinals and Sisinnius.

A light push on his back diverted his attention. "Do you see anything interesting?" Borgia asked, half-joking.

"I am not sure what I am seeing these days." Valentinus's tone was sounding a little depressed.

"Cheer up." Borgia patted him on the back. "This will be over soon."

"*Sì*, that is what I am afraid of." Valentinus glanced at Borgia then focused on Irenaeus. "*Scusami*." Before Borgia could answer, Valentinus darted across the room to break up Irenaeus's conversation.

Cardinals Jean Bodin from France and Everard des Barres from Turkey stood with Irenaeus and Cardinal Clemente Sisinnius, looking quite serious, judging by their facial expressions.

"*Scusami*, gentlemen," Valentinus interrupted. "I was hoping you could give me an update on the last part of the congregation."

"Val, I was looking for you this morning. I hope you are well," Irenaeus flaunted with a smug grin.

"*Sì, sono. Grazie.* I had some errands to run for Pope Gregory." Valentinus lied to sound more important in his duties.

"Oh, His Eminence, how is he?" Cardinal Jean Bodin was sincere enough.

"Valentinus, this is Cardinals Bodin and des Barres." Cardinal Sisinnius gestured.

"He is well. *Grazie.*" Valentinus nodded and spoke with authority. "He is concerned, of course, about our visiting cardinals' views regarding the current state of our church, given all the scandals swirling above." He motioned, his finger swirling in a circle. "I assured him the conclave is in no danger of being lost to gossip, that our cardinals are focused on only truths. And that we would all be loyal to God, our church and to each other. Cardinals, can I count on you to be loyal to the truth?" Valentinus stared them down.

Valentinus studied their every move, wanting to see if he could sense whom he could count on.

"Of course, *per favore.* Relay my best wishes to Pope Gregory and let him know he can count on me," Cardinal des Barres responded straightaway.

Cardinal Bodin worked with Clemente Sisinnius in Syria for a time and glanced first at his longtime friend before answering. "Of course. I pledge my support to our beloved church. Gossip shall not be a distraction keeping me from performing my duties, I can assure you."

"And what about you, Valentinus?" Irenaeus taunted his foe. "Do you have any distractions hindering the performance of your duties?"

"I can tell you that I am loyal to *mio Santo Padre* and my church and to Gregory." Valentinus stood fast. "And I will do everything in my power to protect them."

"I am sure you will, Valentinus," Sisinnius acknowledged Valentinus's efforts. "Now, if you will excuse us."

Sisinnius pointed to the Great Hall door. "Irenaeus, we must be going back to our seats...And I am glad you could join us, Valentinus. I was afraid you were not well."

"You mean you like seeing me distressed," Valentinus thought to himself as he nodded farewell.

Cardinal Bodin joined them, leaving Cardinal des Barres, who leaned into Valentinus. "Cardinal de Marcosi, I am afraid this conclave will not have a favorable outcome," he voiced his concern in a whisper. "*Per favore*, know I will try to do all I can to help you. My heart also belongs to our Blessed Mother." He winked before walking away.

Valentinus stood there for a moment, remembering his own commitment to the Blessed Mother. "*Per favore*, Blessed *Madre*, help me," he pleaded before finding his seat in the Great Hall.

The speakers wore Valentinus out. His mind could not focus. He was too busy watching the visiting cardinals, their reactions to the speakers, and to one another.

"It is a sight to see, the traditionalists fight against the progressives," he thought. "God's work is lost to the ego."

"Finally the congregation is over. It is time to mingle and get to know these people." Valentinus hurried to introduce himself.

He noticed a few cardinals from Asia, Africa, and Cardinal Perez from Latin America standing together.

"*Buon pomeriggio*, Cardinal, I trust you rested," Cardinal Jose Perez asked. "You will need it. I understand Gregory is upset about the *gay lobby* leaks." Perez gave him a point-blank stare, waiting for a response.

"*Sì*, he is...I mean, it is upsetting at the very least. Knowing we have a traitor among us is distressing, wouldn't you agree?" Valentinus was just as forward.

"*Sì*, it is personally upsetting." Cardinal Perez softened his tone. "I was one of the people on the phone with the pontiff when our conversation was hacked."

Valentinus stood back, stunned. "Really, I did not know."

"*Sì*, we are working with Gregory, and as I understand it, you are also." Perez focused on Valentinus. "And I am told we can trust you."

211

"*Sì*, Cardinal Perez. With all my heart, I want to help Gregory leave a lasting legacy and to help rebuild our church to its proper glory in praise to our *Santo Padre*." Valentinus's sincerity overwhelmed him.

"Can you meet with us later? I will let you know where and what time. Is that all right?" Cardinal Perez's invitation didn't seem to leave Valentinus with many options.

"I will be glad to. This is my direct number." Valentinus handed him his private business card.

Perez took the card and put it in his pocket, then gave a faint smile. "I will call you." He nodded before he walked away with the other cardinals.

Valentinus looked around to see if he should talk with anyone else. However, the cardinals wanted to eat dinner, rushing to leave the Great Hall.

"I guess I should eat too." He was reminded by his growling stomach. Going back to his room before dinner, he called Korsig. "Did you find what you were looking for?"

"Are you hungry?" Korsig answered him with a question.

"I am starving!" Valentinus responded sounding desperate.

"Meet me in my office. I just ordered Italian. If that is all right?" Korsig hoped he would have company.

"I would eat my own hand right now," Valentinus anxiously replied, thinking if Perez called him, he would leave Korsig early. "I am on my way."

Valentinus did not have far to go, and he was glad for that. "I hope the food is already delivered when I get there."

He was not disappointed.

"I am sorry, my friend, I could not wait." Korsig was already eating a spaghetti dinner with meat sauce. He dipped his large piece of bread in the sauce to prop up the spaghetti on his fork. "*Per favore*, take a plate and dig in…*Bon appétit*."

"Do not worry, I will help myself." Valentinus beamed. The food trays were spread out over Korsig's desk. "*C'è odore delizioso*."

"*È delizioso* and have some *vino*." Korsig pointed to the bottle. "*è il buon vino*…and I think we could both use it."

"*Sì, grazie.*" Valentinus said a small prayer before taking his time to enjoy every bite. "*Questo è meraviglioso il mio amico.*" He was appreciative of his good fortune.

"*Sì,* it is wonderful. I am glad you like it." Korsig enjoyed his meal but then focused on the business at hand. "Did you know that a Catholic Church was burned yesterday on the banks of the Galilee Sea? It was the Church of the Multiplication." Korsig's emotion grew serious. He picked up his glass of wine.

"No! *Dio mio.*" Valentinus was shocked as he drank his own wine. "The site of Jesus's miracle where he multiplied two fish and five loaves that fed five thousand people. It is gone?" Valentinus put his glass down.

"*Sì,* our history is being destroyed by Muslim radicals, Jewish settlement extremists, and others. It is not a good time for our church or our people. China not too long ago, as you know, has also burnt or destroyed many of our churches. I just cannot help but feel we are in terrible danger. The world is a dangerous place." Korsig finished his meal with a bitter taste left in his mouth.

"I share your feelings," Valentinus agreed with him. "Have you found out anything regarding Cardinal Rosotti or the traitor?" He was just as eager to know about the traitor.

"So far I have found that Irenaeus has pledged his allegiance to Cardinal Sisinnius." Korsig focused his words and frowned. "And while there are a few other hopefuls, it seems he is the serious front-runner."

"I have sources who tell me that Sisinnius has been working with cardinals from around the world to gain their trust and their confidence long before this conclave." Cardinal Korsig belched. "*Scusami.*"

"*Bene,* I could have told you that he was a front-runner. I saw him at work during the congregation. He was making sure he and Irenaeus spoke to just about everyone," Valentinus conveyed his observation. "He was fishing for votes."

"Val, have you heard of the Kairos Palestine Document?" Korsig moved his empty plate to uncover a folder he had under it.

"No, I don't think so," Valentinus replied as he put down his fork after taking his last bite of pasta.

"The document declares the Israeli occupation of Palestine is a sin against God and against humanity. It calls on churches and Christians all over the world to believe that Israel should be punished." Korsig opened the folder and shared the report with Valentinus. "The writers of this paper want to call for the boycott of all Israel."

"I have not heard of this document, but this seems like old news, no?" Valentinus poured another glass for each of them.

"*Bene*, what is new is that these leaders call for the beginning of systematic economic sanctions and boycotts to be applied against Israel. This Kairos Palestine Document reportedly states that the isolation of Israel will cause pressure on Israel to abolish all of what it labels as apartheid laws that discriminate against Palestinians and non-Jews," Korsig continued. "The problem is that this document was written by Palestinian Christian leaders who call it The Moment of Truth."

"Christian leaders?" Valentinus questioned in disbelief. "Don't people see how even the EU accuses Palestine of corruption and mismanagement, squandering nearly two billion euros of European aid when they were supposed to be helping their own people? Palestinian leaders watched their own people starve while their soldiers built tunnels to help them kill people. What kind of Christians could they be to stand for this behavior?"

"The worst kind. They do not mind that the likes of Hamas in the Gaza Strip promote violence. And now we have the possibility of electing a pope from Syria. That is a new concept, wouldn't you say?" Korsig was sarcastic and very serious.

"There is a growing consensus that Israel should not exist. The problem is growing more with each day from prominent leaders, fanatics, and extremists on many sides. Muslim radicals, these so-called Christian leaders, and these church-burning Jewish settlers, are only a few sources telling of a larger danger."

"How does this tie in with Cardinal Clemente Sisinnius?"

Korsig continued but not before opening another bottle of wine, "Sources tell me that Sisinnius is working with some of these fanatics. One such person is a Rabbi Abiyhum Shemer, who was recently arrested."

"Rabbi Abiyhum Shemer was tried in a Tel Aviv District Court and sentenced to five years in prison for bribery associated with the illegal activities between him and the former head assistant of a Lahav 444 police anticorruption unit."

"And…" Valentinus still did not understand.

"And Shemer and Sisinnius are related by marriage," Korsig expressed his concern. "Sisinnius's sister converted, and there is talk, I am told, that Sisinnius made promises to help isolate Israel so his brother-in-law would receive a lighter sentence for his crimes."

Valentinus looked suspicious. "Do you have proof of any of this?"

"I am working on that." Korsig sat back in his chair. "I can tell you that there is something deeper going on, but I need more time. I should have more information before we go into conclave."

"*Bene*, we would definitely need proof." Valentinus drank his wine. "We will need hard evidence if we are going to knock Sisinnius out of the running."

"I understand." Korsig drank his wine. "I will get back to you as soon as I have any more information."

"I will look forward to it," Valentinus answered him eagerly.

The men made small talk before Valentinus grew tired. "I really must be going. I am exhausted!"

"I do understand that feeling well," Korsig acknowledged with a nod. "Then I will see you tomorrow."

They parted ways, and Valentinus went back to his quarters, thinking of his options.

"If I could get rid of Sisinnius, perhaps there is still a small chance for me yet." He dreamed as his head hit his pillow. He was fast asleep until he woke to the sounds of people walking past his room.

"This day came faster than I would have liked. I am still so exhausted." He had gotten ready, feeling his heavy eyes and sore bones. He walked back into the Great Hall. Sitting down, he peered over his congregational handouts.

He could see who was talking to Irenaeus, Sisinnius, and their cronies. "*Per favore*, Blessed *Madre*, help me," he pleaded.

"Valentinus, how are you today?" Cardinal Borgia came up to him and sat down in the empty chair next to him. "May I sit with you?"

Sitting up straight, Valentinus gestured. "*Per favore.*"

"I won't stay." Borgia leaned in and whispered, "I just want to warn you. Perez may not be able to be trusted. I know you were counting on his allegiance, but be careful."

Valentinus looked a little surprise. "Are you sure?"

"At this point I am not sure of anything." Borgia looked more than concerned. "I have never seen this much division within these walls as I see today."

"I will—" Valentinus was interrupted by an assistant bishop.

"*Scusami*, Cardinal Borgia, but we need you downstairs," Latin American Bishop Taren advised Borgia.

"*Va bene*, I am coming," Borgia responded looking annoyed. He looked at Valentinus. "Just be careful." He left with Bishop Taren.

Valentinus watched Borgia walk away, feeling more alone then before. He got up and walked out into the corridor.

"This is incredible. Who can I trust?" He wandered about the corridors, pacing. There were a few cardinals walking around him, but he didn't take notice.

Cardinal Antonelli tapped his shoulder. "Cardinal de Marcosi, are you all right?"

Valentinus turned around. "*Sì*, Giacomo. I am just a little distracted. That is all."

"I can see that." Giacomo looked concerned. "You look like you are talking to yourself."

"I am sorry. I guess I got caught up in the moment," Valentinus replied sounding a little confused.

"Well. I hope this helps. Cardinal Korsig called me." Antonelli smiled. "He wanted us to know that he needed to see an old friend and that he will meet us at my office at nine tonight. Can you join us?"

"*Sì*, of course. *Grazie*, Giacomo." Valentinus was grateful for the message.

"Oh, and he said grace will be swift and dismiss the corruptor," Giacomo uttered his words with confusion.

216

"I am not sure what Korsig meant. Do you know? Unfortunately, after that we were cut off."

Valentinus thought about it for a moment. "I am not certain, but we will speak to him later," he assured Giacomo. "I will meet you tonight."

Giacomo half smiled. "*Bene*, I have other duties I must attend to now. I will see you tonight." He turned and walked down the corridor.

"Hmm...*grande.*" Valentinus again spoke to himself. Thinking about it more, he called Korsig on his mobile but it went straight to voice mail. A moment after leaving a message, his phone rang. Thinking it was Korsig, he answered, "*Ciao*, I just left you a message," without checking the incoming phone number.

"You left me a message?" Cardinal Perez asked, confused. "When?"

Valentinus realized it was not Korsig. "Oh I am sorry, Cardinal Perez." He recognized his Latin American accent. "Never mind."

"*Bene*, Cardinal de Marcosi. I know we were supposed to meet, but I need to postpone our meeting. Unfortunately I had something unexpected come up. I am sorry." Cardinal Perez was short in his tone. "I will, however, see you tomorrow in conclave."

"Conclave?" Valentinus was upset. "I thought we were supposed to talk before conclave!"

"*Sì*, we were, but this cannot be helped. I will see you tomorrow, and we must be discreet."

"I am a little surprised that we cannot—"

"I am sorry, but I must go." Perez closed the conversation. "I will see you tomorrow."

Valentinus did not understand what was going on but remembered Borgia's warning. "I guess I will see you tomorrow then." He spoke into the silenced phone.

Looking around the corridor, he felt there was only one thing to do. "I need to get away from this for a while." He headed back to his quarters to do the only thing that gave him peace.

"*Caro Santo Padre* in heaven, *Cara Madre*," Valentinus pleaded. "*Per favore*. Help me to see Your light of truth."

217

"Per favore, help me to see Your intentions." Lost in sorrow, he prayed for hours until the alarm on his watch buzzed. It was almost nine o'clock.

"It's time to go." He departed to meet Antonelli and Korsig.

"I am glad you could make it." Cardinal Giacomo Antonelli was waiting in his office when he saw Valentinus coming through the open door.

"*Sì, bene*, I didn't see much choice." Valentinus tried to be polite, but he did not forget Giacomo's outburst at their prior meeting with Borgia and the other special guests.

"*Per favore*, sit. I just called Korsig, but it went straight to voice mail again." Antonelli looked a little startled. "I am starting to get a little concerned."

"Let's just wait and see. I am sure he is fine." Valentinus tried to be reassuring. "Where did you say he went to visit this old friend?"

"He did not tell me." Antonelli picked up his phone and dialed Korsig for the fourth time. "But I know he has many friends in and out of the church, so he could have gone anywhere."

Ring, ring, ring...

"You have reached the voice mail of Cardinal Korsig..." Antonelli hung up the phone. "I am getting a little more than concerned."

"Giacomo, I am sure he is fine." Valentinus was starting to feel uneasy himself but wanted to assure Giacomo. It was better than thinking of other possibilities.

The next hour went by slowly. "Giacomo, I am not sure what happened to Korsig, but I think we should call the authorities. Something is not right. I doubt he would be an hour late for a meeting he called without so much as a phone call."

"I will go by his office and see if I can find out where he went and call the authorities from there." Giacomo got up and grabbed his coat. "You must retire and prepare for conclave. You look exhausted."

"Is that another way to tell me I look like hell?" Valentinus jested.

"You said it. I was only trying to be polite." Giacomo smirked.

218

"*Va bene*, I am going to my quarters, but *per favore*, before conclave starts, tell Korsig to call me. It is essential that I speak to him." Valentinus bore a serious expression, grappling with the idea of going into conclave, which was as much of a concern as Korsig's well-being.

"I will contact you with any news, or Korsig will meet you to apologize personally, I am sure." Giacomo wanted to believe in a more positive explanation of Korsig's no-show appearance.

"*Arrivederci,*" Giacomo bid farwell as they left his office together.

Chapter 12

THE MAN BEHIND THE SHROUD

Traveling to Turin by train, Sophia dressed for the inclement winter weather. She arrived outside the former Councilman Roberto Callesino's office building just before eleven. Sitting in a taxi across the street from the storied building, she waited for Ben. She knew the time and location of Ben's appointment and just hoped he would understand her intrusion.

"Oh, there he is," Sophia whispered then turned to the driver. "*Per favore*, wait for me. I will be right back." She quickly opened the door and ran across the street to stop Ben.

Ben had just gotten out of his own taxi and started walking toward the office building door.

"Stop! Wait, Ben!" Sophia fast approached him. "Ben, I was waiting for you. I am glad—"

"Sophia, what are you doing?" Ben interrupted her. He was surprised and annoyed. "You know you cannot come in here with me."

"I know. I will be waiting for you in that taxi across the street." Sophia pointed. "After your appointment with Mr. Callesino, we have business with Councilman Salvatore Moretti." She sounded proud of her improving investigative skills.

"What are you talking about?" Ben was puzzled and still annoyed.

"I will tell you after your appointment. Now go, you do not want to be late," she assured him, displaying a little sarcasm.

Ben gave her an annoyed smirk, one usually reserved for his sisters when they agitated him. He turned away, glancing back once and sighing under his breath.

Sophia went back to her taxi and waited patiently. Her driver, however, was running out of patience.

"Lady, do you see the meter?"

"*Sì*. I can assure you that I will pay you." She was confident. "But after my friend comes out, you need to take us to another location. We need to go to the Turin City Council building. It is not too far."

"I know where it is," he caustically responded.

More than twenty minutes passed.

"That's if your friend ever comes out," the driver mumbled under his breath. "This lady is crazy."

Sophia did not appreciate the comment and gave him her disgusted look. A few more minutes passed by.

"Look, there he is." Sophia could see Ben walking out the building. "*Per favore*, wait."

"Yeah, yeah, yeah. Let's just get going already." The driver sat up, ready to take action as soon as Ben was in the car.

Hastily, an annoyed Ben sat next to Sophia and closed the door. "What the hell—" he tried to say, turning toward her.

"*Per favore*, take us now." Sophia turned to the driver.

"I am already on it." The driver took off as if he was in a race.

"Where are we going?" Ben demanded as he fell back in his seat.

"You will see, and I promise then I will explain." Sophia gave him a coy expression. "And how was your trip?"

"As pleasant as it could be," Ben cynically replied. "Now, what is going on?"

"I will show you in a few minutes." Sophia wanted to surprise him. "I think I have another lead."

"A lead? Are you playing detective?"

"No more or less than you are," she replied with a smirk. "Look, just be patient for a few more minutes, and I promise I will tell you."

"Tell me now," he demanded.

"Sh. You never know who is listening." She put her fingers to her lips.

The driver looked through his rearview mirror at Ben and Sophia, being somewhat bothered.

After a fifteen-minute ride, the taxi driver announced, "Lady, you are here."

He pulled over to the corner of a street. It was a main thoroughfare in Italy's first capital city, crossing over IV Marzo Street.

"Hey, did you know this is the oldest part of the city?" Sophia quizzed Ben as the taxi stopped. "Look, there is the City Hall Square, and that building, Turin City Hall. That is where we are going."

The City Hall Building dominated the square as a historic landmark that presented visitors with its long past.

"That is where we are going?" Ben was still annoyed but appreciated Turin's rich history. "I understand that Torino is now an industrial center. On the train here, I read it is home to the Fiat and Lancia plants, which provided a boom to Turin's economy."

"*Sì*, an *importante* history lesson." Sophia handed the driver her credit card, then motioned for Ben to get out of the car. After she paid the driver, she joined Ben, standing on the busy city square street corner.

There seemed to be thousands of people rushing around the city of Turin. They saw people walking, riding in taxis, pedaling bikes, and straddling Vespas, for those braving the weather. It was busy everywhere.

Ben was pushy. "Now tell me why we are here!" He took notice of the large city square.

"Because Salvatore Moretti is the attorney who signed the adoption papers for the orphanage," Sophia went on to explain enthusiastically.

"What orphanage? What are you talking about, Sophia?" Ben raised his voice to cross-examine her.

"The orphanage where my brother was adopted from," she replied as a matter of fact.

Ben was confused. "Your brother…" He hesitated. "You have a brother?" He trotted after her, following from behind.

Sophia led Ben to the front of the Turin City Council building.

"*Sì*." She stopped, turning to him. "In deed, I may have two."

Ben almost ran into Sophia, not expecting her to stop short, but he did not expect a lot of things from Sophia. "Any girl who climbs into a dusty spider-ridden ceiling vent is a girl filled with surprises," he remembered, thinking to himself.

Inside the city hall building, the security line was long enough that Sophia had time to offer Ben an explanation.

"Wow. You could be one of triplets!" Ben shook his head.

"*Sì*, and Councilman Moretti took former Councilman Callesino's seat. He is also the attorney for the orphanage. I am taking that as an omen." Sophia was unrepentant. "We could see what he knows about Callesino's son and, if I am lucky, if he knows anything about the baby left at the orphanage."

After passing through security, they made their way to the elevator heading toward Councilman Moretti's office.

"How do you know he is in? You may not get to talk with him." Ben's doubt of Sophia's intuition was obvious.

"I called his office this morning, so I know he is in. At least that is a start." Sophia had a million thoughts circling in her head about how to get to speak to him.

The elevator opened, and Sophia hurried down a hallway leading to various official business offices as people rushed in every direction.

"Moretti may be able to answer—" Sophia was turning the corner and suddenly stopped short again. This time Ben did run right into her.

"What the hell—" Ben bounced off her. Sophia was frozen.

"*Cazzo!*" She was spooked, turning around and pushing Ben back into the hallway they had just come through. Sophia slowly took another look around the corner then gave Ben a ghostly stare.

"What is it?" Ben went around her to sneak a peek around the corner. Just as he got a glimpse, Sophia grabbed him.

"Let's go! We have to go now!" Sophia pushed him back.

"What is the matter, Sophia?" Ben was more than curious.

She sprinted toward the elevator.

"Sophia, what is the—" Ben touched her arm gently and noticed the fear in her eyes. "You can tell me," he assured her.

"I just saw my uncle Egidio talking to…He was shaking hands with Moretti." Sophia's face flushed white.

"That could mean anything." Ben was trying to reassure her.

"This is all wrong. I can feel it." Sophia was sure of herself.

"Yeah, OK." Ben snickered, dismissing her claim.

"Seriously, we need to leave right now." Sophia was not laughing.

The questions swirled in her head. "How does he know Moretti? They looked too friendly. Does Uncle Egidio know about the orphanage or the baby left there?" She was thinking of ways to approach her uncle, her very private uncle.

"Sophia, are you all right?" Ben sensed Sophia was really upset. Not answering him, she nudged him down the hallway toward the elevator they came from and frantically pushed the down buttons.

"No, no." Sophia shook her head, talking to herself. "How long did he know Moretti? Uncle Egidio was the one who helped my mama and papa adopt me. Did he also know about my brothers?"

"Sophia, what's wrong? You look like you saw a phantom." Ben was startled by how affected she was by seeing her uncle Egidio.

The elevator door opened. Sophia tried to rush in, but the people stepping off stopped her. She grew more nervous as she waited for a short bald man in an expensive suit and a middle-aged woman who was impeccably dressed to move and go around her. They took notice of Sophia's anxious behavior before walking down the same hallway in the direction of Moretti's office.

"Sophia, you need to calm yourself." Ben touched her arm. "Please, you will give yourself a heart attack," he half-joked.

She did not say a word from the elevator door to the front door that took them outside. Ben tried to respect her privacy but couldn't.

"What do you think your uncle was doing with Moretti?" He was confused.

"I don't know." She desperately tried to put the pieces of the puzzle together in her head. "But I will find out!" Her determination was obvious.

Standing on the corner waving for a taxi, Ben noticed Sophia's inner strength was being revealed, even if she was at the moment unsure of herself.

As a taxi pulled over, Sophia grabbed the door and rushed in.

"*Per favore*, take us to the Turin Cathedral," she instructed the driver.

Ben just barely got seated when the taxi took off.

"The cathedral? Why the cathedral?" Ben was surprised by her request.

"I told you already. My friend Eme told me we have to go there to get answers to our questions," she responded flatly.

"Oh yeah, your friend Eme." He downplayed it, not wanting to disrespect the deceased.

"What did Callesino say to you?" Her sharpness returned, and she gave Ben an intent stare.

"As a friend of Mrs. Potter, he mentioned that his reelection bid was in trouble only after his mum backed out of a real estate deal. His mother owns property in Apulia and changed her mind, not wanting to sell her family property to a solar company. Callesino had the council's support despite his son's ordeal regarding the deceased American student. However, after his mother refused to sell her property in Apulia to this Solar Star Development Corporation, things went from bad to worse in a hurry." Ben adjusted his position. "It seems there was a power struggle, and he lost. At least that is what he said."

"Apulia?" Sophia mouthed. "What in southern Italy could provoke a power struggle here in Torino?"

"He told me that he could not discuss the details due to a pending investigation." Ben turned to face Sophia and whispered, "It seems that the Cosa Nostra may be involved, and he wants to protect his family."

Sophia listened while taking in the familiar sights she remembered as a child, when she would visit the cathedral with her family.

"That is interesting indeed." She nodded.

"Hey, didn't you have to work today?" Ben just remembered.

"*Sì*, I called in sick. I acted sick when I last saw Carmine, so he should be fine." Her expression changed. "Although when I called in sick, I spoke to him directly, and he didn't sound like himself."

"Wow, do you know that your eyes change color with your expression?" He was flabbergasted. "Hey, you are like a live mood ring. My sisters loved them when they were young." He laughed.

Sophia's facial movement was twisted. Ben's tone changed to serious as he recognized his friend's concern.

"And so…How was talking to Carmine?" he prompted her.

"Honestly, it was painful," she confided in him. "It is difficult to be in the same room with him, pretending everything is fine. Talking to him on the phone was not any easier." Sophia got herself together as they neared the cathedral. "You know, I have noticed that he seems nicer to me. I don't know if he knows that I know he tried to hurt me or…" She turned to Ben. "I don't know. He just seems a little sweeter, *è pazzesco*!"

The taxi arrived at the Piazza San Giovanni, where the Cathedral of Turin attracted millions of tourists, just as it started to rain.

"Brr... This rain is making my bones freeze." Getting out of the taxi, she wrapped her coat tightly around her. "It's really miserable out."

Ben paid the driver and joined her on the cold sidewalk in front of the cathedral. "Yes dammit! It is cold!"

He pulled his coat tight, clasping the buttons, as he looked up at the massive buildings before them.

The piazza was large, having a series of buildings that were set back in the square, with the central building's many stone steps leading up to the main door entrance. The faded white stone exposed the cathedral's age. Three tall wooden doors were centered at the front of the main building, with the largest door having a huge oval-shaped sculpture above it.

"That reminds me of the scales of justice in its design. It must be the main entrance." Ben pointed to Sophia.

"Impressive, isn't it?" Sophia unequivocally remarked.

"It's huge." Ben's breath was visible in the cold air.

"It was built in 1490." Sophia hurried toward the entrance, with Ben following her every step. She turned halfway and pointed to an attached tall bell-towerlike building. "And that part of the building over there is known as the Campanile. It was built even earlier."

"It is pretty amazing, isn't it?" She hurried to the front door entrance.

Ben glanced at the building Sophia pointed to, but it was too cold for an outside tour.

"Ah, yeah." He nodded in agreement with her anyway.

They reached inside the nave of the cathedral, along with other tourists who gazed upon its magnificent beauty. Old wooden pews lined up on both sides of a marble floor aisle that led up to the altar, which seemed a great distance from where they stood.

Stained-glass windows on each side of the cathedral were intricate in their details. While the clouds hid the sun's reflection, some light still shone through the glass, making prisms of yellows, reds, greens, and gold illuminate all around the cathedral.

"There used to be three churches a long time ago. They were dedicated to the Holy Savior, Saint Mary of Dompno and the main building, of the three, was for Saint John the Baptist, Jesus's cousin. Their history is long, and after they were demolished, they were rebuilt." Sophia could see Ben's awe as she brushed the rain from her coat.

"They even had an assassination take place in here. The Duke of Torino was killed by some crazy church follower. That's interesting, don't you think?" She led Ben to the side aisle, continuing her monologue.

"What are you? A tour guide?" Ben was intrigued.

Sophia giggled. It was her first sign of released tension. "No, for my religious studies class I did a report on the cathedral when I was in high school. And my family would come here for mass when we visited my cousins in Torino." She pointed. "Look there, behind the altar. Do you see that paneled painting? It replicates the original viewing on the Cappella della Sacra Sindone with the Altar of Bertola."

"The what?" Ben looked confused at what he was supposed to be seeing.

"Cappella della Sacra Sindone. You might know it as the Chapel of the Holy Shroud. Unfortunately, it was seriously damaged during a fire back in the late 1990s." She sighed.

"But you can still see the Holy Shroud of Jesus Christ, at least when it is displayed...Ha, maybe I do sound like a tour guide." She laughed quietly.

"Boy, you Christians spare no expense, huh?" Ben could see the altar and the surrounding extravagant décor.

Sophia shrugged her shoulders and continued walking.

"Hey, why are we here anyway?" He realized he was not on a tour. "What is so important about this church?"

"We are looking for something." Sophia's answer was short as she wandered around the right side of the cathedral. Going around the large, white marble pillars that held up the arched ceilings, she thought of Eme's words about finding answers. She stopped in front of the cathedral organ near the right transept, and gazed across the cathedral to the left transept, where she could see the Chapel of the Holy Shroud in the distance.

"You will find the answers to your questions," she repeated in her mind over and over. "Eme, *per favore*, show me."

"What are you looking for?" Ben asked again while looking up at the stained-glass art above his head.

"I am not sure." Sophia was starting to doubt herself.

"*You* are *not* sure!" Ben raised his voice. "I don't understand."

"Sh, keep your voice down." She turned around, putting her forefinger to her lips. "I will know it when I see it."

Sophia faced forward and could see a marvelous stained-glass picture of the Blessed Mother holding an infant Jesus. Closing her eyes for a moment, she prayed, "*Per favore, Santa Madre* and Eme, You said you would help me. *Per favore*, tell me that I am not going crazy."

"I think it is a little bit too late for that!" Ben quipped.

Sophia didn't realize that she spoke her words out loud. Now embarrassed, she walked away, going toward the front of the altar to cross over the Chapel of the Holy Shroud. Finding herself at the Cappella della Sacra Sindone, she strolled along, stepping on the large, white, circled marble tiles with smaller inlaid black squared marble tiles that echoed each of her high-heeled, thumping footsteps.

She followed her instincts as they went to the chapel.

"Sophia, where are we going?" Ben followed her, growing more annoyed at what seemed to be a waste of time, even while he admired the beauty that surrounded him.

"This is the Chapel of the Holy Shroud," Sophia explained to Ben as he followed her.

"It is beautiful." Ben said the only words he could think of.

"*Sì*," she barely acknowledged him, looking around for a seat in a pew directly in front of the altar. In the second row she noticed an old couple sitting at the far end. Sophia scooted in with Ben beside her.

The altar was small in comparison to the altar in the main part of the cathedral. It was set behind two half-size marble balustrades that were fashioned with a red velvet rope between them. In the middle, in front of the rope, a beautiful, dark, wooden prie-dieu with artistic detail allowed visitors to kneel and pray to the shroud of Jesus's face hanging behind a glass window above the altar.

Sophia stared at the shroud. Jesus's face captivated her. His eyes were closed as if he were sleeping. The outline of his hair, nose, beard, and mustache were also visible as well as what appeared to be wounds on his forehead. Staring at it, Sophia could see something on the top of his head almost resembling two thin lightning rods shooting in or out of his head. She stared at the motionless picture, being transformed into another time.

"Sophia, what are we doing?" Ben elbowed her in her side.

"Sh." The agitated old lady at the end of the pew shushed Ben.

"Ben, *per favore*, just give me a few minutes," Sophia pleaded after being disturbed from her trance. "*Per favore*, just a few minutes!"

"Fine, just a few minutes." Relenting, he could see desperation in her eyes. He sat back in the pew and started to look around. Some visitors sat in front and to the left side of them, praying rosaries, while others quietly whispered to one another in their foreign tongues.

"I wonder what they are thinking." Ben liked to people watch.

A middle-aged woman stood in front of the prayer candles with her hands clasped. Her floor-length black skirt complemented her light blue-jean jacket and white tank top. She wore a long flowered scarf on top of her head that also covered her shoulders.

The man standing next to her lit his candle and sealed it with the sign of the cross, then blew a kiss to the statue of the Virgin Mary holding a baby Jesus. The woman followed his lead, lighting her own candle, and they walked off together.

"There is just something magical about this place." Sophia spoke quietly. "What am I missing?"

Ben looked at Sophia. He felt sorry for her. "At least I knew my father. Even if I lost him, I knew him. And I have my mother and sisters. Poor Sophia doesn't know any of her biological family."

Sophia closed her eyes and said a prayer again. "*Per favore*, help me." Those were the only words she could think of. Starting to feel foolish about dragging Ben on a wild-goose chase, she opened her eyes.

"*Bene*, let's go." She unclasped her hands quickly as if giving up. "I don't know what I—"

Just as the words left her mouth, she saw the woman sitting at the end of their pew with a church bulletin. She tilted her head as if confused.

"Sophia, what is the matter?" Ben tried to show some patience.

"I…" She stood up. "I need a bulletin."

"A what?" Ben followed her down the cathedral aisle.

"A bulletin. You know, like a church newsletter." Sophia walked toward the front entrance. Bookshelves stood on both sides of the doorway, and on top of each bookshelf laid a few cathedral bulletins.

"This one is for me." She quickly picked one up in her hands and walked out of the cathedral. She scanned through it as she walked, until the rain started to wet the paper.

"Let's get a taxi to the train station, shall we?" Sophia folded the bulletin and put it in her pocket.

"Sophia, did you get what you were looking for?" Ben followed her again.

"I hope so." She tried to sound confident and signaled for a taxi. Wincing from the cold, she could see her breath. "*Dio mio*, it is cold!"

"And wet," frustrated Ben agreed.

On her first try, a taxi came to their aide. "What luck!" she happily acknowledged as she and Ben climbed in.

"*Per favore*, take us to the Porta Nouva railway station," she directed the driver.

Getting somewhat settled for their short journey to the railway station, Sophia remembered to ask Ben, "By the way, when you spoke to Callesino and asked him about his family not wanting to sell their property in Auplia, did he mention who he spoke to in the Solar Star Company?"

Ben thought about it for a moment. "I should not be telling you this, but..." He hesitated but somehow he felt compelled, "he spoke to a man from Rome, a Joseph Grillo. Why do you ask?"

"When I speak to my uncle Egidio, I want to know if he knows this person." Sophia lowered her voice in response, "in his former position he has come to know many important people who know people, if you know what I mean." She looked out the window looking at the approaching signs for their intended stop.

Ben nodded, "I hope it stops raining soon, it just makes everything more miserable."

"This is fine... let us out here," Sophia motioned to the driver.

Once left on the corner, they ran into the main entrance to buy their tickets back home.

"Ohhh, there's a train leaving in five minutes," Ben noticed in a hurry. "We can make a run for it or wait another hour."

"Let's run!" Sophia shouted. "It's this way." She pointed over Ben's right shoulder.

"OK, last one there buys the first round!" Ben was sure of himself as he darted out in front of Sophia.

"*Sì, bene.*" She took off running. "*Scusami, scusami,*" she apologized to the people she was bumping into.

Ben ran faster. His lanky legs made him look like an oversized school boy running in an expensive business suit.

Sophia looked at her surroundings and saw her opportunity. She ran past a marble column and then in front of a man briskly walking toward his train.

Ben looked behind him and didn't see her. He snapped his head back when he bumped into a woman holding her child in her arms.

"Oh my, I…I am," he stammered almost knocking them all to the floor, "I am so sorry."

The woman stood, holding Ben so she would not fall back. "You better watch where you are going!" she protested in a high-pitched yell.

"Yes, I will! I am sorry, please excuse me," he gushed and was again off like a shot.

He arrived at the train, looking around for Sophia. "Where is—"

"Ben, over here," Sophia announced as she waved her arm to summon him into the train, where she stood a winner.

As Ben stepped onto the train, the doors shut behind him.

"Oh, and I got us seats too." She was proud of herself.

Ben jolted as the train took off and fell into the seat beside Sophia.

"All right, you won this time, but—"

"*Sì*, I am a winner, so you will buy the first round!" she cracked, taking the crumpled bulletin from her pocket.

A picture of the cathedral adorned the cover. Mass schedules were listed below the picture. Turning it over, she could see the many advertisements from cathedral sponsors. It had only about a dozen pages. Sophia thumbed through it, hoping to see something, anything that would help her to find answers.

Ben moved toward Sophia as if he was going to kiss her. "What are you doing?" Sophia quickly shifted in her seat.

"What?" He moved back into his seat, taking his own bulletin from his back pocket. "I wanted to see what it looks like." He sat back, thumbing through his own.

The first few pages listed parish news, program schedules, and Shroud Museum updates. A letter from the archbishop of Turin was published on the inside cover reminding visitors to respect the cathedral and its property, like a father reprimanding his children.

Sophia read the article. "It's such a shame that people have to be told to respect—" Sophia stopped short, then screeched, "*Dio mio!*"

"What is it?" Alarmed, Ben looked up, then down at his bulletin. Sophia was frozen, focusing on one page. Ben looked down to see if they were on the same page.

"There are announcements of upcoming programs within the parish and an advertisement of an upcoming lecture. What is the big deal? What is it, Sophia?" Ben questioned her again, this time more forcefully to bring her back to reality. "Sophia?"

She seemed distant. Sophia's mind raced back until she was sitting at her laptop in her flat. Remembering the DVD from Dennis, her mind processed, reviewing it in slow motion.

A man on the steps of the orphanage was bending down and placing a cardboard box in front of the door. Her finger hit the button to make him pick up the box, then click…He put it down. Over and over she replayed the DVD, studying the profile of a man in a black hat and coat.

"Sophia, what is it?" Ben nudged her.

"*Santa schifezza,*" Sophia murmured under her breath.

"What, what is holy crap?" Ben was desperate to be in the loop.

Sophia reached into her purse and pulled out a picture of the same man on the DVD. She held it in front of her, then looking at the bulletin. Back and forth, her eyes studied the man in the lecture advertisement and the picture in her hand.

"Sophia, for *Parameshvar's* sake." Ben grew frustrated. "What—"

"Look at this picture and look at the man in the bulletin." She gave the picture to Ben, and he compared it to the bulletin.

"Doesn't that look like the same man?" Sophia was astonished, excitedly pointing to the picture in the bulletin.

Ben looked at one, then the other. "I don't know." He shrugged his shoulders. He read the advertisement. "It says there is a lecture at the Polytechnic University here in Turin next week."

Ben read the lecture title out loud. "'Renew Your Faith through History.' Hmm, that sounds interes—"

"Look at the picture again!" Sophia demanded. "He has the same profile. It's the same man! I just know it!"

"This man, this Cardinal Valentinus de Marcosi, have you ever heard of him?" Ben was curious.

"No, never." Sophia slouched back into her chair.

She noticed the train moved so fast, passing farms, buildings, and homes. It was just a blur.

"Its kind of like my life, it is all a blur but I just know it is the same man," she said, refocusing on the bulletin picture again. She looked at Ben. "I can feel it."

"Yeah, OK, I wish I could share your confidence, but I can't say that it is him for sure." Ben was trying to be supportive but also realistic. "This picture is grainy at best. I am sorr—"

"Don't apologize, Ben. I am going to the lecture and will find out for myself."

"Have you ever been to this Polytechnic University in the Castello del Valentino? Do you know where that is?" Ben's tone was sincere and concerned.

"*Sì*, it's in the northwest part of Torino. I have been to the Parco del Valentino, where the castle is, when I was younger. Do you want to go with me?" Sophia smiled, hoping he might consider it.

"I am not sure I can." Ben did not want to give false hope.

"Listen, I also have this man on a DVD video." She stressed her point. "The video shows him standing in front of one orphanage dropping off a cardboard box. The picture is taken from when he dropped off a different box at another orphanage." Sophia leaned over in Ben's face. "I was a baby in one of those boxes!"

Sophia's eyes changed to a dramatic dark green, a shade Ben has not seen before.

"Wow." Ben shook his head. "I can't believe—"

"You better believe it!" Sophia slouched down as she continued to interrupt Ben, taking back the picture from his hand. "Do you see they both have a thin face, long sideburns, and high cheekbones?" She was trying hard to convince Ben.

"Sophia." Ben wanted to believe her, but his lawyer instincts would not allow it. "Look, a lot of men have thin faces, sideburns, high cheekbones, and wear black hats." He gently shook his head. "But you really cannot tell from this picture. I am sorry. I am afraid your imagination is getting the best of you."

The bulletin advertisement measured only three by five inches. A small profile picture of Cardinal Valentinus de Marcosi was in the corner as he faced inward toward the words that announced his lecture.

"Cardinal?" Sophia studied the man's face and the article for any clues. "Maybe you are right. He is a cardinal, but his face is similar. Can you at least grant me that?" With sarcasm in her tone, she looked up at Ben for any encouragement.

"All right, they are similar." Ben took back the picture from Sophia's hand. "They both have a long nose, and it seems the chap in the photo has a long neck like your cardinal. But I do not see anything else."

"OK, I can live with that." Sophia put the bulletin in her pocket along with the photo Ben returned to her. She sat back and allowed her mind to drift as the train passed through various towns, admiring open green lands and homes on their way home to Trastevere.

Ben gave her some time in her thoughts before nudging her. "Sophia, I can only go so far with you. I am getting off at the next stop."

"Ben, why?" Sophia knew the answer but didn't want to accept it.

"It's better this way. Until we know who went through my hotel room, I don't want you to be at risk for me." Ben patted her on her knee.

Sophia looked at the window again, almost in a trance. "You know this Cardinal de Marcosi will probably be in conclave tomorrow."

"Yes, I would imagine he would be," Ben decidedly agreed.

"Ben, are you going to be all right? It is scary thinking someone is following you." Sophia sounded concerned for Ben's safety.

"The hotel trashing certainly unnerved me, but I have good people taking care of me, so don't worry about me. Just don't you be following anyone, and call me after you speak with your uncle."

"Ha, now you sound like Dennis," Sophia joked.

"Well, I mean it." Ben smirked, not really kidding.

"You know, Ben"—Sophia's eyes changed to a soft green—"We have not known each other a long time, but I feel like I have known you for years. Isn't that strange?"

"No, I don't think it's strange." Ben's tone softened. "I feel that way also."

235

Then he thought for a moment, and the big protective brother came out. "Which is why you need to be careful too!"

"*Sì*, I will," she assured him. "Should I use the mobile you gave me to contact you with an update about my uncle and Moretti?"

"Yes. I will let you know when you cannot." He smiled as he got ready to leave.

"All this spy stuff…I don't know whether to be excited or nervous." Sophia gave him a half smile.

"You should be cautious. That is all," he assured her just as the train stopped. Ben stood. "All right, this is where I get off. Just be careful. I will contact you by Wednesday, OK?"

Sophia nodded. "*Sì, bene*. You be safe too."

Ben smiled and turned to walk away. Once on the platform, he watched Sophia through the window as the train pulled away.

Sophia waved to Ben, then looked around the train carriage and noticed the people around her for the first time.

Travelers with suitcases sat a row in front of her. A small family with a mom, dad, and two toddler children sat across from her, while business professionals were scattered about, filling up the train only halfway.

Some people got on and some got off as the train pulled into other stations heading toward her stop. When she was not people watching, she just stared out the window.

"These are strange days. I don't understand what is happening." Sophia closed her eyes. "These strange happenings are worse than before. Eme, *per favore*, help me." She pleaded for some comfort.

Taking out the bulletin and the photo again, she stared at each one. "I just know it is the same person!" The train jolted to a stop that made Sophia look up.

"Home, let's go home, chaps, shall we?" Sophia joked to the picture and the bulletin as she pulled herself together and left the train.

The day wore Sophia to the bone. After a short taxi ride, she was finally at her door.

"*Grazie a Dio per il vino*." She was tired and hungry. "The first order of business is to open a bottle of Cabernet."

236

"I am glad I buy *vino* by the case. It comes in handy on days like this, especially when I need a glass or two or three."

After her first sip, she rummaged through her cupboards and refrigerator, throwing a leftover chicken cutlet on bread for a sandwich. She grabbed her wine and her dinner, then retreating to her living room to relax, she sighed in relief.

She sat on the chair next to the sofa, which her new painting rested on. Chewing her chicken sandwich, she gulped her wine in between each bite, all the while staring at her expensively elaborate work of art.

"I cannot believe the money I paid for you to come home with me." She chuckled. "This new artist, Makaria, can really paint. Usually I wouldn't pay that kind of money for a picture, but there is something about you, isn't there?"

Staring at the painting in between bites and sips of wine, she imagined the colors swirling around the stars.

"Swirling colors, it is almost like the picture is underwater." As her focus shifted, the stars and swirls of colors got bigger, then smaller, with each swirling wave.

"It's like a picture is on top of a picture." Sophia was overtired and dazed by the wine. She yawned. "Maybe I am looking at you too hard. Maybe tomorrow you will want to talk to me," she teased herself, then yawned again.

"It's time. I have to get some rest." She stood up, covering her mouth with her right hand while stretching. Sophia got ready for bed, putting on comfy PJ's, then followed her predictable routine of brushing her teeth, washing her face, and taking the last pee before she hit the sack.

"Maybe lighting this candle will help me sleep better," she told herself, placing it in a safe manner on the side table. Sitting on the bed, she started to get under the covers as she looked up at the bedpost.

"Hmm." Sophia reached for the rosaries that hung from the bedpost. "Maybe I…"

She held them in her hand and stared at them for a moment, then played with the bracelet on her wrist that Mariam had given her.

The candlelight caught the shining beads, making beautiful colorful prisms form around her.

"If I could find my family, *mio Dio…*" She closed her eyes and prayed.

Ring, ring, ring…

She reached for her phone, looking at the number calling her. Sophia realized the weekend had gone by so fast, she had not personally spoken to her parents as she usually did.

"*Ciao*, Mama, I am so sorry I could not join you for supper this weekend. I did leave a message. I hope you got it."

"*Ciao, amore mio. Sì*, we did, but we have not heard back from you, and we were worried." Mama's concern had the right touch to make Sophia feel guilty.

"I know, Mama. I am sorry." Sophia pressed on. "I will see you this upcoming weekend for Sunday dinner, and I will call you during the week to see how you are doing." She tried to make up for her neglect.

"That would be wonderful. I will tell your papa. He worries so about you." Mama gave one last guilt dig.

Sophia smiled, having played this game many times before. "I know, Mama, I know. Anyway, how was your weekend? What did you do?"

"Your papa is working on the kitchen. He is going to paint it. Just like I have wanted for the past three years, and now finally he is going to finish it." Mama's voice sounded excited. "Don't you think it needed it?"

"*Sì*, I think so, Mama," Sophia agreed, remembering the faded, gold-colored walls.

"I understand you saw Rosey this past Saturday. She told Aunt Rose you had a *buon tempo*." Mama was fishing for more gossip.

"*Sì*, we did have a good time." Sophia cringed, thinking about what Rosey could have told them about their girls night out.

"Did you meet anyone special? Rosey said you met a young man," Mama prodded.

"*Sì*, he is American, so don't worry, Mama," she quipped.

Sophia acknowledged her parents' wishes for her to settle down with a nice Italian boy.

"*Sì*, maybe next time. *Bene*, I am *contento* that you went out at least." Mama was readying herself for the next line.

"*Sì*, Mama." Sophia cut her mama short. "*Sì*, maybe I will go out with Rosey again."

"That sounds good," Mama agreed.

They made small talk before Sophia let out a big, loud yawn.

"*Va bene*, my little Flaming Star, twinkle in the sky at night, then rise up with the sun in the morning light, and forever…you shall shine so bright." Mama's voice was comforting. "*Dormi bene amore mio, ti vogliamo bene.*"

"*Sì*, Mama, you sleep well too, and *per favore*, tell Papa I am thinking of him." Sophia remembered all the nights when Mama would tuck her in bed and kiss her on the forehead while saying those very words.

As they ended the call, Sophia paused. "*Bene*, I liked to hear her voice." A warm feeling filled her heart.

"I love you, Mama, and you will always be my Mama." Lying down, she sighed.

Still having the rosaries in her hand, she prayed, "Is it wrong that I want to find my blood family?" She yearned.

A grateful feeling overcame her. Memories of her mama and papa invaded her mind. She prayed silently.

"See, Eme, I remembered." Sophia smiled to herself.

As she prayed, her mind drifted. She contemplated going back to work and taking in the events of the weekend. Being distracted, she could see the lineal outline of the bulletin she had placed on the table near her sofa.

"Now if you could help me find my brothers." She paused. "And let me understand what Carmine is mixed up in. Amen!"

"Breathe deep, in…then out," she repeated to herself over and over. Sophia remembered Mariam's angel cards, Raphael, in particular. "*Breathe.*" Concentrating, she could feel each breath leave her body and then replenish with fresh air and new energy.

Despite all the confusing and colliding thoughts that penetrated the crevasses of her brain, she fell asleep quickly. Exhaustion provided her a natural sleep aide.

In the middle of the night, rolling from one side to another, her nose smelled a familiar odor. A burning whiff caused Sophia's nose to twitch. She rubbed her nose as if a feather had touched her nostril.

The fervent aroma got stronger. She twitched her nose again.

"Fire?" her sleepy brain starts to awaken. She rolled over. "*Fire*!" Sophia realized what her mind had just said.

Springing upright, she opened her eyes wide, looking around. "The living room! *Dio mio*! It is on *fire*!"

She tried to stand, but her legs would not move. The flames were spreading quickly. The sofa was burning. Her new painting was burning. The table leg broke, and the bulletin slid off into the fire.

Screaming at the top of her lungs, she desperately tried to get up. The red, the yellow, the orange glow was intensifying.

"HEEEELLLPPP!" she screamed louder.

Behind her wall divider, she could see a shadow of movement. "*Dio mio, per favore*, help me!" she desperately called out.

Two arms were stretched out holding an empty wastebin. Then appeared the body to which they were attached.

"Carmine!" Sophia's eyes bulged. "*Santa Marada*! Carmine!"

Sophia could not do anything as she watched Carmine throw the empty wastebin into the flames that now surrounded him. In amazement, he did not scream.

Even though she had been gazing into his eyes for a second, it felt like years had gone by. She was not afraid for herself any longer.

Carmine did not look afraid either. The expression on his face was impassive, drawing a blank stare. His eyes were focused on his fate. The flames started to melt his skin, his hair, and then eventually they engulfed his body. But still he did not scream out.

"Carmine! No! Carmine!" Realizing his fate, Sophia cried out to him.

Her right leg started to move. She frantically threw her body around, trying to stand up.

"Carmine, no! Don't!" The flames grew higher as her cries to Carmine got louder, watching him wither into the flames.

Hearing her own voice, she startled herself. Her body was violently tossing and turning.

"Carmine!" she cried out again. "Carmine!" As the words left her mouth, she opened her eyes.

Her head was still shaking from left to right and back again, but she could now see she was in her flat.

"*Dio mio*, it was a dream!" She sighed heavily.

She put her hand over her forehead. "*Dio mio*, *per favore*, don't let me dream like that again."

Sitting up in her bed, she could see the candle had gone out, and nothing was really burnt. The flat was still, almost eerie. The silence was deafening.

The light from outside her window gave her a glimpse in the otherwise darkened flat. Looking down at the floor next to her bed, she could see a faint sparkle from her rosaries, which had fallen next to her slippers. She picked them up and held them close to her chest.

"*Dio mio*, it was only a dream." Sophia murmured a small prayer. "*Per favore*, I know Carmine tried to hurt me, but if you could watch over him, you might be able to save his soul."

The thought of forgiving Carmine was foreign to her, yet the words came out of her mouth.

"And if you could help me deal with him today, I would greatly appreciate it." Sophia made one last request.

She tried to go back to sleep, but she was too startled. Her nemesis, restlessness, was back.

"I might as well go in early." She got up and got herself ready for work.

"*Per favore*, you promised you would help me." Sophia bargained with Eme as she walked back into her lab and opened the door. The room was dark. Carmine was not in yet.

"Hmm, I cannot believe I beat him here." Sophia talked to herself while turning on the lights and readying her computer.

"I guess even the lab rat can be late." She shrugged.

The usual pile of case files had been left for her, so there was no reason for alarm. She picked up her files and began her normal procedures.

One folder, testing materials and jotting down her notes, turned into two folders, then three. The hours trickled by. Before she realized it, three hours had gone by and still no Carmine. Not even a word.

"That's strange, not even a phone call," Sophia thought.

Her legs were beginning to cramp. "Let me do my stretches." She got up and went into her first yoga position, the warrior one pose, and then into her downward-facing dog.

Just as she was looking under herself, seeing the computers upside down, the door flew open. It startled Sophia. Stumbling to her feet, she could see it was Mr. Lorino, who was shocked to see Sophia's position.

"Oh my…I am sorry. I try to stretch. It helps me…"

She could see that Mr. Lorino was not amused. His facial expression bore his grief and concern.

"Mr. Lorino, is everything…" Sophia tried to ask.

He looked around the room and walked over to Carmine's desk. His head bowed. "He is dead."

"*Che cosa*?" In shock, Sophia didn't understand him.

"Carmine." Mr. Lorino looked back at Sophia with teary eyes. "I am sorry to say that Carmine is dead. He was killed in a house fire."

"*Santo Merda*! I mean, *Dio mio*." Sophia knees buckled.

Mr. Lorino ran toward her and grabbed her as she fell.

"No…I just can't believe it! No, no." Her dream raced through Sophia's mind.

"Sophia, *per favore*, sit down." Helping her to her chair, Mr. Lorino comforted her.

"I can't believe it." Those were the only words Sophia could say over and over as she shook her head. She hardly realized Mr. Lorino had called her by her first name.

"Do you need some water? Can I get you anything?" Mr. Lorino was sincere and concerned.

"No, no, *bene*. I just…" Sophia could only see her dream. It was so clear. "He did not scream."

"*Che cosa?*" Mr. Lorino was surprised by Sophia's comment.

She looked at him with a blank stare. "How, I mean, how did it happen?" She just had to know.

"The fire marshals and *polizia* are still investigating, so I do not have details. I am sorry." He gave her a tissue from Carmine's desk.

Mixed emotions filled her head and her heart. She could not feel tears, but she was still saddened. She was angry but felt sorry for him.

"I…I will understand if you need time to collect yourself." Mr. Lorino bumbled his Mr. Nice Guy sincerity. It felt awkward to him.

Sophia sat silent for a moment.

A distant memory came to her, when she was talking with her mama about becoming frightened by a premonition she had when her grandfather passed on. Her mama calmed her fears. "Sophia, don't be afraid when the angels speak to you. They are messengers of God, and they will never put you in danger."

"I know, Mama, but the dream was so scary. Grandpapa was in so much pain, and I could not help him," Sophia cried, sitting on her mama's knee.

Mama patted her chest over her heart gently. "Oh, my little one, you must trust in God. He loves you. He gives you messages he knows you can understand. God gave you special gifts, and he will be there to help you use them, I promise." Her mama was always trying to comfort her when she had disturbing dreams or visions.

Sophia's mother, not being her biological mother, could not relate to some of the mystical happenings that occurred in Sophia's childhood, so they largely tried not to make too much of her "gifts," as her mother referred to them.

"Sophia, are you all right? If you need…" Mr. Lorino raised his voice to get her attention.

"No, no. *Sto bene*." Sophia snapped back in the moment. "I am just stunned and saddened. I just can't believe it."

She looked over at Carmine's empty chair. In a low, sad tone, she said, "I just need a moment."

Mr. Lorino was uncomfortable when dealing with female employee issues. "Ah, *bene*. Well, if you need to go home, just let me know."

He looked at the case files she was working on and added, "And from now on, *per favore*, report directly to me. *Va bene?*"

"*Sì, sì*, of course." She was trying to process the dream and Carmine's fate.

"Sophia, did you hear me?" Mr. Lorino asked politely.

"*Sì, sì*." Sophia looked up at Mr. Lorino. "*Sì*, I did hear you. I will report to you after I finish these files."

"If you need time…" He tried to be gentle but firm. "Just let me know when you are finished."

"*Sì*, I will." Like a machine, she replied, "I will report to you."

"If you need more time," he added once more.

"No, *va tutto bene*, I only have these two files to finish, and then I will give you the reports." She began coming back to her senses.

"*Va bene*, I will see you shortly." Mr. Lorino nodded and turned to walk out of the room, but not before standing at Carmine's desk for a few seconds.

As the door shut, she glanced over at Carmine's desk. A deep chill crept up her spine.

Now that she was all alone, she could feel how cold and lonely the lab room really was. It was devoid of any human emotions.

Gazing around the room, she could not sit there any longer. "I need a break." She left the lab to refresh herself in the ladies room.

After a while, she walked back to her lab through the maze of white hallways.

"The corridors feel like they are closing in on me again." The sound of her footsteps echoed until she stopped at her door. Tilting her head up, she saw the ceiling and the vents.

"Oh, Carmine," she thought, remembering how he had tricked her and had given her the date rape drug. "Why?"

Opening the lab door turned her stomach. She could feel the emptiness. She could sense everything was wrong.

"Maybe…" she flipped the light switch off, then on. "Maybe I can change the energy." Realizing it was a silly thing to do, she walked in. Walking past his desk, she felt a breeze pass through her.

"Brr..." She stopped in her steps and turned around. Out of the corner of her eye, she thought she saw Carmine sitting at his desk.

"*Santa schifezza.*" Scared, she jumped back. Sophia turned her head again, but there was nothing there.

"Let me finish these files and go home. I need some *vino.*" Sophia bartered with herself.

She sat down in her chair and took a deep breath. "Breathe in…then out." Thinking of the Raphael angel card, she repeated the word *breathe* over and over in her mind until she felt some relief.

Then a thought crossed her mind. "I should call Ben." Sophia went into her purse to retrieve the mobile phone Ben had given her.

Ring, ring, ring, ring.

"That's funny, no answer." Her stomached turned again. "*Dio,* I hope he is all right." She tried calling again, with no better results.

With nothing more she could do, she put the phone away and decided to try him a little later.

"*Bene,* you can do this!" She looked at the two remaining case files and took a deep breath as she opened the first one.

It was a slow process, working through the first case file and the information needing to be tested then updating her notes.

Getting to the pointed results was more difficult than she imagined. Her brain zoned in and out of the events over the last few weeks. She found it difficult to concentrate.

Waiting for the test results gave her more time to think. "And how do I approach Uncle Egidio to find his connection to Moretti?"

"*Per favore,* just let me get through these files," she pleaded with God. "Eme, where are you? I need you now."

The time dragged on, but finally she only had the last case file to finish.

"Whoa, that last one took forever. Only one more to go."

"Hopefully this one will go faster." She opened the folder. "*Che cosa?*"

Inside the folder lay a white piece of paper, a letter folded in three as if it were ready to be placed inside an envelope.

"*Che diavolo...*" Sophia picked it up and unfolded the paper. "*Merda!*" She was amazed, immediately recognizing Carmine's handwriting.

"Carmine, what did you do?" she called out into the empty room. Her hands began to shake as she read it to herself.

> Sophia,
> If you are reading this, then I am dead.

She gasped in disbelief. "*Dio mio...*"

> I believe you know I was the one who put the GHB in your *caffè*. For that and many other things, I am truly sorry. *Per favore*, know that I NEVER meant to hurt you.

Sophia's eyes started to get teary.

> I would never have done something so dastardly, but I was being blackmailed. It was not only about me, which I could have dealt with, but this monster was hurting the love of my life, and I could not stop it any other way.

"*Merda!* Carmine. You had a love life?" Sophia was shocked.

> Unfortunately, the monster made us do things, and my love was recently arrested. Our once nice, quiet life was destroyed. There is no other way out. I know you, and others, considered me to be a lab rat, but...

"*Sì*, I did." Sophia chuckled and gently nodded, wiping a tear from her eye.

> On the contrary, I did have a life, and it was wonderful. It does not matter that I tell you this now. You will find out soon enough. My love, Cardinal Meade Rosotti, is not evil. He was forced into this Vatican banking scandal, and he was forced to go to Switzerland. He did not know about the laundering until it was too late. So you know the truth. He did not want me to get hurt, and the monster promised to kill me if my love did not submit to the demands placed upon him. It was not his fault, and I believe someone needs to know that.

"This is surreal." Sophia sat back in her chair, trying to take in the words in his note.

> The devil works in mysterious ways, don't you think? I know the devil works in the Solar Star Development Corp. I know we will pay for our sins. I fully expect to, but before I left, I needed to ask for your forgiveness. I hope you will find it in your heart to give me this last request.

Sophia's heart sank, bowing her head. "*Sì*, Carmine. *Dio mio*!"

> You have always been nice to me, and I wanted you to know I appreciated that. *Grazie*, Carmine.

Sophia stared at the letter. Turning it over, she could see words on the back.

> And check with James Scala, the security camera man.

"The camera man!" Sophia's eyes grew wide.

247

She thought of Ben's comment: "Carmine would have needed help with the camera not recording him while leaving the lab after Sophia was poisoned."

"*Santo Merda*, this is crazy." Sophia memorized Carmine's confession. "What if he was murdered?" She was frozen in fear.

The notion that Carmine could have been murdered or even committed suicide made her sick. She could feel the color draining from her face as she broke out in a cold sweat.

"Breathe, Sophia, breathe." The voice in her head was trying to calm her, but the emotions were too much. Sophia leaned over the wastebin and threw up.

"*Bene*, now breathe. Just breathe in…then out." Self-soothing was helping her gain some control. She wiped her mouth off. Her thoughts were running wild.

"I have to call Ben." Sophia reached for the phone Ben had given her once again.

"*Dio mio*, I have to call Dennis!" She remembered Dennis had followed Carmine and had seen him with someone, maybe his lover before he was arrested. "I have to know more details."

Just as she opened the phone, Sophia could hear the door handle jiggling.

"Just stay calm, Sophia," she told herself, "just stay calm."

"Sophia, I just wanted to make sure you were all right," Mr. Lorino said politely as he walked into the lab. "Sophia, are you all right? You look like you have seen the devil." He stood a short distance away.

Sophia's eyes were fixed on him as she put the phone behind some paperwork and stood up.

"*Sì*, I am a little shaken, but I finally finished another case," she assured him. "And, and, and…"

"Sophia, what is it?" Mr. Lorino could see she was very upset.

"Should I give him Carmine's letter or not?" Sophia's mind was racing as a million thoughts overloaded her brain all at once.

"Sophia, what is the matter?" He came a little closer.

"And I found this letter. It is from Carmine, addressed to me." The words fell out of her mouth.

"It was in the last file when I opened it." Sophia's hands were shaking as she handed him the letter. Nervously she reached behind her to grab Ben's phone and quickly put the phone in her lab coat.

"Oh, Sophia, I am sorry for this. Did you tell Carmine you knew he was the one who gave you the GHB?" Mr. Lorino read the letter, briefly looking up at Sophia.

"No, I didn't, because honestly, I was not sure." Sophia could not explain to Mr. Lorino that she had climbed inside the ceiling vent.

"Well, I think we need to give this to the authorities. *Per favore*, follow me." Mr. Lorino started to lead her out of the lab.

"But, but what about this last case file? I have not even started it." Sophia's automatic pilot kicked in, wanting to make sure all her work was done.

"Don't worry. I will have another technician come in. *Per favore*, follow me."

"Wait, Mr. Lorino, I have to clean this…" She leaned over to get the wastebin.

"No, no, Sophia, just leave it. I will have maintenance come and take care of it." He gave her a half smile and led her out of the room.

"Where are we going?" she asked as she grabbed her belongings.

"To my office, where we will call the *polizia*. They really need this."

Once the authorities came, they took possession of Carmine's letter. She stood by her account that she never confronted Carmine and that he must have had a guilty conscience.

For several hours the police questioned Sophia in Mr. Lorino's office, going around and around with questions.

"Well, I guess we are finished here, Ms. Pistisi. Here is my card in case you think of anything else." The tall white-haired superintendent of detectives handed her his business card.

"Sophia, why don't you go home to get some rest," Mr. Lorino added with a bit of sincerity.

"*Grazie, bene*. That sounds good." Sophia was glad it was over. She was exhausted from the deep and conflicting emotions she had carried throughout the day.

"*Sì*, take the next few days, and we will see you next Monday." Mr. Lorino was reassuring her.

"Are you sure?" She looked uncertain about taking him up on his gesture.

"*No problema*. I think you have earned it." He smiled.

"*Va bene, grazie.*" She stood up and gathered her things. "*Grazie*, Mr. Lorino."

He nodded his head in approval as she left the room, leaving the police and Mr. Lorino to finish their discussion.

"I am still feeling sick to my stomach," she thought as she walked down the corridor. "It feels weird. Something is not right." The thought came to her and nagged her until after she left the building. Not understanding the feeling that nagged her, she called for her taxi and waited.

"Hmm, let me try Ben again." She took the mobile Ben gave her and tried it once more.

Ring, ring, ring…

"*Ciao*," a drowsy man's voice answered.

"Ben?" Sophia was not sure if she had the right number.

"*Ciao*, Sophia," Ben replied in a sleepy-sounding tone.

"Ben, what is wrong? You sound terrible." Sophia was honest and concerned.

"I am in the hospital. A bus hit my taxi." Ben's voice sounded a little more like himself.

"*Merda*, Ben. What the…" She hesitated. "Are you OK?"

"Yeah, you should see the other guy." His medication was clearly kicking in.

"What?" Sophia raised her voice in concern. "What other guy? Ben, what hospital are you in?"

"I think it is Fatebenefratelli near Rome…" Ben tried to finish his sentence.

"I am on my way, Ben."

She ended the call as her taxi arrived. *"Per favore*, take me to the Fatebenefratelli Hospital," she quickly requested the driver.

Sophia imagined the worst: broken bones, ruptured disks, surgery. Forgetting about her own sour stomach, she hurried to the hospital. She could not get there fast enough.

The nurse at the hospital entry desk was helpful, giving her Ben's room number after Sophia pretended to be his sister.

Upon reaching his room, she could see the door was open. Peering in, she noticed a bandaged leg in a pulley over a bed.

"Oh my…" She stuck her head in to see Ben lying in the bed with his broken leg in the pulley contraption. "Ben! *Dio mio*, are you OK?"

Sophia saw he was not alone as she entered the room. Five other injured men wearing hospital gowns shared the same space. There were three beds on each side, with Ben being the first on the right side closest to the door. The curtain was drawn next to Ben's bed, so Sophia could only see the end of his neighbor's bed, which seemed empty. The one after that was occupied by an elderly fellow.

"Ciao, Sophia. How are you?" Ben was sitting up, looking very uncomfortable.

"Never mind how I am. What happened to you?" Her concern was evident.

"I was in an automobile accident. I have screws in my knee. Want to see?" He was obviously medicated.

"Not now, Ben. First tell me what happened." She walked closer to him to get a better look.

"I was in a taxi, and the bus hit me." His eyes went to the ceiling. "Or the taxi hit the bus. I am not quite sure." He dopily chuckled as his eyes rolled around before trying to focus on Sophia.

"Wow, thank God you are all right." She gently touched his shoulder.

"Yeah, I will be…" Ben closed his eyes for a second. "Yeah," he repeated before he drifted off.

Sophia stood there watching Ben try to fight the urge to sleep, but it was no use. He dozed off.

251

She turned her attention to the other people in the room. The man across from Ben had his wife or girlfriend helping him to the bathroom with his injured leg. While another man was calling for a nurse, another was fast asleep.

Two televisions at each end of the room were on a sports channel and a news station.

Returning her focus to Ben, she saw the intravenous tube and the heart monitor that made his injuries seem much worse than a broken leg.

She rubbed his shoulder gently.

Opening his eyes, Ben was happy to see her. "Hey, Sophia, you know what?"

"What, Ben?" She tried to comfort him.

"I found out who Joseph Grillo is." He smiled like a proud peacock. "He is Moretti's cousin who appears to be connected to Cosa Nostra. How about that?" He smiled a big, silly grin.

"Wow, Ben, *fantastico*. You did good work." Sophia comforted her friend before getting serious. "Ben, I have something to tell you."

"Oh yeah. I bet you thsink I am Superman," Ben teased.

"Ben, Carmine is dead." She did not know another way to break the news.

"Wow, Carmine is dead," he repeated. "Wow, Carmine. Poor Carmine."

"Yes, poor Carmine. He was killed in a house fire. The *polizia* are investigating it." She was not sure how much Ben was able to process.

"Dead? Wow, dude." Ben looked at Sophia.

"*Sì*, Carmine is dead," she reiterated to try to get him to understand the gravity of the situation.

"Dead. Wow, Sophia, that is terrible. Now we won't know whom he is working for." The reality was setting in for Ben.

"Carmine wrote me a letter saying he apologized for poisoning me with the GHB and that he and his lover were being blackmailed by a monster." Sophia gave Ben the short version.

"Wow, he wrote a letter?"

"*Sì*, and you know how you questioned the security camera, how Carmine wasn't seen in the security camera the night he gave me the GHB? Carmine's note told us who helped him. The *polizia* are talking to a James Scala in security as we speak."

"That is good work, Sophia."

"It was not me. It was Carmine. I am sure the *polizia* will arrest Mr. Scala."

"Wow." Ben's eyes rolled back.

"And there is more. Carmine mentioned that a Solar Star Development Company—"

Ben started to snore.

"Well, OK then, I will check that out, and you…well, you just rest." Sophia glanced around. The television broadcasting the news channel showed a news report with a Vatican vote update.

An Asian anchorwoman spoke into the camera while a projection of the Vatican smokestack showed behind her left shoulder. Sophia could not hear as the volume was turned down, but she could see there was no smoke pouring from the chimney.

"Conclave is set to Begin," the caption under the newscaster read.

Sophia read the newswoman's lips. "And we will keep you updated. This is Yin Quan reporting to you live from the Vatican."

Sophia could see all the people gathered in Saint Peter's Square. Many looked like they were praying. Some were singing, and others were holding signs declaring their desire for peace in the world.

"Hmm, I wonder what Cardinal de Marcosi is doing right now." She let her mind wander for a moment before gazing back down at Ben. "*Va bene*. I will be going."

Smiling on him like her little brother, she gave him a gentle stroke on his shoulder. "I will see you tomorrow."

Turning around, as if in a dance, she went to take a step, but she bumped into a man coming in from the hallway.

"Oh, I am sorry," she clamored realizing that she knew the man she just bumped into.

"Oh…Michael! What are you doing here?" Her eyes widened, turning a soft green as her face tinted red from embarrassment.

Michael, the American soldier she had met on Saturday night, held an intravenous pole in his left hand that was connected to him by a tube. His right shoulder was in a surgical sling, while a pronounced bruise darkened the left side of his face. He was wearing a hospital gown.

"I was in an auto accident. On the way back to my base, my bus was hit by a taxi," Michael flirted.

"*Questo è pazzesco.*" Sophia could not believe Michael was standing in front of her.

Michael was alert, unlike Ben, the sleeping beauty.

"I agree it is crazy. This taxi came out of nowhere." He pointed to his shoulder. "I needed a pin in my shoulder."

He stood taller than Sophia and very close. "You know, I could use a private nurse to help me heal faster."

"Ha, that's funny." Sophia scoffed at his gesture. "But you know what is funnier? My friend Ben was in the taxi." She pointed over to Ben.

"That is funny. What are the odds?" Michael took a step closer. "I guess it is meant to be that we get to know each other better." He marveled at his good fortune, given another chance to be with Sophia. "You know what they say. It is a small world after all."

Michael was taken with Sophia's beauty. Her black hair lay like silk around her face and shoulders. He was captivated by her green eyes. They sparkled like the stars. He stared at her for a long moment.

"*Sì, bene…*" Sophia broke the awkwardness as she caught a glimpse into his blue eyes. "I have to go. I hope you feel better." She tried to go around him, but his muscular build prevented her from stepping to the side.

They danced to the right, then to the left, before Michael relented to let her pass.

"Well, I hope to see you again very soon." He softly nodded to her. "I hope you still have my number."

"*Sì*, hm…I still have it." Sophia stumbled on her words as a warm tingle went up her spine. It was an unfamiliar, sensuous feeling that got her attention.

She headed for the doorway before turning around. "And *per favore*, be careful."

"Oh, I will." Michael smiled like a little boy. "Hey, hey…"

"*Sì*, what is it?" Sophia asked keenly, remembering their dancing encounter a few days earlier.

"Hey, I mean, would you have dinner with me sometime?" He finally got the words out.

"Well, I guess." Nervously, she didn't know what else to say. "That would be lovely." Sophia looked into his deep-pooled blue eyes, thinking, "He is nice to look at."

"Here, let me give you my number again. In case you may have lost it from last Saturday night." He stumbled to his bed.

Looking for a piece of paper, he took a newspaper on his hospital tray. He tore off a corner piece and wrote his phone number on it, using the pen he used for his crossword puzzles.

"Ah, isn't that nice?" Ben yawned, seeing Michael hand the piece of paper to Sophia.

"Ben, you are so funny this way." Sophia took the paper from Michael and moved toward Ben's bed.

"Michael, this is Ben, and Ben, this is…" She started to introduce the two men, but when she looked at Ben, he was back to his slumber.

Sophia and Michael both laughed.

"He is really funny…and really sweet." She tilted her head in approval of Ben's disposition. "He is a really good friend of mine." She pulled the blanket up to Ben's chest.

"Well then, I should take really good care of him," Michael keenly replied.

"You should just take care of yourself." Sophia laughed, looking back at Michael. "Well, I should go. Take care." She almost winked before walking out of the room.

"What was that? I almost winked. That was stupid." Sophia laughed to herself as she walked down the hallway and into the elevator.

The taxi ride home seemed as swift as the thoughts in Sophia's mind.

"It was a crazy day, poor Carmine but at least Ben is all right, and I literally bumped into Michael again." She snickered. The driver took notice of her talking to herself when he glanced at her through his rearview mirror.

Sophia also noticed the driver. "He looks foreign, perhaps Russian." Sophia recognized the music coming from his radio. While she could not speak the language very well, she could understand it.

"With a diverse community, you need to understand more than your own language," her papa told her many times growing up.

"That is how you can avoid being taken advantage of, do you understand, Sophia?" Sophia could recount the games they played in various languages. Crossword puzzles and converting the words of food into languages at meals made it more fun at supper.

"*Per favore*, can you turn this up?" Sophia asked the taxi driver. "The news mentioned something about the conclave."

"You are Catholic?" The Russian accent was verified.

"*Sì*," she nodded.

"And so am I," he leaned over to turn the volume button up in his old car.

"The last of the visiting Cardinals have arrived," the newsman announced, "the first vote will take place early tomorrow."

Sophia turned her thoughts to Cardinal de Marcosi, "I wonder what he is doing." Sophia took out her mobile to search the internet for information about him.

"OK, *signorina,* we are here," the driver pulled up in front of her building.

"*Grazie*," she paid with cash and a smile.

Opening the door after getting her change, she turned to see a familiar man standing in front of the main entrance of her building.

"Dominic," she lost her breath. He wore a black leather fitted jacket showing off his muscular physique. She stopped for a second, sitting back in the car.

"Is everything OK, *signorina*?" The driver asked as he focused on Dominic holding a small brown box in his hands and a bottle under his left arm.

"Oh yeeah, *grazie*," she took a deep breath, got out and went toward Dominic.

Dominic's eyes never left her, staring into her. She struggled to walk without looking nervous.

"Dominic what are you doing here?" She suspiciously questioned him as she put her phone in her pocket.

"Well." He made eye contact and would not let her go. He smiled. His sexy Italian demeanor could touch her soul. "I was in the neighborhood. I was going to eat alone and thought how much you liked sushi. So I thought…I was hoping you would like to eat dinner with me?"

He held the box a little higher. The bottle of wine under his arm started to slide down. "Oops."

Sophia grabbed the bottle. Getting closer to him, she could smell his cologne.

"He smells so good." Her nostrils wafted. Her knees felt weak. "*Dio mio*, you cannot do this right now," her inner voice proclaimed.

"*Per favore*, join me." His glance reminded her of their youthful days. "You look hungry. I bet you haven't eaten all day. *Dai, per favore.*"

Sophia shot back a little bit. She was surprised to remember that she hadn't eaten all day. "I am so exhausted, but the food, now in front of me…it smells as good as Dominic."

"Ah, I sense your hesitation, Sophia," he teased playfully. "You can trust me. I will be a true gentleman." He smiled while raising one of his eyebrows. It was that one thing that got her to do whatever he wanted.

"I promise. Sophia, I have changed. *Per favore*, won't you give me a chance?"

"I cannot cross my heart with the food in my hands, but I will if you want me to." He was playful and sexy.

It was a bad combination against Sophia's willpower. In spite of her better judgment, her stomach won out.

"Umm, that would be great." She hesitated. "I am starving."

As she opened the door, with Dominic studying her every move, in her mind she could hear the confession she made to Eula during their sleepover.

"If I am with him, I am afraid I will have sex with him." She could feel his eyes on her. "No, Sophia, be strong!"

Once inside her flat, Sophia walked over to her kitchen and put down her keys. Dominic followed, putting down the box of sushi.

"I will get glasses and dishes." Sophia turned away from him, taking off her jacket.

"Here, I will take that." He gently touched her hand as he reached to help her.

"*Grazie*." Her inner voice returned. "Mama always taught me to be polite, so that is what I will do and no more."

He opened the wine while she readied the dinnerware. Having a small kitchen placed them nearly on top of each other while they prepared their plates.

"We can sit over here." Sophia moved around him toward the sofa. "Oh, wait a minute. Let me move my painting." Sophia put her dish down to pick up the painting.

"Oh no, let me, *per favore*." He gently grabbed her arm, then moving in front of her, "Where do you wish me to put it, *il mio amore*?"

"Over there will do for now." She pointed near her bed.

"I will place it on your bed because it is beautiful, like you." He smoothly swayed back to join Sophia on the sofa.

Picking up her glass, she gulped more than half of it down.

"I am glad I brought your favorite Cabernet *vino*. I knew you would enjoy it," he said, motioning to toast her.

"*Il cibo profumo delizioso*." She inhaled the sushi's aroma. As politely as she could, she fought hard not to give off any other signs that could be interpreted as leading him on.

"Roberto Voerzio. I don't recall drinking this." She picked up the bottle and poured another glass for extra courage.

"*Sì, bene*, I upgraded." He toasted her, clanking her glass. "I have never enjoyed sushi the way I did with you." The meal did bring back memories. "We used to eat this all the time."

"*Sì*, sometimes twice a day, breakfast and supper." She giggled.

The ice was melting away between them with each sushi roll and each sip of wine.

"Anyway, how did you know when I was coming home?" She was curious.

"Well, I didn't. I took a chance…Yesterday I waited for over an hour." He bowed his head as if he had just been caught in a lie.

"*Che cosa*," she said. "You were here yesterday?" She was shocked by his confession.

"*Sì*. As I said, I took a chance. The sushi did not make it yesterday, but today it is *delizioso*!" He happily grinned as he put an entire sake maki roll in his mouth. "And I am glad I did," he added with a mouthful of food.

It brought back endearing memories when she was totally in love with him.

"To two old friends," he toasted. "It is really something special that I am able to see you again, Sophia. I hadn't realized how much I missed you until I saw you."

"To old friends, Dominic." She was making her move. "Because that is all I can give you. I hope you understand."

He looked saddened. "*Sì*, I do understand nothing can be as it was. Which in one way, I am happy about." He shrugged his shoulders. "I was a bad boy back then. But now I am a good man. I hope you will see."

"He is saying all the right things," her inner voice warned. "Sophia, be careful."

"How are things going in your gallery?" Swiftly she changed the subject.

"They could not be better." He sat back, finishing his last roll. "I am a very lucky man."

"*È fantastico*," she agreed giving him a smile.

"And how is your family?" he wanted to know as he put the glass to his soft-looking lips.

"*Sì*, they are well, *grazie*," she said, and then her mind raced. "Be polite, be polite, but no more." She reasoned with herself even though she could sense a tingle in her neck as she tried not to notice his lips.

"Hey, do you remember when we went to Venice for that long weekend?" He sat up straight so they would be very close on the sofa. "*Tu eri pazzo*, convincing the concierge that you were a real royal princess. We ate like royalty, at least until the check came in."

Sophia giggled. "It was pretty funny." She sipped her glass. "It was probably one of the best weekends of my life."

"Mine too." He smirked.

"And we sang karaoke in front of a wedding party, having them believe we were their main performers." Sophia almost choked, she was laughing so hard.

"Well, you dared me." He poured another glass for each of them. "You could always get me to do things."

"No, I could not," Sophia contended. "You had a mind of your own."

"Oh yeah, when you dared me to put on your panties for the weekend, I did it for you."

"But it was not just for me, now was it?" Sophia laughed harder and playfully bantered with him.

"Perhaps it was for both of us." Dominic coyly smiled.

"Perhaps." She was playing hard to get.

Sophia turned her attention to her new painting to get another conversation going. She got off the sofa and walked over to her bed. "Maybe you can help me hang this up." She put down her glass of wine and picked up the painting. "I was going to hang it above the sofa. What do you think?" She didn't really care how he answered. She just wanted to move away from him and his sweet masculine aroma.

"I think that is a great idea." Dominic stood up to help her.

"Do you have a hammer and nails?" He walked over to her and gently took the painting from her hands, making sure he made contact with her.

"I think I have what you need." She walked around him and knelt down in front of the sofa.

"What are you—" Dominic started to ask before Sophia pulled a pink toolbox from beneath the sofa.

"This is a present from my papa." She smiled as she stood up and opened the toolbox. Inside were small tools, a pink-handled hammer, matching pliers, and a screwdriver, along with other small home-improvement items.

"My papa always wanted me to be prepared." She laughed.

"Well, he is a smart man." Dominic smiled, putting the picture on the sofa and reaching for the box. "Hmm, let us see what we have here…"

"I was thinking right here." Sophia gestured to the exact point where she thought the painting should hang.

"*Bene*, I think I have what I need." Dominic picked out his needed tools and took off his shoes. "I need to—"

"We can simply move the sofa." Sophia giggled at his attempt to help. "You don't need to step on the sofa."

"*Sì*, that is true." He was a little embarrassed. Dominic put the hammer and nails down to help move the sofa.

"OK, so right here." She pointed.

Dominic took control of the hammer and steadied the painting on the wall. Moving a step back, he admired his work.

"Well, I think it looks good right here." He was pleased with his accomplishment.

"*Sì*, I think it does too. I was so drawn to it when I first saw it." Sophia tilted her head to gaze upon the painting again.

"It speaks to me as well. I confess when it first came into the gallery, I thought of you straightaway." Dominic looked at Sophia. "*The Flaming Star*. I told myself there was only one Flaming Star in my heart."

Sophia felt the room temperature go up. It was getting steamy.

"*Grazie.*" Sophia felt awkward and moved to pour another glass of wine for each of them, finishing the bottle.

"*Prego.*" He took up his glass to toast her again.

"You...you know," Sophia nervously stuttered feeling a little tipsy. "I mean, you know, Eula loves your gallery. She is especially into all the stars and stuff."

"You mean astrology?" He smirked affectionately.

"*Bene,* she can get pretty weird about it." Sophia moved into the kitchen to start cleaning up the dinner mess.

"Here, let me help you," he offered, picking up the dishes and dirty napkins.

The tiny space left no room to move around. Sophia was getting flushed being so close to him. The wine did not help matters, but it did give her some courage.

"I can do this. Tell him I have to go to work early," she argued with herself. "*Dio mio,* Carmine," she remembered.

"Sophia, what is it?" He touched her hand. "I can tell something is bothering you."

"Oh no, it's nothing..." She paused, throwing the napkins in the trash then turning to grab a dish to put in the sink.

Dominic grabbed her hand before she could touch the dishes. "*Per favore,* tell me. I want to know how you are feeling."

"Um, it's, it's..." She was so mad at herself for being nervous. "It's just that my boss died this morning. He was killed in a house fire."

"*Dio mio,* Sophia. That is terrible." His eyes were sympathetic. His lips looked soft as he spoke to her in his smooth, understanding, sexy way.

"*Sì,* so I guess I am not good company tonight." Sophia was surprised that she gave herself such a well-timed out.

"Oh, I would be upset also. Were you friends?"

"I wouldn't say we were friends." She thought of Carmine's letter to her. "But I..." She thought about it for a second. "I am not sure how I felt about him, really."

"Ah *bene,* I see." Dominic picked up a dish and moved closer to her.

He reached his hand around her, placing the dish in the sink. "I can help you with them. I am good at doing house chores."

He was within kissing distance, and Sophia's face blushed red. It was hard to breathe with him standing so close in front of her.

"Look away, Sophia." A hard tingle, like a spasm, went down her spine. She tried to look away.

His eye contact went through her. "He can see my soul. *Per favore*, no, I can't," her inner voice whispered below the sounds of her heart beating so fast.

Letting go of the dish, his hand gently moved up Sophia's arm.

"Oh no." The tingles were all over her body.

"Sophia." His voice was soft. "I can help you if you want me to stay." He raised his right hand to lift her chin closer to his face.

"Oh *mio*…" Sophia started to shake inside. "Here it comes…"

Dominic reached closer to put his lips on hers, kissing her ever so gently. "Oh…" She could not control herself. "I think I just…"

He kissed her again, passionately but still very gently.

"*Merda*! I…" Sophia had not had slept with anyone in a long while, and she was nervous, but old feelings of lust started to creep in.

Dominic's left hand found its way into Sophia's hair, holding her head gently but persuasively up to his.

"Um, kiss, um, kiss. His lips are so soft." She felt his body getting closer to hers, his chest almost pressed against her breasts. There was little space between them. He crowded her, getting even closer.

They stood there kissing. "It's just like it used to be but better." She felt him completely. "But I can't—"

"Sophia, I have missed you so much." He kissed her again. "*Per favore*, let me stay. I will be good to you. I promise I will not hurt you." His sincerity struck a chord.

"Dominic," she whispered, "I can't…" She tried to fight the urge. He kissed her again and again as he moved his hands over her body, touching all the old trigger points he had known so well in years past.

"*Per favore*," he begged like a little boy as he continued to kiss her softly. "Look, let me show you something."

263

He pulled away from her by a short step and unbuttoned the first two buttons of his shirt, then reached in.

"Oh, that looks good, too good. Sophia, you can't..." Her inner voice murmured in the distance as if it were talking to someone else.

"See, this is the *Santo* Dominick medal you gave me years ago." His eyes peered into hers. "I still wear it. Over the years it has meant more to me. He is the patron saint of hopeful mothers, and it was always my hope that he would help you find your mother."

"Oh, Dominic." She looked back into his eyes with tears. "That is so sweet."

He reached for her again, this time a little more forcefully. He kissed her harder, his tongue finding his way into her mouth.

"Oh..." She could not resist his touch. It was too much for her to deny. She kissed him back.

He felt her response. Their tongues did the communicating now, moving in and around, searching for the triggers that would send them into another world.

Dominic's hands were all over her body. Finding the opening under her shirt, he reached under to touch her bare skin. It was soft, smooth, and inviting. Reaching for her bra clasp, he played with it to see her reaction.

Kissing, their lips interlocked, Sophia could not resist him. She was surrendering. He was passionate, as he always was. He knew her body better than anyone and ran his fingers up and down her spine so she would feel each and every tingle.

"Oh." She was starting to perspire and kissed him again.

That was his sign. He unclasped her bra, then moved his hands in front of her shirt and caressed her breast while he kissed her.

"Mmm." He was starting to sweat. Sophia could feel the heat generating from his body. They were igniting their forgotten desires. He reached for the buttons on her shirt. With one hand he managed to get three of them undone. It was with the last two buttons he experienced a little difficulty as they swayed back and forth, kissing eagerly, awaiting the next stage.

Sophia was all in. "Let me help you."

264

She pulled back slightly and pulled off her shirt and bra. When she realized what she had just done, she got embarrassed. Standing in her tiny kitchen with her 34D breasts exposed, she blushed.

Moving his hand to hold her chin to his face, he leaned in and kissed her ever so gently.

"*Sei così bellissimo,*" he whispered in between each kiss. "Let me do the same." He smiled and took a step back to take off his shirt.

"Oh, *mio…*" Sophia had almost forgotten what a ripped body he had. His clothes did not do justice to the naked body under them.

He pulled back again. "Sophia, I am going to carry you to your bed." He wanted to make sure it was all right with her. Kissing her again, he reached under her legs, quite literally sweeping her off her feet, and walked her across the room.

Standing over her bed with her in his arms, he gently placed her on top of her covers. Kneeling beside her, he kissed her lips then kissing her face, he moved to her chin and down her neck.

Sophia ran her fingers through his black, wavy hair. Lying anxiously, toward the bottom of her bed, she could feel his energy, his heat.

"He feels so good. Mm." She moaned without realizing it.

As she squirmed back and forth in anticipation, her mind brought back memories of their past lovemaking sessions. Dominic was no stranger to her desires.

"I have missed these titties. They speak to me. They have been calling my name ever since I saw you," he whispered.

"He will know I am enjoying this." She felt the dampness in her panties and started to get self-conscious, but there was no time to dwell.

Dominic focused on her lips as his right hand slowly moved in light touches, in circles until he reached her pants. Teasing her, he moved his hand in under her pants, watching her reaction to his touches.

"Mm." He kissed her lips again and again.

He leaned closer to her body. "Oh, I can feel him through his pants. Mm." She let out a louder moan. Dominic played with her for a good long moment before unfastening her pants. He stood up and gazed upon her beauty.

"Sei così bella," he whispered.

When he took off her pants, she was completely naked. Sophia lay on the bed looking up at Dominic, wanting him but hesitant at the same time.

His pants slowly and deliberately came down to rest at his ankles, revealing his small black briefs hiding a rather large bulge.

"Oh, *amore mio*, I have missed you." He moved in slow, lying down with her. Following her to the upper part of the bed, he mounted himself on top of her, feeling her hot, sweating body under his weight. She was trapped under him.

"You are mine now and forever, *il mio amore*," he whispered as he kissed her gently.

"Oh, I have missed him too." She felt every bit of him. "I am his."

Oscillating up and down, swaying back and forth, she could feel him so alive inside her. Kissing, moaning, and sweating together brought them back to old times.

"Groan. I have to…oh…" Dominic stopped thrusting and kissing her back. "Oh, *mio Dio*, Sophia, I had to."

Sweat trickled down his forehead as he stroked her face. "Oh, I can't move. I think we are stuck this way forever."

"Ha, but we have to…I need air." Her breath was labored as Dominic tumbled beside her.

"Wow. I have not done that in a long time," Dominic blurted out.

"Really?" Sophia's head rested on a pillow. She turned toward him, surprised by his confession.

He looked into her eyes. "No, after my wife died, I did not. I could not." He shook his head.

Sophia had almost forgotten that his wife had died. She thought of him as her old boyfriend, not a widower.

"Oh, Sophia. I am sorry I came in you. I never asked you if…" His face was a little panicked by the afterthought.

"Ha." She smirked. "It is OK. I am on the pill. It helps regulate me."

He sighed. "I do not want to cause you any troubles."

"No trouble at all." She smiled, shaking her head, thinking about the sex they just had.

"Ha." Dominic moved closer to her. "I only want to be here if you want me here." His small kisses were passionate and soft.

"*Ti amo*...No, no, no, you cannot say you love him!" Her inner voice was louder, trumpeting over her new, relaxed state. "OK, I will not say it, but I was thinking it."

"What are you thinking about?" Dominic stopped his tender kiss to look at her. "I can tell you are thinking about something."

"Ah, nothing. Actually, I have to go to the ladies room." She politely ended the conversation to go and relieve herself.

But once in the bathroom, she was haunted by her conflicting thoughts. "Why did you have sex with him? Because he has changed. How do you know he has changed? I just know." Thoughts racked her brain.

As she looked in the mirror, the inner interrogations continued, and the questions swirled. She bent down and splashed water on herself. Rising to stand up, she looked in the mirror and got a shock.

There was a large shadow behind her.

"*Dio mio*..." She turned around as fast as lightning...But there was nothing there. "Wow...I need to get a hold of myself."

"Sophia, *stai bene*?" Dominic stood just outside the door. "I heard you shout. Is everything OK?"

"Ah, *sì*...I just slipped." She opened the door to see him stark naked standing in front of her. He was just innocently standing in front of her, with that hard muscular chest, trim body, and strong arms.

"He looks so good, how can it be wrong?" She kissed him. "Your turn."

"Ah, *grazie*, I think I will." He chuckled and hugged her, spinning her around so that he was now in the bathroom. "And then I will rejoin you over there." He gestured toward the bed.

Sophia got a glass of water before returning to her bed. Putting it down on the side table, she noticed her rosaries had fallen on the floor. She picked them up and got a sharp pain in the palm of her hand.

"A cramp. *Merda*." She put the rosaries on the table next to the water and shook her hand out to ease the cramping pain. "That really hurt." She rubbed it to help relieve the pain.

Sophia climbed in bed and threw the covers on top of her. Waiting for Dominic, her conflicted thoughts returned. "Stop! I will be fine," she shouted inside her head to her inner voice.

"Anything I can get you, *il mio amore*?" He returned with a sweet grin on his handsome face.

"No, I got us a glass of water." She pointed, taking notice of his every move.

"*Bene*, I need that." He reached for the glass. "I see you still have your rosaries. I thought after Eme, you—"

"I know." She sighed, admitting, "It is a recent development. I am not sure what I am doing with them."

"*Bene*, if I can help you." He climbed into bed and snuggled up to her.

She laid her head of the left side of his chest, facing the living room. "Dominic, I am not sure of a lot of things these days."

"Oh, *il mio amore*, don't worry. I think it was God who put us back in touch so maybe we can help each other in these difficult times." He caressed her head and kissed her forehead.

"I don't know. I have had some pretty strange things happen around me lately. I don't know if—"

"Sophia, as I remember, you have always had strange things happen around you." He chuckled. "But that is why I loved you so much. Life was never boring with you." He smiled and softly kissed her. "Now tell me what strange things have happened lately."

She hesitated. "I don't know."

"Tell me. I want to know how I can help you. *Per favore*, let me help you."

His tone was so sincere, she gave in. "Well, I had this dream about my boss dying in a fire, and when I went to work, I found out he did die in a house fire."

"Oh, that sounds terrible." Dominic tried to comfort her.

"And that's not all." Sophia went on to tell him about Raphael saving her. Something told her to stop there, not to reveal too much about her uncle Egidio, Ben, or Michael.

"Wow, that is a pretty amazing story," he said. "Well, now I am with you, and I will protect you. *Per favore*, do not worry." He gave her a comforting hug. His strong arms wrapped around her, providing a shield. "Nothing could pierce my arms to get to you. Breathe deeply, my love, *tutto andrà bene*." He kissed her again.

"Well...*grazie mio eroe*," she jested, playing with the few strands of hair on his chest.

They were in their own little world, snuggled into each other's bodies as they fell asleep.

At one moment during the night, Sophia felt she could not breathe. She moved her body to loosen Dominic's grip, but he was sleeping heavily. She started to struggle but was distracted by a light emanating from behind her. Turning her head, she could see the light coming from the window was getting stronger.

"I cannot move." Her body restricted, while her breathing was labored from Dominic's tight grip on her.

The light was almost blinding as it moved closer. It became stronger, causing Sophia's eyes to flutter. Then in a flash, as fast as the light grew, it dimmed.

"What the...," she whispered. Within the dimmed light, a woman stood staring. The woman with short red hair scowled at Sophia, glaring down on Sophia in bed...not saying a word.

"Wh-who are you?" Sophia nervously asked. Still the woman did not answer but slowly glided closer toward the bed.

Sophia could now make out some of her facial features—her blue eyes, small cheeks, and slight body frame.

"What do you want?" Sophia demanded.

The woman put out her hand as if to push Sophia.

"Oh. *Dio mio...*" Sophia's head slipped backward. She could feel herself starting to fall.

With difficulty, Sophia could turn her head slightly, enough to see she was falling into a black hole.

Glancing back toward the frightening redheaded woman, fear started to overwhelm her.

"Oh…" She had to get free and tried desperately to move her arms. Falling so fast, she could feel herself losing her breath.

"Sophia, *stai bene*?" Dominic woke up and lifted his arms.

"No." Sophia sprang up. "*Merda* I just had a crazy dream." She sat up with her knees to her chest, rubbing her forehead.

"What was it?" Dominic was startled.

"I, I, I think…" She fought to get the words out. "I think your wife pushed me into a black hole."

Dominic looked at Sophia with saddened eyes. "Oh, Sophia, *stai bene*?" He did not know what else to say.

"*Sì*…oh, Dominic, I am sorry I brought her up. I did not mean to upset you." She was now trying to comfort him.

"*No problema, il mio amore.* Come here." He lay down and rubbed her back to encourage her to lie with him.

Without saying another word, she put her head back on his chest. Slowly she started running her fingers up and down his chest and stomach, contemplating her thoughts.

"I know Christina, and I can tell you she would never hurt anyone. I know she wants me to be happy." Softly he stroked her hair.

As he tenderly kissed her forehead, his one kiss grew into another and then another. He targeted her lips using the fullness of his own lips.

Sophia felt his other hand making circles on her arm, then tracing along to reach her breast.

"Mm," she moaned.

Teasing her was Dominic's favorite pastime, and he did it well. Her nipple got harder as the urge to feel him between her legs grew stronger. Before long they had sex again.

Finding herself lying on top of him, she could feel his body as if they were permanently joined together. Their kisses were deep and passionate like time had never separated them.

"I can feel your heart beating through my chest," she teased.

"I can feel your blood flowing through my veins." He kissed her again tenderly.

Sophia smiled, sliding over on her side, exhausted.

Their lust was replaced by a profound gratification, leading them into a relaxed slumber.

Ring, ring, ring, ring…

"Yawn." She stretched, not quite back in reality.

*Ring, ring, ring…*Her mobile seemed louder.

"I think your cell is ringing," Dominic announced with a hint of sarcasm.

Sophia looked around. "I wasn't dreaming?" She stretched as she moved around him to get her phone.

"*Ciao…*yawn," she answered.

"*Ciao, il mio amore.* Sophia, did I wake you?" Mama wanted to know.

"Oh no, Mama, you didn't." She covered herself, being embarassed talking to her mama stark naked. Dominic laughed, getting up from the bed to check his own phone.

"*Bene.* I just wanted to make sure you were coming for dinner this Sunday." Mama was exploiting her natural right to make her daughter feel guilty.

Sophia watched Dominic put his things together. "He is sooo handsome." She got lost in her thought.

"Sophia," Mama called out to her.

"Oh, *Sì*, Mama. I will be there," She remembered she was on the phone with her mama. "How is everything? How is Papa?" She tried to act normal.

"He is fine. I told him to see a doctor about his knees, but you know him. I don't know what I am going to do with him. He complains, but he won't go to the doctor."

Sophia smiled. "OK, Mama, I will talk to him on Sunday." She watched Dominic put his clothes on…one naked thigh at a time was being covered up until even his manhood disappeared.

"*Bene*, we should have a new pope by then too." Mama reminded Sophia of conclave.

"*Bene*, I am sure we will." Sophia encouraged her mama's hopes without insult. "OK, Mama, I have to go to work, so I will call you later."

"*Bene. Ti amo*, Sophia." Mama's voice was always comforting.

"*Ti amo anch'io*." Sophia blew a kiss through her phone. "*Addio*."

Ending the call, she could see Dominic was looking for something. She leaned over to pick up the tie she had been sitting on.

"Are you looking for this?" She teasingly swayed it back and forth in front of him.

He stepped closer to her as she stood up. "*Sì*, I was." He kissed her lips softly and pulled her closer to him. "I have an appointment I must keep, but I was hoping to see you later. May we can have dinner tonight?"

"I can see what my schedule looks like." She playfully kissed him back. "How about I call you in a little while and let you know?"

"*Bene*." He took his tie from her hand and kissed her again. "I wrote my number on the note pad on the counter. I will be waiting for your call with anticipation."

She walked him to the door, where they kissed like old lovers. "*Va bene*, I will be calling you later." She smiled back at him before shutting the door behind him as he left.

Chapter 13

A NEW LEADER HAS EMERGED

Tired and restless, Valentinus headed toward Saint Peter's Basilica with the other cardinals. His night was filled with worry for Cardinal Korsig, who was supposed to meet with him the night before.

Buzz, buzz, buzz. His pocket vibrated.

Exhaustedly, he answered his cell phone. "*Ciao*, Cardinal Antonelli. Have you heard from Korsig?"

"No, no, I haven't. But I did find out that he traveled to the city of Brindisi, although I still do not know why or whom he met with. His assistant has not yet heard from Korsig either and has alerted the authorities." Giacomo's concern was alarming. "This is not like him. I am afraid for his safety." Then he hesitated. "…And I had to tell Cardinal Borgia so he could name a substitute for Korsig, someone who could take over his responsibilities as dean of the College of Cardinals at conclave."

"Giacomo, I am sure he is fine." Valentinus did a terrible job trying to reassure Giacomo. "Look, I have to go. They are taking our mobile phones, so I cannot contact you until later. I will be saying extra prayers for Korsig and the conclave."

Giacomo was silent.

"What is it?" Valentinus asked, knowing there was more bad news.

"They are talking about Irenaeus taking over Korsig's role at conclave." Giacomo delivered his update with some consideration.

"*Cazzo!*" Valentinus was enraged, drawing attention to himself. Looking around at the cardinals staring at him, he smiled, trying to downplay his outburst.

"The first vote will be early this morning, and considering Pope Gregory's limited options..." Giacomo paused.

"I believe he and the majority of the consistory will go along, giving Irenaeus his blessing," he sighed. Giacomo tried to break the news without causing too much more distress.

"There is nothing, nothing, I can really do at this point." Valentinus surrendered. "Listen, I have to go, *addio*." He ended the call feeling an apple-sized pit engorge in his stomach.

"*Scusami*, Cardinal, we need your mobile," the Swiss Guard officer asked politely.

"Oh, *sì*," Valentinus replied trying not to act out of sorts as he handed it over. Feeling the pain in his stomach, he was more desperate.

"Now it's just me. *Per favore, mio Padre* in heaven, help me to tend the weaker sheep and keep watch over the wolves."

The cardinals were gathering and taking their seats for what they believed would be the opening comments and initial prayer service.

Pope Gregory entered near the tomb of the Apostle Saint Peter, where before the prayer service began, Irenaeus stood in the wings.

"*Buongiorno*, my fellow shepherds." He was greeted with resounding applause. He gestured for silence. "*Grazie, grazie...per favore*, we have an urgent matter that needs to be addressed."

The cardinals quieted, and Gregory continued. "Our dear friend and colleague Cardinal Korsig is missing."

Gasps echoed around the holy walls.

"Authorities are searching for his whereabouts, and we pray for his safe return. However, this important hour in the history of our church cannot be delayed." Gregory's solemn tone could be felt with each word. "It is with regret that I stand here now and ask that you allow Cardinal Irenaeus Smyrna to conduct this special prayer service, and if Cardinal Korsig is unable, then to also have Cardinal Smyrna perform the duties as our dean of College of Cardinals during conclave, until we have more information regarding Cardinal Korsig."

Valentinus stared with disdain at the cardinals voting for Irenaeus. He was too distraught to vote at all.

"Irenaeus seemed well prepared to take Cardinal Korsig's place for the mass on such short notice, don't you think?" Cardinal Perez whispered to Valentinus after the mass.

They walked in the procession from the Pauline Chapel to the Sistine Chapel in a state of prayer.

"Perhaps too prepared," Valentinus offered up in frustration, walking the fifty yards from the Rite for Entrance into Conclave through Regia Hall, giving them just enough time to make their insinuations.

Arriving in the Sistine Chapel, the cardinals' pageant was prearranged, guiding each of them to his place at the long rows of tables on each side of the chapel.

Two long rows of narrow tables were staged on each side of the chapel, adorned with neatly appointed dark camel-colored table coverings and long red skirts underneath that draped to the floor. The tables were impeccably organized with place cards, name tags, and relating conclave materials at each place. The altar centered the room, and one by one in order of seniority, the cardinals would approach the altar displaying the chalice paten and cast their vote.

Valentinus found his place, which allowed him a close look at Irenaeus and Cardinal Clement Sisinnius.

"At least I have a good seat for the show." Valentinus's mind flashed to the earlier prayer service, where Irenaeus presided over the Missa Pro Eligendo Romani Pontifice. Watching his foe perform Korsig's duties at the Mass for the Election of the Roman Pontiff made his blood boil.

Chanting the Latin hymn, *"Veni Creator Spiritus,"* Valentinus desperately prayed with the words of the song. *"Per favore,* come, creator spirit, I need you."

The cardinals took their oath, promising to abide by the rules of conclave before Irenaeus stood to give his opening remarks.

"There are unprecedented challenges for our new leader, who must be able to stand with world leaders of today and unite all Christians," Irenaeus lectured his audience. "And while we love our former leader, we cannot continue his legacy, which is associated with scandal. We must elect a new pontiff who can overcome these indignities and bring the flock of Christ back to his beloved church." He then gave them instructions. "After folding your ballot down the middle, you will drop your ballot into the chalice and make history."

"He directly attacked Gregory." Valentinus could see the each side starting to take aim.

"Even the newly elevated cardinals having voting rights given by Gregory's own hand may not be enough to sway this den of wolves against Sisinnius." Valentinus sighed heavily.

He continued to assess the possibilities. "Cardinal Giuliani della Rovere of France is a strong contender, as is Cardinal Ascanio Sforza from Germany," Valentinus thought, "but I doubt they can beat Sisinnius. The lines are being drawn deep in the sand...The traditionalists are out to slaughter the progressives."

The first vote was cast. Black smoke rose from the chapel chimney stack. It was time for a break.

"I am glad we are making progress." Irenaeus's voice bellowed behind Valentinus.

"I see what you call progress, and it does not impress me," Valentinus flatly stated as he stood up, getting ready to leave the chapel. "But let's see how the next session goes, shall we?" Valentinus nodded to his foe, quickly turning back around, not wanting to hear Irenaeus's response.

Valentinus continued out the door and down the corridor. Walking through various empty hallways and desolate corners, he found himself alone. After looking around, he pulled another mobile from his inside pocket.

*Ring, ring, ring, ring...*He called Giacomo's mobile.

"*Merda!*" Valentinus was losing his patience.

"*Ciao...*," Giacomo finally answered in a hushed tone.

"Giacomo," Valentinus was hasty.

"Sorry, I didn't recognize the number," a surprised Antonelli answered.

"Giacomo, I don't have time. Did they find Krosig?"

"*Sì*, but Valentinus, it is not good," Giacomo tried to explain.

"What happened? Is he all right?"

"He is in a coma. He was found in his car. The *polizia* say he went off Strada Statale Adriatica. It is a long road, and it appears he was on his way back to Rome, based on the direction his car was faced."

Giacomo was solemn. "His car was found in an old wine vineyard. He was unconscious when they brought him to the hospital."

"*Dio mio*." Valentinus put his hand to his forehead in disbelief. "What are the doctors saying?"

"They are still doing tests, but it looks like he has a lot of internal bleeding, so we just don't know." Giacomo was trying to be hopeful. "Look, I will let you know what they are saying later, after conclave."

"*Per favore*." Valentinus was starting to feel sick. "Giacomo, what hospital is he in?"

"Casa di Cura Salus. I will let you know anything I find out. Just keep yourself together. Remember, you are supposed to be helping Gregory and our church, right?"

Valentinus paused for a moment. "*Sì*. I am trying." He sounded less confident.

"Valentinus, you need to be strong." Giacomo wanted to give him a pep talk. "You are supposed to be looking for a traitor. Have you found out anything?"

"No...not really." Valentinus felt emotionally void. "But I will see what I can find out later and during the next sessions," he said, wanting to offer a little encouragement.

"*Va bene allora*, we both have a job to do. I will speak to you later." Giacomo was anticipative.

"*Sì. Addio*." Valentinus ended his call just in time. Hearing footsteps behind him, he turned to see a Swiss guard.

"*Scusami, signore*, you are not supposed to be here," the tall, hulking guard announced. "You must leave and return to the chapel area."

"*Sì, grazie*. I just needed to stretch my legs." Valentinus hid his mobile and briskly walked away.

***

"Black smoke rises from the Sistine Chapel smokestack," the media reported. Sophia had been watching the news on her laptop.

"Geez, it is going to be a long process," she thought.

Ring, ring, ring…

"*Ciao*, Ben. How are you feeling today?" Her mobile ring tone distracted her from the news.

"Good. I am being released later today." Ben sounded better than he did on her last visit. "I kind of remember you being here yesterday. What did you say? Something about a solar company?"

Sophia giggled. "*Sì*, Ben. Listen, I will see you shortly. I am on my way now." She shut down her laptop and grabbed her coat. "We can talk when I see you."

"But…," Ben tried to say. "Sophia, are you still there?" He was talking to himself, as she had already ended the call. "She is going to drive me crazy," he said, putting his mobile down.

The nurse had just entered the room, ready to dole out his pain medication. "I was just thinking of you."

"I am sure you were," the nurse smiled, handing him a small cup with two pills inside. He took his medicine with a shot of water and started to rest.

When Sophia arrived, Ben had his eyes closed.

"Sleeping again. You must be related to Sleeping Beauty," she jested, putting down a bag of curry chicken treats. She leaned over him, wanting to see if he was asleep.

"Groan." Ben moved his head. Sophia could see her friend was still in pain.

"Ben, are you OK?" she whispered, but he didn't answer. Looking around, she saw the curtain was pulled to hide Michael's bed.

"Hmm." She wondered where he was or if he was listening to Sophia talk to Ben.

"I am glad you came." A woozy voice spoke from below her. "Ah-hmm." Ben's eyes were now open as he tried to move on his own.

"Wait, let me help you," she insisted.

She reached under him to help him move his pillow.

"Ouch, that hurts…son of a devil," he mumbled under his breath.

"I am sorry." She felt bad for him.

"No, it's not you. It's this leg." Ben was curt. "I am not a good patient."

"Except for when they give you your pain medications, you mean," a familiar voice sounded from behind the curtain.

Michael, already in his street clothes, pulled the curtain away to find Sophia helping Ben to sit up. Ben's face grimaced with pain as he struggled to straighten out his body.

"Ben, are you all right? You don't seem fit to be leaving." Her concern was genuine.

"I am fine!" he shouted as he leaned back against the bed. For a moment his face froze.

Sophia and Michael stared at Ben for a second, not believing his unnatural nasty tone.

"Oh, Sophia, I am sorry." Ben focused on her. "It's the medication talking." He lowered his voice. "I am really fine. The doctor has given me his blessing."

Sophia looked at Ben and then Michael. The energy they generated reminded her of the relationship she shared with her cousins, especially when they were playing tricks on her.

"Hmm, I see." She left the topic for a moment. "Well, is there anything I can do for you? How about some curry chicken?" She picked up the bag from the chair.

"Actually, that sounds good," Michael replied enthusiastically.

"I am sorry. I didn't know you liked curry." Sophia glanced at him as she pulled the hospital bed table over Ben's bed and began taking out the food.

"That is OK. I will share mine," Ben generously offered.

"Wow, are you guys dating or something?" Sophia joked.

"Something," a witty Michael quipped while standing up over the table of food.

"Hey, do you mind?" Ben bellowed.

"You guys are going to spill food over me." Ben's concern went unacknowledged.

Michael opened a container of chicken curry and held it in under his nose to smell it. "It does not look great, but it smells good. Thanks." He picked up a fork and started to eat it out of the container, over Ben's objections.

"Hey." Ben looked disappointed.

"Don't worry, Ben. I have something better for you." Sophia took out another container and with a fork gave it to Ben. "Look, your favorite, chicken tikka marsala."

"Ah, and it smells great. Thank you, Sophia." Ben's face lit up like a child receiving a present.

"I hope you like it." Sophia took a third container of rice from the now empty bag and started to pick at it.

Michael realized that he had taken her food. "Here, let me give you some chicken for your rice." He dumped a little of his chicken in her rice container.

"Oh, no thank—" She tried to respond before Michael spilled a few drops of sauce on Ben's blanket.

"See, I told you that you would spill—" Ben began.

"No worries, buddy." Michael jumped into action to clean it up, only to smear it deeper in the blanket's fabric.

"Stop, stop," Ben shouted. "You are only making it worse!"

"Both of you calm down. Here, let me." Sophia's motherly tone made them pause. She put down her container and cleaned Ben's blanket, at least making it not as noticeable.

After Ben scarfed down his meal, he was ready. "Sophia, can you please hand me my clothes? They are in the wardrobe behind you." He pointed to small, numbered wardrobes built into the back wall. "I am number one."

"Ben, are you sure the doctor—" she started to say just as a nurse came in to check on the patients.

"Hmm, it smells good in here. I like curry too," the nurse teased as she entered the room. "Mr. Dhara, I have your papers, but again the doctor believes you should stay another day for monitoring. Therefore, *per favore*, you need to sign our waiver," the nurse insisted.

"Hmm, it seems I also told you that you should stay." Sophia's eyes darted a not surprising look at Ben.

"I have to leave, so please give me my clothes." Ben took the forms from the nurse and signed them. "Thank you, and please thank the doctor for me. I will be fine."

The nurse gave an unkind smirk and walked out. Ben continued. "Sophia, please, my trousers and shirt." He moved the bed table away while steadying himself to get out of bed.

"Ben, I don't think it is—"

"OK, then I will do it myself." He started to get his injured leg off the bed.

"OK, OK. I will help you, but don't say I didn't warn you if you don't heal properly."

"Oh, mother hen, he will be fine," Michael chimed in.

Sophia swiftly turned and sneered. "Don't mother me. You don't know me, but I can tell you, I can be a motherfu—"

"All right, if you could please just hand me my clothes," Ben caught her in mid-sentence. "And by the way, did you say something about a real estate development or solar company yesterday? I was not sure if I was dreaming when you were here." Ben took the trousers from Sophia.

Sophia giggled. "*Sì*, I did." She looked over at Michael. "But perhaps we should talk privately."

"Hey, I can take a hint," Michael said with a pout.

"It's OK, Sophia. It turns out Michael and I have some common interests," Ben assured her.

"Common interests? What does that mean?" Sophia was puzzled.

"I can show you." Michael started toward Sophia.

"Back it down, cowboy." She put her hand up to stop him.

"Sophia, what about this solar company?" Ben raised his voice to bring them back into focus.

Seeing Ben's trust in Michael's role as a confidant, she continued. "*Sì*, Carmine mentioned it in his letter. The Solar Star Development Corporation. It is the same solar company in Apulia."

"The one you mentioned regarding Callesino's mother. It is getting a lot of attention from authorities lately. And guess who the manager is?" She stood up with a sly smile on her face.

"Who?" Ben asked, putting on his shirt.

"Joseph Grillo, the same man who you found out just happens to be Moretti's cousin." She looked at Ben, who was having trouble getting his clothes on. "Here, let me help you."

"No, no, I can do it." However, his frustration was growing as he tried to reach his pants over his casted leg.

"Here, let me help you, buddy." Michael stood up and went around the bed. "But if you don't mind, we will need a bit of privacy." He motioned for Sophia to step back, then drawing the curtain back.

"OK, let's see what we can do." Michael's voice carried over the curtain. "Here, I have this."

"Ouch, damn it," Ben shouted.

"Sorry, buddy," Michael responded gently. "OK, how about this?"

"Children." Sophia stood on the other side of the curtain listening to their exchange and shaking her head. Looking up, she saw a news channel on the television was reporting on the conclave. "Hmm." Her attention wandered but was distracted by the sound of clothing tearing.

"Hey, those are my good trousers." Ben raised his voice in concern.

"You will not be able to wear them with your leg in a cast. Listen, you could either go without your pants or go this way." Michael took charge.

"Shit…" Ben's voice trailed off.

A few moments passed before Michael opened the curtain to reveal Ben's new fashion.

"Ha, ha, ha, ha." Sophia could not contain herself.

Ben was standing beside his bed wearing his shirt and his pants. One leg was cut above the knee, while the other pant leg was normal.

"Are you having a good time?" Ben asked Sophia, looking serious.

"*Dio mio*, I am sorry. It just looks..." She shook her head. "Hmm...I am sorry," she said letting out one last giggle.

"Well, buddy, I think you look good," Michael assured Ben. "Besides, we need to be ready." Michael gathered Ben's belongings.

"Ready? Ready for what?" Sophia asked wanting to know their secret.

"For our ride," Michael answered smugly.

"Our ride?" She was surprised. "You are leaving together?"

"Yes, we have business to attend to." Michael was patronizing Sophia as Ben sat down on the bed resting his leg.

"Business?" She quizzed them.

"Yes, we have some...work to attend to," repeating Michael, Ben tried to explain.

"Work?" She was feeling left out of the loop. "What about this solar company Carmine mentioned and Moretti's cousin?"

"Great job, Sophia," Ben assured her. "I will look into it."

"You will look into it?" She was lost for words. "What about me?"

"I was hoping you were going to ask," Michael wanted to add his two cents. "What are you doing for dinner tonight? I was hoping we could—"

Sophia glanced at Michael in frustration. "I am sorry but no, *grazie*." She knew she sounded short-tempered but she did not care.

"Please, you would make an injured soldier feel better. It's just dinner." He gave his best impression of puppy eyes, trying to make her feel sorry for him.

"Where are you going, Ben, in case I have to reach you?" She turned her attention on Ben.

"I am staying with a friend. I will call you tomorrow." He had just finished his sentence when a tall, burly man in a dark suit entered the room, followed by the nurse with a wheelchair.

"Ah, great! Our ride is here, buddy." Michael stood closer to Sophia. "Well, how about it?" He looked into Sophia's surprised eyes.

"How about what?" Sophia was bewildered watching this display of friendship unfold.

"Dinner tonight?" Michael tried to be suave.

"I am sorry. I am busy tonight." Sophia didn't want to hurt Michael's feelings.

"Well, what about tomorrow night?"

"I am sorry, I am busy then too." She was stern but subtle.

"How about the weekend?" Michael persisted but used his charm on her.

"The weekend?" Sophia thought about Dominic. "No, I am sorry, but I can't."

"OK, OK, I can take a hint. You have my number, and you can call me anytime." Michael tried to show his hurt feelings without going overboard.

"Well, Mr. Dhara, are you ready?" the nurse interrupted their chatter.

"Yes, I am." Ben was anxious to get out as he stood up, leaning into the wheelchair. "Let's go."

Sophia looked bewildered and stared at the well-suited man who accompanied the nurse. He did not say a word as he moved back for the nurse to wheel Ben out.

"So you will call me, right?" Michael was hopeful.

"*Sì, bene.*" Sophia was not paying attention. "Ben, I will let you know what happens after I speak to my uncle Egidio. Call me tomorrow."

"Yes, I will," Ben promised her. "And thank you for the curry chicken. I did appreciate it." He warmheartedly glanced at her before focusing back on the busy corridor ahead.

"*No problema.*" Sophia felt a little better that perhaps she was not being kicked to the curb after all.

They made their way through the corridors and to the main exit, where a black limousine was waiting.

"Don't worry, I will talk to you tomorrow," Ben affirmed as he was being helped into the car.

"Yes, and I will talk to you before the weekend." Michael winked at Sophia.

The car doors shut, and the car took off.

Leaving Sophia standing there by herself, she looked around and suddenly felt out of place.

"*Mi scusi*, do you need a taxi?" a security guard asked, seeing she looked a little distressed.

"*Sì, grazie*," she politely acknowledged.

A white taxicab pulled up, and she got in thinking about Ben and Michael. "Buddy?" She was talking to herself.

"*Mi scusi*," the driver asked.

"Ah…nothing. *Per favore*, take me to the rail station," she answered him.

On the train she changed her focus. Sophia started to think about Carmine and how she would confront Uncle Egidio about knowing Moretti.

"I cannot accuse him of anything," Sophia thought, "but what are the odds he knows Moretti, the same attorney who worked for the orphanage? They did look like old friends."

Before long the train arrived in Infernetto, Latium, and she hailed a taxi to see Uncle Egidio.

"And perhaps I can also go up the block to visit Mama and Papa," she thought as the taxi pulled up to his home. However, as she got out of the car, she started to second-guess herself.

"Maybe I am making something of nothing." She shook her head, feeling foolish. "I'll just go and say hello," she tried to convince herself.

Walking up to his stately two-story red and white brick house, the five-foot-tall wrought iron fencing looked as intimidating as a twelve-foot wall. Her anxiousness was starting to get the better of her.

"You need to know. Just go," Sophia mumbled.

The oversized wooden front door was styled to resemble the doors on an old castle.

She used to love the feeling it gave her when she visited her uncle as a child. The bowed windows on each side of the large wooden door gave off an elegant appearance. She used to pretend to be the princess of the manor, visions of long ago were faded in her memory.

After standing at the gate for a long moment, she took a deep breath before opening it and walked up the steps, taking her time to approach the front door.

"Maybe I will come back another day." She started to turn around when a noise behind her made her cringe.

"Sophia, what are you doing here?" Uncle Egidio's soft tone harmonized with the low swish of the door opening. "You look a little lost, *il mio amore. Va tutto bene?*"

"Oh, ah, I am fine. I was just in the neighborhood." Slowly turning around, she could sense her uncle's curiosity.

"*Ebbene, venite, entrate.*" He opened his arms, giving her a kiss on each cheek. Then he moved aside to make room for Sophia. "*Per favore*, come." He motioned for her to follow him.

"I was"—she prayed for the right words as she followed him—"I was visiting a friend and thought of you."

"Well, I am glad you did. *Per favore*, come and sit." He led her into his kitchen, pulling out a chair under the marble island countertop. "I just made some *caffè*. Would you like some?"

"*Sì, grazie.*" She sat down and watched him move around his customed chef's kitchen, staring through him as he poured the cups of coffee.

"Sophia, what is it?" He looked at her sincerely.

"Well, I guess I am feeling a little lost." She looked up at him. "My boss died yesterday."

"*Mio Dio*, Sophia! I am sorry." He brought the cups over to her and placed one in front of her. "That is terrible."

"*Sì*, it is." She took a sip of her coffee and paused. "You always make the best." She relished the taste in her mouth. Sitting still for a moment, her thoughts came back to reflect on Carmine.

"Sophia?" Uncle Egidio prompted her. "If you don't mind me asking, how did it happen?"

She felt a little dazed. "In a house fire," she said flatly.

"A house fire? I heard something on the news about a house fire last night, but the deceased man's name was not released."

"His name was Carmine. It's funny. He was not the nicest person, but I feel sad that he died."

"The news did not say it was suspicious. Do you know if it was?"

Sophia sat straight up, looked her uncle in the eyes. "I think it was, and if you promise not to laugh or think I am strange, I will tell you why."

Uncle Egidio took his pointer and middle finger, kissed them, and placed his fingers over his heart, their sacred sign for holding a secret. "Sophia, I promise. You know I have always believed in your special abilities."

She recalled telling her uncle of the many strange dreams.

Some of her experiences were frightening, like believing she could see and talk to dead people's souls. However, her uncle would comfort her, telling her magical tales of faraway lands to make her feel better. It was their secret, and it made her feel special. Their secrets were sealed with a finger kiss and locked with the crossing of their hearts.

"Well," Sophia confided in him, "I had a dream." She concentrated on her words. "It's strange. I did not see that Carmine lit the fire. I feel he was already dead when it started." She shook her head. "I don't think he killed himself. I think he was murdered." Her gut feeling and her inner voice guided her. "But maybe he caused his own murder."

"I see." Uncle Egidio looked on her with pity. "I believe you have these dreams for a reason, Sophia. And if I remember correctly, you were rarely misguided by your intuition. So trust your instincts."

"*Sì,* I do, but I wish I knew more. The dreams are scary at times." She took another sip of her coffee, thinking of a way to change the subject. "But it's puzzling, because he wrote what I believe was a suicide note. He explained he was being blackmailed and a politician named Salvatore Moretti was involved." She waited for his response.

When he didn't seem to acknowledge the name, she continued, "I don't know what he was talking about or who this Moretti is." She hated lying to her uncle, but her intuition, as he mentioned, was rarely wrong.

Taking the last sip of her coffee, she held her cup out. "May I have another? It was just what I needed." She felt the delicious taste in her mouth more than she felt sorrow for Carmine.

"*Ovviamente*." Uncle Egidio took her cup and walked over to the coffee machine.

Sophia watched his reactions. "Do you know a politician named Salvatore Moretti?"

"He wrote a suicide note to you?" her uncle asked. "Why would he write to you?"

"I don't know. Maybe because he felt he did not have anyone else." She was just as surprised by Carmine's note.

"Were you close to Carmine?" Uncle Egidio took a long sip from his cup.

"No, not at all." She looked up at him and paused. "I think it is sad that I am only a coworker, and the only person he felt he could reveal his tortured soul to." She took her new cup of coffee and held it tightly.

"Let me see the note. Maybe I can help." Uncle Egidio put his cup on the counter.

"I can't. I gave it to my superior. Carmine left the note at work, and I had no choice but to give it to Mr. Lorino, my supervisor." She took another sip of her coffee.

"Oh, I see."

"So, do you know a man named Moretti?" she pointedly asked him again. "I want to understand what was so bad that he was being blackmailed and who this Moretti guy was and what he had to do with Carmine."

"Sophia, you said you gave the note to your superiors, and I am sure they contacted the authorities, so *per favore*, let them do their jobs. You did the right thing by giving the note to them." He looked at her, taking a sip from his cup like an old man who was giving wise advice.

"I know the authorities will do their job, and hopefully it will not be as messed up as the investigation into Eme's disappearance!" Sophia eyes changed to a dark green.

"*Sì*, let's hope so," he somberly agreed.

"I thought I remembered something in the news about a Moretti politician in Turin. Have you heard of him?" Sophia was pushing to have his answer.

"Knowing this person is not going to help you. Sophia, you need to let the police do their job. Especially when politicians are involved. They can be dangerous. *Per favore*, let the authorities look into this Moretti person. They will find out if he was involved in your coworker's death."

Uncle Egidio seemed sincere and touched her hand gently. "Promise me, my curious star, you will leave it to the authorities. I can tell the wheels in your mind are turning, but this is just an unfortunate situation that you have no business meddling in."

Sophia focused on her uncle. She could tell by the way he avoided answering her questions that he knew Moretti, but she wondered why he was being so evasive. "I will figure out this mystery," her inner voice assured her.

"Don't worry, Uncle Egidio, it's not like I can do much anyway. I am just curious. It's not like you get these types of notes every day."

"*Sì*, quite." He sipped his coffee again. "*Sì* indeed, strange happenings." He shook his head as he got up to pour himself another cup.

Sophia finished her cup. "Uncle Egidio, I wanted..." She stopped.

He turned around to look at her. "*Sì*, Sophia, what is it?"

"Umm, I was searching on the Internet and came upon a story of a man who found his long-lost siblings forty years after being adopted." She looked down at her now empty cup.

"*Sì*, and..." He was making her ask the question, although already knowing what she was going to ask.

Sophia started to get a little nervous. "Well, I was wondering..." She felt herself starting to sweat. "I was wondering if you knew if I had any siblings."

"Siblings!" he declared, not really asking a question. "I think when God created you, he broke the mold." He gave a little laugh.

Sophia looked at him laughing. She just stared at him.

"Oh, Sophia. I am sorry. I did not mean to offend you." He could see she was serious. "Oh, my child, I am not sure of anything. I am sorry." He tried to give her some measure of comfort.

She eyeballed him with a curious and undeterred grin.

"Hmm…Are you looking for your birth parents again?" He already knew the answer.

"It's just something I wondered about." She pushed on. "It's only natural. Don't you think?" Sweetly she buttered him up.

"*Ovviamente*. I just wish I could give you more help," he countered with his own degree of genuine sincerity. "You have always meant the world to me. You know that, don't you?"

"*Sì*, I do." She was surprised by his question.

"If you want to look for your biological parents, I will help you. You do know you can trust me?" He gently patted her hand.

"Of course." Baffled, she hesitated to be totally honest with him. "I do want to search for them, but I have a lot going on right now."

"I understand." He drank his coffee.

Glancing away, she saw the edge of a dark, hard-covered book with lighter lettering on the binder. Resting on the countertop, it was almost concealed by a newspaper. Sophia could barely make the title: *The Hypostasis of the Archon*. Her head tilted slightly, trying to read the book binding. The memory of her conversation with Mariam about the Gnostics came rushing back.

"Do you believe in archons?" She surprised herself in asking him so straightforwardly.

"What?" He looked stunned, given the change of topics.

"Archons," she repeated as she stood her ground, wanting to see if he knew.

"Where did you hear about them?"

"A friend told me about them. Do you believe they are real?"

"Sophia, I am not an expert on such things. I do not—"

"I noticed your book." She pointed to the newspaper in the corner.

Uncle Egidio turned to see what she was referring to and moved the newspaper.

"Oh, this." He picked up the book. "It was given to me by a friend. He thought I would find it interesting."

Sophia looked at the hardcover black book with the tan letters. "It looks old, like it has been in a basement." She looked back at him. "Well, do you?"

"Do I what?"

"Find it interesting?"

He changed his body language, leaning more into the counter, and was uncharacteristically bashful. "Well, I have to confess I have not read it." He picked it up and fumbled it. "Here, would you like to borrow it?" He handed it to her.

Quickly Sophia took it from him. "Hmm... *The Hypostasis of the Archons*." She looked a little puzzled. "It's funny because I have never heard of these archons before a few days ago." She looked up at her uncle. "I will return it after I read it."

"*Bene*." He smiled.

Ring, ring, ring...

Uncle Egidio's mobile interrupted them. "*Ciao. Bene.* I will call you back shortly." His tone was serious to the person on the other end, and he quickly hung up. "Ah, duty calls, *il mio amore*."

"It's all right. I need to be going," Sophia insisted as she held her borrowed book and grabbed for her belongings.

Uncle Egidio walked her to the front door. "Ah, *il mio amore*." He kissed each side of her cheeks. "I will see you at Sunday dinner."

"Um, *sì*." Sophia hesitated. "I will see you then. And *grazie*...for your book."

"Sophia, I can drive you where you need to go," he said, not seeing a taxi or her Vespa.

"No, no, I am going to visit Mama and Papa." She smiled. "But *grazie*." Putting the book in her pocketbook, she headed up the block as Uncle Egidio quickly went inside, closing his door.

"Huh. That must have been an important call. He usually sees me up the block." She sighed, continuing on her way.

Upon reaching her parents' cobblestone walkway, Sophia turned to look back at her uncle's house. "He is leaving?"

She could see he was getting into the backseat of a black sedan. Slowly she went up the walkway, allowing time for her uncle's car to pass her.

As she waved, she could see a serious-looking man with a deep scar on his left cheek driving her uncle, who was sitting alone in the backseat as he gazed straight ahead with a grimaced expression.

"Hmm." She turned again and focused her attention on greeting her parents. "It looks dark in the house." She realized the lights were off as she approached the front door. "I wonder if they are home."

Taking her keys out, she opened the door. "*Ciao*, Mama, *ciao*, Papa. I am home," she yelled out. "Are you home?" She walked into the hallway. "Mama, Papa? Where are you?"

She realized they were not home. "Let me leave a note for them." She went into the kitchen, looking for paper and a pen. "At least I tried to see them. No guilt here." She giggled.

A notepad Mama used for her shopping list was on the counter, next to a basket of Mama's freshly made biscuits. She smelled one and wrapped a few to put in her pocketbook.

"I guess they went shopping," she answered herself.

Taking the notepaper, she searched in her purse for a pen. Feeling the book, she took it out, placing it on the counter and retrieved a pen to write her note.

> Just stopped in. Sorry I missed you. Will call you later.
> *Ti amo,* Sophia * And the biscuits were *meraviglioso*!

Putting the star next to her name gave her childhood nickname some reverence, letting her parents know she loved them.

After writing the note, she turned her attention to the book. The black hardcover had a texture like cloth, and the tan words were deeply embedded on its cover and on its rim.

"That's strange. There is no author." She noticed. "Hmm." Sophia started to flip through the pages that seemed yellowed by time. On the inside cover was a faded note written in pen: "I have sent this to you because you inquired about the authorities of the darkness."

She read the words and was intrigued but still very confused. Flipping through the pages, she stopped. "The Reality of the Rulers. Hmm." She continued to another page. "The Golden Fleece. The Treasury of Light is found within the profundities of oneself."

Looking closer at the words, she whispered, "*Che cosa*? No wonder Uncle Egidio was not interested in this book."

She flipped through the pages again and started reading the first thing she saw.

"For we wrestle not against flesh and blood, but against principalities, against powers, against the rulers of the darkness of this world, against spiritual wickedness in high places," she read out loud.

Hearing a car pass by interrupted her focus. "I'll have to read this later." She pulled out her mobile and called for a taxi, but as she waited for her ride, the pages of the book called to her curiosity.

"Well, I guess I could read a few more pages." She opened the book again and flipped to another page.

"Our bodies are constructed of lunar matter, and the archons rule within us according to our nature. Only the Twice-born (who have the 'wedding garment of the soul') have Solar bodies: the chariot of Ezekiel." She paused, taking a breath.

"Thus, we who remain dressed with lunar bodies are subject to the wheel of samsara: evolution and devolution." She shook her head. "Yeah, OK." She flipped the pages again…

There are three ways that the Sacrament of Priesthood is expressed:
- Priesthood of Yesod: Sexual Magic.
- Priesthood of Hod: Natural, Ceremonial, or Ritualistic Magic.
- Priesthood of Netzach: Hermetic Magic.

"Sexual magic? *Che cosa*?" She could not believe her eyes. Reading the book out of context made her more curious. "Maybe it's a good thing Uncle Egidio did not read this." She laughed.

A horn sounded outside. Sophia raised her head from the book to see her taxi was waiting in front of the house.

"Oh well, I will get back to you later." She gathered her things and ate another biscuit on the way out. Getting back to her flat did not take much time. "I am ready for *caffè* to go with Mama's biscuits. I think I will wait to call Dominic tomorrow. I am tired."

Knock, knock, knock…

"Who is…" She opened the door. "*Ciao*, Eula. What are you doing here now?"

"Mm, that *caffè* smells good." Eula rushed in.

"I have extra, if you want some."

"No thanks. I can't stay, actually." Eula headed straight for the sofa.

"*Che cosa*? You can't! That is a first." Sophia was surprised.

Eula started moving the cushions on the sofa, then got down on her knees.

"Yeah, I am doing a weekly cleanse of my body and my spirit from toxins. That means *caffè* is out." Eula's face was so innocent, like it was an old habit.

"Eula, what are you doing? Wait, what?" Sophia did a double take.

"A cleansing." Eula was searching frantically for something.

She only briefly looked at Sophia, then starting to explain, "I have an IsAgenix shake twice a day, eat a few healthy snacks, drink lots of water, and eat a big healthy supper. It's good for my mind and body." Eula returned to her search, looking under the sofa, so her words were muffled.

"What are you searching for?"

"Ah, here it is. My favorite earring." She stood up and put it in her ear. "I lost it when I slept over."

"OK, now tell me about this cleansing."

"Actually, I can't stay. I have to get my rest."

"Your rest?" Sophia was confused again.

"*Sì*, I have to get up at three in the morning to get ready for my four a.m. meditation." She was so serious. Sophia dared not laugh at her.

"What are you talking about?"

"Yeah, I joined the Brahma Kumaris, and that is the time we meet at the center to pray."

"Wait, are you telling me you get up at three in the morning to go pray at a center at four a.m.?" Sophia's expression was more than shock. She was concerned. Eula had a tendency to be a follower and had a history of being taken advantage of.

"*Sì*, it's important to me. It means the Daughters of Brahma in Hindi." Eula was intent that Sophia understood her dedication to her new inspiration.

"What are they? I mean who are they? I have never heard of them before."

"Sophia, don't worry." She walked closer to Sophia and rubbed her arm. "They are good. We honor some Hindi traditions and beliefs like reincarnation, which you know I believe in." Eula was educating her friend. Eula then looked into the wall mirror that hung near the door. "Ah, I feel better." She touched her newly found earring.

"What does your group do?" Sophia wanted to understand more.

"It's an eighty-year-old practice of meditation and prayer recognizing one Supreme Soul." She gazed backed at Sophia, who was still trying to grasp Eula's new passion. But Eula was confident. "And we adhere to a vegetarian diet that helps us stay cleansed of toxins."

"Oh." Sophia didn't know what to make of Eula's new friends.

"Sophia, don't worry. You should be happy. The Brahma Kumaris puts women in charge to help create a world spreading inner peace, love, and happiness. Don't you think we need more powerful women in this world to help balance the mess we are in now?" Eula illustrated her defiance toward the status quo.

"Ah." Sophia thought about it for a moment. "I guess. I mean, I see your point." Sophia tried to offer encouragement.

Although it was for something she did not fully understand, she was happy for Eula finding a new outlet to harness her curious energy.

"Sophia, *va tutto bene*. Trust me." Eula could sense Sophia's hesitation. She kissed Sophia on both cheeks. "I have to go."

"Hey, what about that guy?" Sophia suddenly remembered Eula's last passion. "The one we met with Michael. What's his name, ah…Paolo?"

"Ah, yeah, Paolo was not meant to be. I will tell you about it over the weekend. *Addio*." And Eula closed the door behind her.

"Ah, ah, OK." Sophia waved, but it was too late for Eula to notice. "*Accidenti*, she flew out of here like a bird. I guess she really needs her rest." She shook her head and went to the kitchen to get her coffee and Mama's biscuits.

"Mmm, that tastes good. *Grazie*, Mama." She ate one biscuit. "It's just what I needed." She sat down on her sofa to relax with her new book.

Knock, knock, knock…

"Grr. Eula, what did you—" Sophia got up and swung the door open to see Dominic bundled up in his fitted leather jacket, with a box in his hand.

"Oh, I am sorry. I thought you were Eula." She was surprised to see him standing there. "I didn't know you were coming."

"*Sì*, I know, but I thought if you were in, we could have an early dinner." He held up the box of Italian food. "I know you are busy, so I thought we would eat in, if that is all right."

"*Sì*, of course. *Per favore*, come in." Sophia felt guilty for not calling him. "Here, let me help you set up the food in the kitchen."

She was a little caught off guard by his unexpected arrival. "Hmm. I am used to being on my own most of the time, but I guess it is nice to see him."

He placed the box on the counter and started to unload it. "I thought Italian was a little different. I hope you like it." He took the utensils from the drawer as Sophia got the dishes.

Sophia noticed how he made himself at home. "It is like we are an old couple getting ready for our supper. She thought, "I am not sure if I like my space being invaded."

"I got your favorite." He held out the container for her. He used his fork to scoop up the spaghetti with meat sauce on her dish. "Sophia, what is the matter? Are you not in the mood for Italian or company?"

"Ah, nothing, *va bene. Grazie.*" Sophia felt silly. She smiled then took her dish. "It smells delicious," she complemented him, putting the dish on the small table. "I think we need some *vino.*"

"Ah, *sì.*" Dominic pulled a bottle of Cabernet from the deep box. "I do try to think of everything." He turned and pulled out two glasses from her cupboard.

"I guess you did think of everything." She put her book down on the counter and got the table for them to share.

They sat together on her sofa. It was a very intimate setting.

"*È delizioso. Grazie*, Dominic." She was appreciative of his efforts to impress her.

"I am glad you are enjoying it," he smiled before tasting his wine, then toasting her. "I am happy I took another chance to see you. I do not like leftovers."

She laughed, putting her dish down. Taking a sip of her wine, then remembered. "I have to go to Carmine's wake tomorrow morning." A sudden sadness rushed over her. "I am sorry. It must be the *vino.*"

"Ah, *il mio amore*. I know what it is to deal with death." He put his dish down and placed his hand over her lap. "It is never easy."

Sophia looked into Dominic's light almond eyes. He took her hand and kissed it gently, then looked back into her eyes.

She felt a tingle down her spine, turning her eyes a lighter green as if she were a cat ready to purr.

"I have come to realize that death in this world is a rebirth in another." His sentiment was sorrowful and uplifting. "The emotion that brings both worlds together is love." He kissed her hand again.

Her body language let him know she connected to his words and his emotion. He kissed her wrist slowly and tenderly. Moving up her arm, he kissed her again and again until he reached her lips.

She anxiously waited for his lips to touch hers, putting down her glass and moved closer to him.

"Our world order, being one, will unite us, and we will create a new world where death and life invoke only happiness," he whispered in her ear.

A tear came to her eyes as she felt the emotion of his kisses. He touched her hair, moving a few loose strands through his fingers.

"*Sei così bella* and so strong." He turned his attention back to her lips, kissing them softly.

The room was heating up with each kiss. Their passion grew. The stronger the kisses, the more their hands roamed, until Sophia backed up and took off her blouse and bra. He obliged, removing his shirt.

Holding her breast in his hand, he kissed it like a child sucking his mother's tit. Sophia groaned. He responded by taking off her shoes and pants, then his. On the sofa, nude, with their flesh touching, she wanted him, all of him.

"I need him so much right now." Something came over her, and she motioned for him to move back so she could stand up. Bending over the sofa arm and a pillow, she exposed her back to him.

Dominic caressed her smooth skin. "*Mia a'more*, one day you shall be all mine." His hands were soft from the many manicures over the years. A tingle went up her spine as he came closer, teasing her.

"*Per favore*, Dominic, I have missed you," she pleaded. It reminded her of the pleasures they shared when they were younger.

He was happy to indulge her fantasy.

***

Valentinus sat silently in his chair, admiring the works of art in the Sistine Chapel. The second votes had just been counted.

"And now there are even more votes for Cardinal Sisinnius than this morning." In his mind he replayed how the votes earlier in the day were counted. "*Mio Padre*, do you not hear my pleas?" Then he thought of having Irenaeus taking Korsig's place. "He makes me sick to my stomach." He bowed his head.

"*Mio Dio, per favore*, let us not have history repeat itself. This Rule of the Harlots will surely destroy your good name…and your church this time around," he prayed desperately.

Valentinus became aware of shuffling noises as the Cardinals started to leave their seats.

"The first day is done," he thought. "I just have to make it through another day. At least he is not the new pontiff today." Valentinus knew Sisinnius was eager to take Pope Gregory's place, having already made use of the many vital connections in the Curia to prepare for his assentation.

Lost in a moment, Valentinus felt a slap on his back. Startled, he flew forward in his seat.

"Valentinus, there is nothing you will gain by sitting there." Cardinal Perez smiled down on Valentinus, who bore an expression of a little boy who had just put his beloved pet to rest. "Come with me." Perez gestured with his eyes and pointed the way out of the chapel.

"Where?" Realizing Perez was right, Valentinus stood.

"For a walk. You look like you need a friend."

"Are you my friend?" Valentinus asked pointedly, walking behind him.

"It looks like I may be the only friend you have besides Korsig," Perez abruptly replied. "Come on, let's walk."

Having no better ideas, Valentinus followed Perez out of the chapel, where various cardinals were gathered in huddles based on their progressing chosen agendas.

"Look at them. The traditionalists are against change while their progressive challengers are ready to wage a revolt to obtain change," Perez observed and pointed out to Valentinus.

Valentinus added, "And the faithful people are the ones who suffer."

They passed Irenaeus in one group and Sisinnius in another. Valentinus looked straight ahead as if they were not even there, continuing down the corridor toward the exit. They headed for their temporary residence in the Domus Marthae Sanctae, where Valentinus could seek his refuge. It was not a far walk. Still, it gave Perez an opportunity to talk with Valentinus.

"Walking is good for the soul, don't you think?" Perez smiled fleetingly. "I understand Korsig is still in a coma. I am sorry for your friend." He was sympathetic.

"How did you hear of his current condition?"

"I know people." Perez winked. "It's just a matter of knowing the right people."

Valentinus looked hard at Perez, wondering which side he was on. There was a good chance that as a staunch supporter of Pope Gregory, Valentinus faced uncertain hardships in his current position within the Curia. Revenge was something cardinals throughout history had learned to perfect.

"Valentinus, I will not pretend to be your friend. I can see the distrust in your eyes." Perez used a soft demeanor as they continued their walk.

Valentinus did not change his expression.

"However, we do have common goals," Perez continued. "We want what is best for the followers of Christ, to help bring them closer to Him. Am I right in that assertion?" Perez already knew Valentinus's answer.

Valentinus nodded only a bit.

"Listen..." Perez stopped and looked Valentinus in the eyes. "A concerned friend told me Korsig contacted a man in Rome to investigate a connection between the IOR and a solar company that is tied to organized crime and has a possible link to a terrorist group in Libya."

"How do you know this?"

Perez ignored Valentinus's question.

"This man, I am told, goes by a nickname, the Negotiator, and this person told Korsig he would find a lead in Bindisi. That is all I know." Perez could not or would not go into details.

"Who is your friend?" Valentinus was still suspicious because of Borgia cautioning him against Perez.

Perez shrugged and continued walking. "Cardinal Pietro Gasparri is fond of you, and he also understands your relationship with Pope Gregory. He asked me to help you during the conclave." Perez walked slower. "Gasparri agreed that Korsig should go to Bindisi, meeting a contact in the Apulia area, to follow up on this Negotiator's lead, and now Gasparri feels terrible about what happened to Korsig."

"So are you working for Gasparri?" Valentinus wanted to know how far his loyalties went for Gasparri.

"Valentinus, you should know I treat everyone as a friend—perhaps not my best friend, but still enough to be friends." Perez smirked. "Unlike you, who would let his enemies be known rather than keep people guessing about who his real friends are." He stopped walking and turned toward Valentinus. "I will let you know when I am your friend, but I will not let you know when you are my enemy. You will not see it coming. Keep people guessing. It is more useful in obtaining your goals." He casually started his walk again.

"You say a negotiator spoke to Korisg and advised him to go to Bindisi?" Valentinus accepted his honesty.

"Be careful who you speak to." Perez avoided answering the question and leaned into Valentinus as they walked side by side. "Even the bushes have eyes and ears." He pointed to a few bushes along their path. "I understand Irenaeus will pay you a visit tonight. Listen to him." He stepped aside, "Well, I enjoyed our walk, my friend. Get some rest. You look like you need it."

Valentinus stood back and stared at Cardinal Perez as he turned and walked away. His confusion mounted as he watched Perez disappear into the Domus Marthae Sanctae residence.

Looking around, Valentinus took notice of which cardinals were within which groups as they were helped off a shuttle bus and went into the residence. He could almost hear the whispering gossip.

"Oh look, he is upset he will not be pontiff. He is unfit to be our leader. He is Gnostic—a heretic." He could hear the voices in his mind.

The pain in his chest tightened all his muscles. His head began to ache.

"*Mio Dio, per favore*, help me," he prayed on the way back to his second-floor corner room within the residence.

He closed the door securely behind him. Looking at his sitting area, then his separate bedroom and his private small bathroom, he sighed. "I hate being away from home."

In the sitting area, a tall cassock-friendly wardrobe used up space on the corner wall, and two sitting chairs centered a large window. In front of one chair, a small desk served him for both working and as a table for eating his meals when he did not go to the dining hall.

"My modest suite has plenty of square footage, but I still feel claustrophobic." He went to his bed and collapsed, putting his face deep in his pillow.

"Just take me now," he called out in a muffled voice. He let out the air from his lungs, trying to feel the suffocation. To no avail, he gave up his feeble attempt and raised his head.

Resting his head on his pillow, he closed his eyes as one tear flowed down the side of his cheek. He rested, breathing in and breathing out for some time.

Knock, knock, knock...

Valentinus stirred begrudgingly and got up as if he were an old man.

He looked around the foreign room in a daze. Hearing the knock again, he came back into his reality. He opened the door and immediately remembered Perez's words. A smug Irenaeus stood in the doorway.

"Valentinus, you look terrible. Are you feeling well?" Irenaeus sounded almost cheerful.

"What can I do for you, Irenaeus?"

"Can I come in? Or are you going to leave your guest standing outside here?" Irenaeus was sarcastic.

"You are no guest of mine, but if you must." Valentinus gestured as he held the door open.

Irenaeus walked past Valentinus, measuring up his foe.

"So what do you want?" Valentinus closed the door, analyzing Irenaeus's every move.

Irenaeus turned toward Valentinus. "I will get to the point. You know I am a member of the Catholic Popular Party, and we wish to restore order not only in Mother Church but also in the world. This new election may give us an advantage that no other time would allow. You know the world has become an unstable place for Christians, Jews, and even Muslims alike." He stated the obvious.

"What is your point?" Valentinus grew impatient.

"Valentinus, we would like you to join forces with us. I know you and I have had our issues, but we share a love for our Mother Church that is stronger than the bond of hate."

"Spare me your politics. I do not subscribe to the brand of socialism within your party." Valentinus was intentionally rude. "And even if I did, I would not trust you as far as I could throw you."

"I can understand that." Valentinus's stare made Irenaeus a little uncomfortable. He turned his back. "But this goes far beyond me and you, Valentinus. Terrorism is replacing faith with fear. It is replacing life with death. It is—"

"I said spare me your rhetoric!" Valentinus impatiently yelled. "What do you really want?"

"Listen, I am here to try to help save our church, whether you want to believe that or not." Irenaeus paced the floor. "There is a plot to rid the world of our church and our traditions."

"There is always a plot to rid the world of our church. Tell me something new."

Irenaeus bowed his head as if defeated. "I am here because they believe you will listen to me. It is not easy to be humbled to you, and they knew that. Still, here I am asking for your support, because it means that much that we work together to save our church."

Standing still, Irenaeus lectured like a teacher. "It was not my idea to stand before you and divulge information that I believe is above your stature." Irenaeus still found a way to insult him.

"To hell with you and those who sent you!" Valentinus shouted, exposing the large veins in his neck.

"No, Valentinus, to hell with Mother Church!" Irenaeus shouted back as he pointed his finger at Valentinus. "That is what the terrorists are saying right now. Christians are being killed…murdered…because they are Christians, just like in years past. We need to save these people and our church by working together."

Valentinus stood silent for a moment watching Irenaeus's theatrics.

"There is another fear," Irenaeus divulged as if revealing a revelation. "Russia has already invaded Crimea and has secretly made a deal with Iran to back its current leader. As you know, Iran's leader is a terrorist. Russia can create confusion while it takes control over more territory. There is speculation Russia wants to control the supply of energy and electricity over the Baltic States which could give them leverage over Poland and even Germany." He raised his voice and used his hands fanatically to make his point. "A casualty of this scheme is our church. Mother Church is being infiltrated by many who want to destroy us from within." Irenaeus lowered his tone as if someone else was listening in.

"*Sì*, and you are part of them!" Valentinus stopped him in his tracks.

"No, Valentinus, I am not," Irenaeus pleaded as sincerely as he could. "We do not see things the same way, but this is a very different time in history. This is a very different world. We have already been rocked with scandals, with more to follow, but these infiltrators will turn the flock against us. You already see the IOR has experienced huge losses. If we continue on this path, we will see our financial demise, and where will people turn for charity, their faith, and redemption?"

Valentinus listened and understood those concerns very well.

"If we lose sheep, others will gain sheep," Irenaeus warned. "Souls of mankind are at stake."

"So you want me to vote for Sisinnius because he can save us and Mother Church? Is that it?" Valentinus asked the question already knowing the answer.

"I want you to see a bigger picture, Valentinus." Irenaeus tried to sound like a voice of reason. "I am hoping and even praying that you will see what has to be done. Sisinnius is from the Middle East. He understands their culture. He is our best chance of saving souls. Russia is spearheading terrorism through a backdoor, and Muslim extremists vie for control that is spreading throughout the world."

"You don't know that Sisinnius can be a more effective leader than Sforza or Della Rovere. You don't know that Russia will succeed in this plot you speak of," Valentinus said.

"*Sì*, we do!" Irenaeus stood his ground. "We have intelligence at very high levels, and they are telling us that the Americans are backing away from conflicts. The Russians believe the Americans are fools and are weak." Irenaeus lectured his student.

"The United Nations has done little to curb the violence in Crimea, and even as Russia now prepares to take over more of the Ukraine, the UN does nothing. They have also failed at stopping the spread of Muslim radicalism. So, what I am telling you is that these concerns from within these walls are very real. Why do you think Pope Gregory resigned? He knows he is old and could not accept this challenge." Irenaeus offered no apologies for his judgements.

Valentinus took a step closer as if to threaten Irenaeus.

"I am sorry. Truly I am, Valentinus." Irenaeus held up his hands to fend off whatever blows Valentinus wanted to punish him with.

Valentinus saw Irenaeus's willingness to be sacrificed, then stopped short.

"*Per favore*, Valentinus, you know I am right. I love Gregory also, but I love my church more, and I am sorry if that truth hurts. I have been asked if you would consider joining the Catholic Popular Party and be on our team. Working together, we can help eradicate terrorism, saving souls and Mother Church." He paused, giving Valentinus a sincere enough expression. "There is something else…" He hesitated. "You know there are secrets as much as I do. Many believe the prophecy of Our Lady of Fatima may be on the horizon."

"Ha! I don't believe you, Irenaeus!" Valentinus stood back and laughed in his face.

"Fatima prophecy or not, this Roman System will not change with the likes of you or Sisinnius." Valentinus shouted louder. "You stand for self-preservation more than church preservation. Now, if you don't mind, I have heard enough. *Per favore*, leave me," he ordered.

"All right, Valentinus. I will leave you." Irenaeus took the hint. "But just remember this moment when you had the chance to help Mother Church and you ignored your calling." Irenaeus sternly warned him.

"Get out," Valentinus hissed, pointing his figure toward the door. "You can tell your groupies that I will do what I am called to do by God, not your Popular Party."

Irenaeus went to the door, opened it, and turned to Valentinus. "You are making a big mistake, my friend," he challenged closing it behind him in true theoretical style.

Valentinus remembered the conversation with Perez: "Listen to his words, my friend." He was more confused about whom to trust.

Knock, knock, knock…

"What do you wan—" Valentinus was ready to pounce as he opened the door.

"*Scusami, signore…*I…" The big-eyed red-haired Irishman stood frightened in the doorway. Bishop Murphy was holding a tray of food, his hands trembling from shock.

"Oh, I am so sorry. I thought you…" Valentinus turned red from embarrassment. "No matter. *Sì*, of course, *per favore*, come in." Valentinus tried to regain his composure, taking the tray from Bishop Murphy. "*Grazie*, I do appreciate your bringing me my meals. The dining hall is too crowded, and I need prayer."

"I do understand." Murphy, who sounded more like a leprechaun, was sympathetic. "It is time for much prayer and negotiation." He bowed his head. "If you need anything else, please let me know."

"*Sì*, I will. *Grazie.*" Valentinus was humbled.

Closing the door, Valentinus could smell the steak.

"I am starving!" He was reminded he had not eaten well in recent days.

306

"Mm, this looks good," he exclaimed, picking up the plate cover warmer and putting it on the desk.

Valentinus sat, putting his napkin over his lap, and began to pray. "*Per favore*, my *Padre* in heaven, send me a sign. *Per favore*, forgive me and absolve me of my sins as I continue to serve only your needs. This I pray. Amen."

He took a few bites, enjoying the taste of the mushroom sauce as both the pieces of steak and mushrooms melted in his mouth.

Buzz, buzz, buzz…

The mobile phone in his sock tickled his right ankle. He pulled it out and looked at the unfamiliar number. Hesitating, he contemplated who was calling him before he flipped the top cover over but said nothing.

"*Ciao*, Cardinal de Marcosi. We have not spoken in some time, but I am sure you remember me." The familiar deep-throated, Italian-speaking voice was hushed.

"How did you get this number?" Valentinus put his napkin on his plate and stood.

"You should know I have eyes and ears everywhere," the voice continued. "Korsig may not live. His injuries are pretty severe. So I am sure after Sisinnius is elected pontiff, he will keep Irenaeus as dean of the Sacred College of Cardinals." He paused. "You should not trust them."

"I know this already, but *per favore*, tell me about Korsig. Who was he trying to see in Bindisi?" Valentinus rushed his thoughts. "And how do you know Sisinnius will be elected?"

"I know many things." His answer was short. "Korsig was in Bindisi because I sent him to speak to someone I know."

"Who?" Valentinus was impatient.

"His name is not important. He never met the contact." Flippant, the Negotiator continued. "He did, however, speak with someone I don't know. I believe it was someone associated with a Solar Star Development Company. They have been accused of stealing millions of euros in subsidies from the Italian government, claiming to be small solar fields when actually they are really quite the opposite."

The Negotiator explained briefly. "Korsig was fooled into thinking he was speaking with the man I sent, and unfortunately you know what happened."

"How do you know this?"

"As I said, I know about a great many things." The Negotiator's sarcastic tone came through. "You need to know that WS Asia Capital is a shell company associated with this Solar Star Company. They have ties to Cosa Nostra, who in turn has ties to a terrorist group in Libya. I am trying to find out more information as we speak." The Negotiator was stern. "And I can tell you that the owner of WS Asia Capital also works for my client, and this is a problem for him too."

"Your client is a member of Cosa Nostra?"

"No, a German named Lars Schneider, who runs WS Asia Capital, brought this solar company deal to your Cardinal Rosotti without my client's knowledge. It seems that Schneider and a local Roman, a man named Joseph Grillo, met with Rosotti and blackmailed him into making sure that the IOR would approve a loan for fifty million euros. Grillo and Schneider wanted to expand their supposedly small solar fields, reaping Italian government subsidies, but the money went instead into WS Asia Capital, who owns the Solar Star Company. From what I can see, the scheme was to have many shell companies to move the money around. This WS Asia Capital associates with many companies, some in Libya with terrorist ties." He laid out the concern. "So that means the church directly or indirectly invested in a terrorist-related organization. Do you understand?"

"How can you prove this?" Valentinus was surprised and disgusted. "Who is your client?"

"I cannot say, but I can tell you that you know many of his companies. He is a very wealthy and influential businessman. And he does not want to be associated with this mess. There is an issue that the media may soon find out about."

"What issue?"

"The fifty million IOR loan was secured by fifty million in German bonds that investigators will soon discover never existed."

"What? How?" Valentinus felt as if he were watching a terrible movie. "That is not possible!"

"Ha, you are naïve, Cardinal de Marcosi. Do you not read or see the news?" The Negotiator laughed loudly in Valentinus's ear. "Can you not see fraud is everywhere? Do you not see what deception lies beyond the fraud our own governments perpetrate?"

"I don't understand." Valentinus did not want to sound confused but had no idea where he was going with his comment.

"Fraud is committed at the highest levels. Look what happened to LIBOR. As you may know, world interest rates are set by an organization known as London Interbank Offered Rate. Banks across the world were falsely inflating or deflating their rates and giving the impression they were more creditworthy than they were. They were on the take for years, and how can this happen?" He was getting to his point. "Because people in authoritative positions looked away. The reality in our world today is that people look away when it helps them line their own pockets or further their own causes."

"*Merda*!" Nauseated, Valentinus sighed.

The Negotiator was direct. "I cannot explain this in detail to you now. You only need to know that someone in the conclave has double-crossed my client, and the only way to make good is for Sisinnius to be elected pontiff." The Negotiator stated his business proposal with force.

"What sacrilege! The Holy Father's seat is not for sale!" Valentinus felt the acid in his stomach rising up.

"Valentinus, you know and I know that for over a thousand years, that is exactly what has happened time and time again. Look up your own history." He was smug. "The media will find out about the nonexistent German bonds and that the money, even indirectly, went to terrorists. However, my client is willing to make good on those bonds to cover the IOR loan to Solar Star Development Company." He added, "With interest."

The Negotiator had hoped for Valentinus to understand his role in making sure his client got what he wanted.

"Will this never end?" Valentinus put his hand to his forehead in desperation.

"I am afraid not." The Negotiator was unsympathetic. "Valentinus, we have a history, and you know you can trust me. I need to know what is going on inside the conclave. It is important that I know who has allegiances with or against Sisinnius. Can you do that for me?" He wanted to feel out Valentinus's own alliances. "And I will keep you updated on your friend Korsig."

"How will I contact you?" Valentinus was thinking about his few options.

"I will contact you. I know where you are. And Valentinus, get some rest. You look terrible." Click.

"What!" Valentinus shouted into the mobile but the Negotiator had already ended the call.

Valentinus looked around the room at the chairs, the desk, and the bedroom.

"Is there a camera?" He could feel the invasion of his privacy creeping up on him like a spider in the middle of the night.

"Ouch." He was looking under the lamp, putting his finger toward the on and off button to see if anything was there, when he burnt his finger.

Knock, knock, knock…

His search was interrupted.

"Oh, *Caz.*" He quickly put his mobile back in his sock and reached for the door.

"*Ciao*, Cardinal de Marcosi. I just wanted to make sure you did not need anything else. Are you finished with your tray?" Murphy asked politely.

"No. No, it's fine, *per favore*. Take the tray. It was very good. *Grazie.*" Valentinus tried to act as if he were not too anxious.

"Very well." The leprechaun-sounding Bishop Murphy smiled. "I shall see you early in the morning then." He bowed his head. "*Buona notte, signore.*" And he left the room.

Running his fingers through his hair and down his face, Valentinus gasped in disbelief. "What the devil is going on?"

"*Per favore*, Yeshua, help me," he pleaded again. He paced his room, thinking of the events leading up to this moment.

His thoughts crashed through his mind as ocean waves crashed the cliffs and rocks during a storm.

With pacing, pacing, and more pacing, he made himself exhausted.

"Yawn…" He stretched out his back. "I need to get some rest, as everyone keeps telling me."

"*Per favore, Madre di Dio*, help me." Lying down on his bed, he stared in a daze at the ceiling, praying.

"Lealia, don't run over there. You will—" A young, dark-haired girl about twelve ran in front of the young Valentinus on a farm where the wheat was as tall as she was.

Her long hair swayed in the breeze, and her blue petticoat highlighted her light hazel eyes as she turned to wave to Valentinus.

"Lealia, come back," Valentinus shouted.

Lealia laughed and turned back around. She ran away as if they were playing a game.

"You can't catch me," she yelled back into the breeze of a beautiful summer day. White fluffy clouds dotted the sky as the sun shone brightly.

"Lealia, *per favore*, come back." Valentinus ran toward her as fast as he could, but he could not keep up. "Lealia, *per favore*—"

Her screams gave Valentinus a chill. "Lealia! Where are you? Lealia!" he cried out again, running as fast as he could.

"*Signore, scu…scusa*." Bishop Murphy had nudged Valentinus's shoulder.

"Oh *mio Dio*—" Valentinus jumped up. "What the—"

"*Scusami, signore*, I am sorry. I heard you calling out, so I came in to see if you were all right." His concern was genuine.

"Ah, *sì, sì*…" Valentinus looked around the room, realizing it was morning. He had almost forgotten where he was.

"I brought your breakfast, *signore*." Murphy pointed to the desk. "Remember, conclave starts in one hour. Might I suggest a shower? With all due respect, you look like you could use a little sprucing up."

"*Sì, grazie.*" He sat up on his bed. "I will heed your advice."

Bishop Murphy bowed his head and left Valentinus alone.

Rubbing the sleep from his eyes, he remembered the conversation with the Negotiator as the aroma of eggs filled his nostrils. Valentinus looked at his desk with the tray of food. His stomach growled. Without any delay, he ate and readied himself for the day.

As difficult as it was, he made his way back to the Sistine Chapel.

"Harlots and more harlots!" He looked at his 112 peers and sneered as he sat in his seat.

"*Buongiorno*, Cardinal, I trust you slept well." Cardinal Perez sat down next to him.

"No, in fact I did not," Valentinus snarled.

"Too bad. Sleep will most certainly elude you after today. You had better get some rest when you can." Perez stood up again. "And just remember your enemies are watching, so rest with one eye open."

Valentinus did not have time to respond before the conclave ceremonies commenced.

Everyone took to his seats, and it began with ritualistic prayers and Irenaeus's daily introduction.

"Beware of false prophets who come in sheep's clothing, but inwardly who are ravening wolves," Valentinus mumbled, feeling sick. He looked around, guessing who was voting for which candidate.

When the ballots were read, Valentinus was surprised.

"I can't believe Sisinnius lost four votes, and I gained four votes." He smiled in delight of upsetting Irenaeus's plan before taking the first break of the day.

"I guess he does not know as much as he thought." Valentinus remembered the Negotiator's push for Sisinnius.

As the traditional black smoke vented from the chapel chimney, announcing to the world a new leader had not been chosen, Valentinus took notice of Irenaeus springing into action and racing toward a small group of cardinals. The one from Egypt was looking particularly nervous, while the others, two from Germany, tried to calm him.

Irenaeus looked furious, which amused Valentinus.

"You reap what you sow." He got up to leave and noticed Sisinnius and another cardinal from Cuba looking straight at him.

"I suppose they are looking at you because you were not supposed to receive any votes." A voice from behind him made him turn around.

"Ah, Cardinal Alexander Borgia, where have you been hiding?" Valentinus was sarcastic.

"I have been doing my job, Valentinus. What about you?" Borgia looked annoyed. "Can I tell Gregory you have been doing your job, Valentinus? You were not supposed to get votes. How do you suppose that happened?" Borgia demanded an answer.

"I guess they cannot control everyone." Valentinus referred to Sisinnius and Irenaeus. "*E grazie a Dio.*" Valentinus smiled.

"Come and walk with me." Borgia smirked. "We will walk back to the Domus Marthae Sanctae together. Shuttles are for old men," he joked, being an older man himself.

Valentinus followed Borgia, taking his wounded pride with him.

"You know it is named after Saint Martha the hospitable, who was a sibling to Saints Mary and Lazarus of Bethany," Borgia offered, trying his best to soothe Valentinus's hurt pride.

"What?" Valentinus was distracted.

"The Domus Marthae Sanctae." Borgia wanted to make small talk. "Pope John Paul II built it…when times seemed less complicated." He sighed.

"Hmm." Valentinus hardly acknowledged the lesson and stared ahead, following Borgia like a student following his teacher.

"You know people believe in you, Valentinus." Borgia flattered him. "You must know that."

Valentinus waited for Borgia to unveil himself. They walked through the papal corridors, passing the centuries-old art that embraced them.

When they reached the outside, the sun was shining. The winter had given them a reprieve for today. Valentinus took in a deep breath. Inhaling the fresh air expanded his lungs, giving him a new lease on life, or at least on that moment.

A light, chilly breeze moved Valentinus's hair, sending a tingle down his neck. He hardly noticed Borgia talking to him.

"Valentinus, are you listening to me?" Borgia stopped and poked him.

"Uh, *sì*." Valentinus then admitted, "I am sorry. My mind is elsewhere."

"Well, you had better listen and get back to reality," Borgia stressed. "There is another media story that will be breaking, and it will not look good for us or Mother Church."

"*Sì*, I know." Valentinus did not give his words a thought.

"You know? What do you know?" Borgia was agitated.

"Ah I mean, I know there is always a media story coming out. What else is new?" Valentinus tried to cover his slipup.

"Never mind." Borgia looked suspicious. "I understand Irenaeus paid you a visit last night."

"News travels fast."

"I suppose he mentioned the fear some clerics have?" Borgia was serious. "About the prophecy?"

"*Sì*," Valentinus acknowledged the impractical theory. "There is always some superstition to be afraid of."

"I suppose." Borgia shrugged and touched his arm. "But what if it were true?" He looked grim.

"Ah, come on, you too?" Valentinus looked at his old friend, giving him a half smile.

"Let me show you something." Borgia pulled a piece of paper from his pocket. "A note was found in Korsig's pocket. Look."

"The first attack from the Sons of Darkness shall be undertaken against the Sons of the Light," Valentinus read from the paper. "What is this?"

"I am not sure, but I am told the original note looked like it was written in a hurry. We assume Korsig wrote the note, but we are not sure." Borgia took the paper back and placed it securely in his pocket.

"Hey, how did you get that?" Valentinus thought about it for a second. "We are not supposed to have communication with the outside world."

Borgia smiled. "The same way you knew of a media story coming out."

Valentinus looked guilty.

"Do you know what the words could mean?" Borgia returned to his serious demeanor.

"The Sons of Darkness against the Sons of Light?" Valentinus placed his hand under his chin, thinking. "I will have to do some research after conclave. Or perhaps Korsig can tell us when he recovers."

"What if he does not recover?" Borgia was sincere, respecting Valentinus's feelings.

Valentinus ignored the question. "What does this note have to do with Fatima?"

"Russia is working with Iran to secure the Middle East for their own purposes, spreading their ideals." Borgia sighed. "They aim for the destruction of the Jews and our church."

"Look, I will give that there is a concern about Russia, Iran, and our church," Valentinus admitted begrudgingly. "But to suggest that this prophecy is to be feared, I think it is nonsense to sway the conclave. For all you know, Korsig could have been reading a book and wrote down the words." He turned to continue walking.

"Do you know why Korsig was in Bindisi?" Borgia pressed on, wanting to see what Valentinus would divulge.

Valentinus turned to Borgia. "Sì, he was confirming information that was given to him by an anonymous source. It was something to do with the IOR and an investment with a solar company. That is all I know." Valentinus lied, not knowing whom to trust, even if Borgia was an old friend.

Walking a little slower, Valentinus saw two other cardinals ahead of them and watched them as they walked by. Peering eyes and open ears made Valentinus nervous.

"Do you believe in the Fatima prophecy?" Valentinus asked Borgia out of curiosity.

"Sì, I do." Borgia's face bore witness to his belief. "I think we are in real trouble, my friend, from all sides, and it is at the expense of God's lost souls." Borgia looked as if he could cry.

315

Valentinus bowed his head. "It always is."

"That is why you must help me by uniting behind us, having one leader of Mother Church. People will follow your lead. Sforza and Della Rovere are losing ground, and that will help Sisinnius to lead our church against Russia and these extreme Muslim heretics."

"*Dio mio!* Are you serious?" Valentinus raised his voice in anger, rubbing his fingers through his hair in disbelief.

"Valentinus, I do not trust Sisinnius either, but I have to believe that his experience, especially in the Middle East, could help unite us. This is a crisis of world proportions." Borgia raised his voice to make his point, prompting the cardinals behind them to gasp.

"I am sorry. I didn't mean to get carried away." Borgia realized his outburst, then touched Valentinus's arm in a polite gesture.

"I understand your passion." Valentinus grinned then proceeded walking toward the residence.

"I would not ask you to do this—to go against your beliefs—if it were not important." Borgia stopped Valentinus and looked into his eyes. "At least think about it, my friend. I do know you must follow your own heart."

They arrived at the residence. "Get some rest, Valentinus. The next session will start soon enough." He patted Valentinus on his back. "I will see you later. I also need some rest, but first I must be replenished." He patted his belly.

Valentinus watched as Borgia walked down the corridor toward the dining hall.

"*Scusami*, Cardinal de Marcosi, can I help you or get you anything?" The Irish Bishop Murphy's voice was becoming familiar.

"Ah, no, *grazie*. I am going to my room to rest," Valentinus replied as if on cue.

"All right then." Bishop Murphy went about his business.

Valentinus was happy to be back in the quiet of his room. Lying down on his bed, he closed his eyes and began to pray.

***

Black smoke steamed from the chimney of the Sistine Chapel.

"I wonder how Cardinal de Marcosi is faring." Sophia was sitting at her computer, clicking on various news sites.

While sitting for a moment in thought, her new book lying on the table caught her attention.

"Hmm, let me see what you have to say about this sexual magic stuff." She took *The Hypostasis of the Archons* book in her hands.

"I think I had some sexual magic last night." She giggled as she looked over at Dominic, who was still sleeping.

Sophia turned to the introduction. "The Hypostasis of the Archons, the Reality of The Rulers, is an anonymous tractate of an esoteric interpretation of Genesis, partially in the form of a revelation discourse between an angel and a ruler or archon." She pointed to the word *angel.*

She continued reading. "While the treatise illustrates a wide-ranging Hellenistic syncretism, the most evident components are Jewish, although in its present form, *The Hypostasis of the Archons* shows early Christian features."

She wondered out loud. "Wow, you really did get around—the Hellenistic period with Jewish and Christian roots?" She tilted her head, interested. "OK…Where is Raphael?"

Sophia flipped through the pages. She wanted to know more about the angels. "Why have I only seen him once?" Again flipping the pages, she stopped. "Ah, this is where I left off."

She read to herself, "The sacraments of Priesthood relate to Tiphereth, which is the sixth Sephirah of the Tree of Life. It is related to the heart. These sacraments were instituted by Jesus Christ, who relates to our Nous atom in the left ventricle of our heart. The Eucharistic Priesthood was instituted at the Last Supper. The first initiates who received the power of Eucharistic Priesthood were his apostles. After that, his apostles anointed other initiates."

"*Buongiorno*, my love." Dominic got out of bed and went to the bathroom.

317

Sophia smiled and went back to reading the book. "After his resurrection, Jesus said to his Apostles, "Go therefore and make disciples of all the nations, baptizing them in the name of the Father, and of the Son and of the Holy Spirit (the three Amens, Kether, Chokmah, Binah, related to the first triangle of the Tree of Life), teaching them to observe all things that I have commanded you" (Matthew 28:19–20). Thus, it is required in the Gnostic Church that all those who are to be ordained as priests or priestesses must undergo the previous sacraments and some years of studies of Kabbalah and Alchemy for their spiritual formation."

She recited out loud, "There are three ways that the Sacrament of Priesthood is expressed…"

Interrupted, she felt a kiss on her neck. "*Mia a'more, grazie*, dinner was *bene* and especially my dessert last night," Dominic teased. "I will go with you to your boss's wake if you would like." He offered his support in between kisses.

"Mmm," Sophia responded to his touch, putting the book down. "I don't think you need to go. *Sarò bene.*" She patted his hand on her shoulder and then stood up, having already gotten dressed. "How do I look?"

"*Sei bellissima*, you cannot go alone to a wake." His response was sexy and supportive.

"I must go. I would not forgive myself if I didn't. But you don't." Sophia grinned.

"Then I will not forgive myself if I did not accompany you." Dominic kissed her cheek. "I insist."

"Are you sure?" She was trying to judge if he was sincere or if he just felt sorry for her.

"Sophia, you mean everything to me, so when you are sad, I am sad. It would ruin my day knowing I could have made your day better and I didn't, so *per favore*, let me come with you," he pleaded.

"All right then. We need to be going."

Dominic quickly readied himself, and they left her flat. His style of transportation was classic. A black Ferrari suited him well.

"Nice car," Sophia thought as sat back in the seat.

Sophia liked his car's amenities, with all the fancy buttons and lights.

"If my girlfriends could see me in this," she thought as they drove to the funeral home and she took notice of his driving skills. "And he knows how to use his stick shift."

"I think it is over there." He smiled and pointed to a series of buildings on her side of the car.

Sophia looked at the storefronts that seemed chained together: an Italian leather store, a glass lamp and dish boutique, a fashion store, and the funeral home. The glass windows gave the impression it was another store.

As they walked up, Sophia could see her reflection in the shiny windows. She shifted her hair over her shoulders and looked again.

A dark shadow stood behind Dominic.

"Ah, *mio*..." Quickly turning around, she almost bumped into Dominic. An inner alarm went off inside her.

"*Che cos'è?* What is the matter, *il mio amore?*" He tried to comfort her.

"Ah, nothing. I just thought I saw..." She could see Dominic's surprised expression and nothing behind him. She felt foolish. "It's silly. Come on."

"That happens to me all the time." He opened the door for her.

They were directed into a very small room with a dozen chairs in front of a closed casket. There were no flowers or cards. Just a single casket was all that remained of Carmine.

"*Scusami*, am I too early?" Sophia asked the attendant.

"No, no, madam. You are the only one," he whispered.

Sophia stood silent. She absorbed the sadness of his words.

Turning toward Carmine's casket, she felt sickened.

"I almost died because of you and now to be standing here in this cold room with not a soul in the world to show you compassion..." Sophia wondered. "It's two emotional extremes, like winter and summer colliding. It is difficult to comprehend."

"Sophia, are you all right?" Dominic rubbed her shoulders for support.

"I just can't believe no one is here." She was dismayed. "No one in the world could or would want to say good-bye to him." Her sullen tone sank deep within.

"Sophia, maybe his soul was not *bene*. Some souls are here on this earth to do the devil's bidding...Maybe he was one of them." He sounded sincere in his explanation.

"I guess, but we can say a little prayer for him and his soul." Sophia thought about it and bowed her head.

"*Sì*, I suppose that is why you are an angel." He nodded. "An angel of the Flaming Star." He smiled and gave her a light kiss on her cheek.

She smiled back and gave the sign of the cross. Standing next to each other, they prayed over Carmine's casket for several minutes.

"*Per favore*, have mercy on Carmine's soul, my *Padre* in heaven." She was relieved of a little sadness.

"It's time to go." Dominic rubbed Sophia's shoulders.

She looked up at him. "*Sì*, I think you are right."

They walked out of the room, but not before Sophia gave one last glance at the empty chairs and lone casket in the cold room.

"I know this might sound a bit crass, but are you hungry?" he asked guiltily, not wanting to seem insensitive.

"*Sì*, I am starving." Getting back into Dominic's car, she felt bad for Carmine's situation, but her stomach was not so diplomatic, growling at the mention of food.

As they drove away, Sophia looked back at the storefront funeral parlor. "It's funny. I almost feel like I left something behind, but I cannot remember what it is."

She turned her attention instead to the radio to distract her emotions. Playing with the buttons, she settled on a news station...

"The new leader of the Catholic Church has not been appointed, and we are learning of yet another scandal involving the Institute for the Works of Religion, or IOR, and the Solar Star Development Company." The announcer continued. "Questions are being raised as to the loans given by the Vatican for the expanded development of solar fields in the Apulia area."

Sophia raised the volume, wanting to hear more of the story.

"Police have arrested Cardinal Meade Rosotti, a member of the IOR reform team designated by resigning Pope Gregory. We are following this story as investigators release more details."

She lowered the volume. "I cannot believe it. Did you hear that?" Sophia shouted, almost jumping from her seat.

"*Sì*, so what? It is one of many scandals they are facing." Dominic apparently did not get the connection to Carmine.

"No, that Cardinal Rosotti is…or was Carmine's boyfriend." She was enthusiastic about the connection, although it did not mean as much since Carmine was dead.

"Carmine's lover was a cardinal?" Dominic thought. "Wow, I guess it was a cardinal sin?" He gave a hardy laugh, then looked at Sophia, weighing her response to his off-color joke.

"Uh…" Sophia did not want to laugh, but it just came out. "Ha, ha, ha, ha…" It lightened the mood just for a moment.

"But you know Carmine wrote in his supposed suicide note that he loved this Cardinal Rosotti." She got serious, thinking about it a little more.

"Well, OK, I guess the devil has another soul in his army of the damned," Dominic blurted out.

"What do you mean?" She was surprised by his comment.

"I don't mean anything, just…I was taught when a soul turns away from God, the devil increases his army, which is said to one day return to make their master king." His explanation made him a little embarrassed.

"That is what you were taught?" She discounted his reasoning. "Somehow I don't see zombies walking about hailing Lucifer." She giggled. "You have been watching too much television."

Dominic drove to Rome and pulled up to a five-story corner building covered in ivy on one entire side. The front of the building was completely covered in ivy, only the windows on each floor and the main entrance were exposed.

"*Che sembra meraviglioso.*" Sophia pointed.

"That is where we are going." He parked his car across the street from a building that looked like a hotel and then turned to her. "I hope you are hungry."

"I am starving. You have used up all of my energy," she teased.

Taking her mobile, she texted Ben. "We need to talk regarding Rosotti news."

A moment later he said, "Tomorrow dinner?"

"*Sì*," she texted back.

"Come on, the restaurant is upstairs in the Hotel Raphael. I know the owners, and their food is *fantastico*. I thought you would want to try it." He helped her cross the street.

"Raphael?" she repeated.

"*Sì*. I know he is one of your angels." He smiled, putting his arm around her as they walked toward the entrance featuring two oversized potted palm trees on each side of the main door.

"The upstairs restaurant has a view overlooking the Vatican. I thought you might appreciate that today, considering the conclave and all," Dominic joked as he held the door open for her.

***

Knock, knock, knock…

Valentinus's rest was short-lived.

"*Scusami*, Cardinal de Marcosi, I have your lunch." Bishop Murphy met a somber Valentinus at his door.

"Ah, *sì*, come in." Valentinus was grateful for any nourishment.

"Here you are. This should fix you up straightaway." Cheerfully, Murphy put the tray on the desk.

"*Grazie*." Valentinus sat at his desk ready to eat but instead stared at the tray, lost in thought.

"You know, *signore*, you do not have much time. You should try to eat something."

"I thought I was hungry, but now just looking at it, I am not sure what I am." Valentinus's voice lowered. "Have you ever felt that way?"

Bishop Murphy could see his struggle. "You know, *mi* mum used to say the future is not set. There is no fate but what we make of ourselves. And if you do not eat, I see in your future that you will be hungry," Murphy added with a nod and a wink. "Now please try to eat."

"*Grazie*. I will," Valentinus promised as the bishop left his room.

He ate several bites, trying to bargain with his thoughts over his angry, empty stomach. Finding himself twirling his fork, he was confused and frustrated.

Before long he was twirling his pencil, with a paper ballot laid flat on the table before him. Printed on the upper half of the ballot appeared the words "Eligio in Summum Pontificem," or "I elect as Supreme Pontiff." Below appeared a space for the name of the person Valentinus was to choose. He tapped quietly on the ballot with his pencil, summoning the courage to do what his heart told him.

"If I vote for Sisinnius, I am voting for the devil in sheep's clothing." He thought more. "If I vote for myself, the division will widen."

Contemplating his options, he stared around the Sistine Chapel, with long tables seating the rows of cardinals.

"I cannot believe it has come to this," he prayed as he scribbled a name.

The scrutineers called out the names of each chosen cardinal.

Then piercing each paper ballot with a needle through the word *Eligio*, and all the ballots were placed on a single thread.

"*Dio* help us." Valentinus felt ill with each ballot being stitched.

Sitting back in his chair, he waited and observed. He caught Borgia staring at him intently. Valentinus stared back until Irenaeus got his attention.

"He is the traitor, I am sure of it." Appalled, Valentinus used his eyes to relay his feelings.

"Cardinal Sisinnius has two less votes, Sforza gained two, Valentinus and Della Rovere stayed the same," the scrutineers announced. "We will vote again tomorrow morning."

"There is so much stubbornness in this room," Valentinus whispered. "They act arrogantly, becoming stubborn, and will not listen to your commandments." He shook his head and left for the residence.

The air was cold but crisp, opening his lungs. He could see his breath.

"Breathe in deeply...The tide is coming in," he told himself as he held his breath. "Breathe out...The tide is going out." It was his only real memory of taking yoga classes years ago that paid off when it was part of a Vatican program to keep clergy healthy.

"May I walk with you?" Cardinal Everard des Barres asked in a hushed tone.

His Turkish accent made him recognizable even from behind. Valentinus turned around. "Ah, *sì*, it is a beautiful evening. The stars will be coming out tonight." He pointed up.

"*Sì*, it is," des Barres agreed with him. "It is a very interesting day, don't you think?"

Valentinus looked ahead, waiting his next comment.

"I just wanted you to know I voted for you," des Barres said, leaning in with a soft smile. "For the record, I thought you would have made a great pontiff. You are a natural-born leader." He held out his hand to shake Valentinus's.

Looking a little confused, Valentinus obliged. "*Grazie...*" He was a little shocked by des Barres's confession.

"You are welcome." He bowed. "Have a restful evening." He walked away.

"*Dio ti benedica*, my friend." Valentinus sent a warm blessing his way. He was starting to see some sensibility.

"*Bene*, that was a vote of confidence. While it is still not realistic to be pontiff, it at least gives me some comfort."

"Good evening, Cardinal de Marcosi," Bishop Murphy greeted him. "I will have your supper ready shortly." He happened to be passing by in the main hall, carrying supplies.

Murphy stopped in his steps. "You look better, *signore*."

"I feel a wee bit better," he said, trying to use Murphy's terminology. Walking to his room, he knew his dream of becoming pontiff was not to be, but the sting of devastation was starting to wear off.

"*Per favore*, bestow peace upon me, my *Santo Padre*." In the confines of his room, Valentinus took solace.

Buzz, buzz, buzz…

His mobile made his leg tingle. He reached for it, looking at the unrecognizable number. Flipping it over, he did not say a word as he put it to his ear.

"*Ciao*, Valentinus." The Negotiator tried to calm his nerves. "If you told the truth about having a mobile you would not be nervous," he quipped.

"What do you want?" Valentinus was not amused.

"I know you were expecting Giacomo, but he is busy, so I volunteered to update you." The Negotiator was toying with him. "So you can relax. We are alone."

Valentinus looked around his room again. The spying innuendo put him on edge.

"Listen, I told you the media was breaking a story about the IOR and that solar company." He got to the point. "I am giving you this information so that you may understand what is happening out here in the real world. I mentioned that Cardinal Rosotti was working with a man named Schneider. Do you remember?"

"*Sì*." Valentinus got up and made sure the door was locked.

"I told you that Schneider also works for my client."

"*Sì*, the one with no name." Valentinus returned the sarcasm.

"That's the one." The Negotiator was not joking. "Schneider usually works through my client except in this case. In making a deal with the Solar Star Company and Rosotti, they—"

"What does this have to do with conclave?" Valentinus's impatience grew.

"This energy deal is linked to the Syro-Phoenician Army. They are a terrorist militia group wanting to impose strict Sharia Islamic law across the world." The Negotiator paused. "My sources say they are working through a company in Lampedusa and may have ties to the Benghazi attack on the US consulate. And let's just say they are not nice people. Do you understand? This is the group where your IOR money was funneled to."

"Are you sure?" Valentinus was most certainly alarmed that the Negotiator could trace this information, and at the same time he felt relieved he had shared it with him.

"As I said before, Sisinnius will be pontiff. Do you understand me?" He demanded an answer.

"*Sì*..." Valentinus felt ill once again. He knew the Negotiator held many secrets and knew well-connected people. He could trust his word. "Three people may keep a secret, *Padre*"—Valentinus remembered a past conversation they had—"if two of them are dead."

"My friend, this is what negotiation is all about. The Institute for Religious Works saves face, and my client is happy." The Negotiator raised his temperament. "To think this dirty laundry was exposed due to a little old lady in Apulia who called her Turin City Council politician son because she was being pressured into selling her land to add to a solar field after her husband died. You see, you should not mess with little old ladies. That is the moral of this story." He laughed. "Sleep well, *Padre*. Take solace in knowing that because of you, there will be one less funeral in Rome tonight." And he ended the conversation.

Valentinus slowly put his mobile back in his sock, thinking about the fifty million euro loan to terrorists and the never-existing German bonds.

"If terrorists can infiltrate Mother Church…" He bowed his head. "Oh, *per favore*, Yeshua. Oh, *per favore*, *Santa Madre*. Oh, *per favore*, *caro Padre* in heaven…Have mercy."

He sat back in his chair, staring out his window, and observed a large, dead tree in the rear of the courtyard.

"The tree has not one leaf. They are nonexistent. *Per favore*, Holy Spirit, help us not to wither away into the darkness of evil." He crossed his hands in prayer.

The earlier high he felt was replaced with deep despair. He felt like the naked tree having to endure the harsh winter weather.

He pulled the rosaries hanging around his neck from under his clothes and used them to pray.

"*Caro Padre* in heaven." Slowly, with each prayer and each prayer bead, he felt some small measure of relief from the internal pain that wrenched his soul.

After some hours passed, the emotional drain was felt through his entire body. "I need to go to bed."

Lying there, he continued to pray until finally he closed his eyes and sleep came to him.

A chill went through Valentinus's entire body. He opened his eyes to see Lealia standing over him.

She was beautiful, with her long dark hair pulled up in a bun, wearing her traditional white wedding gown. The sequined bodice glittered with each movement. Her hazel eyes sparkled with excitement.

"Come dance with me." She held out her hand.

Valentinus looked around. He was sitting at a table by himself, wearing a black tuxedo with a purple bow tie. They were alone in the large catering hall ballroom. The lights were dim as the music played their favorite song, "La Solitudine."

"Come on, Valentinus, *per favore*, dance with me. You are supposed to dance with me." She smiled like an angel peering through the heavens.

"Wow, *sei bellissima*." He smiled and slowly stood.

"And you clean up fairly well too," she teased.

327

"You inspire me." He took her hand.

They reached the center of the dance floor, and he held her close, not wanting to ever lose her again. Suddenly there were two hundred guests watching them.

"I think we make a wonderful couple." She smiled, giving him a tender kiss on the cheek. "I think they are jealous," she said, referring to the audience.

"I think you are right." Valentinus hammered it up with the beautiful bride. His smile gleamed through the room. It was the happiest moment of his life.

"Valentinus, you know I love you." Lealia became serious. "You know that, don't you?"

The music slowed as if watching an old movie coming to an end.

"*Sì*. I love you too." He smiled back. "You have always brought out the best in me. You are everything good in my life."

"Then remember this: I will always be with you," she whispered in his ear and softly kissed his lips. "Always be positive. It suits you. You should know you have powerful people on your side, and they will help you."

"Lealia, I…," he went on to say but could not. Lealia was starting to disappear into the night. Her image was fading from his arms.

"Lealia, wait, don't go. I love you!"

The music stopped. There was only emptiness in the silence.

"Lealia, *per favore*, come back." Valentinus began to weep. "Lealia, I am frightened. *Per favore…*" Valentinus fell to the floor, weeping, calling out to her. "Lealia, come back," he begged as his tears rolled down his cheeks.

The movement of his arms and his body jerking woke Valentinus from his deep, troubling slumber.

"Oh *Dio*, that felt so real. Wow." He shook his head, then wiped his eyes. He was disturbed by his dream. He sat up, stretching his aching back.

Knock, knock, knock…

Valentinus was still groggy, but hearing the knock again, he got out of bed to open the door.

"*Scusami, signore*, I have your breakfast." As Murphy set the tray on the desk, he looked at his charge. "Oh dear, Cardinal de Marcosi, you look like you slept in your clothes."

"I guess that is because I did." Valentinus looked down at himself, feeling the sweaty shirt he slept in.

"Can I help you with anything?" a concerned Bishop Murphy asked in his usually friendly brogue.

"No, *grazie*." He did not want Murphy to worry unnecessarily. "I will take a shower. I am sure that afterward I will feel like a new man."

"I am glad to hear it." Murphy nodded. "It is a new day, *mi* mum used to say. May you always have a clean shirt, a clear conscience, and enough coins in your pocket to buy a pint!"

"*Grazie*, I will try to remember that." Valentinus laughed for the first time in days.

"Very well." Murphy was leaving. "And good luck today. I am sure it is not going to be easy, but just as sure…it will be rewarding in the future, perhaps, if not today."

Valentinus looked at Murphy, closing the door behind him.

"He is a strange one," he uttered, taking off the plate covering. "*Bene*, at least breakfast looks good. That is a start." Remembering Lealia's words from his dream, he decided to be positive.

It was very early in the morning. Valentinus could see the sun starting to rise over the buildings. As he ate, he looked out the window and remembered Lealia's embrace and her soft kisses.

***

The taxi was pulling up to the front of Sophia's laboratory building.

"I wish the weekend could have lasted longer." She fleetingly reminisced about her sleepover with Eula and Navaeh and visiting her parents for dinner. Then she thought of lying in Dominic's arms at his flat in Rome. From lying on the bed in his penthouse, Sophia could peer through the large window overlooking Castel Sant'Angelo.

"That building was used as a fortress to hide the sins of past pontiffs from the people, but still...They could not hide their sins from God," she thought. "Ah, but it is a breathtaking view," she whispered.

"Not as lovely as the view right here." Dominic kissed her.

"Mmm," she purred. The hesitations she originally had about getting back with Dominic were fading. "Your flat is amazing with the three-hundred-and-sixty-degree panoramic views of the entire city. How did you find it?"

"You have to know the right people." Dominic kissed her again. "And have a little bit of luck."

His flat had a master suite and a small guest bedroom. The open floor plan combined a moderately sized kitchen and living room. Dark wood floors throughout the flat were highlighted with lighter colored taupe walls. His furniture seemed expensive and modern but with a hint of Italian tradition. Fancy art, painting, and sculptures were focal points in every room.

"It certainly is bigger than my little space. And your decorator did a brilliant job," she teased.

"How do you know I hired a decorator?" He laughed. "All right, I guess you do know me." He put his hand through her hair, getting more serious. "I was hoping you would want to stay here with me, and we can share this flat." Dominic kissed her again softly.

"Dominic, are you asking me to move in with you?" Sophia pulled her head away and looked into his eyes.

"Sophia, we have known each other for many years, so it would not be like two strangers living together." He was serious.

"I don't know." Sophia started to feel pressure. "I need more time. I am sorry."

"That is all right, *mi a'more*. Take all the time you need. I will be right here." Dominic slowly kissed her lips.

He touched her body in all the right places, and she responded.

It did not take long for the taxi driver to bellow, "Hey, *signorina*, are you getting out?"

"Ah, *sì. Grazie*." Sophia looked around she was back in her reality. She paid her fare and took small steps into the building and then through the corridors, hoping to delay the inevitable.

Once at her lab door, she stood for an extra second and took a deep breath.

"Yuck." Glancing up, she noticed the vents that she had previously crawled through and she got a chill down her spine.

"*Tutto ok*, Sophia, you can do this." She reached for the doorknob and turned. As the door was opening, she could immediately see the lights were already on.

"Oh, Sophia, I am so glad you are back." Gabriella, who had once comforted her when she had to work with Carmine, stood by a new desk and greeted her with excitement.

Mr. Lorino was standing where Carmine's desk used to be. "Sophia, come in. We were waiting for you." His relaxed disposition surprised her more than the changes to the lab room.

"I helped straighten up your new desk area. I hope you like it." Gabriella moved to a larger, more modern lab desk and chair. Everything was neatly positioned. "It's ready for you, Sophia. It is a new start."

"A new start?" Sophia mouthed the words as she slowly entered the room, heading toward her new workstation.

"I hope you like it," Mr. Lorino chimed in. "And after you get settled, *per favore*, come to my office so we can discuss your new title and responsibilities."

"My new title?" Sophia put her things on her new desk, turning toward her boss. Still in shock, she was trying to take it all in.

"*Sì*, I will see you in a half hour," he requested her promptness.

"*Sì, grazie*," she gratefully replied as Mr. Lorino left Gabriella and Sophia alone.

"And even better, I am able to work an extra day, so I will be on your team." Gabriella was excited.

"My team?" Sophia was still confused.

"*Sì*, Mr. Lorino is promoting you to supervisor. I thought he would have mentioned it before now."

"My promotion?"

"Sophia, stop repeating everything I say." Gabriella laughed but then got serious. "You are taking over for Carmine, but I think they like you better because they are giving you two forensic investigators and me."

"Wow." Sophia sat in her new chair as a feeling of disbelief came over her, weighing her down.

"I won, so you owe me—" The door swung open. A short, middle-aged Asian man came in first and was in the midst of talking to a taller brown-haired man. "Listen, I am serious, or I will not bet with you again."

"I did not bet with you at all," the younger, brown-eyed, brown-haired man insisted as they entered the room and stopped in front of Sophia.

Gabriella laughed. "Sophia, this is Lee Hung and Simon Ferrara. They are on our team."

"I am Lee, and this is Simon," Lee pointed out in his local Italian accent.

"*Ciao*, Miss Pistisi," Simon introduced himself.

"*Ciao*." Sophia giggled. "It is nice to meet you, and *per favore*, just call me Sophia."

After shaking hands, she watched them go to their own desks and start their work, carrying on the conversation from which they began.

"You did bet me, and you owe me the money!" Lee snapped at his coworker.

"I did not bet you. I do not bet!" Simon stood his ground.

"It is none of my business, but how much did you bet?" Sophia interrupted.

"One euro!" Lee sat in his chair with a huff.

"I see. What did you bet on?" Sophia giggled under her breath.

"Electing a new pope, of course. I said we would not have one yesterday." Lee stood up. "You did bet me." He pointed at Simon.

Simon raised his head from his folder and looked at Sophia. "No, I didn't. He is a gambler, and he bets on everything. But his wife almost left him, so he now only bets one euro on just about everything." Simon smirked.

"Ah, I see."

"We are working on a few cases that Mr. Lorino has been overseeing. We could..." Gabriella reminded everyone of the responsibilities.

"Ah, Mr. Lorino. *Sì*, we will review them, but first let me have my meeting with him." Sophia jumped up and left the room, gesturing she would return shortly.

"OK, no worries." Lee was subtle. "We will be here for you, boss."

"Boss. I like the sound of that." She thought, smiling as she left the room. "Being a supervisor and having my own team is intriguing. I just hope I can do this."

The white corridors didn't seem as overwhelming on the walk to Mr. Lorino's office. He greeted her warmly and asked her to sit.

"You know, Sophia, I was sorry to have missed you at Carmine's wake." His sincerity was obvious.

"You were there?" she screeched, surprised and relieved she was not the only one.

"*Sì*, the attendant told me that I missed you by only a few minutes." He sat behind his very large steel and glass desk.

"There was no one else there." Sophia gave him a smile. "I am happy you went."

"It is a shame all the way around." He bowed his head for a second. "But we must carry on," he stated as a matter of fact.

"Quite frankly, Sophia," She sat up straight, waiting for his next word, "you have shown you are a team player. Your work ethics are exactly what we need, and that is why, based on my recommendation, you are being promoted to team supervisor."

"*Grazie.*" His confidence in her abilities warmed her body down to her toes.

"I have had HR prepare a new contract." He picked up a folder from his desk and handed it to her. "I trust you will be happy with our agreement."

"*Grazie.*" Sophia's grin went from ear to ear.

"*Prego.*" He stood up, signaling the end of their meeting. "Just don't screw up."

She did not know if he was kidding as she stood up and reached for his hand. "*Grazie*, Mr. Lorino. I will not let you down."

"I know," he assured her. "I will see you tomorrow for our weekly audit meeting."

"*Sì*, you will. *Grazie.*" She turned toward the door too fast, almost tripping. Catching her balance, she bid him farewell and was out of there. "*Buona giornata.*"

On the way back to her lab, her mobile went off. "*Ciao*, sorry I had to cancel dinner the other night. How about tonight?" Ben texted.

"Sounds good, 7 p.m. Same Curry house," she texted back.

"Great. See you then." Ben signed off.

***

At the Sistine Chapel, Valentinus's stare into the abyss was interrupted by a pat on his back.

"Valentinus, you did the right thing today. I pray God will have mercy on our souls." Cardinal Perez's expression was that of someone at a funeral, leaving Valentinus to grieve as he walked away.

The conclave was over. A new pontiff had been elected by a unanimous vote. He replayed the scene in his mind…It was an old horror movie.

"And for those who have their doubts, I will work hard to gain your trust." Sisinnius thanked all his supporters.

"The Harlots rule the day." Valentinus closed his eyes. "*Per favore*, Yeshua, have mercy on us."

Sisinnius made his debut to the roaring applause of the world audience, taking the name Innocent XV. History was being made on a universal stage.

"The world has their new spiritual leader." Borgia stood beside Valentinus.

"*Si*, they do, and history will judge us harshly I am afraid," Valentinus quickly retorted.

"Only if we repeat it." Borgia tried to be optimistic.

"We are repeating it. You just don't see it yet," Valentinus said with a sneer. Across the room, Irenaeus stood next to Pope Innocent XV.

Borgia noticed Valentinus's cause of disdain.

"*Scusami*." Valentinus suddenly felt as if he was going to throw up and rushed to find a bathroom.

Weaving in and out of the lined-up cardinals, he rushed to the first bathroom he could locate, down the longest corridor. He pushed the door open and fell to his knees. It took less than a minute before he was vomiting.

"*Per favore*, Yeshua, hold me up," he prayed while his guts were raw with bile.

"Breathe in…then out." He tried to control his emotions. Hovering over the cold toilet, he began to slowly feel steadier. With each breath he felt a little stronger.

He stood up in front of the mirror and rinsed his mouth of the vomit flavor, taking a sip of water from the faucet then spitting it out.

"Devil workers, the army of the damned is working within the curia. Hmm…The sons of darkness are rising. I wonder if that is what Korsig meant in his note." He thought of Irenaeus and Sisinnius and spit one last time.

"I need some rest," he thought, looking again in the mirror. Reclaiming his composure, he left the bathroom and alone found his way back to the Domus Sanctae Marthae.

It felt like it was the longest walk he had ever taken in his life. He could feel his weight dragging him down.

"*Scusami*, Cardinal, you do not look well," Bishop Murphy greeted him. "Can I get you anything?"

"No, *grazie*. I just need to rest."

"If you need me, I am here," Murphy tried to reassure him.

Valentinus locked his door behind him, escaping from the world.

"*Grazie a Dio,*" he sighed upon seeing his bed, collapsing on top of it. However, his gratitude was replaced with restlessness. He rolled from one side to the other, trying to relax.

Knock, knock, knock…

Bishop Murphy yelled from the other side of his door. "I am sorry to disturb you, but I brought you some tea." He hesitated. "And since conclave is over, I brought you a telly."

Valentinus opened the door and watched Murphy steadily roll in a small trolley with an old twelve-inch television set on it and an inviting cup of tea steaming next to it.

"It's not much, but I thought it might ease your troubles. And the tea is *mi* mum's specialty."

"*Grazie*, Bishop Murphy, that is very kind of you." Valentinus appreciated the gesture.

"Please call me John. Everyone else does." Murphy smiled. "Except for *mi* mum, she calls me…well, there is no need for that." He handed the cup of tea to Valentinus. "I hope you feel better."

"*Per favore*, call me Val or Valentinus. That is what my friends call me." Valentinus smiled. "It smells wonderful."

"And *grazie* for the telly," Valentinus gave a faint smile.

"If you need me, I am here." Murphy nodded and smiled as he left the room.

"Mmm, *Grazie a Dio* for Irish tea." Valentinus could feel the tea's steam caressing his face with its warmth. Each sip seemed to settle his nerves.

Looking around the room, the television seemed like his only friend at the moment.

"If I turn you on, you will only upset me." Struggling with wanting to know what the world was being told and knowing the truth, his curiosity got the better of him. He turned it on and started flipping the channels.

"And a new pontiff has been elected," one newsman announced, standing in front of Saint Peter's Basilica. "We are being told Cardinal Clemente Sisinnius has chosen his new name to be Pope Innocent XV."

When he flipped to another channel, the camera spanned through the crowds at the Basilica.

"Thousands of worshipers are praising the cardinals for a relatively quick conclave and are thanking God for his intervention during the process," another newswoman reported.

"Ha, God had nothing to do with this election." Valentinus laughed. "Anything but the pope's election, I cannot watch." Flipping through each channel the new pope seemed to dominate the news.

One news station, however, was midway through a prerecorded program, a special report. An Asian anchorwoman was centered on the screen with a map of the Middle East behind her. Valentinus recognized her face and stopped on the channel.

"In a historic precedent, we are witnessing a strategic collaboration between Russia, Iran, North Korea, and China. Some are referring to them as the Four Horsemen."

Yin Quan looked straight into the lens. She easily connected to the viewers with her eyes, drawing Valentinus into her story.

"While the world stood by, Russia invaded Crimea and the Ukraine under the false pretense of protecting their Russian citizens."

"North Korea has tested ballistic missiles capable of carrying a nuclear warhead to the United States." Yin Quan sneered and continued. China has committed itself to the century-old Assassin's Mace method of economically destroying its enemies, while Iran has on several occasions used chemical weapons on *their* own people."

Yin Quan revolted. "The world continues to stand by while millions of people are murdered and displaced."

"History is being repeated in front of our very eyes, and one has to question if all these happenings are a foretelling of something more terrible to come," she challenged her audience.

Valentinus bowed his head, reaching to turn the television off. He sipped on his tea while praying.

"*Per favore, mio Padre*, have mercy on us." His eyes started to tear up, but he would not give in, taking another sip of tea. With each sip he could feel a lump in his throat.

Knock, knock, knock...

"How was your tea?" Bishop Murphy reentered the room.

"Excellent." Valentinus tried to smile.

"Is there anything else I can get for you?" Murphy was encouraged.

"*Sì, per favore*, get me a car. I am going home." Valentinus stood up and handed the teacup to Murphy.

"You are not staying for the festivities?"

"No, I must return home."

"Are you sure?" Murphy was still very much concerned.

"I am positively sure. *Per favore*, arrange for my car." Valentinus paused. "But inform the driver I must make an important stop before he is to take me home."

"*Sì*, Cardinal...I mean Valentinus." Murphy was still unsure of becoming more personal.

"I will not do anyone any good staying here," Valentinus thought to himself, "and I cannot bear it." One tear escaped down his cheek.

***

In her lab Sophia was busy reintroducing herself to her coworkers and her caseloads when her mobile buzzed.

"*Ciao*, Dennis, how are you?"

"*Ciao*, Sophia. I was hoping we could talk." He sounded serious.

"I am at work right now, but I can excuse myself." Something Sophia would never consider doing working under Carmine. She signaled to Gabriella and left the room.

"What is going on? Did you find out anything more?" Excited, she rushed to know.

"Sophia, I really think we should get together."

"*Per favore*, Dennis, tell me, what did you find out? My time is short. I started back to work." Her curiosity was peaked.

"I may have found a lead," he cautioned her. "Someone who used to work for the orphanage in Turin. She stated that there was a another security tape showing a man dropping a box off at the front door of the building, then ringing a bell and quickly walking away."

"Whoa, Dennis, that is great. Can we see the tape?"

"No, she said it got damaged, but Sophia, she remembers the man was wearing a collar."

"*Dio mio*," she gasped. "A *priest!*"

"Sophia, this woman is elderly, and I only spoke to her over the phone. I have made arrangements to meet with her, and those expenses will be listed for you. That is why I am calling you now. I wanted to make sure it was all right with you. It may cost about five hundred euros."

"Of course it is OK. Where is she?" Sophia tried to get more information.

"I cannot say until after I speak with her. You know people do have rights to privacy that I must respect." His tone was serious enough that Sophia knew not to push the issue.

"When will we meet with her?" She settled for less detail but tried to include herself.

"No, no. *We* are not, *I* am meeting her. That is *my* job."

"*Per favore*, you will not even know I am with you," she pleaded.

"I know because you won't be there." He was using his sarcastic fatherly tone. "But the woman also mentioned she remembers an adoption and an American couple."

"*Merda!*" She was in disbelief. "Really? America? I did not think they would live outside of Italy or…Europe, for that matter." She took in that concept for a moment. "Where in America? Who are they?"

"Slow down, Sophia. I am trying to get more information, and I will let you know the status as usual." Dennis did not want to give her false hopes.

"Ah, what about the other baby?"

"I am having a hard time gathering more information, but I am working on it."

"*Grazie*, Dennis. *Per favore*, keep me informed," she pleaded. "*Grazie* and *grazie!*"

"*Va bene allora*, get back to work. I will talk to you soon." But he didn't forget to say, "And Sophia, it may or may not be a priest, so *per favore*, do not go following anyone."

It seemed as if he was getting to know Sophia's intentions even before she had the thought.

"Promise me." He requested her acknowledgment.

"Ah."

"Sophia, *per favore*, promise me."

"*Sì*, fine. All right."

"I will talk to you soon." Dennis ended the call.

Sophia stood frozen in the corridor. She was silent while absorbing the information.

"*Mio Dio!*" The possibilities seemed endless. She looked up. "*Grazie*," she whispered.

"Sophia, is everything OK?" Gabriella had come out of the lab.

"*Sì, grazie.*" She smiled. "Let me get back to work. I may be going to America." She almost skipped back into the lab, leaving Gabriella to wonder about her new supervisor.

The remainder of the day flew by as Sophia imagined all the possibilities in meeting her brothers.

"I bet you will be early tomorrow by ten minutes." Lee baited her as they were ready to leave for the day.

"No, I don't think so, Lee. I think I will be on time." She smiled back, trying not to laugh.

"OK, I will take that bet," Lee was hard-pressed. "We will see who wins."

"We look forward to working with you tomorrow, no matter what time you show up." Simon shook his head and smiled at Sophia.

Walking out of the lab, Sophia was enthusiastic. Finding her way to the front door, she almost pranced.

"It is a pleasure to have my new coworkers, and they are looking forward to working with me. That's a nice change." Sophia kept smiling. "It was a good day." With a happy, unwavering grin, she made her way to the Curry house to meet up with Ben.

The restaurant was crowded. The dim lights made it difficult to notice Ben was sitting with someone.

As she walked closer, she could see Ben's legs were spread out, giving his casted leg more room.

"Ah…he is sitting with Michael." Her feelings were still mixed about Michael. "Just be cool," she told herself.

"*Ciao*, Ben." She moved to kiss him on the cheek.

"*Ciao*, Sophia." Michael stood up to greet her. He was still wearing his shoulder sling cradling his bandaged arm.

"*Ciao*, Michael." She accepted his polite kiss on her cheek.

"Sit down next to me." He played with her.

She sat in the only chair available. "How are you boys?"

"Better now that you are here." Michael slyly smiled.

"OK." Sophia turned to Ben. "So, how are you? I suppose you have more information about Carmine's Cardinal Rosotti? The media has already started reporting about Rosotti's ties to that Solar Star Company."

"I am OK, although I have a hard time sleeping," Michael chimed in but was ignored. "I guess because I don't like sleeping alone."

"I have heard about Rosotti…and I wanted to tell you that the case involving Callesino's son has been dropped, along with that of the Canadian student. They have been released for good. I spoke to the judges in the Supreme Court of Cassation." Ben looked into Sophia's eyes, giving a big smile.

"Due to a large part of your efforts in helping me, they set aside the first verdicts of Tricia Hendrix and Roberto Callesino based on the grounds that it had gone beyond the remit of the Corte d'Assise d'Appello."

His attorney persona came through. "Because they did not order new DNA tests, and by failing to give weight to other originally ignored circumstantial evidence, the case is now over."

"That is great news! You did a great job, Ben." She congratulated him.

"And it seems I have made new friends." Ben was a little smug in his own achievement. "Judge Rentini, who presided over the retrial, granted the prosecution's request to use your results and analysis of the DNA sample found on Callesino's kitchen knife," Ben shared the praise. "It was because of your C-Y-A files, Sophia."

Ben held up his water glass to toast her. "Your C-Y-A files discredited the court-appointed experts at the appeal trial." He paused. "And Rentini was impressed with our work, so I owe you one."

"I am glad to hear it." Sophia sat back in her chair.

"Sophia, you had your private investigator looking into Carmine and Rosotti." Michael turned serious. "I was just wondering if he found any more information about Carmine or Rosotti. Perhaps your investigator may have seen people whom Carmine was with?"

"What? What are you talking about?" Sophia was surprised by the change in topic.

"Ah, nothing." Ben gave Michael a hard stare. "Let's eat. Dinner is on me. I ordered your favorite."

The waitress came with wine and a tray of various dishes, setting the entrees on their table.

"I ordered for the table. I hope you like it." Ben held his glass of wine for a toast. "To good intentions and hard work," they all cheered.

"It looks great." Michael hinted of his hunger, digging into each dish to put on his own plate.

"*Grazie*, Ben, it does look great." Sophia was grateful for his gesture and kind words but was curious. "Why did you want to know about who Dennis may have seen with Carmine? Didn't you speak to him yourself?"

"We did, but he would not talk to us," Ben answered flatly. "This is good stuff." He tried to change the topic again.

"Oh, I see." Sophia saw her opportunity. "How about we play a little game? It's called I tell you, and you tell me."

"I don't think—" Ben tried to answer.

"OK, I will play with you," a smitten Michael replied.

"*Bene*, you first." Sophia winked at Michael.

"Mike, I don't think you should," Ben warned.

"You trust her, so I trust her, and maybe she can help." Michael was trying to sway Sophia's affections.

"*Sì*, Ben, maybe I can help." Not wasting her witticism, Sophia smiled.

"Rosotti was working with a man named Schneider, who secured a large loan from the IOR for this Solar Star Development Company. This Schneider guy has associates that the U.S. and Italian governments are interested in."

"Associates? Who?" Sophia was intrigued.

"Well, that is what we want to know," Michael said, half-kidding as he wolfed down his meal.

"Well, I can talk to Dennis for you. In fact, I spoke to him today and will be speaking with him again tomorrow." Sophia offered some hope in their quest. "What exactly do you want to know?"

"We have reason to believe Schneider's associates have ties to La Cosa Nostra, who may also have ties to terrorists in Lampedusa and more links to Libya," Michael explained in not too much detail. "Schneider has flown back to Germany and is expected to be arrested soon on fraud and contributing funds to terrorist organizations. These are some very bad people, and it would be questionable if he survives to stand trial."

"The island of Lampedusa is close to Libya, so I guess it is not a stretch to think terrorists are working in Italy," Sophia thought out loud.

"No, it's not, so when you speak to Dennis, *per favore*, see what you can find out for us." Ben resigned himself to asking for her help.

"*Tutto ok*, I will," she agreed feeling a part of their team.

"OK, now we can finish our meal." Ben toasted with a nod.

"It looks like someone already has." Sophia laughed, looking at Michael's empty plate.

"Who said I was finished?" He took another helping from the dishes in the center of the table.

"What…I am hungry." Michael looked up at his dinner companions, who stared at him piling on his food, while making no apologies.

"So you are working together now?" Sophia was inquisitive. "Wait, Ben, did you get the promotion into the antiterrorism investigators unit?"

"Perhaps." Ben was being evasive.

"Oh, and don't tell me you are working for your government in the same area?" she guessed, focusing on Michael.

"Well, ma'am, I cannot rightly say," Michael gave her a poor impersonation of an American cowboy.

"I see." Sophia played along.

"I am so happy you've decided to have dinner with me." Michael looked at Sophia with wanting eyes.

"OK, cowboy, this is not a date." Sophia joked.

"I will take what I can get," he flirted giving her a sexy sort of smile.

"Yeah, OK." Sophia moved the conversation along. "Ben, do you remember I thought the man in the pictures I showed you was Cardinal de Marcosi?" Sophia was electrified. Her energy was turned up.

He nodded with a mouth full of food.

"Well, I was right," she proclaimed. "And I am going to meet him in a few days at his lecture." She was even more determined.

"How do you know it was him in the pictures?" Ben washed his food down with wine.

"I told you I spoke to Dennis today, and I spoke to my uncle Egidio."

"And?" Ben wanted to know.

"As I suspected, Moretti had a hand in one of my brother's adoptions." Sophia took a huge leap in twisting the details based on her intuition. "And it looks like my brother who was adopted in Turin could be in America."

"Your brother's adoption? In America?" Michael was confused but concentrated on one thing. "Wait, are you going to America?"

"*Sì.*" Sophia was short, not wanting to reveal too much. "And I found out that Joseph Grillo, Moretti's cousin, is also involved with a wind farm company in Sicily."

"Sophia, you should not worry about Joseph Grillo. He is a dangerous man." Ben didn't go into details.

"I know, he is connected," Sophia guessed. Her laptop research provided some information, but it has its limits.

"He is also missing," Michael let slip, prompting Ben to shoot a hard stare dart at him.

"Missing or hiding?" Sophia played along, not sounding surprised.

"Sophia, please promise me you will leave this Grillo fellow to the authorities." Ben could see the wheels in her head spinning.

"Ben, my friends will not put me in danger."

"Yeah, OK." Ben dismissed her. "Just promise me."

"OK, I promise." She slyly smiled.

"Wow, when are you going to America? Maybe I can help." Changing the subject, Michael was eager to assist her.

"*Grazie*, Michael, but I do not need an escort." Sophia was almost snobbish. "I am going to talk with Salvatore Moretti after I go to the lecture in Turin."

"Sophia, are you sure?" Ben was concerned she did not know all the facts. "Moretti may be tied to Cosa Nosta."

"I understand." Now she dismissed him. "But he is also a public servant, and as such I will approach him." She stood her ground.

"Well, just be careful," Ben said, knowing there was no way to deter her when her mind was made up.

"I can show you places you have only imagined." Michael displayed his sensual side, but he was joking. "I mean in America."

"I am sure you can." Ben protected his adopted sister. "But I bet she could kick your ass if you try to take her places she does not want to go."

"*Grazie*, Ben. I think I know how to handle cowboys," she joked, "especially when they horse around."

"Ah. Did you really say that?" Michael was flabbergasted.

They looked at each other, taken back by her silly answer, and laughed.

***

Valentinus was happy to be home in the Suburbicarian Diocese of Velletri-Segni. An attached building behind the Basilica of San Clemente was home, at least for the time being.

"Welcome home, Cardinal de Marcosi." His assistant, Monsignor Bairre Walsh, an Irish Dominican, greeted him.

"*Grazie*, Bairre." Valentinus coughed through his greeting.

"That is a nasty cough. Can I get you anything?" Bairre was concerned. "I can bring you some of my chicken soup." He did not rush Valentinus, watching as his boss moved slowly, heading into his bedroom to rest in his chair.

A sitting area in the bedroom, between the bed and the two windows, had a fire going in the fireplace, giving Valentinus a small comfort. The building itself was old, dating back to 1100 A.D., but had been updated to reflect the rich history of the church.

The two large windows centered the room, allowing in plenty of light. His bed, opposite the windows, was king-size, as requested by the previous occupant.

"It takes up too much space." Valentinus often complained to Saint Clemente's picture hanging over the fireplace.

"We are doomed." Valentinus sat in his chair and mumbled to the picture.

"*Scusami, signore*, I am sorry. I did not understand you."

"Nothing…Chicken soup would be lovely." He smiled at Biarre.

"Very well, I will return shortly. Perhaps you need to go to bed. Your health is important."

"*Sì, grazie*." Valentinus was defeated, surrendering to his body's weakness. "At least I am better than my friend Korsig," he thought, reflecting on his visit to the hospital on his way home.

When Valentinus arrived at Korsig's room in the hospital, he was pleasantly surprised that Karl already had a visitor. Sitting in a chair next to Korsig's bed was Giacomo, who was slumped over, snoring lightly.

"Wow, those are a lot of tubes," he whispered. Valentinus could see the many tubes invading Korsig's body and the machines that quietly beeped, showing his vital signs.

"*Sì*, they are." Giacomo woke up. "How are you, Val?"

"Better than Karl. What are the doctors saying?"

"Pray for a miracle." His face did not look hopeful. "Even Pope Gre—I mean, Gregory was here, praying."

"*Caro Dio.*" Valentinus bowed his head. "Is there any more news on what happened?"

"I am trying to find out. I suppose the Negotiator spoke with you?" Giacomo yawned as he stood up. "I know he knows Gasparri very well, and he knows you?"

"*Sì.*" Valentinus did not offer any more details.

"How do you know that guy anyway?" Giacomo was curious.

"I will tell you another time." Valentinus walked to Korsig's bedside. "Right now we must pray." He bowed his head.

The smell of the soup brought Valentinus back into the reality of his bedroom.

"*Grazie*, Biarre." He was appreciative of his assistant.

"Enjoy, *signore.*" He left Valentinus alone in his misery.

Valentinus ate slowly. "Poor Korsig." His mind wandered.

"*Santo Padre* help him," he murmured. Each bite seemed to ease his stomach from churning. One look at his bed, and his body began to ache. He hurried and got himself ready.

"*Grazie* for my safe return." In bed he was ready for his long-awaited slumber. Looking around his familiar surroundings, he closed his eyes and continued to pray.

"Valentinus, wake up. You need to wake up," the sweet young voice of a woman whispered in his ear, "Valentinus, wake up."

"Mm." Valentinus stirred.

"Valentinus, I have brought those who need to speak with you," she said. "You need to awaken your spirit."

Those words resonated with him as he opened his eyes at once. The room was dark. Walls replaced his windows. Lying still, he could see his breath. The room was freezing and strange.

Valentinus shot up. "The cold air is thick with a mist. It's getting even more frigid. Brr."

It was too cold to get his thoughts in order. "I can't see." His heart started to race.

"Valentinus, do not be afraid," the young woman's voice returned.

"Lealia...Where are you?" He now recognized her. Valentinus stood up immediately. "*Per favore*, I need you."

There was no reply.

"Lealia!" he shouted loudly.

Still there was no answer.

"Lealia, where are you?" He started to cry. Tears flowed freely in the freezing dark room. He could feel each iced tear rolling down his cheek. "Lealia..."

The floor was freezing. He looked for his slippers, but they were gone. He turned around, but could not find his bed. Only more blackness. His bed was gone. His breath started to become labored.

"*Per favore*, come back." He turned around again. The walls seemed to be getting closer. The black, cold air pushed up against him and through him. He could hear the sound of crunching metal in the distance, growing louder. *Twist...crunch...*His eardrums began to hurt as it came upon him.

Crunch. Standing there alone, he put his hands up to cover his ears.

"Lealia!" he screamed in fear. "*Per favore*, stop! *Dio* have mercy, *per favore*..." He wept.

The sound suddenly stopped. He turned in a circle, trying to see what was in front of him.

"A pentagram?" he stammered as the shadows of five walls surrounded him, forming a shape. He ran into each wall, trying to escape, but they were made of cold stone.

"*Santo Merda*!" He rubbed his shoulder from the bruising he sustained tackling the stone walls.

"Valentinus, do not be afraid," an unfamiliar soft voice called to him.

"Lealia?" He was afraid and confused.

"We are here to help you," another female voice almost sang to him.

Valentinus desperately looked around, but he did not see anyone or anything—only the five black walls that imprisoned him.

"Wh-who are you?" His hesitated breath could be seen in the air.

"We are the light." The voices were more than two and were simultaneously in harmony.

A bright light appeared above him. It was powerful like the sun but not hot. It grew in intensity and began to warm his body from within, while his skin remained cold and clammy. The warmth grew from within him until it gave him goose bumps.

"Brr..." A weird, unfamiliar energy emulated from his legs up to his neck.

With blinding energy, the light beamed, overwhelming him. From straight above him, it began to bear down on him. Valentinus covered his eyes.

"Ah..." He screamed in fear for his life.

"Do not be afraid. We are with you." The voices spoke in harmony.

The light fragmented above him and began to form five shapes over each of the five blackened walls that held him captive.

Valentinus's eyes were wide. His mouth gaped open as his body shook in fear.

The light transformed into five beautiful women. Each had her own glory. Each radiance did not shine more brightly than the other, but together they unveiled the light of a heavenly star.

Crunch. Valentinus closed his eyes and protected his head as a crushing, twisting metal sound echoed, consuming him in terror. The walls progressed closer so that he could almost touch each one while standing in the middle.

"Ah," he screamed as he opened his eyes and covered his ears. "Ah!"

Within a second the noise had stopped. There was silence.

He was trembling. Taking his hands off his ears, he pleaded. "*Per favore, Santo Padre,* help me. Forgive me, and have mercy on me." He cried like a baby.

"Valentinus open your eyes," one sweet voice called to him.

His fear diminished upon hearing her words. He felt her voice go through him, as if lighting had passed through his body.

"Ah..." His eyes fluttered. The light was so bright, he was mystified.

The walls were transforming, but he was not sure what he was looking at. Bewildered, he turned around in a circle.

"*Che cosa?...*" It was beginning to dawn on him. On each wall there appeared a mosque, churches, and temples.

"*Dio mio,* that's New York's Saint Patrick's Cathedral." Valentinus tried to touch the vision on the wall, but his hand went through it as if it were a mirage.

"Saint Peter's Basilica?" He turned toward the front. "What?" He looked at the next wall but could not comprehend what his eyes were seeing. "Russian Church of Our Savior of the Spilled Blood?

"I don't understand." He stretched his hand out to touch Beijing's Temple of Heaven. "Oh..." His hand went through the wall. He turned around once more. "The Temple on the Mount? *Dio mio!*" He shook his head, his body still trembling.

Suddenly overcome with fear, he tried to run though the wall, but again it was solid.

"W-who are you?" He rubbed his shoulder. His hesitant stance showed he understood that the powers around him were greater than he.

"*Per favore,* I beg...Speak to me." Repenting, he bowed his head and tried to secure his knees.

"I am mother to Yeshua, Our Lady of Light." Over Russia's Church of Spilled Blood, a sweet voice sounded in his heart and gave him clear vision. At that moment he could define the images he was seeing in front of him.

"I am wife to Muhammad, Mother of Believers." Another angelic hush surrounded his body, taking away his trembles. She illuminated over the Temple Mount, spreading her light around Valentinus.

"I am the patient and loyal mother of Isaac," an older, wise voice proclaimed from behind him, hovering over the Temple of Heaven.

"I am sister to Moses. Sing to the Lord, for he will triumph gloriously," another voice sang to him, gleaming over Saint Patrick's Cathedral.

"And I am the apostle Magdalene, companion, wife, mother, and sister." The beautiful glimmering shape of a woman over Saint Peter's Basilica spoke softly. "We have come to help you. We have heard your prayers, Valentinus."

He looked up, turning around to see each woman. Their illuminating shapes obscured their faces, but Valentinus had never seen such beauty. In awe, he felt his fear lessen.

Children's laughter chimed in from behind him, soft but gradually getting louder. Valentinus turned to see children going into the Temple Mount and then the Temple of Heaven. He turned to see children going into each house of worship. Their laughter and conversations were getting louder and louder as the crowds of children filled each building.

"Children?" Valentinus could see them as if he were watching a movie. Various children of all ages, sizes, and nationalities frolicked and walked together. There were thousands of children behind the ones who entered each building. Their voices were filling Valentinus's ears, making him smile.

He turned around, observing each building, studying the children: infants, toddlers, and teens. Some were carried. Some were missing limbs and walking on crutches. Some were impeccably dressed while others were naked or in rags. They were happy and innocent.

"They are all beautiful." Valentinus smiled, staring at each vision before him. "There seems to be no end to them."

"Valentinus, the Father of Israel has called out a sword against all nations, and by the Holy ones of His people, He will do mightily," Khadijah, Muhammad's wife, announced.

"*Per favore, Santo Padre,*have mercy on us all," Valentinus pleaded, turning away from the children for a moment.

"For all nations, let their designs become hardened so that whatever they have conspired shall return upon their own heads," Sarah, Isaac's mother chimed in.

Raising her voice, she continued woefully. "Some have prepared themselves maliciously, but they will find themselves to be impotent, and their offspring shall come to exact their own *price tag* policies."

"W-what? I don't understand." He shook his head, not wanting to believe what his eyes saw and ears heard.

The children were getting louder, Valentinus turned around to see many were crying. Others were silent, staring bewildered. The older ones looked straight in front of themselves, helping others along their journey as fear was settling in.

Valentinus stared at the buildings as the children piled in.

"The buildings, they are…" He could see the seams of each building starting to stretch like elastic. The more children who piled in, the larger the stretches seemed to get.

"*Per favore,* I don't unders—" Valentinus looked up at the glowing women. He could see their stomachs were getting bigger as each building expanded. "*Mio Dio.*" He gulped for air.

"*Per favore,* what can I do?" Unsure what he was seeing, he started to fear something terrible was going to happen.

"*Per favore,* my Ladies of Light and Hope, I am your humble servant. Only say the word, and I shall be at your service." His voice was shaky but determined and desperate. "Indeed my faith is in my Lord, and I shall not fear Him." He clasped his hands together in prayer.

"The Father of Knowledge is the word of knowledge," Magdalene recited. "Children of our heavenly Father can be saved if they come to know their Father. Ignorance can be destroyed upon them because knowledge of their Father will arrive upon them. Let there not be anyone who breathes without knowledge or voice."

"*Per favore,* tell me how I can serve my Father." His words could barely be heard out loud.

"Be enriched in your Father, and receive the purpose of the Most High. Be strong and redeemed by His grace." Mariam, Moses's sister, breathed over him. "Let the Lord direct your mouth by His word and fill your heart with His light. You shall help Wisdom destroy Ignorance and her allies. Wisdom's persecutors will come, but let them not see her."

Valentinus felt the warmth of the light pierce through him as she said the words. He closed his eyes for a second. He felt uplifted, standing taller.

"Behold, the Lord is our mirror. Open your eyes and see you in Him." Khadijah's words opened Valentinus's eyes.

Khadijah prophesied, "The Seers shall go before Him, and they shall be seen before Him. With their help, you shall convert the lives of those who desire to come to Him, and to lead those who are captive into freedom."

"Ahh…" He could see the buildings swelling, as were each of the women's wombs.

"He expanded the heaven and fixed the stars. From the east and unto the west is His Praise, from the south and unto the north is His Thanksgiving," Yeshau's mother voiced in singing praise, speaking to his heart. "Valentinus, He will never leave you."

• "The everlasting crown is Truth. A precious stone for wars were on account of the crown. But Righteousness has taken it and has given it to you, Valentinus." Mariam's light touched the tip of his head.

Their glow intensified. Their bellies swelled as the seams of the buildings became engorged.

Crunch. The twisting, crunching sound of metal began to grow louder.

"Oh no, *per favore*…" Valentinus could see what was going to happen. "*Per favore*, merciful *Padre* in heaven." He covered his ears.

The sounds vibrated under his feet, piercing his eardrums. The noise was unbearable as the glowing light intensified and became blinding.

Boom!

The explosion surrounded him, forcing him to his knees. The twisting metal crunched inches away from him. The children's voices went silent.

Hunched over on the ground, Valentinus shook as he opened his eyes to see black, thick smoke.

He stretched his hands out for something to grab hold of, but there was nothing. Crawling on his knees to find a way out, he could feel the ground was getting wet.

"*Per favore, mio Dio.*" He started to pray.

"Help me, help these children. I beg…" He tried feeling around in the darkness. The liquid was thick and had an awful stench.

"What is thi—" He could not make out what it was through the black smoke.

He stood up as the thick liquid rose higher, and he rubbed his hands on his clothes. Now up to his knees, the liquid rose higher, to his thighs.

"Oh *per favore*, no…" He tried to run, but his feet were stuck. He thrashed his arms and shoulders around, trying to move, but the thick liquid kept him in place, rising to his chest.

"*Per favore*, S*anto Dio, per favore*, no," he cried out, raising his hands to his face. "*Dio mio!*"

He screamed out, "Oh no. *Per favore*, have mercy." He could see his hands were red, covered in thick, red, oozing blood that was rising still higher and higher.

Lifting him up from his feet, the blood was now under his chin. He was panicked, flailing his hands and trying to kick his feet.

Now able to move his feet, he hit something and kicked it up.

"*Mio Dio!*" he shrieked, swatting a child's head away. The baby boy's eyes were closed, but his mouth was smiling. Valentinus could see other bones floating around him. Some were bigger than others, but they were all the bones of children.

"Ah," Valentinus screamed, out of his mind in fear.

Valentinus's mouth gaped open as he screamed, allowing a gulp of blood to flood in.

"Grr, ah." He threw up. Blood and his vomit surrounded him, the blood rising up as if he were in a bottomless pit.

"*Per favore*, save me, Yeshau!" he howled once more before going under.

"*Per favore*, have mercy on our souls...*per favore*," he screamed after coming up covered in blood.

In an instant a powerful flash of light appeared above him.

The light gleamed with the colors of magenta, cobalt blue, yellow, and green as if in a moving prism. A figure came out of the light and held something out to Valentinus.

"Grab hold, Valentinus. Your Father has heard your prayers," a man's stern, deep voice instructed him.

"A sword." Valentinus reached out, seeing a shiny, pointed, thin object. He didn't have time to think and grabbed the sword, not caring if he was cut.

"He has sent me to help you to protect Truth. Grab hold!" the angelic figure demanded.

Valentinus was terrified, but as soon as he touched the tip of the sword, he felt energy like no other radiate throughout his body, and he was transformed into silence.

"Ah..." Opening his eyes slowly, he could see only beauty. A labyrinth of stars shimmered in shapes of constellations he had not known. Nebulas of various colors and shapes, each in its own vibrancy of light, swirled around both near and far.

A floating sensation came over him. When he looked down, his clothes were clean. His feet felt like they were moving, but he saw nothing under him.

The tall, well-built man stood in front of him dressed in illuminated white Roman garb with gleaming chest armor. Light reflected off his chest, veiling his face and leaving only his golden, light, shoulder-length wavy hair glistening with his movements. Valentinus could see his mighty sword at his side.

"Wh-where am I?" Valentinus humbly inquired of the soldier standing a length taller than him.

"You are in Pleroma, the heavens of Logos," the man stated frankly. "Come."

Valentinus could see orbs of different shapes and sizes whiz up to him and then move farther away. The colors of cobalt, gold, emerald, magenta, crimson, and many more were so vivid, so alive. Sheer star-dusted clouds sparkled in wavy patterns here and there, moving as the energy swayed across the space.

"I can feel an energy I have never felt before. What is it?" Valentinus was astounded.

"Love." The man continued forward without turning to him. He stopped in what seemed to be a short distance and pointed to his right.

Valentinus could see children and animals playing in a field of stars as fluffy clouds swirled under their innocent feet. Laughing and running around, the children were happy.

Transcending into another galaxy, others played in a distant field of rich, lush green grass, where flowers and playgrounds abound. Whitecapped purple mountains offered a protective sensation. Bright, almost florescent colors of the rainbow streamed about.

Mature female and male angelic figures watched over all the children as they played, interacting as a happy family.

"It's so bright." Valentinus could barely see from the distance, they illuminated so brilliantly. "They look so peaceful and happy." He stared at them, studying their faces. "Not a care in the world. It looks like millions of them. They are from all over the world—Muslims, Jews, Christians, and…" Valentinus was mesmerized. "There are so many."

"Yes," the solider agreed without emotion.

Valentinus felt a tug on his pants and looked down to see a young Muslim girl wearing a head scarf, her hand stretched out holding a yellow rose. He recognized her when she went into the Temple on The Mount, crying as an older Jewish boy helped her. She stood half Valentinus's size and smiled at him. She gestured for him to take the rose from her.

"*Grazie.*" He smiled back, bowing his head slightly while taking it from her hand.

Giggling, the girl turned around and skipped back to a group of Jewish and Christian children who welcomed and hugged her.

"She is Blessedness." The soldier had admiration for the child.

Valentinus stood holding the rose, smiling at the frolicking children and animals.

"Come," the soldier instructed and pointed to his left.

"I feel like I am flying but without wings." Valentinus smiled as they moved without the use of their feet. However, he could start to feel the energy changing, getting colder and damp as if they were going into a dungeon. The stardust clouds were getting fewer and sparkled less.

Space was abundant. There were no walls, only darker space with stars shaped like dark rocks, sand-like stardust, darkened nebulas, and shapes of substances he didn't know.

"Where are we?" Valentinus looked around him, studying everything. The sound of men and women crying took his attention below his seemingly floating body.

Various orbs of light revealed the shadows of people's bodies, all different but all suffering. Men's faces wore deep worry lines as they stood silent. Women cried out, reaching their hands above their heads, trying to grab on to something.

Their cries and desperation grew louder. A cold, damp feeling grew within Valentinus. He could hear the slow drip of a faucet as if in another room.

Drip...drip...drip. The torturing sound provided the backdrop for the crying women.

The cold air gave Valentinus a chill deep within his bones. He looked at the women's pleading faces.

"Oh *mio Dio*, th-they are crying for their children." Valentinus hesitated to say it out loud.

"Ignorance of the Father caused their agitation and fear." The soldier stood at attention. "Like a dense fog, Ignorance captured their hearts and consumed them."

"We were supposed to help save them." He bowed his head, his eyes tearing up. "The church, w-will we survive?" He was ashamed he could not save the children.

The soldier waved his hand, picking up stardust and moving it in a circular motion. Around and around the stardust cloud grew in the palm of his hand. He stopped waving his hand and blew off the stardust, exposing a dark hole in space no bigger than a shoe box. It was void of stars and color. The soldier nodded for Valentinus to look inside the dark hole.

"Ah" Valentinus gasped. An old, plump, naked man lay still on a metal floor. The surrounding black walls appeared wet, cold, and damp.

"Oh." the man whimpered, mumbling. Valentinus focused on the metal-looking floor and started to make out a design the man rested upon. It was circular like a tarnished coin, having inlaid jagged shapes that peaked up, giving it an appearance of mountains and valleys. The naked man was lying in the middle.

"Ah, what?" As he looked closer, Valentinus recognized the coin of Pope Alexander VI. He could hear the dripping sound of water splashing the coin around the old man. Razor-sharp, freezing-cold droplets sliced his bloodless, ashen skin. The old man cried, jolting and whimpering as each droplet sliced the exterior of his soul.

Valentinus listened more intently. He could hear something else in the remoteness of the dark hole.

"People are screaming and crying." Concentrating on the sounds, he lamented in shock.

"Each tortured soul at the hands of another shall be set free and mark the soul of their torturer for eternity." He pointed to the old man. "The Archons blinded souls from Knowledge. Thus Error found strength without having learned from Truth. Error then took residence in a model form, preparing by means of the power in beauty, a substitute for Truth."

"I am sorry. *Per favore*, forgive me, but I don't understand. Are we talking about a person?" Valentinus cautiously asked.

"Wait, the archons?" Valentinus gave it another thought. "I think I remember." For a brief second he was a young boy. He could see his father arguing with his uncle Marcion about the evil behind some souls they referred to as archons when they were discussing their Gnostic teachings.

"They are the principals who have revealed themselves. You know them." The soldier looked into Valentinus's eyes and straight into his soul. "Baptize with water and oil, and you will baptize them in God's knowledge. You can save their souls." He touched Valentinus's chest on top of his heart. "But be warned, the Craftsmen may hinder your quest. You need only to remember to call upon us, and we will be at your side."

"My quest?" Valentinus was confused. "Who are the Craftsmen?"

"We must go." The soldier laid a hand on Valentinus's shoulder. It grew darker and darker until it was pitch black.

"Oh *Santo Padre*." Valentinus shook back and forth. "Where did you go? *Per favore*, do not leave me!" he wailed desperately.

"*Per favore...per favore*." Feeling alone, he started to sob, shaking in fear. Rocking back and forth, he suddenly opened his eyes.

When he looked straight up, he could see the ceiling of his room.

"It is still here. I am still here." He sighed in relief.

Looking around the room, he patted his chest. "I need a shower." He was drenched in sweat.

"*Grazie, Santo Padre* in heaven, it was only a dream." He took a deep breath in, held it...and released it.

"*Dio Mio*, that was so bad." Slowly he sat up, breathing each breath as if it were his first. Sitting at the edge of his bed, he leaned over, putting his hands to his head, holding his head up as if he had a hangover.

"Mary, *Madre di Dio*, I am your servant," he promised, remembering the glowing women, their light, and their words.

Feeling the urge to relieve himself, he got up and almost fell back, feeling faint and weak in the knees. Steadying himself, he slowly made his way to his bathroom a few feet away.

Splashing water on his face, he felt his sore shoulders and rubbed them. "Hmm...that hurts." He did not want to remember why they hurt.

He turned his attention to his face in the mirror. "I should get dressed and eat."

After taking his time refreshing himself, he opened the bathroom door. The strong smell of roses overwhelmed him.

"Hmm." He looked around his room, but no one was there.

"*In nome di Dio* …" Looking over at his bed, he saw an object out of place. A beautiful large yellow rose lay on his pillow, where his head once rested.

Valentinus walked over, picked it up, and inhaled its fragrance. Suddenly the smiling young Muslim girl came into his mind. Its perfume filled his nostrils, and all at once his path became clear.

"Oh *mio Santo Padre*, I am your servant." He breathed in the rose's aroma.

***

Sophia's taxi was pulling up to Castello del Valentino when the driver adjusted the radio announcing the news...

"And today we have learned Cardinal Meade Rosotti died from an apparent heart attack," the news reporter went on. "He was recently arrested on charges on fraud involving the Vatican Bank..."

"*Santa schifezza!*" Sophia gasped in disbelief.

"Are you all right?" The driver looked through his rearview mirror, alarmed.

"*Sì, sì,*" she murmured.

"OK then. We are here. Is this OK to drop you off?"

"*Sì,* ah...*grazie,*" she answered back, still being startled by Rosotti's untimely demise. "*Bene,*" she said, trying to regain her composure.

Walking into the Castle of Valentino, Sophia was nervous with anticipation. Her stomach was doing flip-flops.

"*Santa schifezza*...sorry, Carmine." She thought of Carmine's lover and them being blackmailed.

Her attention was swiftly refocused, as the entrance and main foyer in the grand Castle was overly crowded. She took each step with purpose before she was stopped.

"Hey, Emelia, do you remember me?" A young woman about her age pulled on her jacket. The woman gasped. "Oh, I am so sorry. I thought you were—"

"*Va tutto bene.*" Sophia could sense Eme's presence in that instant. "Really, *va bene,*" Sophia assured the already embarrassed woman.

"*Grazie,* sorry again." Red-faced, the woman hurriedly walked off.

"Hi Eme, I am glad you could join me." Sophia looked up to the ceiling and smiled.

Sophia watched as people of different races, ages, and genders walked in small groups and talked among themselves. Some were loud, while others whispered.

"I am glad there are unnumbered seats." She watched them as she looked for a good seat.

"Renewing Your Faith through History, given by Cardinal Valentinus de Marcosi." Sophia passed a billboard.

"*Bene*, I am going to find my own history tonight." She smiled. "And they said I was foolish." A flash of the past weekend went through her mind...

Sophia recalled the knocking on the door in her mind. She opened her apartment door to see Navaeh and Eula standing in the hallway.

"*Ciao*, girlfriend, we are here for our sleepover," the tall, slender, beautiful Navaeh announced as they both hurried through her doorway.

"I am so glad to see you." Sophia hugged them both. Catching up was easy enough. They laughed, they gossiped, they drank and drank some more...through the night.

She confided in both of her best friends all her deepest thoughts and feelings.

"And I think this Cardinal de Marcosi can tell me about my family." Sophia was sure.

"Sophia, you don't know that he can." Eula tried to be supportive but truthful as she hiccupped.

"I don't know, Sophia. You have always had a way of just knowing things." Navaeh, clad in her designer pajamas, poured another glass of wine for each of them. "I think you will know the truth if you search for it."

"Wow, I think you are poetic," Sophia slurred.

"I think you are both crazy," Eula said. "Oh no." She held her hand to her mouth. "I think I am goi—" She got up and ran to the bathroom.

"Ha, that will teach Eula to doubt me," whispered Sophia under her breath just as she felt a push from someone behind her.

"Dennis, what are you doing here?" Her eyes grew wide in disbelief as he towered over her.

"I am making sure you do not get into trouble." Sternly he tried to discipline her.

"Ha, that is funny." She laughed at his serious grin. "Hmm, I need to find a seat." She walked ahead of him.

"I have two seats here." He pointed to an aisle seat and the one next to it in the twenty-second row.

"It is centered to the stage so I can get a closer look at him," she thought. "*Bene*, that will do."

"OK, your majesty. I am glad you approve," he mocked her.

"How did you know I would be here?" She sat down in the aisle seat, leaving him to squeeze by her.

"I have experience."

"*Sì*, I know," she acknowledged his confidence, settling in her seat. Looking around the audience, she was like an anxious child. While she was fidgeting and people watching, she could see many younger people like herself and two rows of clergymen in front of the stage. "Look, there are bishops and cardinals lined up waiting to hear Valentinus." Sophia pointed.

"Ah, hmm." He nodded.

"Ah, Dennis, I understand you spoke to Ben." Waiting for the lecture to begin, she was reminded of the conversation with Ben and Michael.

"*Sì*." He was tight-lipped.

"I was just wondering about—" The applause started to drown out her words.

"Sh." He put his finger to his mouth. "Pay attention. You wanted to hear him speak, so now listen." His fatherly tone was obvious as he pointed to the stage.

A short, gray-haired man in a dark suit and grayish bowtie introduced the speaker.

"Cardinal-Bishop Valentinus de Marcosi is, as many of you know, a learned man with over thirty-three years of experience in theology, including a fellowship in our own Politecnico di Torino. His spiritual insight and dedication to the Vatican have proven him to be a true leader."

Sophia listened, anxiously waiting to set her eyes upon him…and finally the moment arrived.

Valentinus walked onto the stage with a confident stride, shaking hands with his host and then turning his attention to the audience.

"*Grazie.*" He appreciated the thunderous applause.

Dressed in a black suit, Valentinus looked the part of a priest but something was missing.

Sophia stared at him, and it hit her. "He is not wearing a collar!"

Valentinus gazed upon his audience, gesturing with his hands for the crowd to quiet down.

"Wow, there are a lot of you here tonight. I am grateful that you wish to hear me…You humble me." He nodded.

Sophia tried in vain to recognize his voice, but it was foreign to her.

"As you know, the Catholic Church has just elected a new pontiff," Valentinus went on.

Again the audience's applause was rampant. Valentinus signaled them to quiet down once more.

"*Sì, sì,* a new leader of the church has been elected. It is a historic event by today's standards. In fact, history is rewriting itself as if Ignorance herself were the author."

The cardinals in the first row turned their heads, talking to one another. Others in the audience seemed confused, not sure what to make of Valentinus's comment.

Valentinus did not notice them as he came from behind his podium to make his declaration.

"For since, through Ignorance, there came about the defect of the whole Roman System. However, Ignorance in her glory is dissolved in gnosis." He stood tall. "Gnosis is the redemption of the inner man and woman. It is not"—he raised his preaching voice—"a redemption of the body, for the body is corruptible. Nor is gnosis physical, for even the soul is a product of the defect. Therefore gnosis must be redemption itself."

Gasps could clearly be heard around the room, along with "Huh?" and "What the—"

Sophia could see the cardinals and bishops talking furiously.

"We need to be transformed by knowledge, the deeper personal knowledge of our Father within our souls," Valentinus avowed, putting his hands over his heart. "This is gnosis...It is the redeemable truth that obtaining knowledge of our Father will save our souls."

A man in front of Sophia stood up and left, as did two cardinals in the front row.

Valentinus started to sweat. He could feel the heat from the spotlights bearing down on him much like the light in his dream.

"*Per favore*, let me speak Your words," he prayed.

"My friends, my words may confuse some, but only because Chaos has been born from darkness and has ravaged our world with scandal, hatred, jealousy, lust, and greed," he pleaded to the crowd. "The lesson has always been that you cannot trust every soul! You need to test souls—these spirits—to see whether they are from our Father or from false prophets who have gone out into the world."

Sophia listened to his words, and while his voice was still foreign to her, she started to understand his point. She glanced at Dennis, who yawned but sat patiently.

"Be sober minded, be watchful. Your adversary, Shaytan, the devil"—he looked at the cardinals directly—"and his army of the damned, who some may refer to as the archons, prowl around like a roaring lion, seeking a soul to devour." He swayed, moving right and left on the stage and trying to engage his audience.

"Army of the damned? The archons?" Sophia immediately played with the bracelet Mariam gave her. She remembered Mariam's words. "Some archons can be dangerous."

Her mind raced back to Dominic's reference to the army of the damned and then to her uncle Egidio at Sunday dinner.

"Sophia, how did you like that book?" he asked over Mama's lasagna.

"Actually I was confused by some of it, and because I started back at work, I haven't had a chance to read more of it," she sheepishly replied.

"Well, when you finish it, perhaps we can talk about it. You can fill me in." Uncle Egidio smiled.

"OK. *Per favore*, can you pass me the *vino*?" She winced at the idea of explaining the priesthood and sexual magic to him.

"Hmm, I'd better read that book," Sophia thought upon hearing Valentinus.

As she gazed around at the hundred or more people watching the master on stage, she could see the remaining cardinals judging every word coming from Valentinus's mouth.

"When the Spirit of Truth comes into your heart...into your soul"—Valentinus showed his dramatic side—"He will guide you into all of the truth...for He will not speak on His own authority, but whatever He hears, He will speak and will declare to you the things that are to come."

"You know, they say there is one truth." He paused. "Only people describe it in different ways." He stood smiling as if telling a joke.

"But these different versions of truth lead souls into chaos and cause souls to separate themselves from our Father. There is a saying that there is nothing wrong in believing in God, but believing in a religion can kill you!" His demeanor quickly changed.

Some of his audience laughed, while others looked confused, wondering if they were in the wrong lecture.

"Religious organizations from thousands of years ago and still today have had a direct link to murder, extortion, greed, and chaos. The Catholic Church, the Jews, and the Muslims have murdered people in the name of a god. In fact, it would be difficult to find a religion that has not been mired in scandal."

"My friends." He went on as if talking in his living room to visiting company. "I say to you that there is no one religion on this earth that is better than another. Nor is there one over the other that will bring you closer to God...the one true merciful incomprehensible God, your Father, who loves you unconditionally!"

Valentinus went behind the podium to lean upon it and continued speaking without missing a step.

"Karl Max said religion is the opiate of the people. And while I don't agree with his politics, the statement is true enough. The world has come into this place…into this chaos."

He stood tall to pose a serious question. "Could it be that souls want to be deceived? Is it easier to believe in the opiates of a religion than to stand alone in knowledge?" There was sincerity in his tone.

"William Shakespeare said ignorance is the curse of God, and knowledge is the wing wherewith we fly to heaven. I would add that there are three parts of essence in every human being that are essential in order to take flight on the wings Shakespeare refers to. There is the irrational carnal soul, an animating rational soul, and a spiritual seed that yearns for knowledge." He used his fingers to make his point.

"When the spiritual seed is peaked by our true inner selves for all who hear His word expressed by creativity and intuition, the spiritual seed grows, *and* it is brought up and elevated *with* the rational soul."

He was happy preaching God's Word. "Everyone has within them the spiritual seed, but unfortunately it is actualized in only a few." He bowed his head.

Valentinus walked back to the other side of the stage, ignoring the clergy in front of him. "The irrational soul or carnal soul is like a drug that makes people forgetful of their true origin, and they become a creature of the lower earthly world," he warned.

"It is as if the spiritual seed falls asleep and finds itself in the midst of nightmares, running toward somewhere unknown." He began to tell his story. "They are powerless to get away while being pursued in hand-to-hand combat."

He raised his voice, using his hands to illustrate his words.

"The spiritual seed is being beaten, falling from a great height. Sometimes it seems that one is being murdered, or they are killing one's neighbors with whose blood one is smeared. Their god is their bodily desires. They think only of things that belong in this world." He stopped in his steps and shouted.

"If we are ignorant, Ignorance herself will sink her roots deep within us and yield her crops within our hearts!" He paused, catching his breath and letting his audience ponder the meaning of his words.

"Ignorance will dominate us! We will be slaves to Ignorance! She will take us captive so that we do the things we do not want and do not do the things we do want. I implore you, worshiping the creation and not the true Creator will keep you in the darkness of Ignorance's shadow."

For a brief second he was back at his seminary practicing and improving his preaching style.

"I share with you…" He paused, letting the audience wait for his words. "Gnosis, or knowledge, it is the process of coming to know our Father through knowing yourself. It is having a deep understanding of your spiritual self. I say to you: you will come to know your Father because you are part of your Father. You are His extension on this earthly plain and in heaven."

He was on a roll, feeling every word, hoping to share his passion with all those who wanted to hear.

"Your Father is within you, and you are within your Father, being perfect, being undivided in the truly good One, being in no way deficient in anything, but you are refreshed in the spirit!"

"Do you understand what he is saying?" Dennis leaned into Sophia.

"Sh." Playfully she put her finger to her mouth.

"Deficiency came into being when your Father was unknown." Valentinus went on with his story, pointing his finger. "But when your Father is known, from that moment on deficiency can no longer exist." He raised his hands above his head. "The deficiency within us and the entire earthly system originated from the curse of Ignorance, but she can and will be destroyed by Knowledge!"

He took a step back, letting his pupils digest his sermon.

"Those who attain knowledge or gnosis will see through the illusion that is the world, and they will rule creation!" He roared, "Knowledge is the key to the restoration of your original condition. It transforms everything!" Tenaciously he was making his point.

"It is within unity that each one will attain himself or herself…and within knowledge they will purify themselves from multiplicity into unity."

"They will consume matter within themselves like a fire in darkness!" Valentinus raised his hands as if he were a brimstone preacher.

His passion was ignited. "Jesus said there are two commandments to hold above all else." Valentinus stood in the middle of the stage and held out his hand.

"One, to love and honor your heavenly Father by whatever name you call him." He held his left pointer finger up.

"And two, to love your neighbor as yourself." He held up his middle finger, creating a peace sign.

"Jesus said this because by following these two simple commandments, all others would be followed...But again Ignorance takes hold, and she forms an allegiance with her allies, Limit and Deficiency."

Valentinus still held up his left hand, displaying the peace sign. "In Jesus's words to us, there was no limit or deficiency, and yet these so-called religions apply many limits on their followers, causing deficiency in us...and in our souls."

In an attack mode, he stated his case by holding up his right hand and fingers to make each of his points. "When religious organizations demand restrictions on your attire or force you to wear certain attire, especially keeping women from attaining their natural states of gnosis; when Jews only allow a woman to become divorced if the husband grants a Get; when the so-called religion restricts what you eat; when Muslims and Hasidic Jews do not allow their children educations that fully expand their minds; when the Catholic Church places limits on gay marriages or decides when a marriage is to never have existed; when Muslims become complacent in the practice of jihad and in murder that displaces millions of people in the name of love for some god. *This* is Ignorance at her best!"

He relaxed his hands and looked straight at his targets, the remaining clergy in the front row.

"My friends, can you not see that these so-called religious organizations are governing people, which is *very* different from administering faith." Valentinus paused and looked at all his audience.

Another cleric in the front row got up and walked out, but that did not stop Valentinus.

"*And* this governance of our souls is keeping our souls away from the fullness within ourselves," he went on with sorrow in his heart.

"It is keeping us away from the fullness of our Lord, God, Yahweh, Allah, or Bythos. It is keeping us away from our Father."

Valentinus could see the remaining clergy getting up to leave and went on. "Our brothers, Yeshua and Jeremiah, have told us there is no earthly purity ritual that will bring us closer to our Father. They have told us that when people ask, 'Is Heaven here or there,' they will not find heaven. For in fact, the kingdom of our Father dwells among us."

Sophia watched and listened. His words rang in her heart like a church bell on a clear day.

"But Ignorance will keep us from experiencing heaven. She is like a witch casting a spell. She fools you into accepting limits from which you then experience deficiency. We cannot attain fullness within ourselves, and we cannot come to know our Father to our fullest extent because of Ignorance's alliance with Limit and Deficiency," he reasoned with logic.

"I believe that what you seek is within you." He pointed his finger and looked at each person who was nearest to him. "You have a spiritual seed yearning to grow and"—he paused, speaking from his heart—"I pray the miracle of love is bestowed upon each one of you, allowing you to reveal your inner spiritual seed. Friends, I know the energy or miracle of love is so powerful, it can transform lives." Without his audience knowing, he was speaking of his dream, and he smiled.

"You know, it is a funny thing that I heard on the news. There are more people today who believe in angels and in miracles, but I believe these same people have less faith in the unconditional love of a truly loving Father." He shook his head. "Because if we truly believed in our all-incomprehensible loving Father, we would not accept religious organizations placing limits on our marriages, our education, and our potential. We would not accept the senseless murders of innocent lives in the name of some god!" He criticized the nonsensical thought of religious-type governments.

Peering into his audience, he added, "I know our Father, our loving Father, wants to know our limitless selves because he created us and he knows our potential. *This*...is obtaining gnosis!"

The last cardinal at the door looked behind him, bearing witness to Valentinus on stage denouncing the church and her beliefs. With force, the doors in the auditorium closed, leaving only those who wished to hear more of Valentinus's wisdom.

Valentinus smiled as if he was holding a secret.

He watched the last cardinal close the door behind him. His mind raced to the letter he had written. He had asked Biarre, his personal assistant, to deliver it directly to the newest pontiff. He could imagine Sisinnius, playing the part of Pope Innocent, opening his letter as Valentinus stood on stage delivering his words of a simple truth to the faithful.

"My friends, I invite you to join me in exploring and achieving gnosis. Truth is in knowledge...truth is in your Father's complete love, and it can only strengthen you. Knowledge can give you fullness without limit! It can avoid chaos, and it will allow your spiritual seed to take root in your heart, in this world, and in heaven!"

Valentinus finished his lecture humbly.

"I want to thank each of you here tonight." He bowed and held up his fingers to show the peace sign, giving them his final blessing. "Be open to truth...and be awakened."

Valentinus obligingly took another bow to a standing ovation and thanked everyone again who came to listen to him.

"*Va bene*. That was interesting." Dennis turned to Sophia with a little sarcasm.

"*Sì*, it was. He was great!" Sophia jumped up from her seat, excited. "I need to meet him. Let's go," she ordered Dennis.

"Wait a minute, Sophia. You can see he has a line of people who want to talk with him. You will have to wait your turn." He pointed to the front of the room.

"I need to see him now!" she demanded, stomping her foot.

Dennis could see she was determined. He looked around the room. "Let's go this way." He pointed to a side door closer to the stage.

"Are you sure?" Sophia gave her best pouting expression.

"I have three daughters, so I know when I have lost the argument. Let's go." He guided her with his own determination.

They walked through the throngs of people who were crowding the aisle to leave or who were getting in line to speak to Valentinus.

Working their way around the room, they reached the backstage guest speaker suite.

"How do you know he will come back here?" Sophia probed Dennis.

They entered the small room with a large mirror and a barber's chair in front of it.

Dennis pointed. "I believe that is his coat and briefcase."

"How do you know that?"

"Because I saw him come in with them." He was smug.

"Oh." She smiled and nodded.

"Make yourself at home. I am sure he will be a while." Dennis gestured for her to take a seat.

"Hmm." She looked at Valentinus's hat and coat. Feeling the brim of the hat brought her memory back to looking at his picture and the DVD.

"I hope he can lead me to my brothers." She sat in the barber's chair and looked at Dennis through the mirror. "*Grazie*, Dennis." Sophia had tears building up. "It is really life changing for me to see where I come from and to hopefully find my family."

"Sophia, it may not—"

The door flew open. Valentinus was being followed by the man who had introduced him on stage. Seeing two intruders in his guest suite made him stop in his steps, having the man behind him bump into him.

"What? Who are you?" Valentinus was shocked by their presence.

Sophia jumped up off the chair too quickly and stumbled toward him. "My name is Sophia Pistisi, and I was hoping you could help me find my family."

Alarmed, the short man with the bowtie shouted at the top of his lungs, "*Mio Dio*! Cardinal de Marcosi should I call the *polizia*?" He was just as startled by the intruders.

Valentinus took a step back. His face flushed white. He was speechless.

Know what is in front of your face,
and what is hidden from you will be disclosed to you.
—Yeshua

About the Author

Like many others, I have had experiences that some may consider strange. It is my belief that some people are sensitive to, or open to heavenly energy more than others. Whether by choice or condition, we see and feel what our minds tell us.

In these pages the miracle story, as I refer to it, is recounted as it really happened in 2012 when my cousin was suddenly stricken with a blood disease known as sepsis. While he was hospitalized in critical condition my husband and I visited the Our Lady of the Island Shrine in Eastport, New York. Curiously, I was given two sets of wooden rosaries by total strangers. Leaving the Shrine we realized we had a flat tire and after the repairs, my husband and I changed our route to the hospital to visit my cousin.

As we drove, we saw a man dressed as Jesus walking in our direction. We were in total shock as he dragged a large wooden cross behind him. Unable to help ourselves, we stared at him so intently it seemed to make him twitch uncomfortably.

When we arrived at the hospital to give my cousin one set of the rosaries we had received, his kidneys started working again which meant his doctor, Dr. Love, (his real name), did not have to start the dialysis treatment already being prepared. From the moment I brought those rosaries to my cousin, it seemed he miraculously started to heal.

But the story and the experience is deeper than saving just my cousin; it saved my own life, as well! I started to question my own life lessons. I had taught religious classes for ten years at my local parish but everything that I knew was fading away into a new reality. Firsthand, I saw that the power of prayer goes beyond the religious sect one might associate with. It is my belief that miracles happen every day. Unfortunately, small ones get little attention and large ones get questioned.

Researching how the Roman Catholic Church and other religions came into being, I questioned social issues involving faith. I wanted to understand why the world was in such a rage.

376

It seems much of the world's chaos stems from the root of "Religion." I began to question what I was taught and what I taught others.

What if the people from so long ago who helped to form our religious beliefs, no matter the religion, were alive today? Who would they be? Would we still have the chaos that has taken over our world?

It was through this quest that I found Sophia. She shares with me a story, a belief, and a mystery: that of a lost soul who was reborn. Through the Gnostic Gospels stored in the Egyptian Nag Hammadi Library, the Gospel of Truth brings us a different version of truth.

I am by no means an expert in religious theory. I am merely an ordinary person who has had the blessings of extra-ordinary experiences. I am a proud Rotarian and a founder of a not-for-profit organization which helps family members with issues such as care coordination with Medicare and Medicaid.

This is my first novel, but I feel so compelled; some would even say inspired; to share Sophia's story, and hope you will enjoy reading it as much as I enjoyed writing it.

I tell my daughters, "You must not simply make waves in this world. You need to make a tidal wave so this world knows you were here!"

Well, here is my tidal wave... Peace and love be with you always.

Continue the adventure with
"On Earth as it in Heaven; Destiny of a Flaming Star"

Please visit our website;
Read our blog with real-life twist of fate updates and view our video.
Enjoy the journey.
www.OnEarthAsItIsInHeaven13.com